BINDER

Harold Robbins

Simon and Schuster
New York

Copyright © 1982 by Harold Robbins
All rights reserved
including the right of reproduction
in whole or in part in any form
Published by Simon and Schuster
A Division of Gulf & Western Corporation
Simon & Schuster Building
Rockefeller Center
1230 Avenue of the Americas
New York, New York 10020
SIMON AND SCHUSTER and colophon are trademarks of Simon & Schuster
Designed by Irving Perkins Associates
Manufactured in the United States of America

10   9   8   7   6   5   4   3

Library of Congress Cataloging in Publication Data
Robbins, Harold, date.
    Spellbinder.
    I. Title.
PS3568.0224S6   1982   813'.54   82–10291
ISBN 0-671-41634-0

Book I

JESUS FOR LOVE

CHAPTER
ONE

"Preacher!" The hoarsely whispered shout hung heavily in the shadowed humid jungle air.

There was a rustle in the underbrush that sent the birds abruptly shrieking into the trees, then silence. Preacher's voice was low and calm. "Where are you?"

"Over here. In the hole. Hurry, Preacher. I'm hurt real bad."

A moment later, Preacher's head and shoulders appeared over the edge of the small crater. He peered down at the wounded black soldier and nodded silently. He elbowed himself forward and tumbled clumsily into the crater, rolled over and sat up, the white band with the red cross on his arm barely visible for the mud covering it. He slipped the medical pack from his shoulders and placed it on the ground beside him. "Where are you hit, Washington?" he asked without looking up from the pack he was opening.

The soldier grabbed at his arm. "I'm gonna die, Preacher," he said in a frightened voice. "Will you hear my confession?"

"You crazy, Joe?" Preacher looked at him. "You're not Catholic, I'm no priest."

"So what?" Joe whispered. "You're a preacher anyway, aren't you?"

"No, I'm not," Preacher answered. "I'm not a minister."

"But they call you Preacher," Joe insisted. "We all know you're always carryin' a Bible with you."

"That doesn't mean anything," Preacher said.

"But you're a Conchie, you won't carry a gun or nothin'. You got to be some kind of religious to make them let you get away with that."

"I don't believe in killing," Preacher said shortly. "That's all." The kit was open in front of him. "Now tell me where you were hit."

"In the back," Joe said. "First it hurt like hell, now I feel the numbness spreading all through my body. That's how I know I'm gonna die. When it reaches my heart, I'm finished. I don't care what kind of preacher you are, you gotta hear my confession. I don't want to go to hell with all them sins on my soul."

"Suit yourself," Preacher said. "But turn over first so I can see where you got hit."

Joe rolled over, groaning as he moved. "Jesus, it hurts," he gasped. "I'm sorry, Preacher. That just slipped out."

"It's all right," Preacher said, looking down. The seat of Joe's pants was soaked in blood. He took a pair of scissors from the kit and began to cut away the material.

Joe began to mumble. "Forgive me for my sins, O heavenly Father. I drank and cursed and took Thy name in vain. I committed the sin of fornication in Saigon with two sisters and sodomized both and made them suck my—"

"You can stop now," Preacher said suddenly. "You're not going to die."

Joe turned and stared up at him. "How do you know?"

"Nobody ever died from getting shot in their fat black ass,"

Preacher said, reaching for a swab and beginning to clean the buttock with an antiseptic.

Joe jumped. "That burns."

"Hold still," Preacher said. "I want to get a compress on it to stop the bleeding."

"Can I have a smoke?" Joe asked.

"Sure thing."

"There's a couple of joints in the pocket of my blouse. Can you get one out for me?"

Silently, Preacher opened the pocket flap and gave him a joint. Joe stuck it between his lips and with his other hand came up with a small lighter. A brief flash and the joint was lit. He took a deep toke and sighed comfortably. "That's better."

A few minutes later Preacher finished taping on the compress. "You'll have to stay on your stomach," he said. "I don't want you to get any dirt on your ass. You can pick up too many infections from this ground out here. I'll send the stretcher-bearers back for you."

Joe leaned on his elbow and looked at him. "You're an okay guy, Preacher," he said, extending the joint. "Care for a toke? This is super shit."

Preacher shook his head. "No, thanks." He began to repack his medical kit.

Joe's voice was very relaxed. "Just what religion are you?" he asked curiously.

Preacher looked at him. "My mother was Greek Orthodox, my father Methodist. But the only church in the town I grew up was Unitarian, so that's where we went. So I guess that's what I am."

"Are all Unitarians Conchies?"

"No," Preacher answered. "That's just what I believe. Christ said—"

Joe laughed. "I was brung up Baptist. I heard all them speeches. You're not goin' to preach to me, are you?"

Preacher looked at him for a moment. "No."

"Think they'll send me home?" Joe asked.

"Probably."

"That's not so bad then. A Purple Heart and a trip home for a shot in the ass, is it?"

"Not so bad." Preacher snapped the medical kit shut.

"I think I'll join up with the Black Muslims when I get back. They the big niggers back home now." He watched Preacher start to get up. "Careful, Preacher, keep your head down," he warned. "Those Vee-yet bastards can see in the dark."

The faint echo of the shot came almost as soon as the words were out of Joe's mouth. The bullet slammed into Preacher's arm, turning him half around and knocking him to the ground.

He lay still for a moment, then sat up painfully and looked down at the blood welling through the sleeve of his blouse. He glanced at Joe. "Now you tell me."

With his free hand he pulled open the kit and took out the scissors again. Quickly he cut the sleeve away from his arm. Blood was spurting from a bullet hole in the fleshy upper portion. "You'll have to help me fix a tourniquet."

"Sure thing, Preacher." Joe crawled over to him and between them they managed to fix a tourniquet and stop the flow of blood. "Jesus, Preacher, I'm sorry."

Preacher managed a grin. "It's God's will." He paused for a moment. "I'll take a puff of that joint now."

The soldier relit the joint and passed it to him. He watched Preacher take several tokes. "Is your arm hurt bad?"

Preacher looked at him. "Not too bad. At least I'll be able to sit on the plane home."

Joe stared at him. "I just thought of somethin'. My balls is numb. You think I got it there too?"

Preacher laughed. "No chance. Not with an ass as fat as yours." He passed the joint back.

Joe sucked on the joint. "How long do you think it will take for them to come and get us?"

"Not long," Preacher said. "They know I came up here."

"Grass always makes me horny," Joe said. "I was just thinkin' about those girls. You know, the ones I was confessing to you about. I think I'm beginnin' to get a hard-on."

"I told you you were all right." Preacher laughed and took the joint from Joe's fingers. He took a few deep tokes and leaned back against the wall of the small crater. "Think pure thoughts," he said. "That's what my mother always used to say."

He dried himself with the towel as he came out of the shower, then spread it over the toilet seat and sat down. Carefully he began to examine his penis. The foreskin was red and inflamed and painful as he peeled it back to examine the glans. That, too, was swollen and purple-veined. It was no use, he thought as he began to spread a thin layer of Vaseline on himself. He was doing it too much. Each day he swore to himself he would stop, but then the very next day it was the same thing all over again. Like just now, in the shower.

He was doing everything just right. Ice cold water. Freezing cold. Then it happened the moment he began to soap his genitals. Almost before he knew it he was doing it, using the slippery soapsuds to carry him away. Then the wildly spurting semen spattered against the white tiles, leaving him empty and ashamed. He stared down at himself. It wasn't what he had wanted at all. Then the urine burst forth, painful and burning and mixing yellow with the water going down the drain. It hurt, it hurt so bad.

He stepped from the shower, his resolution to stop growing firm again. But even as he thought it, he knew he could not stop. It would happen again in school. He would run to the toilet after seeing the girls in their tight little gym suits. And then in the afternoon down at the candy store, where they all met and sipped their Cokes and girls teased with their twitching boobs and asses, sending him back to the toilet again. There were times he couldn't even wait and it would happen while he was sitting at the table with them and he felt the spurting sticky wetness suddenly flooding into his underwear. He was sick. He was sure of it. He was sick.

"Constantine!" His mother's voice filtered through the bathroom door.

He hated that name. His mother was Greek Orthodox, from Chicago, and had named him after her father. He never used it at school. There all the kids called him Andy, short for Andrew, his middle name.

"Constantine! Better hurry. You'll be late for school."

"I'll be right out, Mother," he called back.

He came down into the kitchen and sat down at the table. His mother placed three fried eggs and bacon steaming from the frying pan in front of him. He reached for the hot buttered biscuits and began to eat ravenously. "Where's Dad?" he asked between mouthfuls.

"Your father left early for a meeting down at the Unitarian church," she said. "They offered to make him a trustee if he would formally join the church."

"Is he going to do it?" he asked.

"I think so," she said. "After all, we've been going there for years. Your father says it really doesn't make any difference. It's Christian."

"It's also the only church in town," he said.

She nodded, sinking into a chair across the table from him. "That's true."

"What about you?" he asked. "How do you feel about it?"

"I don't know," she said. "But the nearest Greek Orthodox church is in Chicago. That's six hundred miles away."

He looked at her. "It's not the same thing though, is it?"

She shook her head. "Not really."

"Then what's the fire? We've been getting along fine the way we are."

"Your father's business is getting very important in the town. And the trustees of the church feel he should give them his support."

"And if he doesn't join up?"

"I don't know," she said in a troubled voice. "You know them as well as I do. They could turn cold in a minute. Like they did with that Jew, Rosenbloom. After six years he had to close up his business and move away."

He finished his breakfast and got to his feet. "Maybe it's not so bad."

"Maybe," she said. She looked up at him. "There's something I have to talk to you about."

"What's that?" he asked, suddenly cautious.

She didn't look up at him; her voice seemed suddenly embarrassed.

"*Mandy showed me the sheets she took from your bed this morning.*"

"*What about them?*" he asked defensively.

She still didn't meet his eyes. "*They were all stained. Mandy says it's been going on a long time.*"

"*Why don't that nigger mind her own business and do the laundry just like she's supposed to?*" he snapped angrily.

"*She thought I should know,*" his mother said. "*I didn't tell your father because you know how angry he would get. You have to do something to stop it.*"

"*I can't help it, Mama,*" he said. "*I don't have anything to do with it. It happens while I'm asleep.*"

His mother looked up at him. "*You can help it, Constantine. Just think pure thoughts. Nothing but pure thoughts. That's all.*"

He returned her gaze thinking of all those girls at school with their teasing twitchy little bodies. "*It's not that easy, Mama.*"

"*You can do it, Constantine,*" she said. "*Just think pure thoughts.*"

CHAPTER TWO

The hot bright sun beat down on Fisherman's Wharf as the patrol car pulled into a no-parking area and came to a stop on the opposite side of the street. It was near three o'clock and the lunchtime crowds were pouring out of the restaurants, bright in their tourist shirts and hats, comfortably picking at their teeth and wandering along the streets peering into the souvenir shops and stalls.

"They're doin' business," the sergeant said in a satisfied voice to the patrolman who was driving the car. "Nice to see."

"Yeah," the patrolman said. He couldn't have cared less. The sergeant had been on this beat for years. He got all the gravy.

"DiMaggio's still the big draw," the sergeant said. "They still come to see Joltin' Joe, even now."

"Yeah." The patrolman's voice was still noncommittal. All he wanted was a smoke, but no chance with the sergeant along.

They sat there silently for a moment. "Do you see that?" the sergeant asked suddenly.

The patrolman looked. He saw nothing. "What?"

"Over there. In the crowds off the wharf."

"I still don't see nothin'."

"Those girls with the long granny dresses. They're shakin' tin boxes. There's about six, seven of them."

"So?"

"I never seen them before," the sergeant said.

"There's always kids around beggin'," the patrolman said.

"Not like this," the sergeant said. "They seem organized. Like they have a plan. See the way they split up and hit the crowds? If the first one doesn't nick you, another follows up right away."

The patrolman became curious. "Think they're dips?"

The sergeant watched them carefully. "Don't think so. They keep too far apart and they never come close to the mark. They hold the tin box in their hands way out in front of them."

"They're all pretty girls," the patrolman said. "Clean-looking too. Not like most of the flower children and dopers."

"Yeah," the sergeant said. "I wonder what the scam is."

"We can roust a couple of them and find out."

"No," the sergeant answered. "Let's wait and see what they do."

The patrolman couldn't stand it any longer. "Mind if I have a smoke, Sergeant?"

The sergeant looked at him with a pitying glance. "Okay. But keep the cigarette down. I wouldn't like the lieutenant coming by and seeing it."

"Thanks, Sergeant." There was genuine gratitude in the patrolman's voice. He bent down alongside the wheel and lit the cigarette, drawing the smoke deeply into his lungs. He took another quick drag and then looked sideways up at the sergeant. "What's happening?"

"The kids are doing all right. The marks are dropping the coins right into the slot."

The patrolman took another drag on the cigarette, then carefully pinched it out and straightened up. "Thanks, Sergeant, I really needed that."

The sergeant glanced at him. "You oughtta learn to chaw tobacco. Nobody can ever spot you doin' that."

The patrolman laughed. "Maybe I will."

The sergeant was watching the girls. "The crowd's thinnin' out now and the girls are beginnin' to leave. We'll tag the last one an' see where they're goin'."

The patrolman switched on the motor. "You tell me when, Sergeant."

"Now," the sergeant said. "They're goin' up the side street near the Orange Julius stand."

The patrolman pulled around the corner and came to an abrupt stop. "Shit, Sergeant, it's a one-way street comin' at us."

"I know the street," the sergeant said. "It's a long one. You round the block. We'll pick them up on the way down."

But when they reached the top of the street and looked down it was empty. "They're gone, Sergeant," the patrolman said.

"No, they're not," the sergeant said. "There's an alley half-way down the block. They'll be in there."

The patrolman stopped the car, blocking the alley. The sergeant was right. At the back of the alley was a purple painted van. In large white letters on all sides of the van were the painted words THE COMMUNITY OF GOD.

"Call in our location," the sergeant said. "Ask for a backup car but tell them we don't expect any trouble—we're just going to check out a couple of Marys."

The side panel door of the van was open and the girls thronging around it didn't notice the policemen until they were almost on them. The chatter and laughter suddenly died as they turned to face them.

The sergeant touched his visor politely. "Evening, ladies." He could see the fear and apprehension on their faces. "There's no reason to be disturbed," he added. "This is a routine check. If I may see your ID's or driver's licenses, please?"

One of the girls, seeming slightly older than the others, pushed forward. "Why?" she asked, faintly belligerent. "We weren't doing anything wrong."

"I didn't say you were, ma'am. It's just that you're new here and we have a responsibility to know what's going down."

"We know our rights," the girl said stubbornly. "We don't have to show you anything unless we're charged."

The sergeant stared at her in disgust. The kids today were all street lawyers. "How about begging in the street without a permit, for starters?" he replied conversationally. "Then creating a public nuisance by interrupting the flow of pedestrian traffic and creating a public hazard that could endanger the lives of others? That was a wharf you were on and people might have fallen off into the water trying to walk around you."

The girl stared at him silently for a moment then glanced at the others. She turned to the open side panel door and called inside, "Preacher!"

The man appeared from the darkness inside the van and dropped to the ground. He was wearing faded Levi's tucked into army boots, a khaki work shirt under a worn and slightly frayed GI blouse. He was not a tall man, about five seven or eight, and had long sandy brown hair that fell to his shoulders, held tightly around his head by a wide band of Indian beads. His mouth and chin were covered by a Jesus beard and moustache. At first it seemed as if his eyes were intensely blue and could see into you, but then they seemed to change and grow gray and bland as if a veil had come down over them. His voice was deep, resonant and pleasant as he spoke. "Welcome to the Community of God, Officer. What can we do for you?"

The sergeant looked at him. All he needed on this beat was another Jesus. He saw at least twenty of them a day and most of them were stoned out of their heads. But he'd been a cop for a long time, and nothing of what he thought or felt showed in his voice. "I've asked these young ladies for their ID's or driver's licenses but they don't seem to want to cooperate."

The man nodded thoughtfully then turned to the girls. "It's all right, children. Do as the officer requests."

The backup car arrived and two more policemen came running up the alley as the girls began to produce their cards. "Tom," the sergeant said to his driver, "you gather up the cards, take them back to the car and call them into HQ for a complete check." He turned back to the man, who was still standing in front of him. "May I have your driver's license and vehicle registration also?"

"Of course, Officer," the man said. "They're inside the van. I'll be glad to get them for you." He turned back to the panel door.

"Wait a minute," the sergeant said quickly. "Do you mind if I go with you?"

"Not at all, Officer," the man said easily. He leapt into the van.

The sergeant climbed up heavily after him. He was not as spry as he used to be. The inside of the van was like nothing he had expected to see. Usually they were filthy jumbles of mattresses and dirty clothing that smelled of dope, wine and unwashed bodies.

This van was clean, spare and painted white. If anything, it was more like a traveling office than an RV. Behind the driver's compartment were a small table desk and chair, bolted to the floor so that they would not move. On the wall opposite the panel door were steel shelves from floor to roof covered with packaged reams of paper. On another table, also bolted to the floor, was a typewriter neatly covered, and next to it was a small mimeograph machine with its receiving tray half filled. On the side next to the door were two rows of benches, also bolted to the floor, and each bench was fitted with four sets of seat belts.

The man saw him take it all in. "We can't all sit up front," he said. "And some roads are pretty rough. I like to feel that all the children are safe."

The sergeant grunted and sniffed. He had always said he

could smell dope better than any of the dogs they were training. But it seemed almost too good to be true. Everything was just too straight.

The man sat down at the desk and opened a drawer. He took out the vehicle registration slip and his driver's license and gave them to the sergeant.

The policeman looked at the driver's license first. It was made out to Constantine Andrew Talbot, issued in January 1967, two years before. He glanced at the picture. It was the same man all right but the look was different now. In the picture he had a straight haircut. The man was older than he had at first thought. He had guessed early twenties; his actual age now was twenty-nine. All else checked: hair color, eyes. Just one thing he could not see. "There's a scar on your left arm," he said. "How'd you get it?"

"Bullet wound. I was in Vietnam."

"My son is in the Green Berets," the sergeant said proudly.

"I was in medics."

"How long?"

"Four years. I volunteered."

"Why medics?" the sergeant asked.

"I don't believe in killing," the man answered. "But neither do I believe that a man should shirk his duty to his country."

"I heard the girl call you 'Preacher,' " the policeman asked. "Are you an ordained minister?"

"No, sir," the man said. "But someday I hope to be."

The sergeant put the driver's license under the vehicle registration slip. "Is this Community of God a recognized church?"

"Yes, it is. We have a registration certificate from the State of California."

"Exactly where is this church based?"

"As you can see from the vehicle registration slip, we're located just outside Los Altos," Preacher answered. "But, as my mother used to say, 'The community of God is imbedded in every man's heart.' "

.   .   .

They had eaten dinner in almost total silence. It was when they were drinking their coffee that he spoke. He looked across the table at his parents. "I'm leaving on the weekend."

"But it's only six months since you've come home," his mother said quickly.

"And he hasn't done a thing except lay around the house, go out all night doin' God knows what an' smokin' that pot he got into while he was in the army. Not once did he offer to come down to the store an' give me a hand," his father said gruffly. "I don't know what four years in the army did for him. He's twenty-five now an' it's time he settled down. When I was his age I was already a married man with responsibilities."

"What is it you want to do, Constantine?" his mother asked.

"I don't really know, Mother," he said. "I've got a call. But I'm not sure for what. I feel I have a message from God to bring to people. But I don't know how to do it or even where it belongs. I only know I've seen too many men die without having made any provision for their souls and lose the gift of eternal life that Jesus promised."

His father stared at him. "If that's what you really think, why haven't you come down to the church and talked to the minister?"

"I have, Father. Many times. But he doesn't have the answers for me. To me, God belongs to all Christians, not just Unitarians. It's a greater community than just this small church."

"The trouble with you is that you really don't want to work. You're happy to get your check from the VA, which includes the bonus for being wounded, and just lay around," his father said harshly.

"Constantine," his mother said.

He turned to look at her.

"Is that what you truly believe?"

"Yes, Mother."

She turned to his father. "Then it's not up to us to pass judgment on him, Father," she said. "We must let him go and find what he believes. It could be that he is right, for there is a community of God imbedded in each man's soul."

CHAPTER
THREE

The patrolman stuck his head inside the door. "They're all clean, Sergeant. There are no make sheets on any of them."

The sergeant nodded and handed him Preacher's license and the registration slip. "Run this one through for me."

The patrolman disappeared as Preacher spoke. "You don't trust anyone, do you, Sergeant?"

"It's my business not to," the sergeant said. "How long do you people plan on staying around here?"

"Just the weekend. We need some cash to pay for seed and fertilizer at the Community. Things have been more expensive than we figured."

"What crops are you growing?"

"Alfalfa, sunflower seeds, safflower and snap beans. We try to grow all our own food. We're vegetarians."

The sergeant nodded. It figured. "How many of you are there in the Community?"

"About forty-five now," Preacher answered. "But we're growing. Each week there's one or two more."

"All girls?" the policeman asked shrewdly.

Preacher laughed. "There are about fifteen men among us."

"I don't see any with you."

"We need them at the Community for the heavy work. The girls are the only ones we could spare."

The sergeant stared at him. Preacher was no fool. He knew that it was easier for girls to collect money than men. The average pedestrian was not afraid of them.

The patrolman came back to the door. "Clean, too," he said, passing the papers back to the sergeant.

The sergeant had one last question. "You can't all sleep in the van?"

Again Preacher smiled. "The man who owns the storage room in the alley next to the truck was kind enough to rent us his place for ten dollars a night. The girls sleep there. I stay in the van."

The sergeant got to his feet heavily. "You'll still have to get a permit for soliciting."

Preacher took another paper from the desk. "We already have it, Sergeant. We got it at City Hall yesterday."

The policeman looked at the paper. Preacher had thought of everything. The permit was good for the three days of the weekend. He gave it grudgingly back. "Okay," he said. "Just be careful and keep your girls out of trouble and I'll see to it that the police won't bother you."

Preacher got to his feet. There was a faint hint of a smile in his eyes. "Thank you, Sergeant," he said. "God bless you."

The sergeant was surprised to hear himself reply, almost by reflex, "Thank you, Preacher."

Preacher stood in the door of the van as he and the girls watched the policemen walk down the alley, get into their cars and drive off. When they were gone, the girls, suddenly smiling, looked up at him. He laughed.

"They sure fell for it," said the older girl who had first spoken to the police.

Preacher nodded slowly. "Yes. But we still have to be careful. That sergeant is no fool. He's going to come back for a few surprise visits. You children are going to have to play it very straight until I can make the arrangements and then we'll get out of here."

"But I'm dying for a toke," the girl said.

"You'll hang in there, Charlie," Preacher said. "We have fifty bricks in that storage room to get rid of. Once we do, we can get out of here and have a real party."

"But Preacher," one of the girls protested.

Preacher turned a stern eye on her. "You heard me, Alice. You'll all do as I say. We need the money we're goin' to get if we want to continue doin' the Lord's work." He jumped down from the van. "Which one of you has the keys to the pickup? I want to go downtown and make contact."

Preacher found an open parking meter at the foot of California Street and pulled into it. He got out of the car and put a coin in the meter, then turned and walked down to Grant. The faint smells of Chinese cooking hung in the air like a perfume inviting you to enter the thousand restaurants that filled Chinatown.

He walked down Grant past the restaurants and souvenir shops until finally, a few blocks down, the street became more prosaic—old apartment houses and small commercial taxpayer buildings. He stopped in front of one of them. The street floor was a storefront with painted-over gray-tinted windows and a sign over the doorway. SOONG DING CO. EXPORTS. WHOLESALE ONLY. The entrance door was locked. He pressed the doorbell.

A moment later the door opened and a man peeked out. "Yes?"

"Barbara Soong," Preacher said.

"Who wants to see her?"

"Just tell her that Preacher is here."

The man nodded and closed the door. A few minutes later he was back. This time the door opened wide. "Come in."

Preacher followed him into the store and waited until the man had closed and locked the door behind them, then followed him through the store filled with crates and boxes to the rear. The man pressed the button for the elevator. The door opened. "Third floor," the man said, and waited until Preacher went into the elevator and the door closed.

A neatly dressed man in a dark suit, white shirt and black tie greeted Preacher as he stepped out into the luxuriously furnished third-floor apartment. "Follow me, please," he said politely.

Preacher followed him down a wide corridor decorated with lovely Chinese silk-screen prints and statues of invaluable jade and ivory to an elaborately carved wooden door. He opened the door, gesturing for Preacher to enter.

He followed Preacher into the room and closed the door behind him. He turned to Preacher. "If you will permit me?" he asked politely. "The House of Soong has many enemies."

"Of course," Preacher answered. He raised his arms so that the man could pat him down.

A moment later, the man straightened up, satisfied. "Thank you." He walked to the desk and pressed a button. A door at the other side of the room opened and a young woman entered.

She was tall for a Chinese and was smiling, both hands held out in front of her in a gesture of welcome. "Preacher," she said warmly, "it's been a long time. I thought you had forgotten us."

"Barbara," he said, taking both her hands in his own, "one does not forget good friends." He let go of her hands and his voice grew serious. "I just learned of the death of your honorable father. Permit me to extend my condolences even though it is late."

Barbara walked behind the desk that had been her father's and sat down. "Thank you, Preacher. It is sad. But it is also life. It must go on even if it is difficult." She paused for a moment. "How can the House of Soong be of service to you?"

He remained standing. It would not have been polite for him to sit until he was asked. "You are aware of the arrangement I had with your father?"

She nodded.

"I have fifty bricks," he said.

She looked up at him. "You have come at a difficult time," she said. "There is a glut in the market. It seems that every dealer on the street has more than he can get rid of."

"I can understand that," he said. "I've checked out a few samples. It's garbage they're selling. There's no reason for anyone to want to buy it."

"Still it's there," she said.

"Agreed," he nodded. He smiled. "Then I won't trouble you. I have kept my word to the House of Soong and come here first. I have some contacts in Los Angeles who I am sure will take it off my hands."

"I didn't say we weren't interested, Preacher," she said quickly. "I merely said there was a glut in the market."

"There is never enough of top-quality merchandise," Preacher said. "And I have the best. It's our own crop and we've chemically checked it out. The THC content is forty percent above average."

"What do you want for it?" she asked.

"Five hundred dollars a brick, less your twenty percent commission, of course."

"Too expensive for this market," she said. "The going street price is three-fifty tops."

"I'll have to take it to Los Angeles then," he said. "They have more money to spend for the little luxuries of life down there. Besides I need the money to keep the Community going for another year."

"There may be a way to work it out," she said. "Why don't you sit down and we'll talk it out over a cup of tea?"

The patrol car inched its way through the nighttime North Beach traffic. "Sergeant," Tom said. "Up there ahead. Look."

The sergeant followed the patrolman's gesture. The purple van was parked on the corner, the rear doors open wide; a black curtain with a white cross painted on it hung down blocking the view into the truck. Extending from the door was a small wooden platform from which Preacher was speaking into a hand-held microphone.

"Pull over a minute," the sergeant said. "I want to hear what he has to say."

Preacher's voice was resonant, yet soft and friendly. It came through the speakers mounted on either side of the platform with compelling intensity and conviction. "If you will accept in your hearts the fact that Jesus Christ our Lord died on the cross for our sins, you have taken the first step toward joining the Community of God. For in the Community of God, man has no sins, no guilts, no wars. Only love for God and his fellowman. In the Community of God, man can find true peace within himself and with his neighbors. In the Community of God, you, too, can join hands with neighbors and live with the righteous. Believe in the Lord Jesus Christ and come to live in the Community of God." He paused for a moment and looked down at the people gathered in front of the platform. He raised his hands in a kind of benediction and in the lights of the oncoming cars, the shadow cast behind him seemed like the vague outlines of Christ on the white cross. "May God bless you and keep all of you."

He held the gesture for a moment, savoring the sudden stillness of the crowd, then dropped his arms suddenly as the girls came around the van, holding their collection boxes in one hand and giving out mimeographed sheets with the other. Preacher disappeared behind the curtain.

"He's got quite a spiel," the sergeant said. "For a moment he almost had me believing it."

Tom laughed. "It's not his spiel, Sergeant. It's those girls. All that fresh young pussy can make me believe anything."

A passerby dropped one of the mimeod sheets near the patrol car and the sergeant stepped out and retrieved it. Getting back in the car, he read it under the dashboard light.

For more information about the Community of God, write and mail this form with or without your contribution to:—

The Community of God
P. O. Box 119
Los Altos, Calif.

He looked up through the window. The black curtain was already gone, the platform had been pulled back into the van and the doors closed. A moment later the van pulled out into the traffic. He glanced behind him. The girls were walking down the street, still handing out the mimeod sheets and waving their collection boxes at the crowds.

He glanced at his wristwatch. It was nine P.M. "Time to go in," he said. "Six hours in this car is long enough."

"I'm with you, Sarge," Tom said enthusiastically.

The sergeant was thoughtful. "Let's pay them another visit tomorrow. Something about them is still bothering me."

CHAPTER FOUR

"Do you really believe in God, Preacher?"

He rolled over in bed and looked at her. She was sitting up, leaning back against the silken pillows. The red-gold light filtering softly through the small Chinese lanterns turned her skin into soft ivory. He waited until she finished lighting a cigarette before he answered. "You know that I do."

She looked down at him. "Sometimes I wonder. The things you do. The dope. The girls. Everything seems so free and easy. Doesn't your God say that these things are sinful?"

"It's all interpretation," he said. "Nothing is sinful if it's done with love. If we believe that Christ the Redeemer died for our sins and we give ourselves up to His care, then we can sin no more."

She touched his face, her fingers tracing the line from his cheekbone to his chin. "You're a strange and beautiful man, Preacher."

"Thank you," he said quietly.

"It has been a long time since we were together," she said. "Many times I have thought about you."

"I have thought often about you too, Barbara."

"I wondered what it would be like when you came back. If you came back. Would it be the same as it was before when my father was alive and I did not have the responsibility of the House of Soong on my shoulders?"

"Was it?" He watched her.

She met his eyes. "Yes. And no."

"How is it different?"

"I question now what I did not before."

He was silent for a moment. "Business?"

She nodded. "Yes. Are you with me because of how you feel, Preacher? Or is it five hundred dollars a brick?"

"What do you feel?" he asked.

"I'm not sure," she answered. "You tell me, Preacher."

He placed his hand on the silky softness of her inner thighs and felt the warm moistness of her response. "I'm with you as I always have been, Barbara. For love."

"And the others? Are you with them for love too?"

He looked up into her face. "There can be no other reason, Barbara. We are all children of the same God and all we have to give one another is love."

The ringing of the telephone seemed a strange sound in this room of Chinese silk and tapestry. She answered it. She listened for a moment then spoke rapidly in Chinese. Finally she covered the mouthpiece and turned to him.

"We can move it all tonight if you'll take four twenty-five."

He thought for a moment.

"If you want my advice, Preacher," she said in a suddenly businesslike voice, "you'll take it. Fifty bricks is a lot of shit to sit on and the police in this town are not stupid. Through our contacts at headquarters we've already found out they have you on their daily checklist. The minute word gets out that a big shipment has hit town, they'll come down on you real fast."

He looked into her eyes. "You sounded just like your father then."

"I hope so," she said. "Or I should not be the head of the House of Soong."

"Okay," he said. "When and where do they want to take delivery?"

Again she spoke Chinese into the telephone. "Now," she said to him. "Anywhere you say."

He was out of bed and already dressing. "Tell them I'll be on the corner up the block from your office. Will they have the money?"

"No," she said. "You'll get that from me tomorrow morning."

"Okay," he said easily.

She turned back to the telephone and spoke quickly, then put it down and watched him finish dressing. "Preacher," she said.

"Yes?"

"Make this the last time you do it," she said. "It's not worth it. It's only money."

"I need the money," he said. "How else can I keep my family together?"

"There has to be a better way than to risk going to jail."

He stared at her for a moment. "I'll think about it."

She reached for a kimono and got out of bed. "I'll have to let you out. After eight o'clock at night the elevator works on a key lock."

"Okay," he said. She came toward him and he took her in his arms and kissed her. "Remember what I said. Only for love."

She looked into his eyes and smiled. "Yes, Preacher."

He followed her to the elevator and waited while she placed the key in the lock and pressed the button. The door opened. He held it open with his foot while he spoke to her. "I'm going to give them the keys to a three-quarter-ton pickup," he said. "The bricks are in a false bottom. Tell them to leave it somewhere safe when they've emptied it and I'll get the keys when I see you in the morning."

She nodded. "About ten o'clock, Preacher."

"Ten o'clock, Barbara," he said and pressed the button. She watched the door close, then watched the indicator lights on the panel until they stopped at 1. Then the light went out and she took the key from the lock and walked slowly back to her room.

From somewhere nearby a church bell tolled four times as he walked along the night-mist-covered sidewalk near the wharf. Already the first of the fishing boats were in with their catch of Dungeness crabs being lifted in their nets by the long-poled winches and dumped into the boiling pots at wharfside. He stood there for a moment, watching, then crossed the street and walked up the block to the alley.

His footsteps echoed hollowly on the cobblestones as he approached the van. He paused while searching in his pocket for the key to unlock the door. It swung open and he looked up. "Charlie," he said. "How come you're not sleeping?"

She stared down at him. "I couldn't sleep. I was worried about you."

He climbed into the van. "There was nothing to worry about."

She closed the door behind him. "You were with that Chinese girl."

"Yes."

She came close to him. "I can smell her on your beard."

He laughed. "That's chow mein. I didn't have time to wash."

"That's not funny," she said. "I can tell the difference between cunt and chow mein."

He took off his blouse, then his shirt, and sat in a chair to pull off his boots. "You're not jealous, are you?" he asked in a reproving voice.

She knelt in front of him and pulled at his boots. "No," she said. "I know better than that. Jealousy is a sick thing. But I wanted to be with you."

33

"You are with me," he said. "You know that."

She pulled the second boot off almost angrily. "Don't give me that shit, Preacher. I'm not a stupid kid like the others. I'm twenty-five years old and you know what I'm talking about. They're all happy to wait their turn whenever you want them. But I want more. I wanted your prick exploding and shooting inside me, not in some stupid Chinese hole."

He stared down at her. His voice was cold. "Those are evil thoughts, Charlie."

She began to cry. "I can't help it, Preacher. I love you so much."

He took her hands away from her face. "It's God you love, Charlie. The same God that is in all of us."

"I know," she nodded, still sniffing. "But is it sinful to want you?"

"It is sinful only if it is selfish," he said.

She sank back on her haunches and looked down at the floor. "Then I am sinful," she said in a small voice.

He got to his feet and looked down at her. "You will have to pray that God will forgive your sins, Charlie."

"Do you forgive me, Preacher?"

"It is not I who grant forgiveness, Charlie," he said. "Only God can do that."

She reached for his hand and kissed it. "I'm sorry, Preacher."

He raised her to her feet. "Now, go back inside to sleep. It will be morning soon and we have much to do tomorrow."

The panel door of the van was open as the sergeant walked up the alley. He looked in the door. Preacher was seated at the desk, writing. "Preacher," the sergeant called.

Preacher looked up. "Hello, Sergeant."

"I'm not disturbing you?" the sergeant asked.

Preacher smiled. "Not at all."

"Mind if I come in?"

"Come on," Preacher said.

The sergeant clambered heavily into the van. He glanced at the notes on the desk. "What are you writing?"

"My sermon for tomorrow," Preacher said.

"I heard you speaking last night. You have a silver tongue, as they used to say when I was a boy."

Preacher smiled. "It's easy to speak with God's words."

The sergeant nodded. "The collections going well?"

"Very well," Preacher answered. "We should have almost seven hundred dollars by the time we finish tonight and start home."

"You're not staying tomorrow?" The sergeant was surprised. "Sunday is the busiest day on the wharf. You should get at least twice as much as any other day."

Preacher smiled. "It is also the Sabbath. And on the seventh day He rested from His labors. And we must be back for the Sunday services."

"But you're here already," the sergeant said. "It seems to me it would be a shame to pass up all that money."

"We really don't need that much, Sergeant. Our wants are very simple. The main reason to be here is to spread God's word."

The sergeant stared at him. He seemed to be sincere. Even the police lieutenant in Los Altos that morning seemed to be convinced they were straight. He said they had a twenty-acre truck farm outside of town and even the lieutenant's wife had bought eggs and vegetables from them. The Los Altos policeman said that to him they were more like Jehovah's Witnesses or Seventh-Day Adventists than anything else. They were always quiet and well-behaved as they passed out pieces of literature while making their sales from door to door. Still, the grapevine had it that a ton of marijuana was being dropped on the city and it had to come from somewhere.

"You seem to be alone here," he said. "Where are the girls?"

"Out with the collection boxes."

"I never saw where they were staying," the policeman said.

"The door is open," Preacher said. "You can have a look for yourself."

"Do you mind showing me?"

"Not at all," Preacher said. He got out of the chair and the sergeant followed him to the building. Preacher opened the door and they went inside.

There were ten neatly rolled sleeping bags on a freshly swept floor. Otherwise the small storeroom was bare. The sergeant glanced around. There wasn't the faintest hint of weed in the air. He looked at Preacher. "Very nice. I see they're all ready to leave."

Preacher nodded.

The sergeant went back outside into the alley. He turned as Preacher closed the door behind him. "You've collected a lot of money," he said. "Keep your eyes open in case someone decides to hit on you."

"I don't think anyone will." Preacher smiled easily. "God looks after His own."

"Just be careful," the seregeant said. "If you should need any help, don't be afraid to call us."

"Thank you, Sergeant," Preacher said.

The sergeant turned as if to leave, then turned back. "There's been rumors that a large order of dope has been dropped on the town. Have you heard anything about it?"

Preacher met his gaze. "I haven't heard any rumors."

The sergeant looked at him for a long moment, then nodded. "I guess you wouldn't," he said. "You're all too far out of it." He held out his hand. "You understand. I'm just doing my job."

Preacher's grip was firm. "I understand, Sergeant."

"Goodbye, Preacher. Good luck."

"Goodbye, Sergeant. God bless you."

He watched the policeman walk down the alley to the patrol car parked in the street. Barbara had been right. This would be the last time. He had the strangest feeling that it was only because the sergeant liked him that he was not being pressed. Almost as if he were saying, "Okay, just this one time. But no more."

Thoughtfully he walked back to the van and climbed inside. He stared down at the desk. The heading for the sermon tomorrow stared back up at him: "Go forth and sin no more."

CHAPTER
FIVE

. It was near seven in the morning when he turned the pickup onto the dirt road at the top of the hill that led down to the farm that belonged to the Community of God. He drove past the large NO TRESPASSING—PRIVATE PROPERTY signs placed on either side of the entrance to the dirt road. He turned the curve at the top of the hill, stopped the pickup and got out. He walked to the edge of the road and looked down.

Sprawled out in the small valley below him were the neatly painted wooden buildings that made up the commune. Four buildings. The women's building was the largest because it accommodated the larger portion of the Community's population, twenty-eight women and seven children. The men's building was smaller. Including himself there were seventeen men. Between the two buildings were the second-largest building, which housed the dining room and kitchens, and the smallest building, which held the meeting room and also served as the church and social room. Behind the buildings were large carport-type sheds under which were parked the various cars and machinery that belonged to the Community or their members, and still farther away was the small building in which he lived and which also served as the general office.

A wisp of blue smoke was rising from chimney over the kitchen and he could see the purple van already parked under the shed. He nodded to himself. That meant the girls had had no problems on the drive down from San Francisco. They'd made better time than he, coming straight down on the freeway. He had driven down on the back roads, not wanting to take any chances of being stopped on the freeway. The back of the pickup reeked of marijuana. The Chinese had been very careless unloading the cargo, having broken open some of the carefully wrapped bricks. Or maybe they weren't careless, just checking that they were getting what they paid for. At any rate, one of the first things to be done was to clean out the false bottom of the pickup and hose it down thoroughly. Even better, he would have the false bottom removed completely, because from now on there would be no further use for it.

He went back to the pickup and continued down the hill. It took another ten minutes to negotiate the narrow tire-tracked dirt road and come out in front of the farm. By that time it seemed as if almost everyone in the Community was outside in front of the buildings to greet him.

They smiled and waved as he drove slowly by. "Good Sabbath, Preacher."

He waved back to them. "Good Sabbath, children."

He stopped the pickup in front of his small house. Tarz, the tall, slim, blond young man with granny glasses who was known as the Organizer and was his chief assistant, came toward the pickup as he got out, closely followed by Charlie, who had driven the van down.

"Good Sabbath, Preacher," Tarz said, his teeth white and large in his smile.

Preacher took his hand. "Good Sabbath, Tarz." He turned to Charlie. "Did you have a good trip?"

She smiled. "No problems. It was a piece of cake."

"I'm glad," he said. "The children all right?"

"Beautiful," she said. "They're on a natural high from spreading God's word to the public and want to know when they can do it again."

He smiled. "I know how they feel." He turned back to Tarz. "Would you please put the pickup under the shed for me? I want to shower and clean up before going in to breakfast."

Tarz nodded. "Of course, Preacher." He hesitated a moment. "Everything go well? Did we raise enough to cover this year's mortagage payment?"

Preacher nodded. "You'll be able to make your banker very happy when you go in to see him."

Tarz grinned. "He sure will be. He was getting a bit edgy the closer we got to the end of the month."

"He'll be okay now," Preacher said, starting for his building.

Charlie followed him inside. "You look beat," she said. "Let me heat some water for you an' you can take a hot soak."

"I'll be okay with a shower," he said.

"Just this once, Preacher, do as I say."

He looked at her for a moment, then sighed. "Okay. I am tired." He sank into a chair.

"That's better," she said. She took a joint from her shirt pocket and lit it. "Here," she said, handing it to him. "Take a few tokes from this. It'll relax you while I go and start a fire in the stove. Then I'll be right back to undress you."

He took a deep toke from the joint. "You're acting like I'm a baby."

She laughed. "All you men think you're so big and strong. But a little bit of babying never hurt the best of you."

He took another deep toke as she went into the next room to start the fire. He leaned his head back against the chair. Suddenly he was aware that he was much more tired than he had thought. She was right. A little bit of babying would not hurt at all.

· · ·

Tarz came in while she was pouring hot water from the iron kettle into the large wooden-staved tub placed on the kitchen floor. "Where's Preacher?"

She glanced at him. "In the other room. Asleep in his chair."

Tarz crossed to the open door and looked inside. Charlie was right. His eyes were closed, his head leaning against the back of the chair. He was still in his clothes. The only thing he had taken off was his boots. Tarz came back to Charlie. "They're expecting him down at the meeting house."

"He ain't goin' to make it," she said. "He's been up all night."

"What do I tell them?" he asked.

"The truth," she said. "It's the Sabbath. And even the Lord had to take a day of rest."

He was silent.

"You tell them to pray an' that he'll be with them after he gets some sleep. He should be okay by the middle of the afternoon."

He nodded, looking at her. "Okay. Need any help with him?"

She laughed. "I can manage. After all, he's not that big."

Tarz left the house and she poured another kettle of water into the tub. She took a bottle of colored crystals from the paper bag she had placed on the table and slowly emptied it into the tub. She stirred it slowly with a big wooden paddle and the scent of pinewood perfume rose with the steam. She breathed deeply. It smelled real nice.

He felt her hand on his shoulder and opened his eyes. "I fell asleep."

"I know," she said.

"What time is it?" he asked. "I got a sermon all ready."

"It'll keep until this afternoon," she said. "I already told them. You get out of your clothes. The bath is ready."

He got slowly to his feet and began to unbutton his shirt. He sniffed the air. "What's that funny smell?"

41

"Pine bath salts," she giggled, "I bought up in the city. The drugstore man says it's real good for when you're tired."

"You'll have me smelling like a perfume factory."

"Don't complain till you try it," she said. "It's got to be a lot better than chow mein."

He laughed. "We'll see."

"How is it?" she asked, looking down at him.

He sank even deeper into the tub, his head against its back, and turned to look at her. "Great. I'd almost forgotten how good a real bath could be."

She smiled. "I thought you'd dig it."

"You were right, Charlie."

She gave him a sponge and a cake of soap. "You scrub yourself good and clean. I'll go and get you some breakfast."

He grinned at her. "My mother always used to wash me."

"I'm not your mother," she laughed. "You're big enough to wash yourself."

"Okay," he said. "And while you're out there, tell Tarz I want to see him right away."

"Can't it wait?" she asked. "I wanted you to have some rest."

"It's important," he said.

He was drying himself when Tarz came in. "How are you feeling, Preacher?"

"Fine," he said. "I was just a little beat, that's all."

"Charlie said it was important."

Preacher looked at him. "It is. First thing tomorrow morning, get both tractors and six men. I want field ten completely plowed under. But real good, so that none of the old crop comes up at all. Then I want you to seed it with alfalfa."

Tarz stared at him. "We're not going to make any money with alfalfa."

"We're not going to make any money if the whole Community gets busted for growing and dealing," Preacher replied.

"That money pays the mortgage."

"We'll have to find another way," Preacher said. "We did

well in Frisco. Maybe we'll start a regular collection program and do a different city each week."

"The children aren't goin' to like it. A lot of them are here because they feel the outside rules don't apply. They like the freedom that the Community of God has given them; they like the fact that no one passes judgment on them."

"They'll still be free to do what they want," Preacher said. "We're just goin' out of the business, that's all."

Tarz shook his head. "They ain't goin' to look at it that way. They're gonna feel that you're giving in to the establishment."

Preacher looked at him. "They're not wrong. But the choice is a practical one. I don't think any of them will like the idea of going to jail any more than I do."

"They'll still want to do their own dope."

"That's up to them," Preacher said. "They can do it. All I'm saying is that we're not going to be growing it here. And anyone I catch breaking that rule gets banished."

Tarz stared at him for a moment, then nodded. "Okay. I'll have the tractors out there at six in the morning."

"I'll be out there with you," Preacher said.

"What's the matter, Preacher?" Tarz asked, a hint of resentment in his voice. "Don't you trust me?"

Preacher laughed. "You know better than that, Tarz. I just want to make sure that the job is done right. I'm still the boss farm boy around here. You city slickers don't know it all yet."

Tarz grinned. "Whatever you say, Preacher. But you're goin' to have to explain it to the children. They'll never buy it if I tell them."

"I'll do that too," Preacher said. "All we have to keep in mind is that the only important work we have to do is God's work. Everything else is incidental."

CHAPTER
SIX

He rolled over restlessly in bed and finally sat up. A week
had passed since his return from San Francisco and he had
not yet been able to sleep through a night. A peculiar foreboding hung over him and he was not able to pinpoint the
cause of his anxiety. And nothing he did was able to alleviate
the strange nervousness. Not prayer, not fasting, or doping, or
sex. Though each in its turn gave him a few hours' rest, the
feeling came back to haunt him.

It was pitch-black in the room, the windows were black
with night, there was no moon. He felt a stirring beside him
and reached out with his hand, touching a naked young body.
He tried to remember who had been with him when he fell
asleep but couldn't. He knew there had been several girls with
him but he had smoked too much and his head was still fuzzy.

"Preacher," came the whisper.

"Yes."

"Are you okay?"

"Yes. I just can't sleep." He paused for a moment. "I can't
see either. It's too dark."

"I'm Melanie." There was a whispered giggle. "You were really stoned. We all had to put you to bed."

"All?" he questioned.

"Sarah, Charlie and me."

He felt a movement on his other side as the girl sat up. He knew this voice. "Preacher, are you all right?" Charlie asked.

"I can't sleep," he said.

"You haven't been able to sleep since you came down from Frisco." There was a bitterness in her voice. "You haven't been able to do much else either. I think that Chinese bitch put a hex on you."

"That's blasphemy," he said. "There's no such thing. That went out with the Middle Ages."

Getting out of bed, she said, "I'm going to make you some herb tea." She lit a candle next to the bed. In the flickering light he could see all three of the girls. They were all as naked as he was. She picked up a small bottle from the wooden box that served as a bedside table and handed it to Melanie. "I've been saving this bottle of Kama Sutra Musk Oil. You stretch out and let the girls rub you down with it. It'll relax you."

"I want a cigarette," he said.

"You've had enough dope," she replied.

"I mean a cigarette cigarette."

"You've been off them for over a year now. You don't want to start up again."

"Don't argue with me," he said edgily.

She was silent for a moment, then took a pack from the table. He pulled a cigarette from it and she held the candle for him to light it. He dragged deeply, the acrid tobacco burning its way down into him. He coughed.

"Feel better now?" she asked sarcastically.

"Much," he said shortly, dragging on the cigarette again.

"Then lie back and let the girls take care of you," she said.

He nodded and sank back on the bed as she lit another candle and placed it in a holder on the box. Then she walked to the door. "I won't be long."

He looked at her. "Thanks, Charlie."

45

"You don't have to thank us, Preacher," she said. "We all love you."

"And I love you," he said.

"Turn this way, Preacher," Sarah said, sitting crosslegged behind him. "And place your head in my lap."

He shifted slightly, doing as she asked. He took a last drag on the cigarette. It was real good. It had been stupid of him to give them up—he really didn't know why. He held up the cigarette and Melanie took it and put it out in an ashtray. The faint perfume of the Kama Sutra Oil came to his nostrils as the girls placed some on their hands and then began to massage him.

Sarah, behind him, began to work on his neck and shoulders, while Melanie, who knelt at his feet, began with his feet and worked her way up across his ankles and legs. Charlie was right. Their light touch and the softness of the oil was both relaxing and soothing. He closed his eyes and gave himself up to the simple sensuality of the feathery-light touch that seemed to reach the nerve ends lying just under the surface of his skin.

Sarah's hands slid from his shoulders to his chest, moving in slow gentle circles over his nipples and ribs while Melanie began to knead his thighs. "Don't fight us, Preacher," Melanie said. "Your legs is all tight. Let the muscles go soft and easy.

"How do I do that?" he asked.

"Talk to us about God, Preacher," Sarah said. "If'n you concentrate on Him, it'll take your mind off'n yourself."

He opened his eyes and looked up at her as she leaned over him, her arms outstretched to reach his stomach. He could see the faint patina of perspiration on her body and noticed the faint odor of her sex rising from her lap. "It's not going to be easy," he said. "I can smell you."

She giggled. "Then I'll talk to you about God."

"Okay."

"I don't know," she said hesitantly. "I been having this

dream. But I've been afraid to tell you. It may be blasphemous."

"The only real blasphemy in the Community is the fear of sharing everything. Even your doubts."

"Melanie knows the dream. I told her."

"Then you can tell me," he said.

She began to knead his stomach muscles, her fingers pressing more heavily than they had on his chest. "In the dream, it is night and I am kneeling at the foot of the cross on Calvary. I am praying at the feet of our Savior when suddenly something makes me look up and Jesus is looking into my eyes. I could feel a white brilliance running through my soul. It is so bright that for a moment I can't see and when my eyes clear it is not His face I am looking into but your face, it is not His eyes, but your eyes. I can see so much pain that I want to reach up and touch you and comfort you but no matter how much I stretch and try, I cannot even touch your feet. I begin to cry. Then I wake up."

Preacher felt the tears on his cheeks. He looked up at her. She was crying even as she massaged him. He didn't speak.

"What does it mean, Preacher?" she asked. "Is it a vision? Or are you really Jesus Christ?"

"One thing I do know," he said. "I am not Jesus Christ. Whatever else it is I do not know. All I can feel is that you are seeking our Lord with such intensity that you are subconciously changing His identity into someone closer to you who you can touch and reach."

"Is that blasphemous?" she asked.

He shook his head. "No. All of us seek God, either in ourselves or in recognizable images. The important thing is that we do not create false images to worship, to remember there is only one true God and He has sent us His only Son Jesus Christ, to redeem us and lead us to salvation."

He felt her oil-softened fingers touch his penis at the same moment that Melanie touched his testicles. A fire seemed to begin in his loins.

47

The girls suddenly withdrew their hands. "Turn over on your stomach," Sarah said. "Charlie said for us to do your back the minute you began to get hard."

"Why?" he grumbled.

"She wants you to be completely relaxed when you have your herb tea," Melanie said.

"I'm relaxed now."

"Turn over," Sarah said. "You'll be more relaxed when we're finished."

He was half drowsing by the time Charlie came back. "How do you feel now, Preacher?" she asked.

He turned his head to look up at her. "Relaxed."

"Good," she smiled. "Now sit up and drink this."

He rolled over and sat up, taking the mug from her hand. He raised it to his lips.

"Be careful," she cautioned. "It's hot."

Tentatively he sipped it. He made a face. "It tastes awful. What is it?"

"Drink it. It's good for you."

"That's not telling me what it is," he said.

"Ginseng tea. The real stuff. I made it from the whole root, not the tea bags. That's why it took so long."

"What's that supposed to do?" he asked.

"Give you strength," she said.

He glanced up at her. "The Chinese say it makes you virile."

"That too." She smiled.

He took another sip of the tea. "Do you think I need it?"

"You can use all the help you can get. You haven't been yourself lately."

"I know that," he said. "But did you ever think I might have other things on my mind?"

"Whatever it is, this should help you reestablish your perspective."

He tasted the tea again. "This really is awful."

"Drink it all," she said. "The quicker you finish it, the quicker we can all get back to bed."

"Will this help me to sleep?" he asked.

"You'll have no problem sleeping," she said with a faint smile. She watched him empty the cup, then took it from him and put it on the wooden box next to the bed.

"Do you want us to blow out the candles?" Melanie asked.

"No," she answered. "Candlelight is very romantic." She turned toward him, placing her hands on his shoulders, pushing him back on the bed, her mouth covering his lips. At the same moment he felt one of the girls place her hand on his genitals, then a soft warm mouth encircled him.

"Hey, what is this?" he asked, a half-smile on his lips. "I'm beginning to feel like a lamb being fattened for the slaughter."

"You don't know?" Charlie asked, lifting her mouth from his and looking at him.

He shook his head.

"We want you to make a baby in each of us," she said.

"Tonight?" he asked incredulously.

"Yes," they answered almost in unison.

He stared at him. "What for?"

"That way none of us will ever lose you. Even when you've gone away, we'll still have some of your godliness with us."

"That's crazy!" he said.

"No it's not," Charlie said. "We all know you're going to leave us."

"Where did you get that idea?"

"Things aren't the same anymore," she said. "Not since you plowed under the crop. You've changed, Preacher. We thought if we were all together once again, you would come back to us."

He got out of bed roughly and lit a cigarette. He stared at her. "Who put you up to this?"

"Nobody," she said. "But the Community is real upset. Half of them want to go away before you do."

He dragged on the cigarette. "And you think if you all have babies that would make everything right?"

"That's what we thought," she said.

"I'm not planning to go anywhere," he said shortly. "Now you get your asses out of here and tell that to the others. And you can also tell them that if they have any complaints to bring them directly to me."

Charlie began to cry. He looked at the other two girls. They were crying too. He shook his head in frustration. There was no way he could make them understand.

"You're not angry with us, Preacher?" Charlie asked.

"I'm not angry with you," he said. "You're all my children."

"We love you, Preacher," Sarah said, taking his hand and kissing it.

Melanie took his other hand. "We just want to be with you like we used to be before."

"You still are," he said. "Nothing's changed."

"Then let us stay tonight, Preacher," Melanie said. "We promise not to do anything like this again."

He looked over her head at Charlie. The tears were still running down her cheeks. "All right," he said, in a suddenly gentle voice. "Put out the candles and let's go back to sleep."

But sleep still eluded him and it wasn't until the morning, when he saw the bearded men with wide-brimmed black hats descend from their car in front of the meeting house, that he knew the meaning of his foreboding.

They were Brother Ely and Brother Samuel from the Church of the Sons of God, and he suddenly knew to whom the House of Soong had sold the bricks.

CHAPTER
SEVEN

The white Cadillac convertible was parked in front of the meeting house as he walked toward the building. The top was down, revealing the red leather interior gleaming in the morning sun. He walked around to the driver's side and leaned in over the steering column to read the registration form Scotch-taped to it. The car was registered to the Church of the Sons of God in San Francisco. He straightened up and went into the building.

Tarz was seated at the table with the two visitors. The two men were dressed in somber black, black wide-brimmed hats, black shirts and slacks—even their full beards were black. They rose to their feet as he came into the room.

He didn't extend his hand to them. "Brother Ely, Brother Samuel," he said.

Brother Ely, the shorter of the two men, smiled. "Preacher, it's good to see you again."

Preacher nodded. He neither smiled nor answered.

"We heard you were in town," Brother Samuel said. "Why didn't you stop in to see us?"

"Had no reason to," Preacher said shortly.

"But you were there three days," Brother Ely said. "You should have stopped in. You know Brother Robert thinks highly of you. He feels no one works harder for the Lord than you."

Preacher stared at him for a moment, then sat down in a chair across the table from them. He lit a cigarette and leaned back in his chair, unsmiling. "I'm sure Brother Robert didn't send you down here to tell me that."

Brother Ely glanced at Tarz meaningfully, then back to Preacher. "He wanted us to have a private conversation with you."

"In the Community of God we have no secrets from each other," Preacher said. "You can speak freely in front of him or any other of the children. We have nothing to hide."

Brother Samuel got to his feet. He was a large burly man, well over six feet tall, with shoulders that seemed as wide. "The message Brother Robert gave us was for your ears alone," he said heavily.

Preacher looked up at him. He knew the man's reputation. He'd been bouncer in cheap nightclubs and a collector for loan sharks who reputedly had seen the light and joined the Church of the Sons of God. But his job for Brother Robert was the same as it had always been: to intimidate and keep dissident members in line. "You're wasting your time, Brother Samuel," Preacher said easily.

"Sit down, Brother Samuel," Brother Ely said. "Preacher knows what he's doing."

Brother Samuel sat down heavily, a truculent expression on his face. He clasped his hands on the table and stared down at them silently.

Brother Ely turned back to Preacher. "You may have heard that we have just completed a very successful mission throughout the state and have brought more than two hundred converts into the church."

"I heard," Preacher said shortly. It was true. They had gone up and down the state canvassing small communes and families that were existing on the fringes of starvation, promising to save them from the total collapse and destruction of society that the Sons of God said was coming.

"Two hundred," Brother Ely said importantly. "We're now more than five hundred members, with churches in L.A. and San Diego as well."

Preacher nodded without speaking.

"We're becoming a real force," Brother Ely said. "Soon they won't be able to ignore us."

"Congratulations," Preacher said sarcastically.

"We have over eight hundred thousand dollars in cash and property and we're collecting over a thousand a week. We own small businesses in each of the towns where we have churches. We're really growing."

"You also have Crazy Charlie," Preacher said.

"Not anymore," Brother Ely said quickly. "Brother Robert kicked him out. The things he wanted to do didn't go down with us. We hold with God in our views of chastity. All Charlie wanted was sex and to play Jesus."

"But Charlie followed Brother Robert over from Scientology," Preacher said.

"That's not true," Brother Ely said. "Brother Robert left L. Ron a long time ago. He never knew Charlie there. He told me that Charlie was lying about everything, that Charlie was in jail all the time he said he was with Scientology."

"Where's Charlie now?" Preacher asked.

"Somewhere down near L.A.," Brother Ely answered. "He's picked up a bunch of kids and kooks and keeps them stoned out of their minds all the time on dope and acid. That's the only way he can keep them believing that he's J.C. and can save them on Judgment Day."

"He's a bad one," Preacher said. "Someday he's gonna kill somebody."

"Not him," Brother Ely said. "He's a coward."

"Then he's gonna get some fool kids to do it for him," Preacher said.

"That's his problem," Brother Ely answered. "We don't

have anything to do with him anymore."

Preacher was silent for a moment. "But that's not the reason you came down here, is it?"

"Brother Robert wants you to consider joining up with us," Brother Ely said. "He feels that together we can be real important. Maybe even bigger than L. Ron."

Preacher laughed. "No way. We're a simple Christian community. We don't hold with that amalgamation of Jehovah, Jesus Christ and Lucifer that you do. We believe only in the Holy Redemption promised to us by our Savior Jesus Christ."

"But Brother Robert has already proven that Jesus has brought about a reconciliation between His Father, Jehovah, and his uncle, Lucifer. On Judgment Day, Jesus will gather up the righteous unto His Father's protection and Lucifer will destroy all the others."

"He hasn't proven it to me," Preacher said. "And not to anyone else who believes in what the Bible has taught us. There's no way we can get it together."

"How many children do you have down here?" Brother Ely asked.

"Forty-odd," Preacher answered.

"Join up with us and you'll have more than a hundred in no time."

"Not interested," Preacher said flatly.

"Maybe you should be," Brother Ely said darkly. "The law is already on to you. They know you've been selling the grass up in Frisco. We can keep them off your back."

"They can do what they want," Preacher said. "We're clean down here. They're not going to find anything."

"Come on," Brother Ely said. "Five hundred bricks would take at least five acres of plants."

"Somebody's got it wrong," Preacher said. "There's not a bit of the weed growing anywhere on the place."

Brother Ely stared at him. "That ain't what we heard from the House of Soong."

"You bought grass from them?" Preacher asked.

"Five hundred bricks. At the same time you were up there fund-raising."

"That's interesting," Preacher said. "And that's why you think we're growing and dealing?"

"No," Brother Ely said. "We got it from the source. There are men in the House of Soong who don't like it that you're making it with Barbara. They want her out. A woman's got no place in an important tong like that."

Preacher got to his feet. "That's all bullshit. You can go back and tell Brother Robert that the Community of God is not interested in a deal with him."

Brother Ely looked up at him. "If'n you're a real community, you wouldn't mind letting the children take a vote and decide for themselves which way they want to go?"

"Not at all," Preacher said. "They can go any time they want. But there'll still be no deal with Brother Robert."

"Then don't blame us if the law comes down real hard on you."

Brother Samuel got to his feet again. "I tol' ya, the only way to talk with a jerk like this is to show him the error of his ways," he growled, moving menacingly toward Preacher.

Preacher watched him steadily. "I don't recommend that you try to teach me anything."

Brother Samuel launched a hamlike fist at Preacher's face. Preacher seemed to move his head only slightly and the big man's hand whistled harmlessly through the air past him.

"Why don't you calm down," Preacher said in a flat voice. "You know we don't believe in violence here."

"I'll show you what to believe in," Brother Samuel grunted. He leaped forward, swinging again.

This time, Preacher seemed to turn partly away from him as if he were trying to escape. Brother Samuel pressed forward after him. He never saw Preacher's kick coming at him until Preacher's heavy boot caught him flush on the side of his face. There was a heavy crunching of bone and he was knocked sideways to the floor, blood pouring from his nose and mouth. He tried to raise himself on his hands, staring up in angry

55

surprise at Preacher, but the effort was too much for him. He collapsed to the floor again with a groan.

Preacher looked down at him, then at Brother Ely, still sitting in his chair. "Get him out of here and take him back to Brother Robert with the message I gave you. We want nothing to do with the Sons of God."

"I thought you said you didn't believe in violence," Brother Ely said.

"I don't," Preacher answered. "But I didn't say we don't believe in self-defense. You all forgot I spent three years in Vietnam."

Brother Ely was silent for a moment. He made no move to help the big man on the floor. "All the same, I'd like you to think over Brother Robert's proposition."

"I've already thought it over," Preacher said with finality, and he walked out of the meeting hall.

From the window of his own little building, he watched Brother Ely and Tarz help the big man into the car. Brother Samuel held a big white towel to his face. He muttered something to Tarz, who turned and walked away.

"What happened?" Charlie asked, coming to the window and looking out as the white Cadillac turned and began to drive away.

"Nothing," Preacher answered. He watched Tarz walk back into the meeting house. Something was wrong. Ordinarily Tarz would have come right over to see him. For a moment he wondered if Tarz had been in touch with them before they came down here. Then he resolutely pushed the thought from his mind.

The Community of God was all together. There was no chance that a Judas could be among them.

CHAPTER
EIGHT

He sat in the pickup and waited for Charlie to come out of the post office. Usually he didn't go into town for the mail but today he was restless. The meeting with the two men from the Sons of God had disturbed him more than he cared to admit, even though he considered them nothing but one of the many strange cults that had proliferated in California, attracting and preying on the hippies and the kids who wandered disenchanted with their lives and came searching for they knew not what.

It was the L. Rons, the Brother Roberts and Crazy Charlies that seemed to get most of them, preaching disaffection with society and promising them a utopia. More than one child had found himself bound in virtual bondage to a man or a group that used him only for what could be obtained from him. And even stranger was the fact that the used were happy being used, because it made them feel needed and important.

It was not what God had promised them or even what God had intended for them but it had a strange power that he could not comprehend. The Lord had commanded him to bring succor to the lost and that was what he tried to do. But maybe that was not enough. Maybe there was something that he himself was missing, something lacking inside him. Maybe it was that the authority he preached was God's and the authority they sought was temporal. But he could not pretend to be anything other than what he was. A man spreading the word of God. He could not do what the others did and place himself above them as God's appointed representative on earth, thus commanding obedience from them. They were all God's children and he was one with them.

Through the windshield he could see Charlie coming out of the post office, the mailbag in her hand. She was smiling as she opened the door. "We got more than a hundred letters," she said. "From what I see they all came from Frisco."

"Good," he said, starting the engine. "Those flyers we gave out got some results."

"Oh!" she exclaimed. "I almost forgot. This telegram came for you."

He ripped open the yellow envelope and read the message. IMPORTANT YOU CALL ME THIS NUMBER 777-2121 IMMEDIATELY. BARBARA.

He glanced at the date on the top of the telegram. It had been sent from San Francisco two days before. He should have received it yesterday. Strange that Tarz, who had picked up the mail, didn't bring it to him. But it was possible that it had not been received until after Tarz had already gone.

He opened the door and stepped from the pickup. "I'll be back in a minute," he said.

Charlie read the expression on his face. "Something wrong, Preacher?"

"I don't know," he answered. He started for the telephone booth at the edge of the parking lot.

Through the closed glass door of the telephone booth he could see Charlie opening some of the letters in the mailbag. The coins tinkled down into the slot and the telephone at the end of the line began to ring.

Barbara came on the line after the second ring. "Hello."

"This is Preacher," he said.

Her voice was strangely hushed and nervous. "What took you so long?"

"I just got the telegram this minute," he said.

"You're going to have some visitors," she whispered.

"I already did. This morning," he said. "I threw them out."

"Oh."

"What's the connection between you and the Sons of God?" he asked.

"I haven't any," she whispered. "But my uncle decided that a woman should not be the head of the House of Soong. He was the one who made the deal with them and told them who we bought it from."

"Couldn't you stop him?" he asked.

"There was nothing I could do," she answered. "He's taken over. I'm virtually a prisoner up here, locked in my own apartment. Most of my cousins are already on his side."

"Aren't any of them loyal to you?"

"I have no way of telling. They're letting no one up to see me."

"Why don't you just walk out of there?"

"I tried. But they have two men on the door downstairs. They wouldn't let me out. My uncle has denounced me to the family as a whore because we spent the night together."

Preacher was silent for a moment. "What are they going to do now?"

"I don't know," she answered. "But I'm afraid. He's called for a family council the day after tomorrow. Cousins are coming in from L.A., Chicago and New York."

"What can they do?" he asked.

"They can have me removed," she said. "And there's nothing I could do about it. I won't be allowed to attend the council."

"That's not too bad," he said. "You don't need all that responsibility."

"You don't understand," she said. "That's not what the tong means by removal."

He was shocked. "They wouldn't!"

Her tone was fatalistic. "That's the way it is done. Succession in the tong can only come when the former head is dead."

"You have to get out of there," he said.

"I told you. I can't," she said.

"I'll get you out."

"There's no way you can get up here. They have two men on the elevator door all the time and my uncle has taken away their keys. The only time anyone can come up here, even with food, is when he opens the elevator for them."

"Do you still have your key?" he asked.

"Yes. But that won't do any good. There's no way I can get it to you. If it weren't for this private telephone line I wouldn't even have been able to send you the telegram."

"If I remember correctly, it's an Otis elevator, isn't it?"

"Yes."

"Then get your key. There will be a number on the back of it."

"Hold on," she said. There was a clicking on the phone as she put it down. A moment later she came back on. "I have it."

He had paper and pencil ready. "Give it to me."

"One, 0, seven, two, three, five, K.I."

He read the number back to her.

"That's right," she said. "But what good will that do?"

"Otis will have a record. They always do. Just for emergencies. I'll have them make one for me."

"But you'll have to get past the men downstairs," she said.

"Leave that to me," he said. "I will call you tomorrow night about two in the morning. But whether you hear from me or not, have a bag packed. I'll be there about that time."

She was silent for a moment. "You don't have to do anything. That's not why I called you. I don't want anything to happen to you."

"We all live by God's mercy," he said. "We will both pray for His guidance and protection. I will see you tomorrow night."

"I will pray for you, Preacher," she said.

He put down the telephone. A moment later it rang and the operator came on. "That will be ninety-five cents additional, please."

Thoughtfully he placed the coins in the slot and listened to them tinkle their way down into the box. "Thank you," the operator said. He placed the receiver back on the hook and made his way slowly back to the pickup.

He stretched the black slacks neatly out on the bed, then folded the black turtleneck sweater and black knitted ski mask and flattened them out on the slacks. Quickly he rolled them into a small tight bundle and fastened it with a thin black leather belt, then put it into a brown paper bag. He left the cottage, threw the paper bag into the front seat of the pickup, then walked down to the meeting place.

Tarz, Charlie and about six others were seated at the long table, opening the envelopes from the morning mail, dividing them into three stacks. One stack was for the letters containing contributions, which would get the special deluxe brochure in reply. The second was made up of information requests, which would get the mimeographed stapled information sheets. The third and last consisted of antagonistic messages. They would be answered by a form letter which asked them not to hate but to show true Christian mercy and seek counsel and forgiveness in the teachings of the Bible and our Lord and Savior Jesus Christ.

Tarz looked up as he came in. His voice was filled with satisfaction. "We've collected about a hundred and ten dollars in the mail between yesterday and today. That's pretty good."

Preacher nodded. "What about recruits?"

"Hard to tell," Tarz said. "But we have about two or three possibilities that I think are pretty good. I'll see to it that they get a special invitation to come down here and spend a weekend as our guests."

"Good. That's more important than the money. One soul brought to the Lord is worth more than all the riches in the world."

"Amen," Tarz intoned.

Preacher gestured and Tarz got out of his seat and followed him into the small room at the back of the meeting hall. Preacher closed the door behind them and turned to face him. "I'm going back up to Frisco this afternoon," he said. "I'll be there all day tomorrow and should be back early the next morning."

"Going to see Brother Robert after all?" Tarz asked eagerly.

Preacher glanced at him. Tarz sounded almost too eager. "No," he answered shortly. "This is personal business. Besides, you heard me. I've already given them my answer."

"They're goin' to make trouble," Tarz said.

"There's nothing they can do, we're clean."

"I don't mean that," Tarz said. "You know how the Sons of God operates. They'll come down here, a whole bunch of them, and scare everybody with hell and damnation because when the big bang comes we've all been committing the sin of fornication."

"If God didn't intend for us to love one another He wouldn't have made our bodies with the machinery to do it," Preacher said. "Just make sure that if they do show up when I'm not here, they don't get a chance to drop any acid on the children. That could get them crazy enough to do anything."

"What if they bring their whips and cats?" Tarz asked. "You know how they like to lay them on the girls. They're pretty rough and there aren't enough of us men here to stop them."

Preacher looked at him. "You sound scared."

"I am scared," Tarz admitted. "Don't forget I spent a year with them. I know what they can do."

Preacher thought for a moment. "Then the minute they show up, call the police on your C.B. radio. They'll take care of them for you."

"The children won't like that. Most of them hate the cops too."

"They'll like it better than getting beat up," Preacher said. He took a deep breath. "But I won't be gone long. Chances are they won't be coming back before I do. That is, if they do come back at all."

"They'll come back all right," Tarz said darkly.

"What makes you so sure?"

"Brother Ely said that Brother Robert won't take too kindly to the way you beat up on Brother Samuel. He said they'll be back."

"Could be," Preacher nodded. "But you know what to do. Just do like I said and there'll be no trouble."

"Yes, Preacher," Tarz said.

"How much money do we have in the cash box?" Preacher asked, changing the subject.

"I don't know," Tarz answered cautiously. "How much do you need?"

Preacher smiled. Tarz was real cautious with the money. Everybody knew he was a skinflint. "Five hundred," he said. Then seeing the dismay on Tarz's face, he quickly added, "But like I said, it's personal. I'll give you my check for the money."

Tarz smiled. "Well, in that case, I think I can scrounge it up for you."

CHAPTER
NINE

He found an open parking meter in front of the warehouse that served as the maintenance building for the elevator company at a quarter to five that afternoon. He got out of the pickup, put a dime in the meter, his eyes scanning the crowd just beginning to leave work for the day. It only took a moment for him to find what he sought.

He stepped quickly through the crowd and tapped a young Chinese on the shoulder. The young man, dressed in faded blue work jacket and Levi's, turned toward him. "Yes?" he asked, his narrowed eyes sizing up Preacher in a glance.

Preacher held the twenty-dollar bill folded in his hand so that the young man could read the number on it. "I need a favor."

"No dope," the young man said quickly.

Preacher smiled. "No dope."

"You a cop?"

Preacher shook his head. "Not a cop. I just want you to go in that building and pick up a key for me."

"If that's all why don't you go and get it yourself?"

"Because my eyes don't slant like yours," Preacher said. "It's the key to my girl's place and her old man's got her locked in her house. But he won't be there tonight and I can get her out if I have a key."

The young Chinese grinned. "The old man don't like the shape of your eyes, huh?"

"Something like that," Preacher nodded.

"Sure it's nothing illegal?"

"Straight and cool, man. It's nothing but romance. Love crosses all boundaries."

"I know what you mean. A lot of the old folks are like that. You should hear my mother when I date a chick that ain't Chinese. Like three blocks away you can hear her."

"Then it's okay?"

The young man nodded. "Just tell me what I got to do."

"It's simple," Preacher said. He took a slip of paper from his pocket. "Just go to the customer's service desk and tell them you came to pick up the key for Miss Soong and show them this paper with the number on it. When they give it to you check the number on the key with the paper and if it's okay bring it out to me."

"And if it's not?"

"Leave it and tell them you'll be back in the morning, then come out and give me back the paper. You'll get the twenty either way."

"What makes you think they'll have it?" the young man asked. "Those keys have to be made up."

"I called earlier. They said it would be ready by four. It's almost five now."

He watched the young man walk into the building, then went back to the pickup and, leaning against the side panel, lit a cigarette. He had just finished the cigarette when the young man came out, grinning.

Preacher straightened up. "You got it?"

The Chinese nodded. "I got it. No sweat. They even asked me 'cash or charge?' I told them 'charge,' of course."

Preacher smiled. "Good thinking."

65

"I figured it'd be even more fun to stick the old man with the bill," the young Chinese said. He gave the envelope to Preacher.

Preacher took out the key and checked it. The number was the same as on the slip of paper. He handed the twenty to the young man. "Thanks, buddy."

"Thank you." The Chinese stuck the twenty-dollar bill in his pocket. "Good luck. Hope everything goes all right." He went back into the crowd and Preacher watched him until he had turned the corner and was out of sight before he got back into the pickup and drove off.

An hour later he drove off the bridge on the Oakland side, made a sharp turn, went down almost to the bay front and stopped the pickup in front of an old gray house on a tired and beat-up street. He locked the cab and went up the steps and rang the doorbell.

The door opened a little and a tall black man peered from the crack, the light from the hall shining behind him. "Yeah?"

"Ali Elijah," Preacher said.

"Who wants him?" the man growled in a heavy voice.

"Just tell him Preacher is here."

The man nodded and closed the door without speaking. Preacher stood there waiting. A few minutes later the man came back and opened the door. "Follow me," he said in a heavy expressionless voice.

Preacher stepped into the narrow hallway and waited until the man had locked the door and fastened it with a bolt and chain, then followed him up a narrow flight of stairs into another narrow hallway. The man stopped in front of a heavy steel door at the far end of the hall.

He looked at Preacher. "Hol' up your hands," he said. Preacher raised his hands over his head and quickly the man patted him down. Satisfied that Preacher was clean, he nodded. "You kin go in."

He made no move to open the door and stepped behind

Preacher, who turned the knob and opened the door. The room was a fairly large one and whatever windows had once been there were all covered with brick. Light came from an old-fashioned chandelier overhead, the bulbs covered with red cloth shades. A desk was against the far wall and in the slight shadow behind it sat the man Preacher had asked for, a curious expression on his face, neither friendly nor unfriendly, just curious.

"Been a long time, Preacher," he said.

"Four years," Preacher said.

"You don't change," Ali Elijah said.

"I've changed," Preacher answered. "We all have."

"True," Ali Elijah said. "I have found Allah. Allah is Allah and Mohammed is His Prophet."

"We all seek God in our own way," Preacher said. "I have found Him in mine. I rejoice that you have found Him in your own."

Ali Elijah stared at him. "Four years. You haven't changed. You have not come seeking Allah. Why have you come?"

Preacher glanced back over his shoulder. The man who had brought him up was still standing in the open doorway. He turned back to Elijah. "I have your marker," he said, taking a small cloth bag from his pocket. He pulled the small string and emptied its contents on the desk.

Elijah looked down at the three spent and flattened bullets on the desk in front of him. He raised his hand, dismissing the man in the doorway. It wasn't until the door clicked shut that he raised his eyes to Preacher. "I was in another life then. That man was Joe Washington."

"The Lord giveth, the Lord taketh away. You are still here, praise the Lord," Preacher said.

"Thanks be to Allah the Merciful," Elijah said. He picked up the flattened bullets and held them in his hand. He looked at Preacher. "They're so small. I still can't believe how much they hurt when you got them out of me. They felt like cannonballs."

Preacher was silent.

"What is it you want from me?"

"I need help," Preacher said.

Ali Elijah smiled for the first time. "That's a switch. Here we are hidin' out, the whole world after our ass, no money even to buy food for our kids, and you the one who needs help."

Preacher put his hand in his pocket and brought out six fifty-dollar bills. He spread them on the desk. "Whether you can help me or not, that money's for the kids. They don't deserve to suffer for our sins."

Elijah looked down at the money then up at Preacher. His voice was soft. "I was right. You haven't changed." Abruptly, he picked up a fifty-dollar bill and went to open the door. He handed the money to the man waiting outside the door. "Give this to Rebecca and tell her to go down to the all-night market and stock up on some food. Tell her to take the oldest boy with her to carry."

He closed the door and came back to Preacher. "How'd you know where to find us?"

"I just looked in my book," Preacher said. "When you were hurt, you had me write a letter to your mother. This was her address. I didn't know whether you'd be here but I figured this was as good a place to start as any."

Elijah went behind the desk and sat down again. He gestured to a chair and Preacher sat down. "What kind of help do you need?"

"Four non-lethal heavy smoke grenades with red magnesium flares that will look like real fire. One plastic cracker with a ten-second detonator, strong enough to blow out a double-hinged steel store door, and a silk rope ladder long enough to drop from a third-floor window."

Elijah stared at him. "That's a heavy order. That kind of equipment ain't just layin' around. The whole thing has got to be put together."

"I know that," Preacher said. "But I remember in your other life you were a staff sergeant in the demolition engineers. I figure you'd know how to do it if anybody would."

"When would you need it?"

"Tomorrow," Preacher said.

Elijah shook his head. "That ain't much time."

"That's all I have," Preacher said.

"We'll need some extra to get the material."

Preacher took out another hundred dollars. "That should take care of it."

Elijah looked at him. "It must be real important."

"It is," Preacher said.

Elijah was silent for a moment. "You ain't goin' to be able to handle all this by yourself. You're nuthin' but an amateur. You'll wind up blowing yourself to pieces."

"You show me. I learn fast."

"Nobody learns that fast," Ali Elijah said. "I better go along with you."

"This is my baby," Preacher said. "You have enough troubles of your own. You don't need any extra."

"I'm not askin'." The black man laughed. "I guess I haven't changed as much as I thought. I remember back in 'Nam I was always volunteerin'."

"I remember," Preacher said.

"Besides, I ain't been out of this house for two months," he said. "Time I got a little fresh air."

"No way," Preacher said. "You have too many people depending on you."

Ali Elijah picked up the three spent bullets. "I'm not leavin' any markers this time. I'm pickin' up all of them. If Allah, praised be His Name, has seen fit to guide you to our door, then it would be sinful for us to allow you to go into danger alone."

CHAPTER
TEN

There were two cars in front of the old gray building under the bridge when Preacher turned the corner with his pickup at eleven o'clock the next evening. Cautiously he drove past the house and around the block before he stopped. He got out and walked back to the corner and started toward the house. Before he reached it, the door opened and several men came out, each carrying small boxes and suitcases. Behind them two women, also carrying bags, came down the steps. He watched them loading the trunks and back seats of the cars. One of the men went up the steps and into the building.

A moment later he came out again with another valise. Following him was a woman with a child in her arms and behind her several other children. They had already entered the two automobiles when Ali Elijah came down the steps, a small boy in his arms, and went to the first car. He opened the door and gave the child to the woman in the front seat while the man started the engine.

Elijah spoke to the woman for a moment. She nodded and he kissed her, then stepped back, closing the door. A moment later the two cars pulled away from the curb and he stood there for a moment looking after them. He lifted his arm in a half-wave just as the cars reached the corner and disappeared, then started back up the steps to the front door.

He glanced down the street once more before opening the door and saw Preacher walking toward him. He waited until Preacher came up the steps. "You're early," he said in an expressionless voice.

Preacher nodded silently. He followed him into the house and waited until the door was locked behind them. It was not like last night. There was a sudden and strange emptiness about the house as if all life had gone from it. Still silent, he followed Ali Elijah up the stairs to his room and stood there as Elijah walked behind the desk. "Is there anything wrong?"

Elijah looked at him. He started to speak but choked up. He shook his head.

Preacher took a package of cigarettes from his pocket. He held it out to Elijah, who took one with slightly trembling fingers. Preacher took one, then struck a match and held it for him. He waited until Elijah had his lit before he spoke. "You can talk to me," he said gently. "I'm still your friend."

Ali Elijah sank into his chair and blew out a cloud of smoke. "I got to thinkin' after you left last night. You found us first crack out of the box. How long would it be before somebody else remembered the same thing?"

Preacher didn't answer.

"And here we are sittin' with a houseful of women and kids and the next thing you know the house is full of pigs shootin' their guns and swingin' their clubs and some of them is sure to get hurt. It didn't make sense."

Preacher dragged on his cigarette, still without speaking.

"Where did I get the right to let them in for that kind of shit? They had nothin' to do with what went down. So I took the rest of the money you gave me and I sent 'em on down to South Carolina where my woman's family is at. They'll be okay there."

"Where does that leave you?" Preacher asked.

He met Preacher's eyes. "I can always manage. I thought after we finish our little job tonight, I'd move on down to L.A.; maybe the brothers there can make a little room for me." A wry smile came to his mouth. "I hear Ron Karenga's become a big TV star down there and is pullin' down good bread appearin' on all them talk shows. Or maybe go to New York. The Panthers is raisin' big money on the Jew cocktail-party circuit. Maybe they'd come up with some real heavy bread to see a genuine bad-ass nigger."

Preacher put out his cigarette. "Is that what you really want?"

Ali Elijah dropped his eyes. "No."

"Then why don't you go to join your family?"

There was an anguish in Elijah's voice. "Because I got a record, man. The pigs'll come after me and the shit'll fly all over them again. I sent them there to keep that from happening."

Preacher shook his head. "I don't understand it."

"What's there to understand, man?" Ali Elijah asked. "I'm just a grunt, I did all the dirty work, I'm the one the pigs is got a make on. The generals laid back and got all the glamour. Now, they tell me, the revolution is moved into another phase. The negotiating table. They goin' to work it all out there, then everything will be A-okay. But right now they want me to lay low. Don't do nothin' to upset the apple cart. I'm nothin' but a big embarrassment to them."

"I'm sorry," Preacher said.

"Nothin' for you to be sorry for. It's not your problem."

"The problem I brought here wasn't yours either but you're helping me with it."

"That's different. There's nothing you can do with mine."

"Maybe," Preacher said. "But you can stay at the Community with me until you have a chance to think things out and decide what you're going to do next."

"What would your friends think?" Ali Elijah asked. "Most commune people don't like blacks."

Preacher met his eyes. "We're all children of the same God."

Ali Elijah was silent.

"You don't have to make up your mind right now," Preacher said. "Just stick it in the back of your head. You'll be welcome whenever you come."

Elijah nodded, then turned and took a carton from the floor next to him and placed it on the desk. "I got everything you want right here."

It was almost one o'clock in the morning when Preacher slowly drove the truck down the street in front of the store on the ground floor of the House of Soong. He gestured at the doors. "They're the ones we have to blast open."

Elijah looked at them. "They heavy, all right."

"I said they were," Preacher answered. "We have to get them open with the first pop."

"We'll do it," Elijah said confidently. "I had a hunch so I got me some extra charge." He gave a short laugh. "We'll blow the shit outta them."

"I don't want anyone hurt," Preacher said, turning the pickup at the corner.

"Anybody in there?"

"Two men that I know of."

"They anywhere near the door?"

"I don't think so," Preacher answered. "Usually they're in the back, but I can't be sure."

"We'll blow them from the hinges then," Elijah said. "That way the side walls will take the shock and the doors will fall out into the street."

Preacher glanced at him. "Do you have enough to do that?"

Elijah laughed. "I got enough to take out the whole side of the building if you want."

"There's an alley that runs alongside the building to the street behind. I'll park the pickup under her window."

"Three stories on a rope ladder is a long way. I hope she's

fast. If she's not we're goin' to have half the cops in Frisco crawling up our ass."

"I hope so too," Preacher said. He turned the pickup into the alley and cut the motor and the lights. "We get out here and push it the rest of the way. I'm not taking any chance that someone's goin' to hear us."

"Shit!" Ali Elijah said. "I thought it all sounded too easy."

Silently the small truck rolled down the alley. Preacher squinted up at the building. Finally he held up a hand. Elijah came around to his side and looked up. Preacher nodded and gestured. They walked back down the alley to the street behind. He looked at his wristwatch under a street lamp. It was a quarter to two. "I have to make a phone call," he said.

There was a telephone booth on the corner across the street. Preacher went inside and dropped a dime in the slot. Quickly he dialed Barbara's number.

"Hello." Her voice was hushed.

"Preacher," he said. "Everything okay? You alone?"

"Yes."

"Do exactly what I say," he said quickly. "Wear slacks and flat shoes. No heels. No matter what happens downstairs don't panic. Wait at the elevator door until I get there. Got it?"

"Yes."

"Just remember that all you're going to hear is a lot of noise. There's no real danger. Just wait for me."

"Yes, Preacher."

He came out of the telephone booth. Silently they walked back up the alley to the pickup. He held out his arms and Elijah slipped the rolled rope ladder onto his back over them. He then pulled the black ski mask over his head. "I'll hold the grenades until you wire the door," he said.

"Okay."

"As soon as the door is down, we lob in the grenades. I'll go in as soon as the Chinamen in there come out, and you get back to the pickup."

"What if the chinks don't come out?" Elijah said.

"Then I'll have to take them."

"Won't work," Ali Elijah said shortly. "You'll lose too much time. I take them. You go up the elevator."

Preacher looked at him. "Okay. But no killing."

Ali Elijah grinned. "I'll just cool them a little."

Preacher nodded. He checked his watch. Two o'clock. "Let's go."

CHAPTER
ELEVEN

They came out of the alley and waited until an automobile rolled down the street past them. Preacher looked up toward the hill. The street was empty. He nodded to Elijah. "Just one more thing," he whispered. "As soon as I get inside, you get back to the pickup and keep the motor running."

"I'll be there," Elijah whispered. He moved into the shadow of the doorway as Preacher kept walking past the building. Preacher looked up and down the street. It was still empty. He started back toward the doorway.

Elijah came charging out, almost knocking him down. "Get the hell back!" His voice was hoarse.

They hadn't moved more than ten steps when there was an almost muffled explosion. As if in silent slow motion, the doors began to tumble toward the street, the glass windows of the store beginning to shatter and dissolve, falling to the sidewalk.

"Now!" Ali Elijah said, and snatched two of the grenades from Preacher, pulled the pins and lobbed them in through the non-existent windows. Without losing a beat he grabbed the other two and heaved them into the store.

A moment later the inside of the store lit up with an unholy eerie red light, and smoke began pouring from the storefront. An alarm went off, shattering the night with its shrill clanging. Right behind the sound a dark-suited Chinese came running from the store toward the firebox on the corner.

He never saw them standing in the shadows. "You said there were two of them?" Elijah whispered. "That means the other one is still in there."

"We'll find out," Preacher said grimly. Pulling his ski mask over his mouth and nose, he went into the open doorway and through the first line of smoke and ran toward the elevator in the back.

The eerie red flare had turned the inside of the building into a giant flickering hell. He was almost at the elevator when the other Chinese came from behind a stairwell. From the corner of his eye he could see the man raising his hand, the light reflecting from the metal of his gun.

Preacher began to twist away from the man's aim but even before he could complete his move, Ali Elijah hit the Chinese from the side. The gun clattered to the floor. Twice more, Ali Elijah hit the Chinese as he was falling to the floor. He nodded silently to Preacher and started back to the door.

Preacher put the key in the lock and turned it. For a moment, nothing happened, then the elevator door opened slowly. Preacher leaped inside and pressed the button for the third floor. The door seemed to take forever to close and another eternity to rise but when the door opened again, Barbara was there waiting for him.

"Come on!" he said, not giving her a chance to speak. They could already hear the sound of the fire sirens as he pulled her through to the bedroom. Quickly he pushed up the window and slipped the rope ladder from his shoulders. He fastened the metal clamps to the sill and threw the rope ladder out the window.

He stuck his head out the window. Ali Elijah was already standing next to the pickup. He waved and Preacher pulled his head back into the room.

"Out you go, Barbara," he said.

"My bags," she said.

"You first," he said. "The bags can come later."

She looked out the window. Her face was suddenly pale. "I can't—"

"Yes, you can!" He picked her up and swung her over the sill. "Get one foot on the rope, hold on to the line above you and just go down one step at a time. Like this." He took one hand and put it on the rope. "Now, move!"

"I'm frightened, Preacher!" she cried.

"You're better off being scared than dead," he said. He slapped at her hand. "Move!"

Slowly she began to go down the ladder. It swung limply against the side of the building. He stuck his head out the window. "Hold the rope tight and away!" he yelled.

Ali Elijah grabbed the bottom rungs and threw his weight on them. She began to move faster now that it felt more firm. Preacher turned back into the room. There were two valises near her bed. He grabbed them and came back to the window.

Ali Elijah was helping her to the ground as Preacher looked out again. The fire engines were closer now. "Two bags coming down!" Preacher yelled.

Elijah pushed Barbara out of the way. "Okay!" he shouted back.

Preacher dropped the first bag. Elijah stepped aside and let it crash to the ground, then picked it up and threw it in the open back of the truck. "Here comes the next one!" Preacher yelled, letting the bag go and climbing out on the ladder without waiting for it to land, scrambling down like a monkey.

He came off the ladder to hear Ali Elijah's exclamation. "Shit!" He turned to see the valise, one side split open, revealing neat stacks of bills.

Preacher picked up the bag and threw it into the cab of the pickup. "No time to play," he said. "Let's get out of here!"

He ran around the pickup and jumped into the driver's seat while Barbara and Ali Elijah climbed in the other door. He put the truck into gear and they rolled out of the alley, the headlights still out. He turned them on the moment he was on the street. It would be stupid for him to let the police stop him on a technicality now.

They were ten blocks away before he spoke. "Ali Elijah— Barbara Soong."

Neither of them spoke. "We couldn't have made it without his help," Preacher said.

Barbara looked at Elijah. "I'm grateful," she said. "How can I ever repay you?"

Elijah grinned. "Easy, dragon lady. With money."

"A thousand dollars sound okay?"

"Five thousand would sound a lot better," Elijah said. "That there suitcase looks like it's stuffed with a lot more'n that."

"I'm Chinese," she said. "We never pay the asking price. Twenty-five hundred."

Elijah laughed. "That's real fine with me, dragon lady."

She stared at him. "Why do you call me that?"

"You're Barbara Soong, aren't you?"

She nodded, a light dawning in her eyes. "You mean—is that what they call me?"

"That's right," he said. "You're supposed to be real heavy." He looked over at Preacher. "How come you know this lady?"

"We're old friends," Preacher said. "I met her brother in 'Nam."

"Is they anyone's ass you didn't pick bullets out of?" Elijah asked.

"My brother is dead," she said. "It was Preacher who brought his things home."

"Oh," Ali Elijah said. He was silent for a moment. "Think

you can run me home?" he asked. "She can give me the money and we can all split."

"No problem," Preacher said.

There was no traffic at that hour of the night and they made it over the bridge to Oakland in less than twenty minutes. Preacher was just about to turn into Ali Elijah's street when he saw the flashing blue lights. Four police cars and two squad cars were in front of the house. He kept right on going.

They were back on the bridge before he spoke. "That was a squeal."

Ali Elijah, who had slumped down below the truck window and had not come up since he saw the police, grunted. "Yeah."

"Got any ideas?" Preacher asked.

"No." Elijah was silent for a moment. "Good thing I got my family out of there in time." He sat up suddenly. "Think something's happened to them? Maybe they got picked up?"

"I don't think so," Preacher said. "They don't move this fast. That was a squeal. Somebody wanted you on ice."

Ali Elijah was silent.

Preacher turned off the bridge onto the freeway heading toward the Coast Highway. "What plans do you have now?"

"Nothing." Elijah looked at him. "Did you mean what you said? About staying at the Community?"

"I meant it."

Elijah nodded slowly. "Then it looks like you got me." He began to chuckle.

"What's so funny?" Preacher asked.

"I wonder what your children are going to think when you show up with the dragon lady and a Black Muslim all at the same time."

CHAPTER
TWELVE

It was four-thirty in the morning when they pulled into an all-night diner on the Coast Highway. Preacher cut the engine and leaned back in the seat. "I think we can all do with some coffee."

"Food, too," Elijah said. "I ain't had time to get some dinner."

Preacher turned to Barbara. "We take the bag with us. How about the other one? Anything valuable in it?"

She looked at him without speaking.

"We'll take both of them," he said.

They got out of the pickup, locked the cab and, each man carrying a valise, went into the diner. Two truckers sat at the counter; otherwise the place was empty. The counterman was leaning against the register, listening to the radio, while a tired-looking waitress was setting place mats in the booths, preparing for the morning rush.

They slid into one of the booths, placing the valises under their seats. The waitress came up to them with steaming cups of coffee and menus. "Morning, folks. Y'all know what you want?"

"Double order sausages and eggs," Elijah said.

"Hash browns?"

"Lots of 'em. And make the eggs over easy."

"Got it." She looked at Barbara.

"Strong tea and toast."

"Gotcha. Double tea bags." She turned to Preacher. "And you?"

"Western omelet. No meat, only vegetables."

"Sorry. The mixture's already set."

"Cheese omelet then."

"Hash browns?"

He nodded and she walked away. At the edge of the booth near the window there was a small coin insert for the juke box. The speaker was right at the table, enabling each customer to make his own selection. Three selections for a quarter, the small sign read. Just below that was another sign. Ten minutes of radio for a quarter. He fished a coin out of his pocket.

"All-news radio's on seventy-seven," Ali Elijah said.

Preacher spun the dial and the newscaster's voice came unctuously from the speaker. "Police in Los Angeles have definitely come to the conclusion that the murders of Sharon Tate and her friends at her home on Cielo Drive and the LaBianca murders several miles away are the work of the same gang. While the motives for the murders are still unknown, police have determined that the same weapons might have been used in committing both crimes. The police are expecting a break in the case very shortly. A group of hippies have been seen in both areas over a period of time shortly before the crimes were committed and a police spokesman said today that they expect to have them in custody shortly for questioning. Now, time for a commercial break and when we come back we'll have the local Bay Area news."

"The pigs are the same everywhere," Elijah said. "It's always the blacks or the hippies."

Preacher didn't answer, just sipped at the coffee. The waitress came back with the tea and toast for Barbara. "I'll have the gents' order in a minute," she said, leaving again.

The commercials over, the newscaster came back on. "Police expressed fears that a new outbreak of tong war may soon be imminent in San Francisco's Chinatown. Shortly after two A.M. this morning, fire bombs were thrown through the windows of the House of Soong, blowing out the doors and the front of the store that occupied the ground floor. Firemen quickly brought the blaze under control. There were apparently no casualties as the store, primarily used as a warehouse, was vacant at the time. An immediate investigation into the cause of the fire was undertaken and the police were called in when fragments of homemade fire bombs were discovered. The House of Soong is the headquarters for the Wong Dip Tong, one of the largest nationwide tongs in America, and is customarily headed up by a member of the Soong family. The last known head of the tong was Charles Duk Soong, who died at the age of seventy-one last year, leaving the post of tong head open since his only son, the logical successor, was killed in Vietnam four years ago. No other members of the family or the tong were available for comment at this time. Firemen estimate the physical damage to the building at about fifteen thousand dollars. The investigation will be continued."

Preacher looked at Barbara. "No mention was made of finding the rope ladder."

"If I know my uncle," she said, "he got upstairs before anyone else and removed it. He's not about to let the police into any of the family business."

Preacher looked at her. "Does he have any idea of what you took with you?"

"I doubt it," she said. "That was in my private safe. Nobody knew what was in there."

"He's still going to be looking for you," he said.

She nodded thoughtfully. "I know."

The waitress brought the steaming plates of eggs to the table. They were silent while she placed everything on the table. "Enjoy your breakfast, folks," she said and walked away.

The newscaster's voice rose over the sound of eating. "Acting on information supplied by an informant, the FBI and the Oakland police staged a surprise raid on a hideout believed to be occupied by Joseph 'The Engineer' Washington, also known as Ali Elijah, a Black Muslim wanted for questioning in several murders and bombings allegedly committed by the Black Muslims over the past several years. The house under the Bay Bridge in Oakland, which formerly belonged to Washington's mother, was found deserted. Police say that it showed signs of recent occupancy and believe that the fugitive is still somewhere in the vicinity. A search of the area is still being continued."

Preacher glanced from one to the other. "I'm sitting with a couple of celebrities," he grinned.

"Stars, man, stars," Elijah grinned. He shoveled another forkful of food into his mouth. "They said nothing about my family so I guess they got away all right."

"That's one good sign," Preacher said. He picked unenthusiastically at the omelet. It wasn't very good.

"I can't stay with you," Barbara said suddenly.

Preacher turned to her. "What are you talking about?"

"My uncle's no fool," she said. "Yours is the first place he's going to look. And he knows where to find you. He's already told the Sons of God where you are."

"You have no place else to go," Preacher said. "Do you know any Chinese who would go out on a limb for you? Your uncle will have eyes all over."

"He plays for keeps," Barbara said. "A lot of innocent people might get hurt. I wouldn't want to bring that down on you."

Preacher looked at her thoughtfully. She made sense. The Community of God was not an army of fighters. Sooner or later, someone would give her away. He had an idea. He got to his feet. "Wait here," he said. "I have to make a call."

He went to a phone booth at the back of the diner. He put a dime in the slot and gave the operator his mother's number. The telephone began to ring in his ear. "Sixty-five cents, please," the operator said.

He placed the other coins in the box just as his mother answered. Her voice was filled with sleep. "Hello."

"Mother," he said.

A frightened concern leaped into her voice. "Constantine! Are you all right?"

"I'm fine, Mother," he said quickly. "Really."

"It's five o'clock in the morning," she said.

"I know," he said. "And I'm sorry to wake you up. But I need you to do a very important favor for me."

"Are you in trouble?" she asked.

"No, Mother. I just need a favor. A friend of mine, a girl, needs a place to stay and I want you to put her up for a while."

"Is she a good girl?"

"She's a good girl, Mother."

"Is she Christian?"

"Yes, Mother."

"She's not a hippie?"

"No, Mother. I was a close friend of her brother. He died in my arms in Vietnam. Now her father is dead and her uncle wants to steal everything she owns. She needs a place to be quiet until the lawyers straighten things out."

"What's her name?"

"Beverly," he hesitated. "Beverly Lee. She's Chinese-American, Mother. A college graduate. She won't be any trouble. Besides, she'll be good for you. She'll keep you company. With Father gone it will be good to have someone around the house to talk to."

His mother hesitated. "You sure she's a good girl?"

"Yes, Mother. I'm sure."

He could still sense her hesitation. "It would be a real act of Christian charity, Mother. She really needs a friend like you."

He could hear his mother take a deep breath. "All right. I'll do it. But if I don't think she's good, she won't stay a minute."

"She won't be any problem, Mother," he said. "God will love you for it."

"Are you going to bring her down?"

"I can't, Mother. I have some important things to take care of. But I'll see to it that she gets there."

"When?"

"By tonight," he said. "You can give her my room."

"I will not," she said firmly. "She can have the guest room."

"Okay."

"And when am I going to see you?"

"Soon, Mother. Maybe on the weekend."

"She'll be here tonight?"

"Yes, Mother. Thank you."

"Take care of yourself, Constantine."

"I will."

"God bless you."

"God bless you, Mother." He put down the telephone and went back to the table. He stood there for a moment, looking down at them. "I think I have it solved."

"What?" Barbara asked.

"My mother says you can stay with her for a while," he answered, sliding back into the booth. "You'll be all right there for a while. By the way, I told her your name was Beverly Lee. Forget Barbara Soong. From now on you're Beverly. I'll feel safer if there's no connection."

Barbara didn't answer.

"When we get to Los Altos, I'll take you to the bank and you can rent a safe-deposit vault for your money. Then we get you a car and you drive down to Mother's."

"I can't impose on a total stranger like that," Barbara said.

"She's not a stranger," he smiled. "She's my mother."

CHAPTER THIRTEEN

It was almost twelve o'clock when he stopped the pickup in front of his cottage. His eyes were red-rimmed from lack of sleep but he would feel better after a cold shower. It had taken longer than he thought to get Barbara off to his mother. At the last minute he had decided to send Ali Elijah with her so that she would not be alone. She wanted to put the money in a bank near where she would be staying and he didn't argue with her. It was her money and she had the right to do with it what she wanted.

The Community was strangely quiet, but he was too tired to notice. Slowly he went into the cottage and began to undress. Wearily he pumped water into the overhead tank and stepped under the shower. The icy-cold spring water shocked him awake. He took a deep breath and began to scrub himself vigorously, then quickly rinsed the lather away. He grabbed a towel and began to dry himself.

The door opened and he looked up. Charlie came into the room. She had been crying. "Charlie, what's wrong?"

She stared at him. "They went away, Preacher."

"Who went away?" he asked. "What are you talking about?"

"They said you weren't coming back. They wouldn't listen to me."

He gripped her shoulders. "Who?"

"Tarz and the others. They said it wasn't the same anymore. The Community was getting to be just like everywhere else. Nothing but rules coming down. They couldn't be free anymore. So they just got in their cars and took off."

He stared at her. "When did this happen?"

"Just this morning after breakfast," she said.

"Did they say where they were going?"

She shook her head. "They were scattering. Tarz divvied up the money in the safe and they took off." She held up her hand. "I still got my money. See?"

He stared at it. Several crumpled dollar bills lay in the palm of her hand. "Where did he get the money?"

"He took it from the safe. He said it was ours. We all worked for it."

He reached for his Levi's. "Anybody else stay here with you?"

"Maybe about a dozen of us. Only girls. All the men went and there was no more room in the cars. Most of them are getting their things together. They're planning to go too."

He buttoned his shirt and got into his boots. "You get them and meet me over at the meeting hall." He ran out of the cottage.

The safe was open and he stared into it, a sick sinking feeling rising in his stomach. It was empty. Even the mortgage money was gone. Twenty thousand dollars.

He heard the girls behind him and turned around. They were staring at him. "Do any of you know where Tarz was going?"

They looked at each other, shaking their heads. Charlie answered for them. "He never said."

"Who went in the car with him?"

"Nobody. He went in a car by himself."

He was silent.

"What are we going to do, Preacher? They took practically everything with them."

"We're going to manage," he said as firmly as he could. "It just means we're all going to have to work harder, that's all."

"But there's some things we just can't do. We need men for those jobs."

"Our job is to gather souls for Christ," he said. "Women can do that work as well as any man. First thing you have to do is get yourselves together and get the buildings cleaned up. Charlie, you put two of the girls into the kitchen to take care of the cooking. I'm going to run up into town and see if I can hire some Mexicans to take care of the heavy work while we get ourselves reorganized."

"I told you what Tarz said wasn't true," Charlie said to the girls. "Preacher's back. He wasn't going away."

"What's the use?" Melanie said in a discouraged voice. "It won't work. There just isn't enough of us."

Preacher turned to her. "That's not true, Melanie. Remember what John said in his Second Epistle." He felt a strength come into his voice. " 'Look to yourselves, that we lose not those things which we have wrought, but that we receive a full reward.' " He paused for a moment and met their gaze. "And as for Tarz and the others, let them go. Again John says it better than I can. 'Whosoever transgresseth, and abideth not in the doctrine of Christ, hath not God. He that abideth in the doctrine of Christ, he hath both the Father and the Son.' "

He turned and closed the open door of the safe and spun the dial, locking it. "Now, that's behind us. God's work is still in front of us. It's time we began."

He strode past them to the door then turned back to them. "I'll be back in two hours. When I get back, I expect to see each of you getting things in order. By tomorrow we're going to be back on a regular routine. From now on, we're going to work even harder for Christ than we ever have before. Are you with me?"

90

There was a moment's hesitation, then their voices came to him. "Yes, Preacher."

He drove into the bank's parking lot and went into the building. He walked purposefully through the bank into the bank president's office. The secretary looked up at him.

"I'm Preacher Talbot of the Community of God. I'd like to see Mr. Walton, please."

The girl nodded and picked up a phone. She spoke into it, then gestured. "You can go right in."

Mr. Walton was a thin man. He held out his hand, smiling. "Always good to see you, Preacher Talbot."

Preacher shook his hand. "Mr. Walton."

Walton waved him to a chair. "What can I do for you?"

"I'd like a quick check on our balances," Preacher said.

"Of course," Mr. Walton said agreeably. He reached for the telephone. He caught a glimpse of the expression on Preacher's face. "Is there anything wrong?"

Preacher met his gaze. "I don't know. My treasurer left while I was on a business trip and is not returning."

The smile left the banker's face. A minute later Preacher had the balances on a piece of paper in his hand. The accounts were cleaned out.

He looked up at the banker. "Could you find out if the latest installment due on the mortgage was made?"

It hadn't been paid in and was already overdue. The banker was sympathetic. Of course he would be glad to extend the payment date. He wasn't worried at all. The Community property was more than sufficient collateral for the loan.

He left the bank and went right to a telephone booth and called his mother. "Is Beverly there yet?"

"Not yet," his mother answered.

"When she does get there," he said, "would you ask her driver to come right back to the Community? I have some important things for him to do."

He put down the telephone and went down to the employment office and arranged for three day-workers to come the next morning. Then he went back to the pickup and started back for the Community.

There were several automobiles in front of the meeting house when he came down the hill. One of them was familiar. It was Tarz's car. He felt a sudden joy. Tarz had come back. Somehow, all along he had felt that he would. He went into the building.

His arms were seized the moment he stepped inside the door. Brother Ely's voice came to his ears. "Howdy, Preacher."

Brother Ely was sitting on the far end of the table. In a chair next to him, his face bruised and bloody, eyes almost swollen shut, sat Tarz. Behind them the girls were huddled against the wall, two men with heavy bullwhips standing in front of them. The girls stared at Preacher with wide frightened eyes.

Preacher twisted to free his arms but couldn't break the grip in which the two men held them.

"Let him go," Brother Ely said.

Preacher stood there for a moment just flexing his arms to relieve the ache. He stared down the table. "I told you not to come back."

Brother Ely smiled. "We were just doing you a favor. Tarz has been a bad boy. We just thought we'd bring him back to you."

"How did you know where to find him?"

Brother Ely laughed. "Easy. He telephoned us. He wanted us to take him back. But you know Brother Robert. He's a stickler for honesty. He won't deal with crooks." He tossed a package on the table. "We even brought your money back to you. It's all there. Over twenty thousand dollars. You can count it."

Preacher stared at him silently, then walked around the table to Tarz. Gently, he held the young man's face in his hands and studied it. The flesh was almost raw and he was sure that his nose and right cheekbone were broken. "There's a first-aid kit in the back room," he said. "And maybe you can let one of the girls bring me some ice from the kitchen. I can make him a little more comfortable until we get him to a doctor."

Tarz's swollen lips moved slightly. "Preacher. I'm sorry."

"Don't try to talk," Preacher said gently. He looked at Brother Ely. "Well?"

Brother Ely nodded. "I almost forgot you were an army medic." He gestured to one of his men. "Get him what he wants."

Preacher worked quickly. In a few minutes he had Tarz's face clean and small bandages over the cuts. Tarz moaned with pain. Swiftly, Preacher emptied a Syrette of morphine into the young man's arm. A moment later Tarz was asleep.

Preacher straightened up. He looked at Brother Ely. "I don't suppose Brother Robert is doing this out of Christian charity?"

"Of course," Brother Ely smiled. "Would he have any other reason?"

"He would," Preacher said. He glanced at the girls. "Why don't you let the children go about their business while we talk?"

"That's all right," Brother Ely said. "They can hear what I have to say."

Preacher pulled a chair up to the table and sat down opposite him. "Okay."

"Brother Robert feels we can still work out a really good thing together."

"I'm not convinced that we can," Preacher said.

Brother Ely nodded. "He thought you might say that. He has another proposition to make you."

"What's that?"

Brother Ely looked at him. "Barbara Soong."

"What about her?"

"You tell us where to find her and we'll go our separate ways."

"That's easy," Preacher said. "The third floor of their place on Grant Street."

"You know better than that. She disappeared from there last night. Her uncle thinks you got her out of there. And Tarz told us you haven't been here for a couple of days."

Preacher shook his head. "You're giving me a lot of credit I don't deserve."

"Maybe," Brother Ely said. He gestured toward the girls. "There's eleven of your children over there. It seems like a fair enough swap. Eleven for one."

"It would be. If I had the one."

Brother Ely made a small gesture. One of the men standing near the girls stepped back and cracked his whip. It sounded like a rifle shot in the large room. He cracked the whip again. This time it ripped down the front of the dress of the girl nearest him, cutting it as cleanly as a razor, leaving her almost naked. Again the whip cracked. This time a thin line of blood traced its way down her body from just under her throat, between her breasts, across her stomach and disappeared into her pubic hair. The girl caught her breath in a sudden cry, then stared down at herself as if she didn't believe what had happened. She touched her throat with her hand. It came away covered with blood. She turned pale, her eyes rolling back in her head, and she slipped to the floor in a faint.

Brother Ely looked at Preacher. "One down, ten to go."

"You're wasting your time," Preacher said. "I can't make a deal for something I haven't got."

"They're your children," Brother Ely said. He turned to gesture again.

Preacher went over the table, taking advantage of a split second when everyone's eyes were focused on the man with the whip. He wound up on the floor with Brother Ely in front of him, his hands clasped over the man's ears, the needle of the Syrette he had palmed in Brother Ely's left ear.

"Don't move!" he said hoarsely. "That needle you feel is a morphine Syrette. If it breaks you die a little bit at a time as your brain gets paralyzed cell by cell."

Brother Ely seemed to freeze.

"Now, let's get up. Very slowly. We don't want to have any accidents, do we? And tell your friends to stay very far away from us. The casing on this Syrette is less than a fiftieth of an inch thick and can't withstand even the slightest pressure."

"You heard him," Brother Ely said hoarsely.

"Okay," Preacher said. "Now. Very slow." Cautiously, he got to his feet, his hands still clasped over the man's ears. Equally cautious, Brother Ely rose to his feet.

"Now, walk backward to the wall with me," Preacher said. "Still very slow."

A step at a time they went back until Preacher felt the wall behind. "Good enough," he said. "Just don't move." From where he stood he could see the entire room.

There were four other men, all staring at him. Preacher looked at them. He nodded slowly. "Tell them to strip to their underwear."

"You heard him," Brother Ely said in a strained voice.

"But Brother Ely," one of the men said, "I ain't wearing any underwear."

"Tough shit," Preacher said. "Strip anyway."

The man hesitated.

"Do as he says!" Brother Ely almost screamed.

A few seconds later, there was a pile of clothing in front of each man. Somehow they didn't seem as terrifying in their nakedness as they had in their clothing.

"Okay," Preacher said. "Now, brothers, line up, face to the wall, next to the door." He waited until the men were in place. "All right, children, pick up their clothes and throw them in the back room."

Quickly the girls did as he said. "Charlie," Preacher said. "Take care of Jane. There's antiseptic swabs in the first-aid kit."

He looked down at Brother Ely. "Who has the car keys?"

"I have. They're in my pocket."

"Take them out and drop them on the floor. Slowly. Don't forget."

95

A moment later the keys jingled to the floor.

"Where's the keys to Tarz's car?"

"They're still in the car," one of the men said.

"Get them," Preacher said to Melanie.

A moment later she was back with them. "Hold on to them," he said. "And kick these keys on the floor over to the men."

The keys slid along the floor. "Okay, brothers," said Preacher. "Take the car and go home."

"Wait a minute," the naked man said hoarsely. "We ain't got no clothes on. We can't go like this."

"Maybe you better tell them," Preacher said adding a little pressure to Brother Ely's ears.

"Do what he says!" Brother Ely almost screamed.

One of the men picked up the keys and went outside. A moment later the others followed him. The sound of the engine came to Preacher's ears, then the bite of tires into the dirt. "Let's walk to the door real slow," Preacher said.

They reached the door just in time to see the automobile going up the road at the edge of the Community. He stood there until the car crested the hill and disappeared.

"Now what are you goin' to do with me?" Brother Ely asked.

"I haven't any choice," Preacher said. "You'd only keep coming back."

"I won't. I promise," Brother Ely said frantically. "I'll even get Brother Robert off your back."

"Sorry," Preacher said. He clapped his hands sharply and stepped back, letting the man go.

Brother Ely's hand flew to his ear. He stared at the blood on his fingers. His eyes focused with horror on Preacher's face. "You really did it!" he said in a voice trembling with fear.

Preacher looked at him for a long moment. "Not really," he said finally, showing him the intact Syrette still in his hand. "All I did was scratch you a little bit. But, God forgive me, this was one time I wanted to." Almost angrily, he crushed the

Syrette in his hand and flung it out the open door. He pulled Brother Ely back into the room. "Strip!"

"Not me too?"

"You, too." He watched Brother Ely undress, then turned to the girls. "Throw his clothes in with the others and lock him in the storeroom until we decide what to do with him."

Four girls surrounded Brother Ely and none too gently shoved him toward the storeroom. Preacher walked over to Jane, who was sitting up against the wall, and bent over her. The bleeding had stopped.

She looked up at him. "Will it be all right?"

He nodded. "It's just a skin scratch. There won't be any scar." He turned to Charlie. "Get one of the girls to go with you. You're going to have to take Tarz to the emergency ward at the hospital."

"Okay," she said.

He went to the chair and picked up the still unconscious young man. He carried him out to the car and stretched him out on the back seat.

Charlie came up behind him. "What do I tell them when they ask me what happened to him?"

"Tell them he picked on the wrong guys and bit off more than he could chew." He looked at her. "Also tell them that we'll pay the hospital bill."

He went back into the meeting house and sank wearily into a chair at the table. Melanie came up to him. "Thank you for taking care of us, Preacher."

He looked up at her and smiled. "Don't thank me, thank God," he said. "It is only by His mercy that we can do the things we do."

"We all love you, Preacher," she said.

"And I love you," he said.

"Can I bring you a cup of coffee?"

"No, thank you," he said. "I think I'll just sit here awhile."

"Do you want to be alone?"

"Please," he nodded.

Silently the girls left the meeting house. He stared down at the paper bundle on the table. Finally he pulled it toward him and opened it. The neat bundles of bills were bright green against the drab brown wooden table. Finally, angrily, he smashed the bundles with his fist. The paper bands broke and the money scattered over the table, some of it falling to the floor.

He was still sitting there several hours later when Ali Elijah came into the room behind him. The two men looked at each other for a long time without speaking.

Finally Elijah broke the silence. "You look like you been doin' some heavy thinkin', Preacher."

"Maybe."

"You had some trouble here?"

"Some. I got Brother Ely from the Sons of God locked in the storeroom over there."

"What you goin' to do with him?"

Preacher shrugged. "Nothing, I guess. Let him go in the morning."

"You're goin' to have to change your act now."

Preacher looked up at the black man. "What makes you say that?"

"I heard over the car radio on the way down. They just took a bunch of hippies in for the Sharon Tate murders. They called them the Manson family. They had his picture on TV when I stopped for coffee. He got hair and beard like you."

"Something like that was bound to happen," Preacher said. "Crazy Charlie, they used to call him."

"You know him?"

"I saw him around Haight Ashbury once or twice."

"That's a lot of green you got layin' on the table there. The Jesus business has got to be better than the Mohammed business. We never seen no loot like that."

"It's not a business," Preacher said. "We're into Jesus for love."

"You call it what you want. It still looks like big bucks to me. Seems to me that you're sitting on a pile of gold and you don't even know it."

Preacher looked at him. "You really think that?"

"You bet your white ass I do," the black man said. "I still remember my mother down at the gospel meetin'. When that preacher shouted, they just buried him with money. All he had to do was open his mouth and holler Jesus!"

Book II
JESUS FOR MONEY

CHAPTER
ONE

Jake Randle sat comfortably in the back seat of his black Mercedes 600 stretchout, safely invisible from all the world behind its dark brown bullet-proof sun glass. Outside, the bright Texas sun baked the earth with its one-hundred-and-ten-degree glare but Old Jake never felt it. He had the air conditioning thermostat set at a reasonable seventy-eight.

An unlit Havana wiggled in his mouth as he chomped on it carefully so that it would not dislodge his dentures. Half the pleasure of a good cigar was in the chewing, not the smoking. The only thing he didn't like about the cigar was the fact that the Commies controlled both the source and supply. If he had his way he would chase the bastards back to Russia or wherever they came from and turn the island over to people who showed the proper respect for the Americans. Hell, if it weren't for the Americans they would still be sucking the hind tit of Spain.

Idly, he glanced out the window as the car left the main street of the town named after his grandfather and turned onto the specially built road that led to his ranch forty miles away. The last building, an old decayed barn which had stood unused for twenty years since the river near where it had been built had dried into a creek, fell behind him. It was the sign in the field next to the barn that suddenly brought him upright in his seat. Twenty feet long, six feet high, it hung suspended between two poles, its red and black lettering on white canvas glaring in the sunlight.

He tapped on the window of the chauffeur's compartment. "Stop here."

"Yes, Mr. Randle."

The Mercedes pulled to the side of the road and Old Jake put on his glasses and peered out at the sign. The lettering was bold and easy to read.

YOU HAVE SEEN THEM ON TV.

Underneath were four photographs, each with a name over it: Oral Roberts, Rex Humbard, Jerry Falwell, James Robison. Below them was an even larger photograph, but this one had lettering on each side. NOW, IN PERSON, LIVE! C. ANDREW TALBOT. Then below the photograph: THE GREATEST GOSPEL PREACHER OF THEM ALL! THIS SUNDAY 4 P.M. JESUS WANTS YOU, NOT YOUR MONEY. ADMISSION FREE! Smaller lettering ran along the bottom of the sign: SPONSORED BY THE COMMUNITY OF GOD CHURCH OF CHRISTIAN AMERICA TRIUMPHANT, LOS ALTOS, CALIFORNIA.

He had just finished reading the sign when a cloud of dust came up in the field behind it and through it rose the top of a circus tent. When the dust settled, he could see the tractors pulling the ropes tight. At almost the same moment a platform, to which a giant white cross was affixed, rose at the far end of the tent. A few seconds later a forklift bearing rows of wooden benches moved under the top and men began placing the benches in rows in front of the platform. Behind the platform a canvas flap fell, on which there was another portrait of C. Andrew Talbot, his finger pointing at the rows of benches in much the same manner used by Uncle Sam in army recruitment posters, only the words were different: JESUS WANTS YOU!

Looking beyond the tent Randle could see the trucks which had brought all the equipment, parked in a row along the far end of the field. There were also several vans and mini-buses. He looked back into the tent. Everything was moving with an almost army-like precision. Rolls of carpet were being laid between the aisles formed by the benches to a larger semicircle of carpet in front of the platform at the same time as a sound system and lights were being hung from the support poles. At first it had seemed as if there were many men, but then he counted only eight, all moving quickly under the supervision of a large Negro.

He touched the button, lowering the window between himself and his chauffeur and his bodyguard. "Drive onto the field!"

The chauffeur nodded and turned the limousine onto the field. He drove the car up to the front of the tent and stopped. "Okay, here, Mr. Randle?" he asked.

Old Jake didn't bother to answer. He pressed the button lowering the side window near him. Several of the men had stopped working for a moment to look at him, then at a word from the Negro went back to their jobs. Old Jake stuck his head out the window. "Hey, nigger," he said. "Come over here!"

Joe Washington looked at him for a brief second, then came toward the limousine. If he saw the bodyguard in the front seat take his gun from his shoulder holster, he gave no sign of it. "Yes, sir?" he asked politely.

Old Jake stared at him. He didn't like niggers. Niggers and Mexicans, no way you can trust any of them. "What the hell are you doing here?"

"Gittin' things ready foh the gospel meetin', suh," Joe answered, slipping deliberately into a black Southern dialect.

"Who gave you permission?" Old Jake demanded.

Joe shrugged his shoulders. "We got the papers from town."

"I own this property," Old Jake said. "Nobody said anything to me."

Joe shrugged again. "I don' know nothin' about that, suh. I jes works heah."

Old Jake turned to the chauffeur. "Get my property manager on the phone." A moment later he spoke into the telephone. "Did you let Lot Twenty for a gospel meeting?"

"Yes, sir. They paid us two hundred dollars."

"Why wasn't I told about it?" he shouted into the telephone.

"I didn't think it was important enough to bother you about it, Mr. Randle." The property manager's voice was shaking.

"How many times do I have to tell you I want to know everything that's going on here?" he shouted.

"They came with very good references, Mr. Randle. Both Reverend Lydon and Deacon Ellsworth recommended them."

Old Jake was silent for a moment. The two men were the pillars of the local church. "Next time you tell me," he growled. "No matter what it is."

"Yes, Mr. Randle."

Old Jake put down the telephone and turned back to Joe. "Who is this preacher, C. Andrew Talbot? I never heard of him."

Joe put a surprised look on his face. "He one of the mos' pow'ful preachers in the country. Evvybody knows him."

"I never saw him on television."

"You got cable?"

"Not down here."

"Tha's why. He on cable back in California. Believe me, if'n you ever heard him, you would never fergit him. When he preaches the Gospel, dat ol' devil, he jes gits up on his hind legs an' runs."

Old Jake squinted at him. "An old-fashioned hell and damnation preacher, eh?"

Joe nodded. "Yes, suh."

"None of that sweetness and light horseshit."

"No, suh," Joe said. "The on'y thing he interested in is gittin' the sin out an' the people back on their knees to Jesus and salvation."

Old Jake was silent for a moment, then nodded in approval. "That's my kind of preacher. I don't hold with that other nonsense."

"He don' neither."

"I think maybe I'll come back, but first I'd like to have a private talk with him. Where is he?"

"He ain't here jes now," Joe answered. "He's over to the Baptist Church prayin' with the congregation. But he'll be real glad to meet you when he comes back. Maybe after the gospel meetin'."

"Maybe," Old Jake said. He reached into his pocket and took out a hundred-dollar bill. "You hold a bench in the front row for me. I like to sit alone."

Joe looked down at the bill. "Admission is free, suh. I cain't take that money. But I'll make sure to hold the bench for you."

"You do that, boy," Jake said. He leaned back in his seat and rolled up his window.

Joe stood there watching the black Mercedes drive from the field, turn onto the road, and begin to speed its way home.

One of the workmen came up to him. "He sounded like a real prick. I couldn't believe my ears when you begun Uncle Tomming him."

Joe turned a baleful look on the workman. "You got a big mouth, Johnson. If you kept your hands as busy as your face we'd have been all set by now."

Johnson stared after the fast-disappearing limousine. "Man, that's a big black car. If'n it was any bigger it would be on Amtrak."

"That's where you goin' if you don't get back to work," Joe said.

Johnson held up a placating palm. "Okay, boss. Okay."

Joe watched him join the men placing the benches under

the tent, then turned back for a glimpse of the car. But it was gone. He shook his head ruefully as he walked behind the tent to Preacher's Winnebago. The big silver RV with the black-lettered *Community of God* painted on it seemed to sparkle in the sunlight. He opened the door and stuck his head inside. "Beverly, you in there?"

Her voice came from the rear of the van. "Come in, Joe."

He climbed in, closing the door behind him. He stood for a moment, letting his eyes adjust to the dark and savoring the air conditioning after the heat outside, then walked to the back of the van.

Beverly was sitting at the small dining table that also served as a makeshift desk, a pile of papers spread in front of her.

"How's it goin?" he asked.

She looked up at him. "Out of money as usual. We never seem to get ahead. Just enough money from one town to make it to the next."

"You talk to him?" he asked.

"You know I did," she answered. "Until I'm blue in the face. But he won't listen. It's God's work, he says. Nobody's supposed to make money on that."

"He's gotta grow up," Joe said. "The local churches will be satisfied with twenty percent of the collections. He don't have to give them fifty percent."

She was silent.

"You know how much them TV preachers is makin'?" he asked, then answered himself. "Millions. They don't bust their ass preachin' up and down the country, livin' out of a shitty van. They got their own jet planes and they shack up at the number one hotel everywhere they go."

"I know that," she said.

"It's steak or roast beef and potatoes every night for them," he said.

A faint smile came to her lips. "Maybe a little chow mein once in a while?"

He grinned suddenly and shook his head. "I sure don't understand why you're hangin' in there, Beverly. You got enough money. You don't need it."

She looked up at him, her eyes suddenly clear and shining. "For the same reason you and all the rest of us do," she said. "We love him."

He had no argument about that. If someone had predicted that night years ago when Preacher came into his house in Oakland that he would find himself down in the broiling sun of the Texas panhandle with a Jesus freak it would have seemed too ridiculous to even pay it any mind. But here he was. And here she was. And all the rest of them.

Sometimes he wondered if Preacher really knew the power he had over people. The way they listened to him and believed him and opened up to him. He really brought God right into their lives. All he had to do was settle down in one place and follow up on them. The money would keep on rolling in.

But Preacher's head wasn't into that. Maybe he never even heard what they were saying, because when the subject of settling down and building a church would be brought up, a distant look would come into his eyes and he would answer with a patient voice. It was almost as if they were children and did not understand.

"No. A single church is not my scene. The Lord has bid me not to plant my own roots but His and I hear His words even as He Himself has spoken them to His disciples." He would pause for a moment and with the quotation from St. Mark end the discussion. " 'Go ye into all the world, and preach the gospel to every creature.' "

CHAPTER
TWO

By three o'clock Joe had already counted one hundred and eighty-seven cars and trucks parked in the field and four hundred ninety-one people, without counting the children, and there was still a long line of cars down the road waiting to enter the lot. He nodded in satisfaction. There would be a good turnout. Maybe more than eight hundred.

The gospel music from the tape player in the tent blared through the four giant loudspeakers to the road. The beat was modern—gospel country western—and he could see the people responding to it with a warm, almost festive, air. The benches inside the tent were already filling up. There was seating for seven hundred and fifty people. He saw the six girls in their white flowing robes escorting the people to their seats and giving each one a small white-bound program, and smiled to himself. He knew the routine and it always worked.

"Welcome in the name of our Savior Jesus Christ," they would say with a smile as they sat the visitors and handed them a program.

"Amen," the visitor would usually say. "Thank you."

The girl would smile again and hold out her hand. "The charge for each program is one dollar. The proceeds, of course, go to the poor and needy in the name of our Savior."

There would be a moment's hesitation, then the dollar would be forthcoming. Never was a program returned. The level of public exposure was too high and the visitor would be sure that the eyes of all his neighbors were on him.

"Thank you, in the name of Jesus Christ," the girl would say, putting the money in a small bag hung around her waist and turning back up the aisle for the next visitor.

He took a quick last glance at the automobiles moving into the parking area then started back to Preacher's RV behind the tent. This time he didn't knock, just went up the steps and opened the door. "Preacher," he called.

"I'm in here," Preacher answered.

He went into the RV, closing the door behind him. Preacher was seated at the small desk, his sermon notes on small cards spread before him. Joe looked down at him. "Preacher, do you believe in God?"

Preacher's voice was surprised. "That's stupid, Joe. You know that I do."

"If God sent you a miracle, would you recognize it?"

A puzzled look came over Preacher's face. "What are you talking about?"

"I got a feeling," Joe said. "A miracle's goin' to happen out there today."

Preacher was silent for a moment, then his voice grew suspicious. "What are you talking about?"

"A man came by today while you were over at the Baptist Church. He was sittin' in the back of a mile-long Mercedes limousine. He started out by wantin' to throw us off'n his property and ended up by saying he would come to our meetin' if I kep' a front-row bench open so's he can set by himself."

Preacher looked at him. "And did you?"

Joe nodded.

"Is he here yet?"

"No," Joe answered. "But it's early yet. He'll come."

"What makes you so sure?" Preacher was curious.

"He asked me if you were an old-fashioned hellfire and brimstone preacher and I said you were. He said he didn't hold with any of that sweetness and light horseshit. I told him to come back—you were his kind of man."

Preacher shook his head. "You shouldn't have done that. You know better."

Joe looked at him. "Couldn't you do it just this once? A little old-fashioned gospel never hurt nobody."

"But that's not my style," Preacher said.

Joe was silent for a moment. "I didn't want to tell you this before the meetin' but I guess I got to now. The men are all quittin' if'n they don't get paid in full after today's meetin'. Going without ain't their style neither. They got families to feed back home and they're behind four weeks' salary."

"They know they'll get paid as soon as we get the money."

"Sure they do. But they kind of give up ever tryin' to catch up. They see what's goin' down. And they know there ain't enough to go round."

"With a good crowd," Preacher said, "we can raise maybe two thousand today."

"And if we do, it's gone before we get it. Two hundred dollars to rent the lot, another two hundred to the gas station, fifty dollars to the electric company for the power and lights, then half the take, a thousand, to the local church, and what do we have left? Five hundred fifty bucks. Take out the food money and we ain't got enough to pay even one man's back salary."

Preacher was silent.

"You'll have to ask Beverly for more money," Joe said.

"I can't do that," Preacher said. "She's given enough already."

"Then you need a miracle," Joe said. "Would you know one if you saw one?"

Preacher's expression was suddenly grim. "I might. If you pointed him out to me."

"I won't have to point him out," Joe answered without a smile. "He'll be settin' by himself on a bench in the front row. His name is Jake Randle."

After Joe had gone, Preacher stared down at the small cards spread on the desk in front of him. They had come a long way from the God of peace and love that he had preached at the Community. That was a God of tolerance and understanding who reached out and heard the prayers of all men, who sent them His Son as the Redeemer so that all who would accept the Christ could come to Him. But that was a God of another time, another place. A God of a world disillusioned with itself, the materialism of its society, the sickness and horrors of its wars. A God for children.

But the children were all grown up now. And today's God, though the same God, was more the Jehovah of the Old Testament than the Christ of the New Testament. This was the God of vengeance, of punishment, who would condemn to everlasting hell all who would not accept His Son as Christ the Messiah. And no deviation from His word as written would be tolerated, no other interpretation would be allowed. Man was born in sin and would die in sin unless he came to Him and was washed in the Blood of the Lamb and reborn.

Preacher closed his eyes. It was the same God, the same God, the same God. What had happened to Him that he could not see? Or was it that he had been blind and could not see that it had been there all the time until that day that the police cars roared down the hill into the Community?

There had been fourteen policemen in four cars. They came to a halt in front of the meeting hall in a cloud of dust. Preacher had looked around for Ali Elijah but he was already gone, disappeared at the first glimpse of them on the hill road.

Relieved, Preacher went outside as the policemen got out of the car.

A policeman came toward him, pulled his gun from the holster and waved it at Preacher. "You! Turn around and put your hands against the wall!"

Preacher stared at him. "What's this all about?"

"Just do as you're told!" another policeman said.

Silently, Preacher began to turn around as some of the girls came out of the building. "All of you!" a policeman shouted. "Over here!"

They looked at Preacher with frightened eyes. He nodded imperceptibly. Slowly they moved toward him.

"Check all the buildings," another voice said. "There has to be more of them than just these five."

Preacher placed his hands flat against the wall of the building and leaned toward it. Roughly, a policeman patted him down. "He's clean."

Preacher put his hands down and turned toward them. "Now, can you tell me what's going down?"

The policeman who had searched him didn't answer.

"This is private property," Preacher said. "Do you have a search warrant?"

A heavyset man with a lieutenant's insignia on his uniform came toward him. "We have a warrant."

Preacher took it from his hand and looked at it.

"I can save you the trouble of reading it," the officer said. "We're looking for drugs, dangerous weapons and stolen property."

Preacher felt a sense of relief. At least it wasn't Ali Elijah they were looking for. "You're wasting your time," he said. "We're a religious community."

The policeman stared at him. "That's what Manson said when they went down to the Spahn ranch."

"We're not the same," Preacher said.

"Maybe," the policeman retorted. "But all you hippies look alike to me. You even look like him with your long hair and Jesus beard."

"I didn't know looking like someone was a crime," Preacher snapped. He shook his head sadly. "I don't get it. We've been here three years now and never had any trouble. Why the beef?"

The policeman was vague. "We caught a few squeals."

"From town?" Preacher asked. "We've always gotten along with everyone there. Check with the bank. Check with the housewives. Quite a few of them get their fresh fruit and vegetables from us."

"Not no more they won't," the policeman said. "The city council just revoked your vendor's license."

Preacher stared at him. "They had no reason to do that."

"They don't need any," the lieutenant answered. He paused for a moment. "Mind if we look around?"

"I don't have any choice, do I?"

The policeman shook his head. He gestured and the other policemen scattered, two each to a building. Two remained with him. "We would like to see the driver's licenses or ID's of everyone here," he said. "We also want to see registration slips of all the vehicles."

Two of the policemen came back with Charlie and Melanie. Charlie's face was flushed with anger. "The pigs pulled us away from the stove in the middle of making dinner. Now it's going to be ruined."

"Too bad," one of the policeman said sarcastically. He pushed her roughly. "Over against the wall with the others."

"Keep your hands off me, pig," Charlie snapped.

"Take it slow, Charlie," Preacher said softly. Beyond them he could see other policemen coming from the field with the three girls and the Mexican day workers who had been working there.

The lieutenant waited until they were all together. "Are there any more of you?"

Preacher shook his head. "No."

"He's right, Lieutenant," one of the policemen said. "The report said there were ten girls."

"Okay," the lieutenant said. He turned to Preacher. "I'll start with your license."

It took them almost three hours to complete their search and at the end of it, all they had to show was two half-smoked joints found in the cab of the pickup. He showed them to Preacher. "Any more like this around?"

"I wouldn't know, Lieutenant," Preacher said. "I'm not in the habit of saving clinchers."

The lieutenant turned back to the other policemen. "Did you see anything else that might be incriminating?"

"There's a whole bunch of big sharp knives in the kitchen," one of the policemen volunteered.

The lieutenant looked at him in disgust. Another policeman spoke up. "We could search the girls. There's no telling what they have hidden under their dresses. I heard—"

The lieutenant's voice was annoyed. "Don't be a jerk. You know damn well we need a police matron to do that."

"Maybe we can just pat them down?" the policeman suggested.

"You lay a hand on me," Charlie snapped, "and I'll have your ass in court."

"Shut up, Smitty," the lieutenant said. He turned to Preacher. "You're clean for now but we're not finished yet. We're going to keep an eye on you. Just one mistake and we bust the place wide open. We don't want people like you around this town."

They all stood in silence as the police cars drove back up the hill. Finally, they turned to Preacher. Charlie asked the question that was in all their minds. "What do we do now?"

He looked at them for a long moment before he answered. "Go back to work," he said. "I'll go into town tomorrow and get it all straightened out."

But even as he spoke, the policeman's words echoed in his ears. And he knew that he'd meant exactly what he said.

CHAPTER
THREE

The attitude in the town had changed. Preacher felt that the very next day when he went up to the bank. Before the bank president had been cordial and relaxed. Now he was guarded and uncomfortable when Preacher was shown into his office.

"I guess you heard that our vendor's license has been revoked," Preacher said.

Mr. Walton nodded. "I heard something to that effect."

"I don't know why they did that," Preacher said. "I was wondering if you could put in a good word for us. We've never given any trouble to anyone in town."

"The city council makes its own decisions," Mr. Walton replied. "They don't like it if someone tries to influence them."

Preacher stared at him. That wasn't exactly the truth. When he had originally applied for the license, Mr. Walton had been an enthusiastic sponsor. "What's wrong, Mr. Walton? What's changed?"

Mr. Walton didn't meet his eyes. "Perhaps some of the stores complained that you were costing them business."

Preacher shook his head. "You know better than that. Most of the smaller stores dealt with us. Actually they were the biggest customers we had."

The bank president was silent.

"We depend on that income to pay our bills. Even the mortgage payments. We're in real trouble if we can't market our produce."

"I can't help that," Mr. Walton said.

"Then what do we do?" Preacher asked.

Mr. Walton looked up at him. "You could sell the property. The bank would be happy to find a purchaser for you. As a matter of fact, we know of several parties that are interested."

Preacher nodded. The writing was on the wall. Even the bank wanted them out. "But we've put a lot of money into it."

Mr. Walton grew more confident. "We can see to it that you come out whole. Perhaps even make a profit."

"And if we don't sell?"

"That's up to you," the bank president said. "But my loan committee has taken a very strong position. I'm under instruction to see that the loan payments are received on schedule. I cannot extend any further leniency."

Preacher got to his feet slowly. He looked down at the bank president still seated behind his desk. "We're not bad people, Mr. Walton. All we ask is an opportunity to live in peace and pay our own way."

The bank president looked up at him. His voice was low, as if he was afraid that he would be overheard. "I know that, Mr. Talbot. But I'm afraid there is nothing I can do. My hands are tied."

Preacher nodded without speaking. He started for the door. The banker's voice stopped him.

"Keep in mind what I said, Mr. Talbot. If you should decide to sell the property, we have some parties that are genuinely interested."

"I will, Mr. Walton. Thank you," Preacher said and closed the door behind him.

At City Hall the clerk was disdainful. "You can appeal the council's decision if you want but it won't do any good. They already made up their minds."

"I would still like a hearing," Preacher said.

"Okay, if that's what you want, I'll put you down for the next meeting. That will be next month."

"Isn't there anything sooner?" Preacher asked.

"The city council only meets once a month. They already had this month's meeting," the clerk said.

Preacher walked out into the parking lot. There were two policemen standing next to his pickup. One had just finished attaching a ticket to his windshield wiper. He took it off and looked at it. Illegal parking.

He tuned to the policemen. "How come? I paid the meter."

The policeman gestured to the sign at the entrance: NO TRUCKS ALLOWED. Preacher looked at it and then down the lot. There were several other pickups parked there. They didn't have tickets.

"What about them?" he asked. "I see they didn't get any tickets."

"We didn't get to them yet," the policeman replied. He stared at Preacher without moving.

"You going to?" Preacher asked.

The policeman nodded. "Sure. But right now it's time for our coffee break. We'll get to them later."

Silently, Preacher got into the truck and pulled out of the lot. In the rearview mirror he could see them looking after him until he turned the corner. He glanced at his fuel gauge. The tank was almost empty.

He pulled into the gas station they always did business with. "Fill it up, Mike," he said to the man who came out of the office.

"Sure thing, Preacher," the man said, walking to the pump. He stopped there, looking over his shoulder at him. "By the way, you got cash?"

"I've got cash," Preacher said. "But how come? We always ran a charge here."

"New regulations," Mike said without meeting Preacher's eyes. "No more private accounts. Only cash or credit cards." He put the nozzle into the tank of the pickup, locked it on automatic and came back to Preacher. "Want me to check under the hood?"

Preacher shook his head. "It's okay."

Mike went back to the pump and waited until the meter clicked off. "Eight and a quarter."

Silently, Preacher held out a ten-dollar bill. Mike gave him change from his pocket. "Thanks, Preacher," he said. "Have a good day."

Preacher looked at him. "We've been friends, Mike. Maybe you can tell me what's going on here?"

An embarrassed look came over Mike's face. "I don't rightly know, Preacher."

"I won't say anything to anyone," Preacher said. "You can tell me."

Mike glanced up and down the street before he spoke. Even then it was almost in a whisper. "It's the Manson thing. It's got everybody scared. And you all livin' out there in the valley like you do. It's just like them."

"But they know better than that. We never had any trouble before. The complaint had to come from somebody."

"I don't know, Preacher," Mike said. "Honest. But I heard that the sermons in the churches last Sunday were all about the hippies and their godless way of livin' with sex and drugs and all that. That's where the Mansons come from, they said."

Preacher took a deep breath and let it out slowly. That was something he should have expected. He had been rebuffed in every attempt he had made to become friends with the ministers of local churches. "Thank you, Mike," he said. "I appreciate your talking to me."

His next stop was the post office to pick up the mail. This time he saw the sign that said NO TRUCKS, and parked at a meter on the street. He went into the building and opened his box with the key. There were about fifteen letters. He shoved them in his shirt pocket and locked the box. He saw the postal clerk watching him from behind his cage. Usually he stopped and passed the time of day with him, but this time when he caught the clerk's eye the man turned away and acted busy. Preacher got the message and went out without stopping.

He sat in the cab of the pickup and began to open the mail. He stared in disbelief at the very first letter. It was printed in pencil.

GET YOUR FILTH OUT OF THIS TOWN NOW
BEFORE WE COME DOWN THERE AND GET
RID OF YOU OURSELVES.

The letter was unsigned. Quickly he opened the others. They were all pretty much the same thing. And all unsigned. He turned them over and looked at the postmark. All were local and dated the day before. Silently he put them into the dashboard and started the motor. He found it hard to accept but it was almost as if overnight it had become another world.

He glanced into the rearview mirror as he pulled into the road. A police car turned the corner and fell in behind him. Preacher drove carefully, making sure that he followed all the rules. He came to the end of town and turned onto the state highway that led to the Community. The police car was still behind him even after he had passed the city limits sign. He continued on for another mile, then pulled off to the shoulder of the road and stopped.

The police car pulled up beside him. "Anything wrong?" the policeman nearest his window called.

"Nope." Preacher shook his head.

"What you stop for then?" the policeman asked.

Preacher looked at him. They were city police and had no jurisdiction beyond city limits. "I thought you might be interested in knowing that you're two miles outside the city limits."

The policeman's face flushed. He glanced at the driver in the seat next to him, then back at Preacher. "We were just waiting for a safe place to turn around."

"You got it," Preacher said. "Ain't no traffic here."

The policeman glared at him. "What are you? A wise guy?"

"No sir," Preacher said politely. "Just a citizen trying to be helpful. I wouldn't want you fellows to get into trouble with the highway patrol. You know how jealous they can get of their jurisdiction."

The policeman stared at him for a moment without answering, then nodded to the driver. The police car pulled in front of him, made a U-turn and headed back toward the town. Preacher waited until they were out of sight, then went back on the road. Somehow he felt a little better even if he knew it was no victory at all.

It was while they were sitting down to dinner that they first heard the roar of the motorcycles. Preacher jumped for the door just as the first rock came crashing through the window.

By the time he was outside they had made a clean turn through the Community and were roaring back up the hill. In the rapidly fading twilight he could see four motorcycles, their white-helmeted riders hunched over the handlebars.

The girls were pushing their way through the doorway when he turned back to them. "Go back inside," he said. "They're gone."

He followed them into the building. Ali Elijah gave him a note. "This was wrapped around the rock."

It was written in thick black marking ink: THIS IS OUR ONLY WARNING. GET OUT WHILE THE GOING IS GOOD. THE NEXT TIME WE MEAN BUSINESS.

He sat down heavily. Suddenly he was weary. There was no way out, nothing more he could do. He pushed the note toward the girls. "Read that," he said. "I have fifteen more outside in the dashboard of the pickup."

"What does it mean, Preacher?" Charlie asked.

He shook his head. "Exactly what it says. They don't want us around here."

"If we can't stay here, Preacher, where will we go?"

"I don't know," he answered. "Wherever we go will take money and everything I have is tied up here."

One of the girls began to cry.

"What is it, Beth?" he asked.

"You're not going to send us away, are you, Preacher?"

"I don't want to," he answered. "But it's not safe for you to stay here anymore."

"We raised a lot of money in San Francisco," Charlie said. "If we get another caravan, we can all go on the road."

"That won't work anymore. I have a feeling that attitudes toward us have changed everywhere. I don't think people will be as kind to us as they were."

"Because of the Manson thing?"

He nodded. "That's got a lot to do with it."

Charlie was silent for a moment. "There are other ways we can get money."

He looked at her.

"I spent some time with Moise David before I came with you," she said. "The girls raised a lot of money for him."

"Moise David is sick," he said. "He perverts the word of God for his own evil ends. Jesus never asked us to prostitute our bodies for him. We cannot turn the grace of God into lasciviousness, fornication and the seeking of strange flesh, for if we do that we consign ourselves to the eternity of hell, no matter how we seek to justify ourselves."

"But we have made love and it was good."

"Because the reason was love and none other," he said. "What Moise David has his followers do is something else." He was silent for a moment. "We're all tired. Why don't we try to get some rest? Tomorrow when our minds are fresh, maybe we will think of something."

Charlie looked at the other girls, then back at Preacher. "No matter what you decide, just remember one thing. We love you, Preacher."

"And I love you," he said.

He watched them leave and finally he was alone with Ali Elijah. Preacher glanced up at him. "It's not easy," he said.

"What are you going to do?"

"I have no choice. I have to find a place for them and send them away."

Elijah stared down at him. "You don't have to do that. There is a way you can still keep the Community together."

"How?"

"If you can't lick 'em, join 'em," the black man said. "But it means you'll have to change your whole image. Cut your hair, shave, go back to the middle of the road. Then you can go on the road and preach the Gospel just like them-radio and television preachers. You can put on a hell of a show with them ten girls all in white transparent gowns, standing around while you're preachin' against sin."

"It's not as easy as that," Preacher said. "That will take money too."

"Barbara, I mean Beverly, would lend it to you. She got a satchelful settin' up there in your house."

"I couldn't do that."

Ali Elijah laughed. "Why not? You'll still be carrying God's word to the people, and isn't that what you really want?"

Preacher didn't answer.

"You do that, Preacher," he said, "and I'm your first convert. I'll take back my own name, Joe Washington, and forget all the Black Muslim stuff. Man, it'll be like being born again."

"Do you really mean that?" Preacher asked.

"I sure do," the black man answered. "I'm sure that God didn't intend to let this stop you. Not after He gave you all that lovely young pussy to help you spread His Gospel."

CHAPTER
FOUR

Exactly at four o'clock the black Mercedes pulled up before the gospel tent. The bodyguard jumped from his seat beside the chauffeur and opened the passenger door. Jake Randle waved aside the man's extended hand and got out of the car unaided. Walking slowly, leaning slightly on his gold-topped ebony walking stick, he went to the entrance of the tent.

From the far side, Joe gave the prearranged signal and two of the usherettes in long white dresses moved toward the old man to guide him to his seat. First, a silence, then a whisper ran through the crowded tent. "Jake Randle." "Jake Randle." For many it was the first time they ever saw the man whose name graced the town in which they lived.

Silently, they watched as he made his way slowly down the aisle to the bench that had been reserved for him. Now they knew why no one had been allowed to sit there. Oddly enough there was no resentment in them, only an unspoken understanding. It was his right. He moved to the center of the bench and sat down without looking around. The girls gave him a program without asking him for a contribution, and he put it on the bench beside him without looking at it while his body-guard sat down on the edge of the bench, far from him.

Slowly, Randle removed his hat and placed it beside him, revealing a large shock of pure white hair. He looked up at the platform. The giant photograph of Preacher stared down at him, the words JESUS WANTS YOU! shimmering in the reflected light. From the empty platform his eyes turned to the large wooden barrels with golden spigots mounted on pedestals, five on either side of the platform. Then a herald of trumpets and a roll of drums came through the sound system and his eyes turned, following a spotlight to the side of the tent.

The flap rolled up, revealing Preacher standing alone in the spotlight, an almost luminescent black cassock with a white collar covering his suit, his sandy brown hair brushed neatly away from his calm white face, a white leather-bound, gold-engraved Bible in his hand. The roll of drums continued and, after a moment's pause, Preacher walked in measured steps to the platform. He stopped and placed the Bible on the podium just as the drum roll came to an end and looked silently out at the congregation. A deep sonorous voice came through the speakers.

"In the name of our Lord Jesus Christ, welcome to the Community of God Church of Christian America Triumphant. The Reverend C. Andrew Talbot, pastor."

There was a rustle of clothing and movement as the congregation settled back on their seats to await the sermon. Preacher looked out at them for a long moment before speaking. Then his voice came thundering through the speakers, strong and firm, but with a faintly Southwestern twang that made them recognize him as one of their own.

"We are all sinners!"

Now he had their attention. There was complete silence as they waited for him to speak again.

"You look at me and ask, 'How can I be a sinner? Did I not attend services at my church this very morning? Did I not listen to my good pastor preach the word?'

"Of course you did. But mere lip service to the Lord on the

Sabbath is not enough. Look deep into your souls. Think of the days past and the days to come. Can you honestly say that you will be safe from the wrath of God when He reveals it from heaven against all ungodliness and unrighteousness?

"Can you say that you did not turn God from you, so that He gave you up to uncleanness through the lusts of your own hearts, to dishonor your own bodies with unrighteousness, fornication, wickedness, covetousness, maliciousness, envy, murder, deceit, and other evil inventions—sodomy, fellatio, cunnilingus and homosexuality?

"Can you say that you are not guilty of intemperance, of the avid seeking of personal and physical pleasures, of seeking profit or property which is not rightfully yours? Or, even, of simply lusting in your heart after that to which you had no right?"

He paused again and let his eyes sweep the congregation.

"And I say to you, if there is one man among you who will come forth and say that he has not been guilty of any of these sins, then I will say to you that all of you are saved."

He was silent again, looking at them. The silence was absolute. No one moved.

He took a deep breath and his voice came through the speakers with even greater intensity. "Then I will say to you the same words that Paul the Apostle said to the Romans.

" 'I am not ashamed of the gospel of Christ: for it is the power of God unto salvation to every one that believeth.'

"And this will be the subject of my message to you today. The failures of America are not because God has turned His back on us, but because we have turned our backs on Him. This country was founded in His name and will only regain its strength and purpose when we return His name to the country. That is the reason for the Church of Christian America Triumphant. To bring back to the United States of America the blessings of our Lord and Savior Jesus Christ!"

It started as a murmur and turned into a groundswell of approval. The sound echoed against the roof of the tent. "Amen!"

Preacher looked down at them. Not a hint of what he felt showed on his face. But he had them and he knew it. Their faces turned eagerly up to his next words.

"The devil is in you!" he shouted. "And where will you be on that day when the Redeemer cometh to collect our souls? And, believe me, that day is coming soon, it is not far off. Will you go with Jesus up to heaven and stand with Him before the golden throne of God? Or will the devil take you down into the eternal fires of hell and damnation? Only you will know!"

Dramatically, he raised his arms and looked up to heaven. "O merciful Jesus," he prayed, "help me show Thy way to these misbegotten sinners before me. Help me, O blessed Jesus."

This time they shouted even louder, not realizing they were being led and amplified by portions of a prerecorded tape playing through the sound system. "Amen! Praise the Lord!"

For more than thirty minutes, he shouted at them, railed at them, cursed them, threatened them with the most horrible images of the hell they were being consigned to until they were reduced to an almost fearful state of self-abnegation. Abruptly he came to a stop, his face and hair dripping with perspiration, his collar open and wet, his cassock hanging limply against him. Silently, he looked down at them for a long moment.

"I am coming down among you, for in some of you I can see the devil more than in others. I will come down among you in the name of Jesus Christ and with Him at my side do battle with the devil for your souls."

They watched in dread silence as he turned and came down the platform steps. He walked slowly up the first aisle, peering into each face. Finally, he stopped and pointed an out-stretched finger at a young man, who seemed to be trying to make himself inconspicuous. "You!" he cried out. "Come here!"

The young man shook his head in fear. "No."

Preacher leaned into the aisle and literally pulled the young man from his seat. He flung the young man to his knees before him. "Confess! Confess you have sinned!" he shouted.

The young man shook his head. Frantically he tried to escape Preacher's grasp. But Preacher held him fast.

"Confess!" Preacher said. "Confess!" He began to slap the young man's face. First on one side, then on the other. "Out devil!" Preacher shouted. "Loose your grip on this sinner! Out! Let his lips speak the words of his redemption!"

The young man began to shudder, almost spastically. He seemed to be trying to speak but nothing but spittle ran down from his mouth.

"Devil! Loosen his tongue!" Preacher shouted, giving the young man a punishing blow on the cheek, knocking him to the ground almost unconscious. Preacher didn't hesitate. He knelt over him and pulled him again to his feet. The young man's head rolled woozily on his shoulders. "Confess!" Preacher commanded him.

The young man fell to his knees and held up his hands in supplicating prayer. "I confess! I confess. Sweet Jesus, I confess! Forgive me, I have sinned. I drank whiskey and smoked dope and have lain with women. I have despoiled my body and my soul. Forgive me, merciful Jesus!" He brought his hands to his face and covered it, his body wracked with sobs.

Triumphantly, Preacher looked around at the congregation, then gently drew the young man to his feet and began to lead him down the aisle. "Come, my son," he said, almost softly. "Let me wash you and cleanse you in the holy waters brought from the river Jordan at great expense, so that you may once more enter the Community of God and approach your Savior with clean hands."

He came to a stop in front of one of the barrels. He pushed the young man to his knees in front of the barrel and gestured to one of the white-gowned usherettes, who came forward and opened the golden spigot.

The water trickled out and Preacher held his hand beneath it and began to wipe the face of the young man. Then, cupping the water in his hand, he splashed some on the young man's head. "With this holy water from the river Jordan, I baptize thee once, in the name of the Father,"—another handful of water—"in the name of Jesus Christ the Son"—and a final handful of water—"and in the name of the Holy Ghost. Amen."

The congregation roared with him, "Amen!"

Preacher raised the young man to his feet. "Now, young man, in the words of our blessed Savior Jesus Christ, 'Go, and sin no more.' "

He stood there as two of the girls led the young man to the side flap of the tent and let him out, then turned back to the congregation. "Now, are there those among you who will come forth willingly to wash their hands and be baptized in the holy water from the river Jordan, or must I go back among you and drag each of you, willingly or unwillingly, to salvation?"

There was a moment's silence, then a man rose at the rear of the tent. "I will come, Brother Talbot!" Then, another man at the far side of the tent, then a woman, and suddenly the aisles were crowded with people coming for salvation.

Preacher climbed the steps of the platform and went to the podium. His voice rolled through the sound system. "You are washing yourselves in the same water of the holy river Jordan that once washed our Lord Jesus Christ. As I have mentioned, this water has been brought to you at great expense, so use it sparingly, for there is just enough to go around. And to those of you who want to contribute to bringing more of this holy water of salvation to the others who will follow, you may place five dollars, or even more if you wish, in the small box next to each barrel. Our saintly young usherettes will thank you as I thank you in the name of our Savior Jesus Christ.

"And may I also add that half of the money received here today will be turned back to your own First Baptist Church of Randle, Texas, Dr. John Lydon, pastor, at whose kind invitation we have been able to come here and preach the Gospel."

He then came down from the platform and pressed the hands of each person as each turned from the spigots and went out of the tent through the flap at the side. It took more than an hour until the tent was empty of all the congregation except one. Jake Randle was still sitting on his solitary bench, his hands resting on his gold-knobbed walking stick, watching Preacher.

Preacher returned the man's gaze without speaking.

After a moment, the old man got to his feet and turned to walk up the aisle.

Preacher called after him. "Will you not come forward and wash your hands in the holy water, Mr. Randle? Or are you so free of sin that you do not need to?"

The old man turned, leaning heavily on his stick, and looked at him. "You're a fake, Mr. Talbot," he said in a rasping voice. "There's no more river Jordan water in those barrels than there is in that dried-up crick out back."

"If you believe that, Mr. Randle," Preacher said, "then will you come with me for a moment?"

The old man looked at him; he hesitated, then nodded. Preacher led the way slowly through the tent flap. Behind him the girls were already picking up the contribution boxes and taking them to the van where the money would be counted.

In silence, Preacher and the old man, followed by his bodyguard, walked down to the banks of the creek. The old man stared, at first in disbelief, then in wonder. The creek was half full, the water running in a sparkling stream down toward the farmland.

Jake Randle looked at Preacher. "It's a miracle," he said in a suddenly husky voice.

Preacher shook his head. "No, Mr. Randle. It's not a miracle. At one o'clock this afternoon, the sluice gates were opened on the Pecos River Valley Dam for the first time. The water was expected to be here by four o'clock."

Jake Randle was silent for a moment. When he spoke, there was a new respect in his voice. "Will you come to dinner tonight, Mr. Talbot?"

"Reverend Talbot," Preacher said.

"Where did you receive your ordination?" Randle asked.

"Christian Unity College in Sioux Falls."

Randle looked at him shrewdly. "That's a mail-order college."

"Maybe," Preacher said. "But it's a valid Christian school."

Randle nodded. "All right then. Reverend Talbot, will you join me for dinner tonight at eight o'clock?"

"If you will send your car for me, Mr. Randle," Preacher said. "It will be my pleasure."

CHAPTER
FIVE

He stepped out of the closet-like shower in the RV and, taking a towel from the rack next to it, began to dry himself. Charlie's voice came from beyond the curtain that separated the bathroom from the rest of the interior. "Care for a toke?"

"I need something," he said. "I'm wiped out."

She lifted the curtain and came in. She was still wearing the white dress of the usherettes. He took the small rolled joint from her hand and put it in his mouth. She held the match for him.

He took a deep toke and nodded. "This is good."

She smiled. "Nothing but the best. Turn around, Preacher, I'll dry your back for you."

She took the towel from his hand as he turned his back. "What's happening?" he asked.

"Tarz and Beverly are counting the money," she said. "Everybody else is cleaning up."

He moved over to a little window and looked out. The tent was already down and the men were rolling the canvas on the poles. The benches were being moved on the forklift back to the truck. He took another deep toke and turned back to her. "That's enough," he said. "I feel good now."

She looked at him. "That's nothing."

He laughed, taking the towel back from her. "I wouldn't look too good if I showed up for dinner at old man Randle's stoned out of my mind."

"I don't know why you're even bothering with him," she said. "I hear he's so tight that he can squeeze the buffalo off a nickel."

"Where'd you hear that?"

"One of the men who pass the plate up at the church told me. When he does show up for the services, which is not too often, all he gives them is a silver dollar."

Preacher laughed. "Sounds like him."

"Then why are you going?"

"Curiosity, I guess. Besides he asked me. I figure he must have a reason." He wrapped the towel around his waist. "Let's go and see how we're doing."

She took a quick toke, then pinched out the joint carefully and followed him into the rear of the van. He walked down to the end where Tarz and Beverly were sitting at the table, the money stacked in neat piles in front of them.

Beverly looked up at him. "Forty-one hundred and sixteen dollars," she said.

He let out a low whistle. "That's pretty good."

"More than double anything we ever took in before," she answered.

"I wonder why?" he asked thoughtfully.

Joe's voice came from behind him. "You gave 'em what they want, for a change. They don't want sweet talk from their preacher. They want the shit scared out of them by hellfire and damnation."

Preacher looked at him. "You really believe that?"

"I sure do," Joe said. "You didn't see their faces. I did. When you began beating up on Tarz, they loved every minute of it. As far as they were concerned you were beating the shit out of the devil."

"And my teeth still ache to prove it," Tarz said. "I'm glad you don't do that every time."

"I'm sorry," Preacher said quickly. "I didn't mean to hurt you."

Tarz laughed. "I'm not complaining. It was worth the money."

Joe cleared his throat and looked at Beverly. "You want to tell him or shall I?"

"I'll tell him," Beverly said quickly. She looked at Preacher. "We've been talking among us. We think you shouldn't give the church more than four hundred dollars."

Preacher shook his head. "We promised them half."

"They won't know the difference," Joe said. "Charlie found out that they don't even take in two hundred dollars at Sunday collections. That's twice that amount. They'll be happy as pigs in shit."

"It's not honest," Preacher said.

"It's not honest not to pay the men for their work neither," Joe said. "I figger we owe more to our own folk than we do to the others. After all, they didn't do nothin' to help us. We paid for everything ourselves, rent, gas and electricity. Four hundred's more'n enough for them."

Preacher was silent.

"If you agree to that, Preacher," Beverly said, "we can pay each of our men this week's salary plus one week's back pay and still have some left over."

"That way, everybody'll be happy," Joe said. "Don't forget it's goin' to cost us this week. Our next meeting's on Thursday. That means four days without any money comin' in."

Preacher looked at them. "Let me think on it," he said. "We're not pulling out of here until tomorrow. I'll let you know in the morning."

He walked to the front of the RV and pulled shut the curtain that separated it from the rear. He turned to the wall and pulled down the bunk and stretched out on it. He put his hands under his head and stared up at the ceiling. Money. Why was it that it always came down to money?

The curtain rustled and he turned to see Charlie come through it. She sat down at the foot of his bunk. "You're all up tight. I can tell," she said. "Maybe you can use another few tokes."

He shook his head. "I'd better not."

"They ain't all wrong," she said.

He didn't answer.

"I know it's none of my business," she continued. "And the girls ain't complaining, mind you. But I know they're not too happy. It's not just the money, it's that we don't have fun no more like we used to. We're always jumpin' from one place to the next and never get a chance to stay in one place long enough to even see a movie. And we can't smoke or drink or party like we used to because if people catch us, we're all finished. And most of all, we miss being with you. At night, you're always alone in this van and you never ask any of us to come in and pass the time with you."

"You can't preach one thing and be another," Preacher said.

"We're not saying that you should," she said quickly. "But we're none of us saints. What do you do when you get horny? Jack off?"

He stared at her without answering.

"I'm sorry, Preacher," she said quickly. "I didn't mean to be fresh."

"It's okay," he said.

The tears began to roll down her cheeks. "Why did they have to chase us out of the Community, Preacher? Things were so beautiful when we were there."

He took her hand. "I don't know, Charlie. I'm sure God has His own reasons to let it happen. Maybe it was His way to test us."

"It's not fair, Preacher. It's just not fair." She bent over suddenly and kissed his exposed genitals, then rose quickly and went to the curtain. "Don't forget, Preacher, that we love you," she said and was gone before he could reply.

He lay there silently for a moment, then sat up slowly. It

was almost seven o'clock and he would have to dress. The old man's car should be here for him almost any minute now.

The big black car made the forty-mile drive in thirty minutes from the time they left the city until they drove under the weather-beaten wooden arch over the private driveway that had the words RANDLE RANCH burned into it with a hot branding iron. From the road to the giant sprawling ranch house was another two miles.

Preacher, looking out the window, saw the private airstrip and hangar on the way to the house. Three small jets, two helicopters and a twin-engined Cessna sat out on the field. Here, too, as at the main entrance, a uniformed armed guard came out of a small house to look at the car as they went by, his broad-brimmed cowboy hat pulled down over his face. A half-mile further on, they came to a whitewashed split-rail fence surrounding the house itself. This time there was a gate and still another guard came and swung it open for them to drive through.

Now they were no longer driving through flatland fields. This was a carefully landscaped desert garden, complete with shrubs, cactus plants, trees and flowers and a man-made lake that ended almost at the foot of the long green lawn that fronted the house. Slowly the car came to a stop at the entrance. Preacher looked through the glass partition that separated him from the chauffeur and the bodyguard. They sat without moving, without even turning around to look at him or speak to him, just as they had during the drive. A man came down the steps of the house and opened the door for him.

He was a tall man in striped pants, swallowtail jacket, starched white wing collar and black bow tie. He bowed slightly as he opened the car door. "Welcome to Randle Ranch, Reverend Talbot," he said in a faint British accent.

Preacher got out of the car. "Thank you."

The butler gestured. "This way, sir."

Preacher went before him up the steps to the door. Another

man opened the door for them and closed it after they had gone through. Preacher blinked his eyes. It was a tremendous entrance foyer. The beamed ceiling and rustic paneled walls contrasted incongruously with an irregular white and black marble floor and a sparkling crystal chandelier that belonged more in a European palace than in a Texas ranch house.

"Mr. Randle and the other guests are in the library," the butler said.

Preacher nodded. Now he was glad he'd worn his dark suit, white shirt, narrow, neat black tie, and highly polished black Western boots. He paused a moment before a mirror. He looked good. And the lapel pin, a small American flag with a cross superimposed over it, didn't hurt. It combined patriotism and religion into respectability. The butler swung open a massive wooden door.

The library was a large room, all wooden oak bookshelves lining the walls, filled with leather-bound books. They covered three sides of the room. Giant floor-to-ceiling sliding panel windows covered the fourth side. The furniture was heavy—massive, overstuffed, dark leather couch and chairs and Mexican wooden tables. A large desk with three telephones and a massive chair were on the far end of the room, and in the corner was a telex whose quiet clatter formed a background to the conversation in the room.

Three men were standing in front of the winged armchair in which Jake Randle was seated. There were two women seated in chairs opposite him and between them a log-filled fireplace roared the chill away from the night. Conversation stopped as they turned to watch Preacher approach.

The old man didn't rise from his chair. He extended his arm. "Reverend Talbot."

"Mr. Randle," Preacher acknowledged. The old man's grip was firm and strong.

Randle turned to the others. "This is the young man I was telling you about," he said. "Reverend Talbot, I'd like you to meet some of my friends and associates who flew down from Dallas and Houston especially to meet you."

Preacher looked at him. He didn't let the surprise show in his face. "It would be an honor to meet your friends, Mr. Randle."

The old man nodded. "First, the big man near you, Dick Craig, president of Americans for a Better Way; next to him, John Everett, president of Everett and Singer, public relations; the gentleman on the end is Marcus Lincoln, president of Randle Communications. We own and operate five TV stations in major cities and over one hundred and thirty radio stations around the country; before the year is over we'll have our own satellite in operation."

Preacher shook hands with each man in turn, murmuring the man's name so that he would not forget it. He turned back to the old man questioningly.

"Last, but not least, the two ladies. In the chair on your left, Mrs. Helen Lacey, president of the Christian Women's Council."

Preacher bowed over the hand of the silver-haired middle-aged woman. "Mrs. Lacey."

Her glance was appraising, her voice cool. "Reverend Talbot."

"The lady on the right is Miss Jane Dawson, executive vice president of Randle Computer Services, Incorporated. Don't let her pretty face fool you; she's one of the mathematical geniuses of our time."

Preacher smiled as he took her hand. "I'm impressed, Miss Dawson. I've never been able to make a column of figures add up to the same figure twice."

The young woman laughed. "Then obviously, Reverend Talbot, you need a personal computer."

He nodded, smiling, and turned back to Randle. "I didn't expect such distinguished company."

"It was a last-minute idea," Randle said. "Would you like a drink before dinner? We have an excellent bourbon."

Preacher shook his head. "No, thank you."

Randle looked at him shrewdly. "Temperance?"

"No. It's just that I can't handle hard liquor. I'll take a glass of red wine if you have it."

"Bordeaux or burgundy?"

Preacher laughed. "I'm afraid that's a little beyond my reach. Gallo or Christian Brothers is more my style."

Randle chuckled. "Bordeaux. You'll like it. Nothing is better than a good claret. Besides, it will sit well with dinner. We're having Texas steaks from my own spoon-fed beef."

Dinner was a quiet affair. Most of the conversation, initiated by the old man, had to do with Preacher's activities. By the time dinner was over, Randle knew that there were twenty-one people involved in the gospel troupe, that they averaged three meetings a week and were barely able to make expenses. After dinner they went back into the library for coffee.

Cognac and cigars were passed around and all the men joined in except Preacher. He and the ladies lit cigarettes; the older woman also had a brandy.

Randle was back in his chair in front of the fireplace. He looked up at Preacher. "I suppose you're wondering what this is all about?"

Preacher nodded. "I have to admit to being curious."

"Since this afternoon I had a little rundown done on you." From a magazine rack next to his chair he picked up a file folder and opened it. He took a sheet of paper from it and handed it to Preacher. "That's a complete biography on you. Look it over and tell me if it's essentially correct."

Quickly Preacher ran his eyes down the page. However the old man had got his information, he had been thorough. He had it all. His parents, his schools, army service and discharge, the Community of God, the starting of the gospel movement. Even down to the money he had tied up in the Los Altos property, which he still owned, and the investment in the equipment for the gospel meetings. He handed it back to the old man. "It's correct."

Jack Randle looked at the others. "I think I might have the

man we've been looking for," he said. "He's young, thirty-four; Vietnam veteran, wounded, honorable discharge, Purple Heart, almost four years' service. He's devoted himself to bringing young people to Christ since he left the service, first with a religious community, then, when that was not broad enough, he decided to go on the gospel trail to reach more people if possible. He's good-looking, clean-cut, all-American and single, and the ladies fall all over him while men respond to his appearance of strength. I feel we should enter into further discussions with this young man to find out if he can really fill the bill and if he genuinely has the same convictions that we do."

Preacher stared at him. "Just a moment, Mr. Randle. I don't quite understand what you're talking about, what you're looking for."

Jake Randle looked up at him. "We're looking for a religious leader who can rally America around him."

Preacher shook his head. "Why me? Certainly there are others far more well known than I—men who already have strong constituencies and influence. Billy Graham, Jerry Falwell, Oral Roberts, Rex Humbard, even young James Robison. With me, you have to start from scratch. Nobody really knows me."

Randle met his eyes. "That's your advantage. We can make you whatever we want you to be. We have the money and the machinery. It all depends on whether we see things eye to eye."

Preacher was silent.

"All those men you spoke about are good men," Randle said. "But they're wrapped up in their own affairs and are already big business, taking in twenty to thirty million a year. They have no motivation to get involved with someone else where they might lose control of their own thing. Besides, we think the American public is ready for someone new. It's like show business, in a way. Each year television comes up with a new star. I feel that religion is in deep need of the same thing."

Preacher still remained silent.

"Of course, you understand, it's not merely your qualifications that have to be taken into consideration, Reverend Talbot," Marcus Lincoln of Randle Communications said quickly. "We'd have to do some video tests of you and see what the research people think of your appeal. Sometimes the best people just don't come over on the tube."

"That's true," Everett, the public relations man, added. "We'd have to see how well you work from prepared texts, off the cuff, how you handle the press, how fast you are on your feet, mentally that is."

Preacher looked slowly from one to the other. "I'm really flattered by all this attention," he said. "What you tell me is fascinating. But so far no one has mentioned the thing that concerns me the most."

Randle looked up at him. "What's that, Reverend Talbot?"

Preacher looked down at him. "God," he said. "Where does He fit into all of this?"

CHAPTER
SIX

The old man stared at him. His voice turned raspingly sarcastic. "Do you want to know where God fits into all this, young man? I'll tell you." He pulled himself to his feet, leaning heavily on his gold-knobbed walking stick. He gestured out the window of the ranch house. "Many years ago, when I was a boy, every morning I walked four miles to a school just down that road. And do you know the first thing we did every morning when school opened? We gave the pledge of allegiance."

Still leaning on the stick, he placed his right hand on his heart. His voice grew strong. "I pledge allegiance to the flag of the United States of America, and to the republic for which it stands, one nation under God, indivisible, with liberty and justice for all."

He was silent for a moment, then sank back into his seat. "One nation under God. You know there are pinkos and liberals who want those words taken out of our schools? Is it any wonder that we lost in Vietnam? Is it any wonder that our children are into dope and drink and sex and lack of respect for their parents and country?

"No. They've been watching the Eastern intellectuals and do-gooders ever since Franklin Roosevelt engage in a steady giveaway program of this great nation's wealth and assets to the lazy bastards in this country who prefer welfare to work, and to the rest of the world—including Soviet Russia, whose only ambition is to take us over and destroy us, just as they're managing to do in more than half the world already.

"I was thirty years old when Roosevelt was elected and I remember my pappy's words when we got the news on the radio. 'Mind you, son,' he said, 'it's the beginning of the end. First, he's goin' to freeze our money and tax it all away from us. Then he's goin' to take us into war, just like Wilson, to free the world for democracy, and then, after it's over, he's goin' to give it all away.'

"That's exactly what happened and what's been happenin' ever since. Now it's time for right-thinkin' Christian Americans to take their own country back into their own hands. We should have a right to say whether we like what's goin' on or not. We should get our own God-fearing standards back and stop impoverishin' ourselves for the benefit of Reds and Jews and niggers. I, for one, don't want to see what I worked so hard for disappearin' into the hands of people like that."

He stopped, slightly out of breath, and looked around at the others. They nodded and murmured their approval. He turned back to Preacher. "Well, young man, have I made myself clear?"

"Very clear," Preacher said.

"And what do you think?"

Preacher looked thoughtful for a moment. "What were those wines you mentioned when I first came in?"

"Bordeaux and burgundy."

"Well, sir," Preacher said slowly, "it seems to me that you're like a man crying with a bottle of wine under each arm. Imported wine at that.

"Like I said, I'm not much at arithmetic, but I'm willing to bet that you're worth a hundred, maybe five hundred times what you were when your daddy spoke those words to you, so it's difficult for me to really understand what you're crying about.

"All I asked was a simple question. Where does God fit into all this? You haven't answered that."

A silence fell in the room as the others looked at the old man. He stared at Preacher for a long moment. "Are you trying to tell me that I'm full of shit, Reverend Talbot?" he asked in a deceptively soft voice.

Preacher's voice was equally soft. "You said it, Mr. Randle, not I."

The old man's face suddenly broke into laughter. "You got gumption, young man, I got to say that."

Preacher was silent.

Randle turned to the others. "I was right," he said. "This is the man for us. He don't listen to nothing else. Only for what he believes. And that's foursquare for God and country." He turned back to Preacher. "Did I say that right, Reverend?"

"Yes, sir," Preacher nodded. "You said it right."

It was near one o'clock in the morning when the limousine brought Preacher back. As he got out of the car he saw the last of the canvas being loaded aboard the truck. He thanked the driver and started across the field to his van.

Joe left the group of men around the truck and fell into step with him. "How did it go?"

"Fine," Preacher said.

"Beverly and Tarz are waitin' in your van for your decision on how much to give the First Baptist Church."

Preacher nodded, opening the door. "Come on in with me," he said.

Joe followed him inside and they went to the back of the van. Beverly and Tarz were at the table, each with a cup of tea in front of them.

"You look tired," Beverly said, glancing up. "Let me fix you a cup of ginseng tea."

Preacher shook his head. "No. I'm fine."

Beverly looked at Joe. "You?"

"I'll have a beer," Joe said. He took a can of beer from the small refrigerator, popped it open and held it to his mouth. "Man, it's dusty out there," he said, putting down the beer can. "I can have the big truck on the road at nine in the morning."

"We're not going anywhere," Preacher said. "We're staying right here. Tomorrow they can begin setting up again."

"But we've already sent out over a thousand dollars in deposits on the next two dates," Beverly said. "We lose the money if we don't make them."

He didn't answer.

"Then we don't have any choice," she said. "There's no way now we can give the First Baptist half the receipts. We won't even be able to pay this week's salaries."

"You give them the money we promised them," Preacher said. "We haven't cheated before, and I don't intend to start now."

"You've got to be practical, Preacher," she said heatedly. "It's time you realized that you have to give to Caesar the things that are Caesar's and to God the things that are God's. We're going to need that money to live on."

Preacher reached inside his jacket and took out an envelope. He threw it on the table in front of them. "There's ten thousand dollars in there. That should take care of things."

They stared at him. Joe was the first one to speak. "What's going down?"

"Mr. Randle wants us to do another gospel meeting from here."

Joe picked up the envelope and took out the money. "And that's worth ten thousand dollars to him?"

"He's putting it on television," Preacher said.

Joe stared at him. "On TV?"

Preacher nodded.

Joe broke into a wide-faced grin. Excitedly he threw the money into the air, grabbed Preacher, and hugged him as the money fell around them like leaves from a tree in autumn. "It's a miracle! What did I tell you? The minute I seen that man I knew there was a miracle in the makin'."

Preacher laughed. "It's no miracle. He's nothing but a selfish son of a bitch, but he thinks he can use us."

"Who cares what he thinks," Joe said. "As long as he got the money to pay for it."

"I care," Preacher said. "But the good Lord moves in His own mysterious ways. He wants me to carry the Gospel and Randle may just be the way He has found for me to do it."

"Whatever the way," Joe said, looking heavenward, "thank you, Lawd."

Preacher smiled. "It's not going to be easy. This won't be just one of our ordinary gospel meetings. There's a whole lot of people coming down here, starting tomorrow, to help set it up. They plan to make a whole production out of it. Television is a lot more complicated than just talking to a tentful of people."

Joe sank into a chair. "I'm not the least bit worried," he said. "I think I'll write my folks right now to watch for us on TV. We all goin' to be stars."

"No," Preacher said quietly. "Let's not forget who the star of our show really will be."

"I know that," Joe said quickly. "You goin' to be the main star."

"Not me," Preacher said, looking at him. "God."

CHAPTER
SEVEN

He came out of the van squinting in the bright sunlight. Joe came toward him. "They lookin' for you over in the tent."

"I was just on my way there," Preacher said. He looked toward the road. A giant trailer truck was backing carefully onto the field. "Another one?" he asked.

Joe nodded. There were two slightly smaller trucks already on the field. "They takin' no chances. They're bringin' on enough power to light up the city. The money old man Randle gave us has got to be chicken feed to what that equipment is costin'."

"I guess so," Preacher said. "How's it goin' in there?"

"They're changin' the girls' dresses to powder blue from white," Joe said. "They say that fifty percent of the TV's in the country is still black and white and on them white comes out dirty gray."

They came up to the tent. Preacher lifted the flap and stepped inside. The whole of the interior had been changed. Gone were the wooden benches, replaced by velours-covered golden folding chairs. Red carpeting covered all the ground now and there were batteries of lights placed all around the tent. Additional spots were suspended on racks over the platform. The giant photograph of Preacher with words JESUS WANTS YOU! that served as a backdrop had been replaced by a silver-white diorama on which different scenes would be projected through the course of the meeting.

Carefully Preacher picked his way over the cables along the ground to where Marcus Lincoln was standing with a group of men. Preacher nodded as he was introduced to Jim Woden, who was the director, Mike Bailey, his chief assistant in charge of script and continuity, and Perry Smith, the director of photography.

Lincoln smiled at him. "What do you think, Reverend?" he asked, gesturing around the tent.

Preacher returned his smile. "It's something else, Mr. Lincoln. I never thought there was so much work just to film a gospel meeting."

"It's more than just filming the meeting, Reverend," the director said. "We have to keep in mind that we're also giving them a show. Since we go on the air at different times all over the country, we have no way of knowing who our opposition will be and if we don't keep the viewers interested every minute, they'll just flip the channel to a rerun of 'I Love Lucy.'"

"The audience is not like the people who come to the meeting. Those people come because they are interested, but the viewer doesn't have to go anywhere. He just stays in his living room and by turning that dial goes anywhere he wants," Lincoln added.

"Do you have your script—I mean, your sermon—ready, Reverend?" Bailey asked. "It's not that I'm rushing you, but we'll need it so that we can program our shots and camera angles."

"Beverly's typing it now, Mr. Bailey," Preacher said. "It should be ready in about an hour. But mind you, it's not a prepared speech. Just notes on cards to remind me of what I plan to talk about."

"That's good enough, Reverend," Bailey said.

"We've been talking among ourselves, Reverend," Lincoln said, "and we've come up with a few ideas we think will add a positive note to the program."

"We can always use a little help," Preacher said. "I'd like to hear them."

"At the opening of the show, we thought a helicopter shot of the cars pulling into the lot and the people going into the tent would be interesting," Woden said. "We have the helicopter standing by if you okay it."

"I think that's fine," Preacher said.

"We also think those barrels of water in front of the platform look a little phony. They mess up the visual of the shot."

"But they're important," Preacher said. "I need them to get the people to come and be baptized."

"I know that, Reverend," Woden said respectfully. "But you put a crowd of people in front of those barrels and nobody can see what's going on. On a small screen it will look like a bunch of ants crawling all over each other."

Preacher thought for a moment. "I don't know how else to do it."

"You have a stream filled with water out at the back of the tent," Woden said. "That could be like the river Jordan."

"There's no way I can get a tentful of people down there in that creek," Preacher said. "They'll all be here in their best Sunday go-to-meetin' clothes and they don't plan to go swimming in them."

"We have a way to get around that," Woden said. "We won't really need them. If you start by leading the girls down to the stream and begin baptizing them, I can arrange for a hundred professional actors and actresses to be here mixed in with the crowd. They can start going in. It will all look spontaneous and natural. You'll be surprised at what happens then. Once you get them started you'll have a lot more people in that stream than you ever dreamed of."

Preacher looked at him silently. "That's not honest, Mr. Woden. Those people aren't really looking for salvation."

"How do you know, Reverend?" Woden asked. "They'll all

be told what to do. Whether they do it or not is up to them. And if they decide to do it, maybe it *is* salvation they are seeking, whether they know it or not."

Preacher was silent.

Lincoln gestured with his hands. "This program is costing Mr. Randle a lot of money. He's betting it all on you to pull it off. But no matter how good you are, or how convincing you are, it won't be enough. If you want people to come back and turn you on every week, you have to come up with a socko ending. There isn't a program on the air that doesn't need it, because that's what keeps them coming back to you every week. And believe me, Reverend, this is a socko ending."

"I don't know, Mr. Lincoln," Preacher said. "I don't want to do anything that would cheapen the word of God."

"It won't, Reverend. Believe me, it won't. If anything, it should come over on the screen as a massive reaffirmation of faith," Lincoln said quickly.

Preacher still hesitated.

"I have an idea," Woden said. "Supposing I bring fifty people down here tomorrow morning and we try it. Then we can see it on the playback and if it doesn't work, we'll forget it."

Preacher looked at him for a moment, then nodded. "I'll agree to that. But if I don't like it, it won't go."

"You're the boss," Woden said.

Preacher looked at Lincoln. "Anything else?"

"That's all we have for the moment," Lincoln answered. "We'll check with you if we come up with anything else."

"Then I'll get back to my van," Preacher said.

"Don't forget to have Beverly give me the sermon as soon as she finishes, Reverend," Bailey said.

"I'll take care of it," Preacher said. He turned and went out of the tent.

Joe fell into step with him. "What do you think of the idea, Preacher?"

"I think they're crazy," Preacher said.

"I don't think it's so bad," Joe said. "After all, it's no worse than when you faked beatin' up on Tarz."

Preacher stopped and turned to face him. "I think you're missing the whole point. I didn't say I didn't like it. I think it's the greatest thing to come down the pike since the Model T. I only hope they can pull it off. But I still think they're crazy."

"Okay, Reverend," Woden said. "I know you did this many times before, but never for the camera. Now, when the tent flap goes up, you step in. You have the Bible in your hand, you don't look down, you don't look up, not sideways, just straight ahead past the camera that will be moving in front of you. Make sure you stay on the white chalk marks so that we don't lose you. Go up the steps slowly, put the Bible on the podium, then look out at the audience and go into your greeting. Welcome to the Community of God Church of etcetera, etcetera. Got it?"

Preacher nodded.

The director retreated behind the tent flap. His voice came from inside. "Go!"

The flap went up. Preacher stepped inside. He walked slowly, doing exactly as he had been told. He began to speak. "Welcome to—"

"Okay, stop!" the director called. "Very good." He paused and someone whispered in his ear. He looked up at Preacher on the platform. "That was perfect, Reverend, but do you have any objection if we put some makeup on you? You show up much too pale."

Preacher looked down at him. "Is it really necessary?"

"Come and see for yourself," Woden said.

Preacher came down from the platform and followed him to a small monitor standing nearby. "Okay, roll the replay," Woden said.

There was a blur, then Preacher came on the screen. He stared at himself for the first time. It was very strange. He never realized his skin was so white. "I'm really not that pale," he said.

"The camera picks up skin tones we don't see with our naked eyes," Woden said. "It happens quite often. A little makeup will fix it."

"Okay," Preacher said. He looked at Woden. "When will the tape we took this morning be ready? I thought you said we'd be able to see it right away."

"It needed a little editing," Woden said. "Some of the girls' dresses were just a little too sheer. We had to cut away from them. We should be ready in about another ten minutes. If you want to go back to your van now, I'll call you."

Preacher nodded. He knew what the director meant. Sheer wasn't quite the word for it. When those girls came out of the water their nudity practically leaped through their dresses. But he had almost forgotten about it when the other people began to leap into the water. In a peculiar way he himself had become caught up in their fervor. It had become almost real. Their cries "Praise the Lord! I'm saved! I'm born again! Thank you, sweet Jesus!" still rang in his ears.

"Okay, I'll be in the van," he said. He walked out of the tent.

"Reverend Talbot," the girl's voice called.

He looked up. "Yes, Miss Dawson?"

"I have the recording tapes you made that we're hooking up to our computer phones," she said. "Would you like to hear them?"

"Yes, thank you."

"Do you have a quiet place?"

"My van," he said. "I was just going there."

She followed him into the van. "Very nice," she said, glancing around.

"Not much," he smiled. "But it's home." He led her to the table. "You can put the tape player here."

She placed the tape player flat on the table. "You know how this works," she explained. "When the phone rings, the tape answers it automatically, then transfers the call to the first operator free."

"They told me that." It was all part of their audience check.

Throughout the program, the announcement would be made that if listeners just called the toll-free number and gave their name and address and birth date, they would receive by return mail a letter signed by the Reverend C. Andrew Talbot personally, which would contain the names of five great Americans born on that same date together with a special prayer for their guidance written by him, absolutely free. There was no money to send, nothing to buy, not even the telephone to pay for. It was all absolutely free.

She pressed down the play button and his voice came from the speaker. "Hello. This is the Reverend C. Andrew Talbot of the Community of God Church of Christian America Triumphant, thanking you for your call in the name of our Savior Jesus Christ. Now, if you will wait just a moment, I will turn you over to one of our operators who will be happy to take your name and address. Thank you again for calling and God bless you."

She clicked off the button and looked at him. "What do you think?"

"It's long," he said.

"I know that," she answered. "But our research shows that people like it. It gives your reply a realness that makes it very believable."

He shrugged. "You're the expert."

"It's our business," she said. "You know your Bible. We know people."

"The Bible is people," he said.

She shot him a quizzical glance. "You don't seem too excited about all this."

"It's strange," he said. "But I'm learning."

She rose to her feet. "I have the feeling, Reverend, you'll learn very fast."

There was a knock at the door and a voice came through it. "The playback is ready, Reverend."

"Be right with you," he called. He turned back to the young woman. "They're going to show me the baptism thing we did this morning. Would you like to see it?"

"I'd love to," she said.

"We're showing it in the editing van," the man who was waiting for them said, and they followed him across the field.

The editing van was a giant Winnebago trailer filled with machinery. Gathered around the large screen were Marcus Lincoln, Woden, Bailey, and Perry Smith.

"Cut the lights and roll it," Woden said as Preacher and Miss Dawson moved up to the screen.

The lights went down and the tape began to roll. The scene came on and Preacher found it hard to believe that it all hadn't happened spontaneously, it seemed so real. In a few minutes it was over and the lights came back on.

Lincoln turned to him. "Well, Reverend?"

Preacher nodded. "You were right, Mr. Lincoln. It is very good. I have just one objection though."

"What's that?"

"The girls' dresses. They all seem much too nude."

"We're doing something about that, Reverend," Woden said quickly. "We've ordered slips for the girls to wear under the dresses and they'll be here in time for the program. Believe me, there will be nothing to worry about then."

"You've been right so far, Mr. Woden," Preacher said. "I'll take your word for it."

Lincoln was smiling. "We're going to have a good show, Reverend. I feel it in my bones."

"I hope so, Mr. Lincoln," Preacher said.

"Reverend Talbot," Bailey, the assistant director and writer, called.

"Yes?"

"I've taken the liberty of having your cue cards retyped," he said quickly. "I haven't made any changes in your text or subject. I've just added notes in red so that you know which camera to turn to for emphasis on particular points. I think you'll find it helpful. You look them over and if you have any questions, just call on me and I'll try to clarify them."

Preacher took the cards from him. "Thank you, Mr. Bailey." He glanced at the others. "If there's nothing else I'll get back to my van."

"You're all clear now, Reverend," Lincoln said.

He went out of the trailer and Jane Dawson followed him. "What are you going to do now, Reverend?" she asked.

"I don't know," he said. He shrugged his shoulders. "So much has happened, I feel like getting out and getting stoned."

She stared at him in surprise. "Why, Reverend, I didn't know preachers even *thought* of things like that."

"We're only human, Miss Dawson." He laughed. "And besides, what do you think St. Francis was doing all that time he was in the desert? He ate of the wild plants of nature and saw great visions."

She met his eyes. "I never thought of it quite that way."

"Don't forget I spent three years in Vietnam, Miss Dawson. And I would have to be real stupid if I didn't discover many things out there."

She stared at him for a moment. "I have some dynamite grass back at my hotel."

He shook his head. "It wouldn't be wise for me to go out there."

"I happen to have a few joints in my bag," she said.

He smiled. "Well, in that case, why don't we go back to my van and just go over that recording a few more times? Who knows? We might even be able to improve it."

CHAPTER EIGHT

Ten days after the program was taped, he was back at the Randle Ranch. But this time it wasn't for dinner. It was for a business meeting at ten o'clock in the morning.

The same people who had been there the first time he had come were there. They sat around the conference table in a private room just behind the library. Jake Randle sat at the head of the table, chewing comfortably on his Havana cigar, a pleased expression on his face.

"You can review the figures, Mr. Lincoln," he said.

Marcus Lincoln nodded and opened a folder in front of him. "We ran the program twice on our own stations. On Tuesday morning at eleven o'clock and on Thursday night at ten o'clock. Tuesday morning we averaged an eleven share of the audience exclusive of the network stations, and on Thursday night we averaged a fifteen share of the audience exclusive of the network stations. We also cut a half-hour radio tape from the program and ran it daily for five days at various times on one hundred and seven of our own stations, forty-two of them FM. In each case we reached a greater share of the audience on each successive rerun. We started as low as a six share on some stations and went as high as a twenty-two share on some stations by the end of the week. For the whole week on radio we averaged a better than sixteen percent share." He closed his folder and looked up. "I think those results are very encouraging. They indicate a positive potential audience for this program."

Randle looked at Miss Dawson. "Miss Dawson."

"Mr. Randle." She picked up a sheet of paper. "The television showings resulted in a total of one hundred and eleven thousand five hundred twenty-one telephone calls—which is an extraordinarily high response based on the viewer share of the audience quoted by Mr. Lincoln. On the radio programs where we asked for mail-in cards we are still in the process of receiving and counting them. At this point, however, we estimate that we will receive slightly more than two hundred thousand postcards and letters. This, too, is an extremely high average response based on Mr. Lincoln's figures." She put the paper down. "All in all, I feel safe in saying I feel we have had a very successful program."

"Thank you," the old man said. He turned to Dick Craig. "I know a lot of your people looked at the show. How did they feel?"

"The Americans for a Better Way felt very positively about the program, Mr. Randle. They felt that the program could help provide a very satisfactory outlet for the projection of their point of view."

"Mrs. Lacey," Randle said.

"The members of the board of directors of the Christian Women's Council feel that Reverend Talbot is an outstanding example of a fine young Christian American and we would be very proud to sponsor his program in every way we can."

Randle turned in his chair. "Last, but not least, Mr. Everett."

The public-relations man cleared his throat. He looked around the table. "You understand, of course, that we approach our surveys in quite a different manner than you. We examine a program for reaction to the image projected by its star performer." He paused for a moment to give his statement a greater importance. "We find that the reaction to Reverend Talbot from both men and women is an extremely good one. The men see in him the qualities of strength and leadership they admire, and the women see in him the strength and idealism which appeals to both their mother-instinct combined with a subtle, almost sexual response." He paused again and looked around the table. "It is my considered opinion that, while nothing is easy, it should be relatively simple for us to establish a national image for Reverend Talbot that will fit into all our objectives."

"Good." The old man nodded. He looked down the table at Preacher. "Reverend Talbot, you look as if you have something to say."

"I have, Mr. Randle," Preacher said. "Everything I've heard here is very interesting but I still have a question to ask. What do we do next?"

"A good question, Reverend, but that is a question that you and I will answer between ourselves." He rose to his feet. "Ladies and gentlemen, thank you very much for your time."

The meeting was over and after the goodbyes were said Preacher and the old man were the only two at the table. The old man looked at him silently, still chewing on his cigar. Preacher returned his gaze without speaking.

Randle took the cigar from his mouth and looked at it. "I could make you bigger than the Pope," he said, almost reflectively.

Preacher still didn't speak.

"Of course, it would depend a great deal on you."

Preacher was still silent.

"You would have to clean up your act. Get rid of that big nigger you have hanging around and that chink girl. They don't fit into your image. People don't like niggers and chinks. And those ten little girls you got washing your feet like you were Christ. They talk too much. By now, everybody who's been around that show knows you've been fucking all of them. They got to go too."

"Is that all?" Preacher asked.

"No," Randle said. He turned from looking at his cigar to Preacher. "You also got to stop fucking Miss Dawson. You got her head so turned around, she's neglecting all the other work I got for her to do. Besides that, I have a very personal interest in that girl."

Preacher rose. "Mr. Randle, I thank you. I've learned a great deal."

The old man peered up at him. "What did you learn?"

"That I don't need you. I can do it on my own."

Randle snorted. "Where you going to get the five million dollars it will take to put you over?"

"I heard the same reports that you did, Mr. Randle. That show went a lot of places. You're not the only game in town."

"Nickels and dimes," the old man said. "It'll take you years before you see any real money. Son, I can have you makin' thirty, forty, maybe even fifty million a year so fast it'll make your head spin."

"I'm young yet, Mr. Randle," Preacher said. "I can wait. I'm in no hurry."

"What's so difficult about doing what I asked?" the old man questioned. "Those people are not that important. They can be replaced."

Preacher looked down at him. "Mr. Randle, you don't understand. There's a great deal more between those people and me than just what you're looking at. There's love and faith and trust. Those people have been with me for years through all the struggle and shit and have never once betrayed my faith in them. Judas betrayed our Lord for thirty pieces of silver. Do you really think you can ever offer me enough to make me betray them?"

Randle stared at him silently for a moment, then stuck the Havana back in his mouth. "Sit down, young man, sit down," he said. "We have to find a place to build a church for you."

Preacher sat down. "I have a place in Los Altos, California."

"Won't work," Randle said. "Everybody thinks all the nuts are out in California. We got to find a place for you in the South or Southwest." He chewed on the cigar reflectively. "A city, not too big, not too small. One with good travel connections. And one that ain't already got a preacher of its own on national television."

"What about New Orleans?" Preacher asked. "The location is good and I always liked that town."

"Nope. Too Catholic."

"Atlanta? That's a wonderful city."

"Nope. Too liberal."

"Memphis? That's central."

"Uh-uh."

Preacher stared at him. "You're playing games again, Mr. Randle. You already have a place picked out."

"That's right," the old man said.

"Then let me in on it."

The old man looked at him shrewdly. "You'll stop fucking Miss Dawson?"

"I already have," Preacher said.

"Then I have the perfect place for you. Filled with our kind of people." The old man smiled and put a match to his cigar. He looked across the table at Preacher through a cloud of smoke. "Right here. Randle, Texas."

"You got to be kidding," Preacher said. "There's two churches here already and neither of them has enough money to stay alive, with only about three thousand people to draw from."

The old man looked up at him shrewdly. "You're forgettin' two things. One, it's my town and I own it, so whatever I want gets done. Two, the ministry that we're startin' up ain't for Randle alone. It's for the whole United States."

"We'll still have to get people here," Preacher said. "It's only a bus stop on the Greyhound line."

"You tend to your preachin'," Randle said. "Leave the rest to me. I'll get them here."

CHAPTER
NINE

It was after one o'clock in the morning when the stretchout dropped Preacher in front of his van and pulled away. He paused for a moment and looked up at the sky. The stars were twinkling brightly in the blue velvet Texas night. "I'm frightened, Lord," he said aloud. "I don't know where You're taking me and I do believe that You will protect me. But I'm still frightened."

He stood there for a moment listening to the silent sky, then drew a deep breath. "I don't want to seem doubting and blasphemous, Lord, but I am only a simple man who wants nothing but to bring Your Gospel to the people as Your Son Jesus has commanded. I implore You, O Lord, give me a sign so that I may know it is Your work I am about to do and that I am not being led astray by the venal temptations of the devil."

He waited, searching the silent sky, and was just about to turn and climb the steps into the van when he saw it. A shooting star flamed across the heavens over his head and fell beyond the horizon. His breath caught in his throat and he felt a strange warmth pour into his body. Then another shooting star flamed through the sky, following the exact path of the first, and when that was gone, a third shooting star, even larger and brighter than its predecessors, flamed overhead, seeming to hang over him for a moment before it too fell beyond the horizon.

He felt the tears flood into his eyes and he sank to his knees in the field. He clasped his hands and bowed his head. Three stars flaming over his head. He knew them. The Father, the Son and the Holy Ghost. All had come to reassure him.

"Thank you, Lord," he prayed. "Forgive my doubts and fears. I am no longer afraid. I pledge my life to do Your bidding and bring to all the message as I was commanded to by Your Son Jesus Christ, who died on the Cross for my sins and those of all mankind. Thank you, Lord. Amen."

He knelt in the field for a moment longer, then rose to his feet. He felt curiously strong and refreshed. Somehow everything now seemed new and bright. A faint smile came to his lips as he went up the steps and opened the door of the van.

Beverly and Joe were at the table playing cards. Beverly had a pile of coins in front of her, and as Joe threw his cards down in disgust, she swept the coins from the center of the table toward her.

Joe looked at Preacher. "She's a mean lady. Don't you go playin' cards with her or she'll have your ass."

Preacher seemed not to hear him. He nodded absently, then turned and went forward to his bunk, pulling the curtain closed behind him. He took his Bible from the shelf and sat down on the bed. The curtain was pulled open before he could open the Bible.

Joe and Beverly looked down at him. "Are you all right?" Joe asked, concern in his voice.

Preacher's eyes were still distant, almost as if he were looking into a world beyond their ken. "We're going to build a church here."

Joe stared at him. "All this asshole town needs is another church. They can't pay for the ones they already got."

Preacher was silent.

"Randle's got you hypnotized with his money," Joe said. "But his money alone won't make the church. A church is got to have people and there ain't enough people around here."

"I know that," Preacher replied.

"Then don't be stupid," Joe said. "If he wants to give you money to build a church, at least build it someplace where you got a chance."

Preacher met his eyes. "Here is where God wants it. Here is where we'll build it."

"What makes you so sure God wants it here?" Joe asked. "He tell you Hisself?"

"Yes," Preacher answered simply.

Joe stared at him. "You been smokin' or drinkin'?"

Preacher shook his head. "I asked God for a sign and He gave me it."

"Wait a minute," Joe protested. "Remember it's me you're talking to."

Preacher got to his feet. "It's true. Outside, before I came in, I prayed to God to give me a sign that this was what He wanted me to, that I was not being led by the devil, and He answered me. He sent the Holy Trinity flying over my head. Three shooting stars, one after the other, each brighter than the one before, and when the last one hung over my head for a moment I felt His knowledge come into me and I was bathed in His warm glow."

"You sure you not imagining it?" Joe asked. "This is the Panhandle. The sky here is always filled with shooting stars."

"Not like these," Preacher answered. "I know what I felt."

Joe stood silent, looking at him. After a moment Beverly put her hand on his arm. "Come, Joe, we're all tired. Let's go to bed. We can talk in the morning."

Joe nodded. "Yes." He turned back to Preacher. "Sure you all right? Anything I can get you?"

"I've never been better," Preacher said.

"Okay," Joe said hesitantly. "Well, then, good night."

"Good night, Preacher," Beverly said.

They let the curtain fall in front of his bunk and walked back to the table. Joe turned to her. "What do you think?" he whispered.

"I don't know," she whispered back.

"You come to the window," he said. "In an hour, I'll show you a hundred shooting stars."

"Maybe," she said, still whispering. "But they won't be the stars he saw."

"Then you believe him?"

Her eyes were large as she turned to him. "Of course I believe him. I always did. And so did you. If we didn't, what other reason would we have for being here? None of us are getting rich by doing it."

"Do you love him?" he asked.

"Of course I love him. Don't you?"

Joe nodded. "I guess I do."

"But I'm not in love with him. That's something else," she said.

"I know that," Joe said. "I'm not stupid."

She met his eyes. "Well, you're sure acting like it."

"Hey," he said. "I thought—"

"Stop thinking," she said, placing a silencing finger on his lips as she came into his arms. "It's not good for you."

He was sitting on his bunk, the Bible still unopened on his lap, when he heard the door of the van close behind them. He rose to his feet and began to undress slowly. So much was happening. It was as if he were caught in a tide that he could not control, a tide taking him to a distant shore that he could not see.

He stretched out naked on his bed, propped his single pillow behind his head, and turned on the small reading light on the wall next to him. He picked up the Bible and, opening it to the First Psalm, began to read, mouthing the words softly to himself.

> *Blessed is the man that walketh not in the counsel of the ungodly, nor standeth in the way of sinners, nor sitteth in the seat of the scornful.*
>
> *But his delight is in the law of the Lord, and in his law doth he meditate day and night.*
>
> *And he shall be like a tree planted by the rivers of water, that bringeth forth his fruit in his season; his leaf also shall not wither; and whatsoever he doeth shall prosper.*

Preacher put down the Bible, snapped out the light and stared up into the dark. He crossed his arms behind his head. Some of his doubts were answered. Was it not written that whatsoever he doeth shall prosper? There was nothing wrong if he should benefit from the spreading of the Gospel; he was doing God's work.

But there were still some faint doubts lingering in him. Could it be that he was deluding himself in order to justify doing what he wanted to do? He rolled out of the bed and knelt beside it and clasped his hands in prayer before him. His voice echoed in the empty van, his words were the final words of the 139th Psalm.

> *Search me, O God, and know my heart: try me, and know my thoughts:*
>
> *And see if there be any wicked way in me, and lead me in the way everlasting.*

Still kneeling, he crossed his arms on the bunk and rested his head on them. He remembered what his mother had once said. "You're not like the others, Constantine. You will not be able to preach your vision of God until you stand on the pulpit of your own church. Then you will touch the world."

At the time he did not understand what she was saying. But now he did. His God was a very personal God, his Jesus was a very human Son of God, filled with an understanding of the weakness of man because He was one of them and so could find in Himself the forgiveness for them and the strength to take all their sins into Him and die for them so that all could find absolution in Him. No threats, no wars, no punishment. Not like the vengeful Lord, His Father. Only forgiveness and absolution in the acceptance of Him.

He did not hear the van door open, and not until the curtain of his bunk was drawn back was he aware that someone had come into the van.

"Preacher." Charlie's voice came from behind him.

He turned to look up at her. She was wearing a faded woolen robe over her nightdress. "Yes?"

"Beverly and Joe are fucking in the back seat of the car next to our van," she said.

He rose and sat on the bunk. "Why tell me?"

"I got jealous," she said. "They were having such a ball it made me horny."

Suddenly he laughed. Nothing had really changed. People were still the same, still children. For the first time that night he felt a weight lifted from his shoulders. "I can understand that."

"You do?" she asked in a wondering voice. "I thought you didn't get horny anymore."

He got to his feet and, taking her hand, guided it to his erection. "What made you think that?" he asked.

CHAPTER
TEN

The rotors of the helicopter were turning slowly as the black limousine pulled up to it. The chauffeur opened the door and Preacher got out.

Randle stuck his head out of the cabin door of the copter. "Come on, son," he shouted above the noise of the rotor. "We ain't got all day."

The pilot stuck his hand out the door to help Preacher into the cabin. "The seat next to Mr. Randle is yours, sir," he said, sliding the door closed.

As soon as Preacher had fastened his belt, the copter began to lift off. It was a six-passenger Bell and besides Randle and the pilot there was another man sitting in front of him.

Randle chuckled. "Got you up early, didn't I, son?"

Preacher glanced at his watch. Seven-thirty. "Yes, sir."

"Get up at sun-up, I always say. A man does his best work early in the morning," Randle said. "Figured I'd get you out before that li'l girl had a chance to drain your morning juice."

Preacher looked at him silently.

Randle met his eyes. "Told you I know everything that's going on down there."

Preacher was silent.

"I suppose you're wonderin' where we're goin' this morning that's so important?"

Preacher nodded.

"We're goin' to look over the site where we're goin' to build the church."

"We couldn't drive there?"

"Easier this way," Randle said. "It's forty miles north of town." He leaned forward, tapping the shoulder of man seated next to the pilot. "Got them plans ready, Chuck?"

"Right here, Mr. Randle." The man turned and handed a large clipboard to the old man. He glanced at Preacher.

"Chuck Michaels, Dr. Talbot," Randle said, taking the clipboard. "Chuck is president of Randle Construction Company."

They shook hands as Randle fastened the clipboard to the back of the pilot's seat. He turned to Preacher. "Know how to read a map?"

"Some," Preacher answered. "Needed to in 'Nam in case I got cut off from our troops."

Randle glanced from the window, then pointed to a line on the map. "We're here now. We'll go over the city, then north along Highway Ten." His finger pointed to the upper right-hand corner of the map. "That's where we're going."

Preacher leaned forward and read the small print. Churchland, an incorporated city. He looked at Randle. "I never heard of a city around here called Churchland."

Randle chuckled. "That's because there ain't any."

"I don't understand."

"You will," Randle said. "I told you that I work fast. I don't have the time you young 'uns have to develop somethin'. I been waitin' a long time to find the right man for the kind of church that will lead America out of the wilderness. Meanwhile I been planning."

He flipped the top sheet over, revealing another map beneath. Across the top was the printed word CHURCHLAND. Preacher looked at it. It was a complete plan for a small city. He turned to Randle. "That's heavy," he said.

Randle looked puzzled.

"It's big," Preacher explained.

"Just as easy to do somethin' big as somethin' small," the old man smiled. "I got more'n a thousand acres out there that's God's own wilderness and just crying to be made Christian use of. I intend for this to become a shinin' light to America." He leaned toward the window and looked down. "We're almost there," he called to the pilot. "Come down over Highway Ten. There's somethin' I want Dr. Talbot to see."

"Yes, sir." The copter began to descend toward the road.

"There." Randle pointed. "Look."

The giant billboard was at the edge of the road. The copter came down and hovered just above it. Preacher read the sign.

CHURCHLAND

THE FUTURE HOME OF

THE COMMUNITY OF GOD CHURCH OF CHRISTIAN

AMERICA TRIUMPHANT

DR. C. ANDREW TALBOT, PASTOR

DEDICATED TO THE SERVICE OF GOD AND COUNTRY

OPENING IN MAY 1976

Preacher looked at the old man. "That's less than two years away. It will take longer than that to build a ministry. Oral Roberts, Shuller, Falwell, Pat Robertson, they all took years to do that."

"They started before television," the old man answered. "Once they got into TV they grew in spite of themselves. And they still really don't know what they have, they're feeling their way. But we know what we have. We have the experience and the equipment. We'll build this ministry like a TV network builds a hit series. Everything will be tested and worked out by the time we open. Market studies, test programs, public relations, everything fed into the computers and all merged together. By May '76 you're going to be the best-known preacher in America."

Preacher was silent. He looked out the window as the copter rose again and began to cross country. They lifted over a small forest of trees and in the fields beyond came over a scene of what seemed to be frantic activity. Small trucks were racing to and fro across the flat fields, leaving behind them a trail of white lime lines. He stared for a moment, then turned and looked at the map on the clipboard. Suddenly he understood what they were doing. Everything he saw on the map was being chalked out on the ground. He looked at Randle.

The old man was smiling. "I told you I didn't intend to waste time." He paused for a moment. "Chuck will explain the layout to you when we get back to the ranch."

The enlarged map was mounted on a wallboard that covered the length of Randle's study at the ranch. The butler brought them coffee on a silver tray, then retired discreetly, closing the door behind him.

Randle nodded to Michaels. "You can begin now."

The burly constructor picked up a wooden pointer. He looked at Preacher. "Just as a bit of background, I thought you might like to know that this is not a half-baked idea that was conjured up at the last minute. Mr. Randle and I have spoken about this project over a period of several years and this plan is a result of those conversations. The preliminary drawings have been revised over those years until we have what you now see on the map before you.

"Let's begin with what you see as you drive up the road to Churchland after leaving the highway. You pass a park, carefully landscaped, small lakes, flower gardens, trees. The first building is a twin-towered seven-storied building, the towers of which are joined by a giant cross that extends another five stories into the air and should be visible day or night for a distance of thirty to fifty miles. This will be the main building which will house the church. The church itself will actually be a large theater auditorium with a seating capacity of one thousand five hundred people on the main or orchestra floor and an additional six hundred people in the balcony. There will be a completely electronic stage with automated platforms that will raise, lower, move forward or backward on command. The entire theater will have built-in television facilities that can scan and broadcast everything that happens in the church, from the stage to any portion of the audience, all operated from a remote-control room located in the proscenium arch over the stage not visible to the audience. The interior height of the auditorium will be five stories. In the remaining two stories above that will be offices and visitors' and guests' rooms for those who are to participate in the programs. There will be ample parking behind the building for seven hundred cars."

He moved the pointer to a group of buildings set in a semicircle behind the twin-towered church. "The large building in the center of the semicircle will be the parsonage, in which the pastor will live with his staff. Three stories high, it will contain on the top floor the pastor's own nine-room apartment. The floor below will have several apartments of two and three rooms each. The entrance floor will consist of offices and meeting rooms.

"The smaller buildings, two each flanking the parsonage, will be chapels where visitors of different faiths may go to meditate. One building each for Catholics, Protestants, and the Hebrew and Islamic faiths.

"In addition there are planned two motels, each with a three-hundred-room capacity and complete food and recreational facilities including swimming pools, tennis courts, miniature golf, and children's special day-care camps and amusement facilities. There will also be one hundred individual cabins available to families who wish to visit or vacation.

"Two hundred acres at the far end of the section have already been approved by the Federal Aviation Administration for the construction of a private airfield licensed for jet aircraft up to the size of Boeing 727s. Also, a special side road will be built to the airport reception center for buses bringing visitors via the highway. All visitors planning to stay will be registered at that reception center and then transported to their facilities by internal buses.

"There are many more details I could add but this, I think, is pretty much the overall picture. I will be glad to discuss any further questions or ideas you may have."

"Thank you, Mr. Michaels," Preacher said. He turned to the old man. "You've got my head spinning."

The old man smiled. "I think we've thought of everything."

"Maybe I wouldn't be so nervous if we were starting smaller," Preacher said. "I'm not Billy Graham. Why should anyone want to come all the way out here to see a nobody?"

"By the time we open you ain't goin' to be a nobody. Arrangements are being made right now for you to appear and preach on every major religious television program in America. Not once, but several times. People will know you, all right."

"But why should any of them put me on the air?" Preacher asked. "Surely I can't bring them anything they haven't got already."

Randle chuckled. "There ain't one of them who don't have the shorts one way or t'other. All it takes is money."

CHAPTER
ELEVEN

"We have thirty days to get our act together," Marcus Lincoln said. "Pat Robertson's '700 Club' is the highest-rated religious TV show in the country. It wasn't easy to get them to be the first show to put you on."

Preacher looked at him. "I don't understand it. I'm a preacher, not an actor."

"You're going to have to be both," Lincoln said. " 'The 700 Club' is a talk show. Robertson mixes guests and sermons. If you don't want to be just another testimonial, we'd better come up with a different kind of approach."

"Why can't I tell them how I feel about God?"

"That's what everybody does. We have to have a theme as well as a different approach. Talk is not enough. Television is a visual medium. Let's not forget that."

"I don't know," Preacher said.

"Neither do I," Lincoln added. "That's why I brought the boys with me. I figure between us we'll come up with something."

Preacher looked at the others—Jim Woden, who had

directed the filming of the gospel meeting, and Mike Bailey, who had coordinated the script. He shook his head. "God should be enough."

"With all due respect, Reverend," Woden said, "not for television. Don't forget He's already got a lot of exposure there. You're the one we have to establish."

"I wouldn't know where to start," Preacher said.

"Supposing we start with you telling us about your life," Bailey suggested. "In your own words. Maybe we'll find our theme there."

Preacher smiled. "It's really not much. It seems to me that all my life I've been searching for a God whose word I can carry to the people."

Bailey smiled. "That's a beginning. The theme could very well be 'Seeking God.' We could begin with photographs of when you were a boy, then of you in Vietnam, then of you coming out and starting the first Community of God, followed by your decision to hit the gospel trail."

Preacher laughed aloud. "That sounds great, but I don't have any photographs."

"That's no problem," Woden said. "I know a couple of photographers that can take care of that."

"I looked different in those days," Preacher said. "Most of the time my hair was long and I had a beard. It would take a year to grow that back."

Woden shook his head. "That isn't necessary. Wigs, false beard and makeup will take care of it." He turned to Lincoln. "If that idea appeals to you, let's try to get up a storyboard on it."

Lincoln nodded. "Okay. Try it. At least it's a place to start."

Less than three months later, he sat in the small green room watching Katherine Kuhlman on the monitor as she floated across the stage of the Shrine Auditorium in her billowing white gown to the off-screen mellow voice of the announcer. "Ladies and gentlemen, the world-famous inspirational teacher of the Gospel, Miss Katherine Kuhlman!"

The camera panned the applauding audience, then back to Miss Kuhlman as she smiled at them, slightly bowing, holding her arms over her head, a soft red-leather-covered Bible in one hand. She walked to the small podium just before reaching center stage and placed the Bible on it. She looked out at the congregation as it grew silent. When she finally spoke, it was in a soft gentle voice that the sound system carried throughout the auditorium. But there was an authority in it that held everyone's attention. She glanced down at the Bible, then up again as the camera moved in close on her face.

"From the First Epistle of John, Chapter Four.

> *No man hath seen God at any time. If we love one another, God dwelleth in us, and his love is perfected in us.*
>
> *Hereby know we that we dwell in him, and he in us, because he hath given us of his Spirit.*
>
> *And we have seen and do testify that the Father sent the Son to be the Saviour of the world.*
>
> *Whosoever shall confess that Jesus is the Son of God, God dwelleth in him, and he in God."*

She was silent for a moment, then moved slightly away from the podium. "Confess and testify," she said. "The key words. How many of us have been willing to do that? Not one or the other, but both. Not just once a year, once a month or once a week, but every day of our lives. How many of you upon awakening this morning said to yourself, 'Jesus is the Son of God, Jesus is my Savior, Jesus died on the cross for my sins and for the sins of all the world'? And then gone down to breakfast and testified that to your wife and to your children?"

Again she was silent looking at them. "Not many of us, I'm afraid," she said in gently reproving tones. Then her voice lightened. "But today we have a very special young man with us. A young man who has carried the message of God to many strange and difficult places, through the quicksand of sin and corruption, only to find that his strength came not from himself but from the Spirit of God that dwelled in him, and his first thought each morning was to confess and testify that Jesus was his Savior. His story has been an inspiration to me, as I know it will be to you, and that is why I have asked him here to tell it."

The door of the green room opened and a young man entered. "Dr. Talbot, Miss Kuhlman is almost ready for you. Will you follow me, please?"

Preacher got to his feet. He glanced at Joe and Marcus still seated on the couch. Joe looked up at him, grinned, and held a thumbs-up fist. "Go tell 'em, Preacher."

Marcus turned from the set. "Emphasize the fleshly temptations a bit more with her. Don't forget she pulls her audience from the same group that watches the morning soaps from Monday to Friday. I made up a special group of photos for her. Pick up your cues from them."

Preacher nodded. He felt the young man's hand on his arm and turned to follow him. He followed the man through a corridor and they came out behind a drape.

The young man put his hand on the drape. "When you hear your name you enter. Pause for a moment to let the congregation see you, then turn toward Miss Kuhlman, who will be seated on a small couch center stage. You sit on the end of the couch opposite her. You will be at right angles toward her for better camera positioning. You will find a pitcher of water and glasses on the small table in front of you. I'll pull the curtain for you."

"Thank you," Preacher said.

Her voice came through the loudspeakers overhead. "My friends, give a warm welcome to . . . the Reverend C. Andrew Talbot."

The curtain was pulled back suddenly and Preacher stepped forward into a blinding battery of lights.

Gushing. Thick syrupy sweetness and light. And still, underneath it all a steel-like sense of purpose came through as she repeated his answer to her every question, turning it to the point she wanted to make. He felt nothing but admiration for her. This seemingly frail woman was made of tempered steel. It was her pulpit. She was the star. And she never let you forget it.

Star quality, Marcus had called it. That was the one thing they all had in common—an indefinable presence that made them rise above the crowd of ordinary ministers. It was different in each one but nevertheless it was there.

In the two months Preacher had been on the TV gospel trail he had appeared on all their programs: Pat Robertson expressed the kindly interest and warmth of every American's ideal next-door neighbor; Jim Bakker, the round-faced boy next door; Jerry Falwell, the sincere, friendly neighborhood president of the local Chamber of Commerce; Robert Shuller, the cheerful, uplifting smile of the neighborhood doctor who always brought the brighter side to your attention; Paul Crouch, with his brightly colored sport jackets, was the man next door ever ready to jump into his van and set off on adventures in the great outdoors or far and wonderful places; Oral Roberts, the intense visionary of the neighborhood with wonderful ideas to remake the world; Jimmy Swaggart, the bleeding heart of the neighborhood, who cried for all the suffering people of the world; Rex Humbard, the stern taskmaster; and, last but not least, Billy Graham, the father all could turn to in times of trouble.

All different. All star quality. All with their own personal relationship with God and His only Son, Jesus Christ, the Savior of mankind.

Katherine Kuhlman had it too. She was the aunt who came to you in times of trouble. With home-baked cookies. Or chicken broth. Everything to make you feel better.

The message light on the telephone was blinking when they got back to their hotel after the services. "Want me to find out who called?" Joe asked.

"Please," Preacher said. He walked into the bedroom and threw himself across the bed. He was tired. He was also bored. He had gone over the same story so many times, he himself was tired of hearing it. The only consolation was that this had been the last stop of the current tour. Tomorrow he would be back in Randle with his own people.

Joe appeared in the doorway. "It's that lady who works for Randle, Jane Dawson, who called. She left a call-back number in Dallas. She says it's urgent."

"I'll call her later," Preacher said. "It can't be that important. I haven't seen her in months."

"The message said urgent," Joe said.

"Okay. Get her for me."

Joe went back into the other room. A moment later he called into Preacher's room. "She's on the line."

Preacher picked up the phone and leaned back against the pillow. "Hello, Jane. What's so urgent?"

Her voice was strained. "I have to see you."

"You know we can't do that," Preacher said. "I told you how he feels about it."

"You can stop in Dallas on your way back. He doesn't have to know about it."

"No. I gave him my word." He began searching for a cigarette. "What's so important that you can't tell me about it on the phone?"

"There's always a chance that someone could be listening in."

"Not on my end."

"I'm not that sure. Sometimes I think my phone is bugged."

He couldn't find a cigarette and began to grow annoyed. "I don't give a damn whether anybody's listening in or not. You tell me what this is all about or forget it."

She began to cry.

"Cut it out," he said. "You're acting like a baby."

"I—I can't help it," she said. "I'm pregnant."

"Shit!" he exclaimed, sitting bolt upright. He thought quickly for a moment. "You get yourself together. I'll try to get a plane out of here tonight."

He slammed down the phone and got out of bed. Joe heard the noise and came to the doorway. "What's wrong?" he asked.

"Now we're fucked. Really fucked," he said angrily. He turned to Joe. "Get on the phone and see if you can get me on a plane for Dallas tonight."

CHAPTER
TWELVE

She was waiting at the gate as he came through the ramp. Her face was pale and drawn, her eyes anxious as she looked up at him. "Preacher," she said in a small voice.

He bent and kissed her cheek without speaking.

"Do you have any luggage?" she asked.

"No," he answered. "I sent it on with Joe."

"My car is in the parking lot."

He nodded and followed her silently onto the moving walkway that took them toward the main entrance hall. The airport was almost empty. He glanced at the clock on the wall. It was one-forty in the morning.

She looked up at him. "You're angry with me."

"I'm more angry with myself," he answered shortly. "I figured you for having smarts. Even a high-school girl isn't stupid enough to do anything without protecting herself first."

She fell silent and they didn't exchange another word until they arrived at the apartment house in which she lived. She got out of the car and gave the keys to the doorman. Preacher followed her into the lobby. In the elevator she pressed the button that took them to the penthouse.

It wasn't until she opened the door to the duplex penthouse apartment that he realized that she lived in what was probably one of the most expensive apartments in the city. The apartment covered two floors, each with its own terrace outside large floor-to-ceiling french doors. It was furnished in a very expensive contemporary fashion and he recognized some of the paintings hanging on the walls as modern masters.

"Can I get you something?" she asked as they enetered the living room.

"I could use a drink," he said, his eyes glancing around the apartment.

"What would you like?"

"A Scotch, if you have it," he said.

"I've got it," she answered, turning away.

He called her back. "Is that real or a copy?" he asked, pointing at a Picasso.

"It's real."

"I never realized you made that kind of money," he said. "The only other Picassos I've ever seen were in museums."

"I'll get your drink," she said.

He was outside on the balcony looking over the city when she came back with the drink. He took the drink from her hand and turned back to the city. "There's a lot of lights out there."

"Yes," she said. "That's why I chose this apartment. It has a beautiful view."

"I never saw an apartment like this except in the movies. Randle pay for it?" he asked.

She nodded silently.

"If you're smart enough to make that old son of a bitch keep you like this, how come you got stupid enough to blow it?" he asked sarcastically.

"I thought I was protected," she said. "My doctor took me off the pill for a while, so I was using the suppositories."

He thought quickly. It was almost three months since they had been together last. "How far gone are you?"

"The doctor said I'm at the end of my third month."

"What took you so long to find out?"

"I told you. I thought I was protected. Besides, I was never very regular and it was nothing for me to miss a period or even two occasionally. It wasn't until this week when I began to wake up feeling nauseous in the morning that I thought something might be wrong."

"Oh shit," he said, taking a deep swallow of his drink. "Did you ask him about an abortion?"

"He wouldn't do it."

"Why not?"

"Doesn't believe in it."

"Catholic?"

"No. Baptist with deep convictions about the right to life."

He swallowed the rest of his drink. "Thank God he isn't the only doctor in the world."

Her voice was shocked. "You'd be willing for me to have an abortion?"

He stared at her balefully. "You bet your ass I would. For the first time in my life I've got the opportunity to get my own church together. How would it look if it turned up that I got a little bastard running around? And how long do you think you could live like this if it comes out? Randle would tie a can to you so fast you wouldn't know what happened."

She was silent for a minute. "We could get married."

He shook his head. "I'm not the marrying kind. Marriage was never part of my plans." He held up his glass. "Where's the bar? I could use another drink."

Silently she led him through the french doors and into the living room and gestured. The bar with the bottle of Scotch on it was in a small alcove at the corner of the room. He poured himself another drink and came back to her. "Chances are you're too well known around here to do anything about it. California would be our best bet."

She sank into the couch and looked up at him. "I can't believe what I'm hearing," she said. "You say that you're a minister of the Gospel. What do you preach with, your mouth or your heart?"

"I preach the Gospel and even the Baptists in their convention of '68 said that abortion is an individual choice," he said angrily. "You tell me where it says in the Bible that I got to marry every girl I knock up."

Her voice grew cold. "There have been others?"

"How the hell do I know?" he asked. "But I've always been with girls and you're the first one that ever came to me with the problem. And how do I know that it's even mine? It's been almost three months since we've been together. You could have been with someone else the very first day we were apart."

The tears began to roll down her cheeks. "I wasn't."

He was silent for a moment. "Okay. So you weren't. That still don't make any difference."

"Does it make any difference that I love you?" she asked.

"The Lord tells us to love one another," he answered.

"That's not what I mean and you know it," she insisted.

He took a swallow of his drink and sank into the couch opposite her. "Lord, you're making it difficult for me. What do you think's going to happen when old man Randle finds out? He made me promise to keep away from you. He's going to kick us both out on our ass and we blow everything—I blow the church and you blow living like this."

She smiled. "Maybe it won't be like that at all. Maybe he'll be real happy about it."

He stared at her. "What the hell are you talking about?"

"Why do you think he wanted you to stop seeing me?"

"He said I was screwing up your head and that it was interfering with your work. That he had a very personal interest in you."

"And all you could think was that I was his whore?" She was angry now. "You stupid idiot, what man in his right mind would want his daughter to get involved with a jerk who's willing to give up everything in the world just to preach the Gospel?"

"You mean—?" Her words were sinking into him just as the telephone began to ring. He turned to look at it.

She made no move to pick it up. "It's probably him right now."

He stared at her without speaking.

"Answer it," she said. "He probably wants to talk to you. I told you I thought my phone was bugged."

He picked up the phone. "Hello," he said in a tentative voice.

The old man's voice boomed through the receiver. "Andrew?"

"Yes."

"Congratulations, son." Randle's voice echoed in his ear. "I don't want you to worry about a thing. I've got the wedding arrangements already made!"

CHAPTER
THIRTEEN

Jake Randle had kept his word. Churchland was ready by May 1976, as he had said it would be. But the official opening was planned for July Fourth in order to coincide with the nationwide bicentennial celebration.

By eleven o'clock in the morning the computers at the reception center had registered two thousand four hundred and twenty-one visitors. Thirty-one buses were in the parking lot. Seven private jet planes, three DC-9's and one Boeing 727-200 were already on the airfield. Over seven hundred automobiles were jammed into the auxiliary parking lots and fifteen buses and three more big chartered planes were expected before two o'clock.

Preacher was standing at the window of his office high in the seventh-floor tower of the church. Below him he saw the crowds of people walking around Churchland, families, men, women, children, all in their Sunday finest. They all seemed to be enjoying themselves, a bright festive air about them. The buzzer at his desk sounded and he went back to it. He pressed a button and spoke into the speakerphone. "Yes?"

"Your wife is on the phone, Dr. Talbot," his secretary said.

He picked up his private line. "Good morning, Jane."

"Hello, darling," she said. "I missed you this morning."

"I got out early. You were sleeping so peacefully I couldn't wake you up."

She laughed. "Isn't it exciting? I couldn't believe all the people I saw when I looked out the window."

"Almost twenty-five hundred people here already," he said.

"How many more do you expect?"

"I don't know," he answered. "Nobody has told me yet."

She laughed. "Silly. You don't need anyone to tell you. That's why the minicomputer is on your desk. It will pick up all the information you want from the central bank."

"I don't know how to work it."

"It's simple. Just punch the code into the machine. The information will flash on the screen automatically."

He shook his head. "I'm hopeless, I'm afraid. I forgot the code."

"You have your code book?"

"I can't make head or tail out of it. It's too complicated for me."

"It must be a mental block. You can remember every word in the Bible but you can't even read a simple code book. I'll give you the code—21-30-219-17."

He pressed the numbers on the computer keyboard. The answer flashed on the screen immediately. "Three thousand four hundred sixteen."

"You can't get all of them into the church," she said. "Good thing the chapels are equipped with projection TV screens. They'll be able to handle at least a thousand people."

"I'd better let reception know about it," he said.

She laughed. "You don't have to do anything. The computer prints out all the seat assignments. It's programmed to divert visitors to the chapels as soon as the church is filled up."

"I don't know what I would have done without you," he said.

She laughed. "That's a backhanded compliment. You'd

still be a swinging bachelor, not the father of two children."

He smiled. Little Jake was almost fifteen months old, and Linda Rae would be three months old next week. "How are they this morning?"

"They're fine," she said. "Their grandfather is up in the nursery with them. I've never seen him having such a good time. But that's not why I called. I was wondering if you would have time to join us here for lunch."

"I don't think so," he said. "I've still got a lot to do. Right now I have to go down and say hello to Ruth Carter Stapleton."

"Who is she?"

"She's the sister of Jimmy Carter."

"I don't know who he is either."

"He's the governor of Georgia who's running for the Democratic nomination for President. He's a born-again Christian and she's a preacher. Right after that I have to be at the airfield. The governor of Texas is due in on his private plane."

"I'm sorry," she said. "When will we see you?"

"It's an old saying but it's true," he laughed. "See you in church."

"If I didn't love you, it would be easy to hate you."

"I love you too," he said, putting down the phone.

The buzzer sounded again; his secretary's voice came from the speakerphone. "Mr. Lincoln is here."

"Tell him to come in."

The producer came into the room, a loose-leaf bound script in his hand. He was smiling. "I think we've got it."

Preacher smiled. "I hope so."

Marcus placed the script on the desk. "You'll find everything you need in there. We've left you fifteen minutes for your sermon."

"That's all?" Preacher asked. "What happened to the rest of the time? I thought we had an hour and a half."

Marcus laughed. "Forty-five minutes get used up so that you can introduce the guests and give them a chance to say a few words."

"That still leaves a half-hour open."

"Film clips of Churchland, inserts of you appearing on other programs, establishing shots, things like that." He sank into a chair opposite the desk. "But you don't have to worry about that. The most important thing is to remember that we have to start exactly at three o'clock and finish exactly at four. That leaves us four hours to edit the program and get it on the wires. We go on the air at ten o'clock in the East, seven in the West."

"Okay," Preacher said.

"Jim Woden will keep you clued on the timing. Just follow his directions and we won't have a thing to worry about." He rose from the chair. "If you have any questions, I'll be in my office downstairs. I've made arrangements to have everybody on stage fifteen minutes before we start."

"Good enough."

Marcus smiled. "Good luck."

"Thank you," Preacher said. "We'll need it."

The faint roar of a jet plane filtered into the office. He went back to the window and looked out. A jet liner was just banking into its approach to the airfield, the bright sun shining silver from its wings. He took a deep breath.

It was almost two years since that morning he had come from Dallas with Jane. They had landed at the old man's private field in one of his Lear jets. He didn't go up to the ranch with her; instead he had the limousine take him directly to his van just outside the big tent which was still standing in the field next to town.

News traveled fast. Joe and Beverly were waiting for him in the van. "How did it go?" Joe asked.

He tried to be noncommittal. "Okay."

Joe looked at him. "When's the wedding?"

He couldn't keep the surprise from his voice. "How do you know about that?"

"There ain't no secrets," Joe said. "She called here first to find out where you were."

"That didn't mean anything."

"She was crying when I spoke to her," Beverly said. "I asked her what was wrong and she told me she was pregnant." She reached for a cigarette. "Then first thing this morning Charlie came in here very upset. She'd been dating Larry, Randle's bodyguard. He came by to see her about three o'clock this morning and told her that you were going to marry the old man's daughter."

Preacher was silent.

"Did you know that she was his daughter?" Beverly asked.

He shook his head. "I just found out last night."

"Are you going through with it?"

He looked at her. "Do I have any choice? If I don't we blow it all."

Charlie's voice came from behind him. "The bitch!"

He turned in surprise. He hadn't heard her come into the van.

"The bitch!" she repeated. "She set you up for it."

"No she didn't," he protested. "It wasn't her fault."

"Nobody's so stupid they wait three months to find out if they're pregnant," Charlie said. "Would you say that if any of us pulled that on you? You'd hustle us off to the nearest doctor."

He was silent.

"You're not even in love with her," said Charlie accusingly. "The old man's money has you buffaloed."

"Abortion's a sin," he said. "It's against the Scriptures."

"Bullshit!" Charlie said vehemently. "I'm getting tired of you pulling out the Scriptures and quoting them at me whenever it suits your purpose. Why don't you admit the truth just once—that it's the money you want?"

"It's not the money," he protested, "it's the chance it gives me to do God's work."

"You can believe that if you want to," she said balefully, "but the girls and I don't. We believed in you once but not no more. You're no different from nobody else. You just blew us off. We're getting out of here this morning."

"Wait a minute," he said. "Give me a chance. Nothing's going to change. We're all still going to be together working for Jesus Christ."

"You are dumb," she said contemptuously. "You can't even see that it's Jake Randle, not Jesus Christ, you're working for."

Before he had a chance to say anything, she had turned and run from the van. He turned back to Joe and Beverly. "Go after her," he said. "Maybe you can make them understand."

"Joe and I have been talking to them all morning," Beverly said. "We can't change their minds. They feel you betrayed them. Only Tarz is staying."

He was silent for a moment. "And you?" he asked.

"We're staying," Joe said. "We don't object to gettin' in on the gravy."

"Do you think it's the money that's making me do this?"

"I don't really care," Joe said. "You're a preacher-man and you gotta preach. Any way you take to do it is okay with me."

"And how do you feel?" he asked Beverly.

She smiled slowly. "I made my choice to go with you a long time ago. What you do is not important. Besides, a Buddhist has no right to pass judgment on a Christian."

"The real important thing is, do you want us to stay?" Joe asked.

Preacher looked at him. "You know I do."

Joe looked at Beverly. "Then we stay."

Preacher glanced at her. She nodded her head. "Good," he said. "I'm glad."

"We'll stick out like a couple of sore thumbs," Joe said. "They'll be pushing you to get rid of us."

"Nobody can make me do that," Preacher said.

"While all this marryin' talk is in the air," Joe said, "do you object to me and Beverly gettin' married?"

"What about your wife and kids in Carolina?" Preacher asked.

"We were never really married, and besides she married up with another guy," Joe said.

Preacher looked at him. "Then I have no objections."

Joe grinned. "Then we all got nothin' to do but congratulate each other."

Preacher took a deep breath. "Not yet. First, I want to go over and talk to the girls myself. I just can't let them leave. Not like that."

CHAPTER
FOURTEEN

He had crossed the field to their trailer, climbed up the three steps and knocked at the door. The voice came muffled through the door. "Who is it?"

"Preacher."

"Go away. We don't have nothin' to say to you."

"I have something to say to you," he said.

"We don't want to hear it. Go away."

He tried the door. It was locked. "Unlock the door," he called.

"No."

He took the doorknob in his hand and twisted it. At the same time he kicked the door with the bottom of his heavy boot. The lightweight door sprang open and he walked through it into the trailer. "Sorry."

The girls were standing near their bunks. There were cardboard boxes and valises on the floor next to them. A faint scent of grass hung in the air. Slowly he looked at each of them in turn. They stared back at him in silence. "Okay," he said. "Who's got the joint?"

No one answered.

"Don't be selfish," he said. "I could use a toke myself."

They exchanged glances, then Melanie held a half-used joint out to him. He took it from her hand and lit it. He sat on a chair near the door and sucked two tokes deep into his lungs. He nodded thoughtfully without speaking, then took another toke and silently gave it back to her.

She took a hit and passed it to Charlie, standing next to her. Charlie dragged on the joint and passed it on. By the time it reached the last girl it was gone.

None of them had said a word until then. Finally he spoke. "Got another?"

"Is that the reason you kicked the door open to get in here?" Charlie snapped.

He met her eyes. "After what you just said to me, can you think of a better reason?"

Her eyes fell; she didn't speak.

He looked from one to the other before he spoke again. "It just happens that I do have a better reason to bust in here than that. We've known each other too long, we've been through too much together and I love you all too much to let you walk out just like that."

Once again it was Charlie who spoke for them. "You don't need us anymore. You're goin' someplace else."

He met her eyes. "I'm not going anywhere that I thought you would not come with me. I need you more now than ever before."

"If that's so true how come you been goin' all over the country while we been sittin' here twiddlin' our thumbs? And then when you did show up for a day or two, you never even talked to us, always at some meetin' or other. Next thing we know, you're marryin' up with that rich cunt."

He stared at her. "I didn't know that not marrying was the reason we stayed together. I thought that the love we have for each other and for Jesus was what counted."

"You keep talkin' about the love you got for us but it's her you been ballin' all the time."

"You know better than that, Charlie," he said.

"I don't know what to think anymore," she said, turning away swiftly but not before he saw the tears welling into her eyes.

He rose from his chair and took her hand, turning her to him. "Charlie."

She hid her face against his shoulder. "Why don't you just let us go, Preacher? What do you want from us anyway?"

He stroked her hair slowly. "What I always wanted, Charlie," he said softly. He looked at the others over her head. "Remember what I said when we left the Community at Los Altos? I wanted for us to build a ministry together. A place where we can help people find the Lord. And that I wanted you to help me."

He paused for a moment. None of them spoke.

"That hasn't changed. And I haven't changed. I still want you to help me. I still need you. I need your faith, your trust, your love. Without that, I can't do it myself."

It was Melanie who spoke now. "We've been hearing stories, even before this happened, that you were going to send us away."

"Where did you hear that?" he asked.

"From the locals," she said. "They said that old man Randle was after you to get rid of your harem."

"Why did you listen to them?" he asked. "Why didn't you come to me?"

"We wanted to," she answered. "But you were always too busy. You'd be in and out all the time."

He was silent for a moment. "I'll make you a promise. Any time you want to talk to me about anything, you come to me. I promise I'll make time for you." They were all looking at him. "Now, will you stay?"

Preacher looked down at the computer printout on his desk, then at Beverly, seated opposite him. "Over six million dollars?"

"That's right," she said. "That's what the Randle Foundation put into Churchland. They own the land and the buildings and they've leased it to us for a ten-year period at six hundred thousand a year and we pay all maintenance and service charges."

"That comes to fifty thousand a year plus," Preacher said.

"We also owe them over five hundred thousand dollars they advanced for P.R. and TV time purchases."

He shook his head. "That's a big nut to start out with."

"That's the deal," she said without expression. "You signed the agreement. If we make it, Randle will do pretty good for himself."

"And if we don't?"

"They can throw us out and take it all back."

"Then what will he do with it?"

She shrugged. "I don't know."

Suddenly he began to laugh. "There's nothing he can do with it. If we don't make the payments he won't throw us out. He'll wind up sticking the whole place up his ass if he does. This is one time I think he got too smart."

Her face was still expressionless. "Maybe."

"When does the rent start?" he asked.

"It already has," she answered. "We owe him a quarter of a million dollars already."

"Good," he said. "Let's run it up to a million before we pay him anything."

"How can we do that?" she asked. "There's almost three hundred thousand dollars of collections in from the first three mailings already and we haven't even opened officially yet."

He looked at her. "You're the church treasurer, aren't you?"

"Yes," she said.

"Who gets to count the money first?"

"I do."

"It's no different than when we were traveling around with the tent," he said. "Whoever counts the money decides what and who to pay."

She stared at him. "That's not what you used to do then."

"This is different," he said. "I'm sure the money can be used better for God's work than to make my father-in-law any richer."

"Okay," she nodded, beginning to pick up the papers on the desk in front of her.

His secretary's voice came from the speakerphone. "Mr. Woden called from the control booth. He says it's one hour to showtime and wants to know if you want the makeup girl to come up now."

"Tell him fifteen minutes," Preacher said. He gestured to Beverly, who was getting to her feet. "Just a minute."

She stood there looking down at him.

"Do all our receipts go into the computer?"

She nodded.

"Is there any way we can fix it so that some part does not go into the computer?"

"It won't be easy," she said. "That is Jane's department. And your wife knows her business."

"I'm sure she does," he said dryly. "But I'm not asking her, I'm asking you. Is it possible?"

"It won't be easy," she said quietly. "But it's possible."

"You work it out then," he said. "I want ten percent of the receipts in an account that only you and I know about."

"Okay." A brief smile flitted across her face. "You're getting very Chinese."

"No," he answered. "Just cautious. Too many churches have been taken over by unscrupulous people. I just want to make sure this doesn't happen to us."

He watched her leave, then picked up the telephone and tapped out a number. Charlie's voice came on the line. "How are the kids doing?" he asked.

Her voice was filled with excitement. "Just fine. We just finished dressing and we're going down to makeup."

"Good," he said. "You all straight?"

"Sure," she answered. "We're not taking any chances."

"Fine. I'll see you all downstairs. We'll get together after the show to have a smoke."

"That will be lovely."

"God bless," he said, putting down the telephone.

He punched the button down on the speakerphone. "Get Brother Washington for me." A moment later the telephone buzzed. Joe was on the line.

"Are you ready?" he asked.

"Got my Sunday go-to-meetin' suit on," Joe said.

"Then come on up here," he said. "I got the makeup girl coming."

"I'll be right up," Joe laughed. "But I won't need any. I'm tan enough already."

Forty-five minutes later he was standing on the small elevator platform below the stage that would bring him, as if by magic, to his position behind the pulpit. He watched the screen of the small monitor built into the shelf before him. He heard the choir over his head as the screen flashed into life.

The first visual was a pan shot from a helicopter over Churchland. The camera zoomed in close on the church entrance with the throngs of people entering, then panned up to the giant cross suspended between the two towers of the building, then abruptly cut inside the church and began to sweep the congregation as the rich mellow baritone of the announcer began to boom overhead.

"From Churchland, Texas, on this two hundredth birthday of the United States of America, the Community of God Church of Christian America Triumphant welcomes you to the grand opening celebration of its first Festival of Faith."

Slowly, the camera began to pan across the dais on the stage, hesitating for a fraction of a moment at each guest so that they could be recognized by the audience, as the announcer's voice continued. "Distinguished guests, ladies and gentlemen, the Community of God Church of Christian America Triumphant is proud to present its pastor . . ."

The tiny radio earphone in Preacher's ear crackled into life as the small elevator shuddered a moment and began to rise slowly. Jim Woden's voice came through. "Hold on, Dr. Talbot, you're on your way to heaven."

Preacher smiled to himself at the faint humor, then as the elevator cleared the stage behind the pulpit, the announcer's booming voice drowned out every other sound. ". . . the Reverend Dr. C. Andrew Talbot!"

The congregation began to applaud. Looking out at them, for the first time, Preacher felt the power that was in him, the power to touch and to reach all these people, the power to change their lives, the power to bring them closer to God. Slowly he looked around the giant auditorium. There wasn't a vacant seat, and each seat was filled with someone who looked toward him for the faith and hope that he would give them.

He raised both hands over his head, palms out until the applause died down and they were quiet in their seats. He turned and looked at the dais behind him for a moment, then back to the congregation. His voice was gentle and reverent but strong with conviction.

"Brothers and Sisters in Christ, let us begin with a prayer." He clasped his hands and looked down, giving the congregation a moment to follow him.

"We thank thee, O Lord, for making all this possible. And we dedicate ourselves and this ministry to Your service and worship in accordance with the Gospel of Your only begotten Son Jesus Christ. And we pledge our minds, hearts and bodies to bring His holy message to all the world."

Book III
JESUS
FOR
POWER

CHAPTER
ONE

"Sorry to be late," Preacher apologized as he entered the board room and took his place at the head of the table, "but when we heard the news of President Reagan being shot, I canceled the program under way and turned it into a straight prayer meeting for his recovery and the recovery of his assistant, James Brady, and the Secret Service man who was shot at the same time. We'll be on the air with that program at seven o'clock in the evening Eastern time and four o'clock Pacific. We'll be the only television ministry with it. All the others run their programs anywhere from one day to a week behind recording. We'll make them all look sick."

"What happened?" Jake Randle asked from the foot of the table. "We've been watching the TV up here. All we know is that the President has been taken to the hospital, but nobody knows had bad he is hurt."

"It may not be too bad," Preacher said. "One of the reports said that he walked into the hospital but that hasn't been verified."

"We could be in luck," Randle said. "If everything turns

out all right our P.R. people will make sure that the whole country knows that our prayers were the first to bring Jesus to the aid of the President."

Preacher looked at him without speaking.

The old man met his gaze. "Right now, I'm glad you were friendly with the Bush people even though at the time I thought you were nuts. If the President dies, Falwell's got to be kicking his own ass for tryin' to talk the President out of pickin' Bush."

"I thought you were in on that," Preacher said pointedly.

"I just gave the committee some money, that's all," Randle said uncomfortably. "Personally I thought Haig should have been the man. Proves just one thing though. We got to make sure that we get control of the House in the '82 elections. If they get the President, then Bush, we got Tip O'Neill and the Democrats are back in the White House."

"The '82 elections are a year and a half away," Preacher said.

"Can't start too early," Randle said. "We got to protect ourselves, elsewise we might lose back everything we've gained."

Preacher nodded without comment and looked around the table. "Time we got the meeting under way and tended to our own business." There was a general assent and nodding of heads. He picked up the gavel and rapped it on the table. "The meeting of the board of directors of the Community of God Church of Christian America Triumphant is hereby called to order." He turned to Beverly, seated at his right. "Will the secretary read the roll call and then the minutes of the last meeting."

Beverly rose to her feet. She ran through the names automatically. "Mr. Jake Randle, Mr. Richard Craig, Mr. John Everett, Mr. Charles Michaels, Mr. Marcus Lincoln, Mrs. Helen Lacey, Mrs. Jane Talbot, Dr. C. Andrew Talbot." She paused for a moment, then picked up a black-bound loose-leaf book. "A copy of the minutes of the last meeting is in the folder in front of each of you. I will now begin to read them."

Randle spoke up. "I move to dispense with the reading of the minutes and approve them as written."

"Second the motion," Craig said.

Preacher got to his feet. "The motion is before us and will be voted upon. All in favor say Aye." The motion was carried unanimously. He nodded to Beverly. "You may now read the financial report covering the last quarter."

Beverly took up another printed folder. "A detailed copy of this report has also been included in your folders. With your permission I will give you the highlights contained therein.

Income from collections and contributions:	12.1 million
Income from dividends, interest and other sources:	4.7 million
Total income:	16.8 million
Less: All operating expenses:	10.5 million
Net excess of income over expenses transferred to surplus:	5.3 million
Current total amount in surplus account invested in bonds, securities and on deposit in various banks:	41.4 million

"I would like to add," she said, looking up, "that the operating expenses of the two months of this quarter that fell within the current fiscal year have increased by approximately one million dollars a month due to the increased cost of television and radio time, mostly based on the new rates charged us by the broadcasting companies since January first."

"What about our income?" Randle asked. "Has that gone up too?"

"Collections and contributions seem to remain at approximately the same level as last year, about four million a month, sir," she answered. "Of course, investment income from the surplus account will rise proportionately but not enough, I'm afraid, to offset the current rate increases and the additional rate increases due to take effect in the middle of the year."

"What you're saying is that we can look forward to a twelve- to fourteen-million-dollar rise in expenses this year with no real compensating offset in income. Is that right?"

She nodded. "Yes, sir."

"Thank you," Randle said. He waited until Beverly sat down. He looked around the table. "That ain't very good news."

No one spoke. They all knew he wasn't finished yet. He looked across the table at Preacher. "It seems to me that it's up to you to find a way to increase our collections."

Preacher met his gaze. "Maybe. But do you have any ideas how I can do that?"

"You can do what the others do. Set up special drives for contributions. Jerry Falwell, Oral Roberts, they do it all the time. They ain't ashamed to get up there themselves and ask for money."

"I'm not either," Preacher said. "With all due respect to the good pastors, I'm not in the business of building monuments to myself in the form of colleges and hospitals. The only monument I want to build is to God."

"Amen to that, Dr. Talbot," Randle said. "But how do you expect to do even that if costs go up and up until they eat away all the money you take in? You have to increase your audience as well as your collections."

"That's easier said than done," Preacher said.

"Falwell's doing it. He brags that he reaches twenty-five million viewers. He didn't do that by sittin' back there on his ass and waitin' for them to come to him. He got out there and made them pay attention to him."

Preacher turned from him to Marcus Lincoln. "Mr. Lincoln, did you bring that Arbitron Company report I asked you about?"

Lincoln nodded and took a folder from his briefcase. He passed it to Preacher, who opened it and looked at it.

"This is a report on the total audience of all syndicated religious programs since 1975, the year before we opened Churchland. In '75 it was 20.8 million. In '76, the year we opened, it was 22.8 million. It stayed like that for two years, then in '79 it dropped a million to 21.4, then another drop of a million in '80 to 20.5. And that's for all of us, including Falwell, who is only one out of a total of sixty-six television ministries." He closed the folder and placed it on the table in front of him. "In that report there is also an audience breakdown which shows that the TV ministries appeal to an audience of fifty and over and a much higher percentage of women than men.

"In view of those circumstances I feel that our maintaining our rate of collections is remarkable. And we have one thing going for us that none of the others have. We don't owe anybody any money. Every bill we get is paid on time and up to date and we still have a large surplus. That's something we can thank the Lord for."

"Amen," Jake said. "So you think we ought to sit still and see what happens?"

Preacher looked at him. "I didn't say that."

"Then what do you say?" Jake asked.

"I say that money sitting out there in banks, stocks and bonds don't do the Lord no good at all. I think that money should be put to work bringing this church, His church, closer to the people." He paused. They were all silent, even the old man. Preacher took a deep breath.

"When I traveled with the gospel tent we used to visit only those towns where the local church would welcome our ministry and help make our stay there a cooperative effort in which together we would bring more people to Jesus Christ. And whatever moneys we collected we shared with the local churches and the money remained in that town for the benefit of its parishioners.

"The television ministry does not do that. We have begun to measure our success in dollars instead of souls saved and brought to the Lord. We can keep track of the money but who among us can keep track of the souls? What follow-up do we have that tells us the souls we brought to Christ remain with Him? The TV ministry doesn't do that. There's no way it can.

"But there is one place that can do what we can't. The local church or churches in all the places our programs reach. What I propose is that we use some of the money we have collected and plow it back into those local churches, many of which are barely able to keep their ministers alive, and bring them into partnership with us in bringing and keeping the message of Jesus Christ alive in the hearts of their congregations."

"Sounds to me like we'd just be throwing away our money," Randle said.

"It's not our money," Preacher said. "It's the Lord's. Maybe if we hadn't taken it, it would have gone to that local church."

"If we didn't get it, it would have gone to Pat Robertson, Jimmy Swaggart, Ernest Angley or Paul Crouch," the old man said.

"You forgot to mention Bob Shuller, Billy Graham and Jerry Falwell among the sixty-six or more ministries that are on the air with us right now," Preacher said. "But the fact remains that we did get the money and it is in our banks. The question is, what we do with it? Keep it hidden and safe in our vaults? Or do we listen to what we were told by St. Luke?"

He opened the Bible before him and looked down at it. "Chapter Sixteen, verse thirteen. 'No servant can serve two masters: for either he will hate the one, and love the other; or else he will hold to the one, and despise the other. Ye cannot serve God and mammon.' "

CHAPTER
TWO

"Daddy wasn't very happy about today's meeting," Jane said as she came from the bathroom.

Preacher was sitting in the bed watching a videotape of one of the most recent Ernest Angley meetings. It was near the end of the taped portion of the show and he was just finishing his healing session and turning toward the camera.

Preacher watched in fascination as Dr. Angley spoke.

"And now, for all of you out there in the television audience who are watching me on your set, do you or one of your loved ones suffer from a problem? Any problem, physical or mental? Have you been unable to expel the demons of drink, drugs, tobacco, lust or the demons of sickness from your body? Remember that Jesus can heal you. Believe me that you can be healed just as these people you just saw were healed, through their faith in Jesus Christ. Remember that He is our sweet Jesus and that He died on the cross for all of us, for all our sins, and our faith in Him will cure all our ills, solve all our problems.

"I will hold out my hand to the camera. You place your

hand on the television screen over mine and repeat this prayer with me." His hand covered the screen. "I believe in the Lord Jesus Christ and that He died on the cross for my sins and in His name I command the demons that cause my ailment to leave me."

Angley's face appeared behind his hand on the screen. The fierce scowling determination on his face was matched only by the strident commanding sound of his voice. "Heal! Hee-all! In the name of our Lord Jesus Christ, hee-all!"

The camera pulled back as he lowered his hand and moved in on his now smiling face. "Thank you, sweet Jesus. Thank you for making me well again."

The screen went to black for a moment and opened on him again. "Join us next week when the Ernest Angley mission appears in Charlotte at the Civic Auditorium, Wednesday night. Meanwhile keep those love gifts and tithes coming in and any extra money you can spare because without your help we cannot bring this ministry to the people. So until that night may the good Lord bless you and in the name of our Savior Jesus Christ, I thank you."

Preacher touched the telecommand. The set went off. He looked at Jane. "What did you say?"

"You weren't listening," she accused. "Don't you have enough religion all day without watching all those preachers at night?"

"There's no other way I can keep up with what all the others are doing," he said. "You can think what you like about Reverend Angley, at least he's doing one thing right. He's getting out there and talking to the people. He's not just relying on the tube to reach them."

She looked at him. "You sound as if that's what you'd like to be doing."

"I kind of miss it," he admitted. "There's something about seeing their faces as you bring them the word and actually touching them and feeling their response to you and to God."

"But you don't have to kill yourself doing that," she said. "You do better than all of them, and never even once have you asked for money yourself the way the others do, so you must be doing something right."

He looked up at her. "If you're talking about bringing in money you know better than that. It's not me. It's you. The way you set up the computers so that they automatically send letters and bulletins to our lists of people is better than anything the other ministries on the air have. They can't even touch us."

"Would you rather I was more like Tammy Fay Bakker or Jan Crouch?" she asked sarcastically.

He shook his head. "I like you the way you are." He smiled. "Besides, you can't even carry a tune."

"Now you're being silly," she smiled.

"Okay," he said, pulling her down to the bed beside him. "Now, what was it you said?"

"Daddy didn't like the way the meeting went today."

He met her eyes. "I know that." He slipped his hand inside her gown and cupped her breast. "Your daddy likes to have things his own way."

She put her hand over his to keep his fingers from playing with her nipples. "I'm trying to be serious, Andrew."

"So am I," he said, feeling her nipples harden to his touch. He smiled at her. "How long has it been since we smoked a joint together?"

Her face went soft and her lips brushed his cheek as she rested her head on his shoulder. "Too long," she whispered.

He kissed her quickly. "I think so too."

She leaned back against the pillow as he opened a drawer in the bedside table next to him. He turned to her with a small wooden cigarette box in his hand. He opened it, revealing it to be filled with neatly rolled joints. She looked at him in surprise. "Where did you get that?"

"Charlie sent it down from Los Altos," he smiled. "Your father got his way on that one but, I guess, none of us are too unhappy about it."

She knew what he meant. It took the old man almost three years to get rid of the Harem, as he called them. At the end, only Charlie and Melanie were left, and when Preacher offered them the chance to go back to Los Altos and rebuild the Community there, they jumped at it, finally admitting they were never happy in Churchland. "How are they doing?" she asked.

"Fine," he smiled. "Tarz just came back from there. They have all the permits from the city and construction will begin soon. By this summer they'll have the camp ready to give a hundred poor kids a week, a real country-farm-type vacation. They've already made arrangements with churches in San Francisco and Los Angeles."

"I'm happy for them," she said genuinely. "But I still don't see why you insisted that you pay all the bills yourself. The church can afford it."

"It's my own thing," he said. "They started it with me and we decided to keep it that way."

He took a joint from the box and lit it, drawing the smoke deep into his lungs and passing the stick to her. He watched while she took a few tokes. "Good?" he smiled.

"Fabulous," she said. Suddenly she giggled. "I've never had anything like this before. Two hits and I feel stoned already."

He laughed, taking the joint back from her. "It should be good. Those two are the best judges of grass in the world."

She watched him draw on the stick. "Do you miss them?" she asked, reaching for the cigarette. She giggled. "Do you miss having your own little harem? A different girl to choose from every night?"

He laughed. "Do you want to know the truth?"

She nodded.

He laughed again. "You bet I do."

She drew again on the joint, then put it down and held her arms toward him. "You come down here, you fool. You're about to find out that a one-woman harem is all you can manage to handle."

He struggled from his sleep to answer the telephone ringing next to his bed. "Hello," he said, his eyes still closed.

His secretary's voice echoed in his ear. "Good morning, Dr. Talbot. Mr. Randle, Mr. Craig and Mrs. Lacey are here to see you."

He opened his eyes. The luminous digital clock on the night table read 8:05 A.M. "Damn," he muttered to himself. Usually he was at his desk before eight o'clock. Just like the old man to show up on a morning he slept late. "Take them into my office and give them a cup of coffee," he said. "I'll be there in fifteen minutes."

He pushed back the cover and got out of bed. Halfway to the bathroom her voice stopped him. "Everything all right?" she mumbled sleepily.

"Fine," he answered, looking back at her. "I overslept."

"I don't know how you can get up," she said, her eyes still shut tight. "I can't move. Maybe you should get the harem back."

"No reason to," he smiled. "We did all right."

"I almost forgot how great a good fuck can be," she said. "It was beautiful."

"It was beautiful," he said. "Now go back to sleep, I've got to go to work."

CHAPTER
THREE

Fifteen minutes later he walked into his office. They were seated on the couch, their coffee cups on the table before them. He pulled up a chair and sat facing them as his secretary placed a cup of coffee in front of him. "Good morning," he said. "More coffee?"

"No, thank you," Randle said. The others shook their heads in agreement.

Preacher looked up at his secretary. "That will be all, Miss Grant. Thank you." He sipped at his coffee until the door closed behind her, then put it down. He came right to the point. "What reason do I have to thank you for this unexpected visit?"

Randle cleared his throat uncomfortably. "Mr. Craig, Mrs. Lacey and I were very disturbed by your defeatist attitude at the board meeting yesterday."

"Defeatist?" Preacher's voice was dry.

"Yes," Randle replied. "We got the impression that you feel nothing can be done to improve our position."

"I didn't say that," Preacher said. "I merely said there is only a limited market for all the television ministries and that the maximum has already been reached."

"We don't agree with you," Randle said.

"Why didn't you say so at the meeting then?" Preacher asked.

"Saw no reason to," the old man said. "Thought this was a matter to settle among ourselves. After all, the others are nothing but employees."

Preacher nodded. "I see." He took another sip of his coffee. "But you didn't seem to respond to my suggestion about investing some of our money in the local churches."

"Mr. Craig and Mrs. Lacey agree with me. It would be throwing the money out."

"You have a better idea?" Preacher asked.

Randle looked at Craig. "Dick, you're closer to the situation than I am. Supposing you tell Dr. Talbot what we recommend."

Craig looked at Preacher. "You know, of course, that Mrs. Lacey and I have a long history of association with many Baptist evangelical churches."

Preacher nodded. "The good work you and Mrs. Lacey have done for the Christian church is a matter of record and very much appreciated. I, too, appreciate your interest in us and will listen most carefully to your suggestions."

Craig smiled. "Thank you, Dr. Talbot."

"Not at all, Mr. Craig. I really mean that."

Craig relaxed slightly. "In our opinion, the real problem facing this ministry is that it has held itself apart from the general Christian evangelical movement."

"You mean what is commonly known as the Christian New Right?"

Craig nodded. "In a sense. For example, we have not committed ourselves to the work of the Moral Majority and taken a strong position with them in trying to bring about a return of the traditional American values."

"I hope you'll forgive me if I appear ignorant, Mr. Craig," Preacher said, "but I fail to see how an affiliation with a political action committee will benefit our ministry."

"Active participation in their work will bring an increased visibility to our ministry just as it has to Falwell. Before that work Falwell was just another minister. Now everybody in the United States knows his name."

"I still don't see where that has helped his ministry. If anything, I have the feeling that Falwell is under heavy financial pressure to maintain the activities of his ministry. If I'm to believe what he tells us, every activity of his ministry is on the verge of instant bankruptcy."

"It's not that bad," Craig said. "Dr. Falwell has cash-flow problems but then so do many of the others—Oral Roberts, Jim Bakker and Pat Robertson. Even Jimmy Swaggart has problems in maintaining his missionary work in feeding and caring for the needy in some of his third-world missions. Money has become very tight. We all have to work harder just to get our share."

Preacher looked at him. "Without meaning to be disrespectful of the good work all these gentlemen are doing, Mr. Craig, is it possible that the overall drop in the audience for the television ministries over the past two years coincides with their entrance into politics and their attempts to impose their versions of morality on the system?"

"I don't think that has anything to do with it," Craig said testily. "What do you advise? That we bury our heads in the sand like ostriches and allow the devils of Communism and immorality to continue to take over our great country as they have been doing over the past forty years?"

"No, I don't believe that, Mr. Craig," Preacher said quietly. "But I do believe that God has given us a greater platform from which to fight the devil than a political one."

"If you're talking about the television tube," Craig said sarcastically, "that's not enough."

"I agree with you that it's not enough, Mr. Craig," Preacher said quietly. "What I am talking about is the churches and pulpits throughout America. It is in His house that we must do battle with the devil."

"Dr. Falwell agrees with that viewpoint completely. Do you know that he has helped more than three hundred graduates of the Liberty Baptist College found their own churches? And that he plans to have thousands more in the next ten years?"

"I have no reason to doubt you, Mr. Craig. It seems to me quite possible, if that should happen, that there will not be enough room left in America for any Baptist church except the Liberty Baptist. It could be a very sad thing if that happened, because to me one of the greatest things about the Baptist faith is that each church and each minister is proud of his independence and freedom to preach the word of God by his own lights."

"But it's the future, Dr. Talbot. It's the American way of big business doing it better than the smaller, ill-equipped and underfinanced independent."

Preacher was silent for a moment, then turned to Mrs. Lacey. "Do you feel the same way?"

"Yes." She nodded vigorously. "We must all unite for a common goal. Together we must stamp out the immoralities that threaten to destroy the American family."

"And you, Mr. Randle?" Preacher asked.

"I see no other way, son," the old man said. "It's the only way we can have the kind of government that we need to safeguard our economy. The only voices that the politicians hear are those that go into the ballot box. If we want further changes in the laws that benefit our interests we have to be in a position to exert even more power than we did to elect President Reagan and gain control of the Senate for the Republicans."

Preacher looked at him. "Would it be impertinent if I ventured that changes in the tax laws and the decontrol of oil prices would benefit your various interests by more than a hundred million dollars this year?"

"It would be impertinent," the old man said testily. "I don't see where it's anyone's business."

"Would it be impertinent, sir," Preacher said smoothly, "if I were to ask your age?"

"That's stupid!" Randle snapped. "Everybody knows my age. I'm sixty-eight."

Preacher smiled inwardly. He knew the old man was well past seventy. "From what Mr. Craig has said, it would take Dr. Falwell ten years to accomplish his plan. Would you be willing to wait that long?"

"What the hell are you getting at?" Randle said balefully.

"What if I were to show you that with the expenditure of ten million dollars or less we can reach the same objectives in two years?" Preacher's voice was deceptively soft.

Randle stared at him. "I'd say you were crazy."

"Kentucky Fried Chicken," Preacher said.

"You *are* nuts," Randle said.

"McDonald's." Preacher saw the light suddenly dawn in the old man's eyes. "Want to hear the rest of it?"

The old man nodded grimly without speaking.

"Franchise," Preacher said carefully. "After TV that's the next step. It worked for them, it can work for us. There are already established at least ten thousand Baptist churches eking out a bare existence in almost as many villages and towns. If we bring them our expertise and methods, together with a reasonable amount of financial assistance, we could have almost as many affiliated franchised Community of God Churches of Christian America Triumphant as we care to take on."

"Son of a bitch!" the old man said in a wondering voice. He caught himself and turned to Mrs. Lacey. "Excuse me, madam." He turned back to Preacher, a broad smile coming to his face. "I knew I was right when I cottoned to you right away. You really are a sneaky bastard."

CHAPTER
FOUR

"I think you've flipped your wig, Preacher," Joe said. "There ain't never been no nigger preacher on national TV except Reverend Ike an' he's a big joke."

"Then it's about time there was one people can take seriously," Preacher said.

"If you do want one, who you gonna get?" Joe asked. "The only one I know is out in Los Angeles. Fred Price of the Crenshaw Christian Center is already on thirty-five TV stations with his 'Ever-Increasing Faith' program. And even if he hasn't gone national yet, he don't need us. He already bought the old Pepperdine University campus in L.A. to build himself a new ten-thousand-seat church for about fourteen million dollars."

"You're right, he's not our man. Mainly for two reasons. One, he's playing to the middle-class blacks with white-middle-class aspirations who are looking for just a mild touch of black gospel preaching. Two, he may be involved already with Oral Roberts. I've heard he's contributed some large sums to the City of Faith Hospital in Tulsa." Preacher picked up a computer printout from his desk. "I have a list of more than eight thousand black Baptist evangelical and pentecostal churches, each with a congregation running between two hundred and fifteen hundred people. These are the people who need us, the people we can help. There's not a one of these churches that is covering its expenses."

"They ain't goin' to listen to us," Joe said. "They goin' to figure it's just another ripoff by the whitey church."

"Sure they will if I go to them. But I'm not going," Preacher said. "You are."

"Now I'm sure you completely gone," Joe said. "I never preached no sermon."

"Then you had better begin practicing. We're planning to tape your first show in two weeks." He stared at the expression on Joe's face and began to laugh. Joe seemed almost dumbfounded with surprise. "It's not really that hard," he added. "Just hold the Bible in your hand, wave it around your head a little bit and slap the pulpit with your other hand every now and then. At the same time you stare the camera and the audience right in the eye and act like you're the man who wrote the good book."

"We'll never fill our church with enough blacks for a TV show," Joe said. "They ain't that many in this part of the country."

"I know that," Preacher said. "Besides, I don't want to use the church. The interior is too well known and will be recognized by the viewers. I'm planning a different look for your show. One more like the churches they're used to, smaller, more intimate. We're shooting your show in the first chapel. We can make three hundred people in there look like they're all packed into a sardine can." He stared at Joe. "What do you say, Pastor? Want to try it?"

Joe looked at him. "What you call me?"

"Pastor," Preacher said. "Can't have just any ordinary man do a show like that."

"Praise the Lord, I've just done been promoted," Joe said, his face breaking into a wide grin. "You bet your sweet ass I'll do it!"

The sign in front of the small white frame church was as cracked and faded as the church building itself. The black lettering was streaked and almost illegible. Preacher read it as Joe pulled the rented car to a stop.

THE LITTLE RIVER BAPTIST PENTECOSTAL CHURCH
Prayer meetings   Sunday School 8 A.M.
every night at   Sunday Worship 11 A.M.
7 P.M. except   Old-Fashioned Gospel
Saturday   every Sat. night 7 P.M.
The Man With the Gifts of Healing,
Prophecy, Tongues and Faith
Parker J. Willard, Pastor

"This Pastor Willard sounds like quite a preacher," Preacher said as he got out of the car.

"Wait until you meet him," Joe said, taking out his brief-case. "Parker Willard built this church thirty years ago. At that time his congregation was more than six hundred people. That's down to about two hundred fifty now."

"What does he say the reason for that is?"

Joe glanced at him. "Television. He says TV preachers make no demands on their congregations except money. He says that it's easier for them to sit back and be entertained than to come to church where they have to participate in the services. He says TV religion is like take-home foods—may not be as good, but there's no work to prepare it and cook it. Just put it on the table and eat."

Preacher looked at him. "He may not be altogether wrong." He paused on the steps of the church. "How does he feel about our proposal?"

"He's interested," Joe said. "That's why he asked us to

come down and talk to him. He's quite honest about it. He says if nothing comes along to increase his congregation to somewhere near its original size, it will take a miracle to keep the church open until the end of the year."

Preacher nodded slowly. "In a way it's sad. All those years, all that work, only to come to nothing." He began to open the door to the church. "The Lord works in His own mysterious ways. Maybe we're the miracle he's been looking for."

Inside, the church was as bare and dilapidated as the exterior. The wooden floors and benches had not been painted for years and showed it. There was a crack in the window on which the cross had been painted behind the pulpit. Parts of the railing before it were broken and missing.

"Pastor Willard lives in a few rooms in the back of the church," Joe said, going to a door behind the railing and knocking on it politely.

A small man with curly gray hair, dressed in a black preacher's suit, white shirt and string tie, opened the door. His face broke into a wide smile, revealing white teeth in his dark face. "Brother Washington, come in," he said. "I was beginning to think you were jiving me when it got to be so late."

"You should know better than that, Brother Willard," Joe said. "Our plane got in an hour late." He shook the old man's hand. "I'd like you to meet Dr. C. Andrew Talbot."

"I feel like I know you." Brother Willard smiled. "I seen you on the TV so many times. You're a mighty talker. With that voice of yours you can sweet-talk the bugs out of the Lord's vineyards."

"Thank you, Brother Willard. I hear you've done some mighty work in the Lord's vineyards yourself."

"I try, Brother Talbot. The good Lord knows I try." He led them through one room into the kitchen. "But I've been given a hard row to hoe." He broke into a smile. "Maybe that's the difference between workin' in the Lord's cotton fields instead of his vineyards."

"In the sight of the Lord we are all laborers together," Preacher said.

Pastor Willard smiled. "I think I hear something of the Corinthians in there, Brother."

"You have good ears, Brother," Preacher said.

The curly-gray-haired man gestured to the chairs around the kitchen table. "Won't you be seated, Brothers? Mrs. Willard baked us a fine pecan pie before she left for work this morning. It will only take me a few minutes to have the coffee ready."

"That's the most pecan pie I ever ate," Joe said, pushing away his empty plate after finishing his second portion. "I'm goin' to have to start dietin' tomorrow."

Pastor Willard smiled broadly. "Mrs. Willard will be real pleased to hear that. She's mighty proud of her pecan pie."

"She should be," Preacher said.

"You can tell her in person," Willard said. "She should be home from work soon." He sighed slightly. "I don't know what I would have done without that woman. If she didn't go out to work, I would have lost this church two years ago."

Preacher looked at him. "You're a lucky man. A woman like that is hard to find. How long you been married?"

"Be three years in September. I'd been a widower for two years before that and even when I asked her to marry me, I never really believed she would."

"Why is that?" Preacher asked.

"I'm not a young man," Willard said. "I'm sixty-three, and she's only twenty-three. Life sure is strange. I remember holdin' her in my arms and baptizin' her when she was only a week old."

Preacher and Joe glanced at each other without speaking.

A reflective look came into the old man's eyes. "I've had this gift of prophecy and faith ever since I was a kid and my mother took me to church and I used to sit on her knee. I always had this feeling of being close to Jesus—that He would let me see things comin' a long time before they happened, things that nobody else saw. Like I always knew that my work would be preachin' his words. And when I was holding that squallin' little baby and immersin' her in the Little River out back of the church, I seemed to hear the voice of Jesus in my head jes as plain as you hear my voice right this moment.

" 'Love this child,' He said. 'Because as you bring her to Me with love, someday I will bring her to you.' "

He looked at them. "I didn't know what He meant then, and in time I even forgot it. But then, on the morning we was to git married and I was on my knees prayin' to Him fer guidance, askin' Him if I, an old man, was doing the right thing and not layin' too heavy a burden on a young child like her, somethin' made me git up and go back into the church records. It was then, when I found the page with her name on it twenty years back, I remembered the words He spoke to me and I was comforted. It was His plan all along that we should be together."

The very simplicity of the old man's words stirred Preacher. He reached across the table and pressed Pastor Willard's hand. They sat for a moment without exchanging a word, then tears came to the old man's eyes and he bent his head, kissing the back of Preacher's hand.

"Why do you weep, Brother?" Preacher asked gently.

The pastor's eyes were still moist. "I don't know," he answered. "Maybe I'm jes tired. Or maybe I'm afraid that I'm too old and no longer have the strength to carry on. That I will lose both, my wife and my church."

"Why do you feel that?"

The old man's voice was husky with hurt. "I know she wants a child. But I have never been able to become a real husband to her."

"Has she complained to you about it?"

Willard shook his head. "Never. She knows that I love her."

Preacher met his eyes. "What makes you think that Jesus will be less understanding than your wife? He, too, knows that you love Him." He was silent for a moment, glancing at Joe, then back to the pastor. "I have to believe that is why He brought us together here today."

CHAPTER
FIVE

Pastor Willard was nervous. He looked at his watch. It was after six o'clock. "Ain't nobody here yet," he said in a worried voice.

"People are still eatin' their supper," Joe said. "The radio commercials said seven o'clock. Stop worryin'. We know what we're doin'."

"I pray to the Lord that you're right," Willard said fervently. He turned and looked down the aisle at the giant television screen suspended from the ceiling over the pulpit. "Man," he said in a wondering voice, "who ever heard of a Monday Night Football prayer meeting?"

Joe laughed. "If you can't lick 'em, join 'em. If the bars and cafés do it because they're losing business on Monday night, why shouldn't the church?"

"People should come to church because they want to hear the word of God," Pastor Willard said.

"The trick is to get 'em here," Joe said. "After that it's up to you to get them to listen to the message."

"Sure that machine will work?" the old man asked.

Joe smiled. "It will work. We checked it all out. It's really very simple." He went down the aisle to the pulpit, followed by the old man. The video cassette player was mounted on the platform. "All you have to remember are those four buttons. They're plainly marked. VIDEOTAPE. BROADCAST. MUSIC. TALK. All you do is press each button according to the schedule on the typed sheet in the slot next to the buttons. And don't worry if you forget to do one of them. The player is already programmed to make the changes."

Pastor Willard looked down at the machine. "That ain't what I'm worried about. I practiced enough to know how to work the machine. But what if somethin' goes wrong and it doesn't work?"

"Nothing will go wrong," Joe said reassuringly. "But if it does—you're a preacher, aren't you?—then preach."

Willard smiled. "That I know I can do."

"The music is programmed to begin at six-thirty," Joe said. "At seven-thirty you go to the pulpit and start the videotape. The tape will run five minutes, then you press to talk. You have twenty-five minutes. Exactly at eight o'clock the machine goes to broadcast automatically. At half time you go back to talk for fifteen minutes, then turn back to broadcast until the end of the game. After that you go to video another five minutes, then talk again and to music when they begin to leave."

"This ain't like no church I ever seen," Willard said.

"It's today's church," Joe said smiling. "Someday all churches will be like this. God didn't give us electronics for nothing but worldly purposes, but also to better serve Him."

"I hear you, Brother," Pastor Willard said fervently. "Amen to that."

The first of the congregation began to enter. Joe looked at them then at the old man. "Might as well start the music, Brother Willard," he said. "And then you can go to the door and welcome your parishioners."

. . .

The small church was filled to the overflowing. Every seat was filled and others were crowded against the wall at the back of the church. Joe sat on a small chair near the door to the pastor's quarters and watched as, exactly at seven-thirty, the old man took his place behind the pulpit.

A moment later, the big screen sprang into life. A small gold cross at first, then growing larger and larger until it filled the whole screen. Title credits in black-shadowed purple lettering began to appear on the arms of the cross as the deep rich radio baritone of the announcer's voice came through the speakers.

> "The Little River Baptist Pentecostal Church, Parker J. Willard, Pastor, in association with the Community of God Church of Christian America Triumphant, presents The Monday Night Football Prayer Meeting. And now, Brothers and Sisters, your very own pastor, in person, Parker J. Willard!"

The sound of applause came through the speakers and automatically the congregation began to join in. Smiling, Pastor Willard stood there for a moment, then, raising his hand for silence, pressed the TALK button with his other hand. The screen went to black. He waited until the congregation finished with their applause.

He placed both hands on the edges of the pulpit and looked down at them for a moment before speaking. His smile took the gentle reproof from his words. "Brothers and Sisters, there are many of you I have not seen in this church for too long a time. I want you all to know I am glad to see you.

"And I'm sure that the good Lord is too. Because the important thing is not whether you came here to see a football game or not. The important thing is that you came here to His house for a prayer meeting.

"What we will see here is a miracle of God. His miracle of electronics, His gift of love to make man's life on this earth rich and fuller so that we may better appreciate the even greater miracle He has given us. The gift of His Son, our Savior Jesus Christ, who died on the cross for our sins and the sins of all, then and in the ages to come, who will acknowledge Him and be washed in the Blood of the Lamb.

"Less than one month ago, I was on my knees in front of this pulpit. I prayed to the Lord to send me a miracle. A miracle to save my church, a miracle to bring my sheep back into His house, so that this church would not disappear from His sight.

"As I rose from my knees, I heard the phone begin to ring. I went into my room and picked it up. A voice I never heard before came to my ear. 'Pastor Parker J. Willard?' 'Yes,' I answered. 'This is your brother in Christ, Joe Washington, speaking. I'm calling you from Churchland, Texas.' 'What can I do for you, Brother?' I asked. 'No, Brother,' he said. 'It's what I can do for you. I want to help you in your work for Jesus Christ.' 'Thank you, Brother. I need all the help I can get,' I said. 'But why of all the churches in the country did you call me?' 'I don't really know,' he answered. 'But when I was lookin' down at the hundreds of churches on the list in front of me, a mysterious power guided my fingers and the next thing I knew I was dialing your number.' "

The old man paused for a moment and looked out at his congregation, then began again. "That was the first miracle. Jesus had heard my prayers." He turned and waved at the big screen behind him. "And what you're goin' to see here tonight is only another one of the never-ending stream of miracles that can come to each and every one of us if we only get on our knees and pray to God."

He looked down at the pulpit for a moment, then back at them, a smile coming to his face. "And now, set back in your seats and enjoy Monday Night Football on our giant screen. I will be back to talk some more at half time." He pressed the button marked BROADCAST and came down from the pulpit to the applause of the congregation and the voice of Howard Cosell coming through the speakers.

He sat in a small chair next to Joe and leaned toward him, whispering. "It's like the good old days. This old church ain't been so crowded in years. I jes hope it'll keep up."

"It will," Joe smiled. "But it's something we'll all have to keep working at. We'll see to it that you'll get all our special programs during the week plus our fifteen-minute video sermon on Sunday, which you can put on before you speak. We also have a twenty-minute episode, 'The Story of the Bible,' for your Sunday-school class. You also receive all our literature plus our own special edition of the Bible to be given free to your congregation. We'll even send in men to help fix up and paint the church so that it all looks better and you can feel proud of it again."

The old man looked at him. "You people are spending a lot of money jes to help a poor church like mine."

"We don't intend for it to remain a poor church." Joe smiled. "That's why we have that franchise agreement between us. You become an affiliate of the Community of God and agree to give to us fifty percent of your collections over the first two hundred dollars a week you collect. That way you help bear the cost of this expensive work we're doing."

"We haven't collected two hundred dollars a week fer two years now," the old man said. "What if we don't git more'n that?"

"We'll take our chances," Joe smiled. "After all, money isn't the only thing. The most important job we have is to serve our Lord and bring His people to Jesus Christ."

"Amen," the old man said.

"Then you'll sign the agreement?"

"Right after the prayer meetin'," Willard said. He turned his head to look up at the big screen. "Look at that picture. Ain't the Lord wonderful?"

"He is. Praise the Lord." Joe began to get to his feet. "Is it all right if I call Dr. Talbot to tell him that you'll sign the agreement? He'll be real pleased to hear that."

"The phone is in the kitchen. You go ahead," the old man

said, without taking his eyes from the screen. "And ask Mrs. Willard fer a cup of coffee if you want."

Mrs. Willard was seated at the kitchen table. She rose to her feet when he entered. "Brother Washington," she said in a soft Southern voice.

"Don't let me disturb you, Sister Willard," he said quickly. "I just came to use the telephone."

She gestured to the wall. "It's over there. Would you like me to fix you a cup of coffee?"

"I would appreciate that, Sister Willard," he said, picking up the telephone. He watched her while the call was going through. She was a tall girl, more than a head taller than her husband, slightly lighter in color than he, with curly hair that resisted attempts to straighten it. He looked with approval at the swell of her full breasts and buttocks straining against her cotton dress. Her body was exactly the opposite of Beverly's, who was thin and delicately formed. Both had their points, but Sister Willard was a lot of woman. Not exactly the kind of woman he thought would marry the pastor. Preacher couldn't be found. Joe left the message with his secretary and put down the telephone just as Mrs. Willard turned and placed the coffee on the table.

"Dr. Talbot wasn't in," he said, sitting down.

"I'm sorry," she said. She was still standing.

"It's all right. I left a message," he said. He looked up at her and smiled. "Why don't you sit down, Sister Willard?"

Without answering, she took her seat across the table from him. He took a sip of coffee. "You make a good cup of coffee," he said.

"Thank you," she said, looking at him.

"It looks good out there, Sister Willard," he said. "If this keeps up, pretty soon you won't have to go out to work no more."

"I like goin' out to work," she said.

"Even if you don't have to?"

233

She nodded. "It keeps me from thinkin'."

He sipped at his coffee. "Thinkin' about what?"

She hesitated a moment, then her eyes fell. "Devil's thoughts," she said in a small voice. "Sinful thoughts."

"We all think devil's thoughts sometimes," he said.

Her eyes still remained fixed on the table. "Sometimes is okay," she said, "but I think them all the time. Pastor Willard is such a good man. I wasn't exactly what you call a good girl when I married him. But I thought if I did, the sinful thoughts would leave. But they didn't."

"Did you pray to Jesus for His help?"

"I do. Every day." She looked up at him. "But the devil is too strong in me. Even when you were standin' there by the telephone, he made me keep lookin' at the bulge in your pants. In my mind it seemed to be gettin' bigger an' bigger."

"It wasn't only in your mind, Sister Willard," he said, putting down his coffee cup. "The devil was in me too."

Her eyes were wide. "What can we do, Brother Washington?"

"We both better get down on our knees and pray together for Jesus to help us."

He knelt on the floor as she came around the table and knelt beside him. He felt her gasp and suck in her breath as their shoulders touched. He clasped his hands in front. "Jesus, look down on us poor sinners and in Your name command this devil of lust to leave us."

She raised her head from her clasped hands and turned to him. "What if He does not hear us?" she asked.

With one hand he turned her toward him while with the other hand, he opened his zipper. "There's more than one way to bury the devil."

CHAPTER
SIX

"Niggers!" Randle said contemptuously. "I thought your idea of franchising was great. But fourteen hundred nigger churches against five hundred and thirty regular Baptist churches is a little too much. Next thing I know you'll have Churchland crawling with them. There won't be any room for white people."

Preacher looked at him. "There's plenty of room and you know it."

"Maybe there is," the old man said. "But what self-respecting white man wants to sleep in the same hotel with a nigger in the room next to his? Or in the same bed that maybe a nigger slept in the night before?"

"How about eating in the same restaurant?" Preacher asked dryly.

Randle missed the sarcasm. "They won't like that either."

Preacher looked at him across the desk. "Maybe they won't like it but they'll have to accept it. Besides the fact that their attitude is un-Christian, it also happens to be against the equal rights laws."

"That's just the laws we're workin' to get rid of," Randle said. "That's just as crazy as the E.R.A., which we ain't going to let get through."

Preacher was silent.

"Don't you see, son," the old man said in a calmer tone, "if you keep on this way, you'll be the ruination of the Baptist church."

"I don't think so," Preacher said easily. "Do you know that of the approximately eighty-odd thousand Baptist churches in the country today, almost half of them are black? Or that more than forty percent of the thirty-odd million Baptists in the country today are black people? As a matter of fact, we ran a few of the latest census figures through our computer recently and came up with a very interesting figure. According to present indications of population growth, in another ten years five hundred and twenty-five out of every thousand Baptists in this country will be black."

Randle stared at him. "I don't believe you."

"I can get the printout for you," Preacher said. "Jane ran this one herself."

"I don't give a damn," Randle said. "I don't want no niggers runnin' around my property."

"You mean Churchland?"

"That's exactly what I mean," Randle said. "I still own the land and everything on it."

Preacher stared at him for a moment. "Would you like us to move?"

"I didn't say that," Randle said quickly. "I just want you to get rid of the black churches."

"Too bad you're feeling like that," Preacher said. "We're already collecting over a million and a half dollars a year from them, and now that we opened up the audience some of the other TV ministries suddenly got interested. Pat Robertson is already planning a show for his sidekick, Ben Kinchlow, aimed at the black audience, and Oral Roberts is helping Fred Price of Los Angeles to raise the number of stations he's already on from thirty-five to a hundred by the end of next year."

"You don't see Jerry Falwell sucking up to them," Randle said.

"That's true," Preacher agreed. "But I've been getting reports from the field that Liberty Baptist College graduates and teachers have been showing up more and more at the black churches offering program help and literature. They're even holding out the promise of some scholarships."

"How'd you hear about that?" Randle asked.

"I didn't until I started getting some complaints from some of the churches about the *Moral Majority Report* they were handing out to their congregations. We checked it out and found that many of the blacks were burned up because they feel that the political aims of the paper are directed against them."

"That's because they're all on welfare," Randle said. "They don't want to work for their money."

"That's not true," Preacher said. "But I won't argue with you. A number of the black churches got together and want to start up their own paper and came to us to ask our help."

"That's too much," Randle said. "I told you they would start takin' over. Of course, you turned them down."

Preacher shook his head. "I couldn't. It's the duty of the ministry to respond to the needs of its congregation. That's a basic creed of the Baptist denomination. Each church has the right to determine its own policies regarding interpretation of the Scriptures and involvement in social affairs. It's for that reason alone there are more than twenty different Baptist bodies in the country."

"That's not answering my question," Randle said pointedly. "Exactly what are we going to do for them?"

"We've already done it," Preacher said, taking an eight-page offset newspaper from his desk and placing it in front of the old man.

Randle stared down at the paper. At first glance it looked

pretty much like the *Moral Majority Report,* even to the type used. But the name in heavy black lettering was different: THE MAJOR MINORITY REPORT. Beneath that in smaller type, THE OTHER SIDE OF THE COIN. In the upper left-hand corner of the first page under the large caption, CREDO, was a photograph of Joe and his name beneath the photo, *The Rev. Josephus Washington.*

The text was in bold lettering:

> **Believing there is more than one viewpoint held by good Christians and believing in the equal rights of all Christians to express those viewpoints and opinions, this paper is founded. We will endeavor to give expression to all Christian viewpoints, regardless of whether they reflect our own personal views or not, as a means of demonstrating the true independence of the Baptist denomination inherent in all its churches and congregations.**

"Holy shit!" Randle said. He picked up the paper and stared at Preacher. "This means revolution. You even put that nigger's picture on the front page as editor and publisher. Why don't you just turn over the whole thing to him, kit and caboodle?"

"I already have," Preacher said. "I didn't think that you wanted blacks here in Churchland—besides, we don't have the physical capacity to handle all the work of the franchise operation—so we're in the process of moving the Community of God franchise headquarters to Los Altos."

Randle stared at him in silence.

"That takes care of your worrying about blacks overrunning Churchland," Preacher said.

"What's going to happen here?" Randle asked.

"We'll be doing business as usual."

"And the money?"

"We'll control that through our computers."

Randle was silent for a moment. "Those niggers have a lot of votes. How do we keep them in line?"

Preacher smiled. "By giving them their own voice and telling them the truth. After that, it's up to them to decide how they go. Don't forget the most important thing."

Randle stared at him. "What's that?"

"Our purpose is to spread the word of God, not to use our pulpit for political doctrine."

"What do you think this damn paper will be doing?" Randle snapped.

"Nothing more than what the *Moral Majority Report* is doing. It is a completely separate and independent corporation with no more official connection with the Community of God than the other has with the Liberty Baptist Church. Our editor-in-chief happens to be Joe Washington and the head of the *Moral Majority Report* happens to be Jerry Falwell."

"You're looking for real trouble," Randle said. "You're going to alienate a lot of our white contributors."

"I doubt it," Preacher said easily. "Our computer studies also show us that there are just as many whites as blacks who feel alienated from our society."

"It seems to me that you trust that computer too much," Randle said.

"Maybe," Preacher answered. "But I remember that you told me once there was no way you could run your business today if it weren't for the computer. And it's worked pretty good for us so far."

The old man rose heavily to his feet. "Our important friends are not going to like it."

Preacher got out of his chair. "Any time they're unhappy they can ask me to leave and I'll go. I have no contract with them. Only with God."

His mother's voice came through the telephone. "You sound tired, Constantine."

"I'm all right, Mother," he said.

"It's not just in your voice," she said. "I saw you on last Sunday's show. Something's gone. You just seem to be going through the motions."

"Maybe I need a vacation," he said.

"I just spoke with Jane," she said. "It's after nine o'clock and you're still at the office. She says the children never see you except on TV. That's not right, Constantine. Children need their fathers too."

"I have so much to do, Mother," he said. "It's not only the show that you see on the air. It's a business that you have to keep after every minute and it never seems to let up. If you do, you find that you lose your audience to any one of a dozen TV ministries."

"How do you keep score, Constantine?" his mother asked. "By how many souls you bring to God? Or how much money you collect from the TV programs?"

He didn't answer.

"How long has it been since you preached to a congregation without having a TV camera pointing at you? How long has it been since you stood in the doorway of a church and spoke to people after your sermon was finished?"

"I don't have time for that anymore, Mother."

"Maybe that's one of your problems. There's a word I hear on panel discussions all the time. Feedback. You get something back from the people you really talk to after a sermon. What kind of feedback do you get from television?"

"We get thousands of letters each week, Mother."

"You don't even read them, Constantine," she said. "They're all answered by computer. Jane once explained to me how that worked. Everything about the letter-writer is programmed into the computer so that when the reply is written all personal references are inserted in their proper places."

"There's no other way to do it, Mother. It's an electronic age and the church has to keep up with it."

"God doesn't need a computer to keep track of all the souls in the world. You answered His call, not a computer. He didn't invent the electronic church, man did."

He was silent.

"Maybe that's why you feel tired and empty, Constantine.

240

Maybe you're beginning to feel like you're just a part of that computer and that you don't really know whether you're bringing souls to God or checks to the bank."

He was still silent.

"I know you, Constantine," she said. "I could always tell when you were happy and when you were troubled. And I know you're not happy now."

"I'll be okay, Mother," he said.

"What you need is to get away from it for a while and have a good rest. Then maybe you can sort things out and discover what you really want to do."

"Nothing's changed, Mother," he said. "I still want to preach the word of God to as many people as I can."

"Maybe that's what's basically wrong," she said. "You could be substituting quantity for quality. I think you were much happier when you could personally take one person by the hand and lead him to the Lord than when you're speaking to thousands of faceless people you'll never see or know."

"There could be another reason, Mother," he said.

"What's that, son?" she asked.

"I'm beginning to doubt my own faith, Mother," he said. "What kind of a God am I serving who allows greedy men, lusting for power, to maneuver people in His name for their own selfish purposes?"

"That's a question only you can answer, Constantine," she said quietly. "I'm your mother, not your conscience."

CHAPTER SEVEN

"We're beginning to lose our audience," Marcus said. "According to Arbitron we've lost over a hundred thousand viewers in the month of December alone."

Preacher turned to Beverly. "What about collections?"

"Down slightly," she said. "But any real drop in viewers won't turn up until the following month or two."

"What about the rest of the ministries?"

"Not as much as us," Marcus said.

"It's the recession," Preacher said. "It's hitting all of us."

"It's not that," Marcus said. "We had A.R.I. in Hollywood run a test on our last few programs. The audience was bored. We have to do something to jazz up our show."

Preacher was silent.

"There's nothing wrong with it," Marcus said. "Did you see the Christmas specials last month? Oral Roberts had the Lennon Sisters, the Krofft puppets, and his son singing and dancing à la Fred Astaire with a chorus of beautiful girls in long flowing skirts on a stairway behind him showing decolletage down to here. Jim and Tammy Bakker at home Christmas Eve with a bunch of guest stars. Robert Shuller with a million-dollar production of the Nativity from the Crystal Cathedral, produced by the same man who did stage shows at the Radio City Music Hall in New York."

Preacher smiled. "I guess we've had it then. Too late for me to learn to sing and dance."

"I'm serious, Preacher," Marcus said. "We're going to have to do something."

"So am I, Marcus," Preacher said. "But what? I'm not an entertainer, I haven't the talent that Pat Robertson has for interviewing people and doing a talk show. I can't heal people on camera like Ernest Angley. I can't even sell square-foot plots on Liberty Mountain like Jerry Falwell does. All I can do when I get up there in front of the cameras is lay my own faith in God on the line for them to see."

"We can't complain," Marcus said seriously. "It worked up to now. But even the best show on television begins to fall off after five years. If you know television, that's a pretty good run. But it's time now to change our format or pretty soon we'll have no audience at all."

"Do you have any ideas?" Preacher asked.

"I'm working on a few but haven't come up with anything to show you yet."

"I have an idea," Preacher said. "Remember that old show, 'Route Sixty-Six,' where those two guys rode around in a Corvette sports car and had an adventure in every town?" Marcus nodded. "We do the same type of show but updated. We have the same two guys, only their names are Jesus and Peter. Instead of a Corvette, they ride a pickup, and their mission is to find the worst sinner in each town and lead him to the Lord."

Marcus stared at him for a moment. "You're not taking this seriously enough, Preacher. I admire and respect you for your sincerity. But, as a friend, I think I ought to tell you that the righteous three on our board are waiting for the first sign of weakness to appear and when they find it, they'll pounce on you like a pack of hungry wolves and tear you apart."

Preacher was silent for a moment. Suddenly, he understood why the man had come to him. "Thank you, Marcus, for alerting me. I'll keep what you told me in mind. Meanwhile you keep on working on your ideas. And I'll see if I can come up with something that might be helpful."

Marcus got to his feet. "Meanwhile, the only suggestion I can offer is for you to try and get some more drama into your sermons. The devil and hellfire have always been the gospel preachers' best stock in trade."

"I'll try, Marcus," Preacher said. "Thank you again."

He turned to Beverly after Lincoln had left the office. "What do you think?"

"He makes certain valid points," she said carefully. "But I keep remembering that he has always worked for Randle. Maybe this is like firing a warning shot across your bows to get you back in line."

Preacher nodded. "Maybe it is. But if they're looking for a fight, I have no way to stop them. I'll just have to deal with it when it comes."

She began to rise from her chair. He held up a hand. "Don't go just yet, Beverly. I'd like to talk to you."

She settled back. "Yes, Preacher."

He looked at her for a long moment before he spoke. "Did any of this turn out the way you thought it would?"

She hesitated a moment, then shook her head. "No."

"It didn't for me either," he said.

"I'm sorry, Preacher."

He smile ruefully. "There's nothing to be sorry for. I chose to do it. Nobody made me."

She was silent.

"Sometimes I wish that we'd stayed with the tent. Even with all the problems, without money, it was more fun."

"You couldn't have done that," she said. "It was time for you to move on."

"I guess so," he said. He met her eyes. "What did you ever do with all that money in the suitcase?"

"I invested it," she said.

"Knowing you, it has to be a small fortune by now."

"It is," she said.

"Then why do you stay if this isn't what you thought it would be?" he asked.

"You. Joe." Her voice was thoughtful. "I guess I'm like you in a way. Neither of us can ever go back to where we were."

"I know what you mean," he said, opening the cigarette box on his desk and pushing it toward her. She shook her head. He lit one for himself and blew the smoke out into the air. "I'm going to be forty-two this year," he said.

She was silent.

"They say that men my age go through a midlife crisis."

She laughed aloud. "That's at fifty."

He smiled at her. "It's a relief to know that. I was getting worried."

"Well, you can stop worrying."

"I will," he said.

"There's something I have to ask you," she said hesitantly.

"Go ahead and ask."

"I'd like to go up to Los Altos to be with Joe," she said. "It's very lonely for me down here. Now that the girls are gone I really haven't any friends. Besides, what kind of a marriage is it when you see your husband only one weekend each month?"

"I can't argue with you," he said.

"Of course I wouldn't go until you found someone who could take over my job."

"I know that," he said. "We can start looking tomorrow."

"Thank you, Preacher," she said.

"We'll have to do something about our private account."

"I've had that all worked out for a long time," she said. "It's in a numbered account in an offshore trust. The only thing I haven't been able to work out is how to continue adding to it."

"I think it's time that we discontinued that operation anyway," he said. "There should be enough in there by now to take care of any emergencies."

She looked at him. "You're a strange man, Preacher. You really don't care about money."

"What makes you say that?"

"You never once asked me how much was in that account. Wouldn't you like to know?"

"Of course I would," he said. "But I never had to think about it. I knew you were taking care of it."

She smiled. "I could have been ripping you off all the time and you never would have known."

"It wouldn't have mattered if you did," he said, "I'd love you anyway."

She blinked back the moisture in her eyes. "You still haven't asked me."

"Okay. I'm asking you."

"Over five million dollars," she said.

He stared at her. "I can't believe it."

"I'll get the passbook for you," she said. "You'll believe it then."

"I never thought it would come to that much money," he said. "Now you really have a job."

"What do you mean?"

"We're going to have to find a way to use that money to help those who need it the most. There are too many sick and hungry in this world where that money would do more good than lying useless in a bank."

"Remember, that account was started for you to use if Randle tried to do a number on you," she said.

He got to his feet and walked to the window and looked out. Below him one of the open-sided Churchland buses had stopped in front of a chapel and the passengers were getting off and going into the building. He turned and looked back at

246

her. "Would you believe me if I told you that it doesn't matter anymore what he does or doesn't do?" he asked.

She didn't speak.

He came back to the desk and stood there looking down at her. "I began this ministry to bring more people to God and I've done that. And with me or without me, there's nothing he can do to stop it."

CHAPTER EIGHT

She opened the study door and looked into the room. He looked up, the papers he had been reading still in his hand. She came into the room. "It's after two o'clock. Aren't you coming to bed?"

"I have to go through all these papers first," he answered. "There's the board meeting tomorrow."

She came into the room and sat in the chair across from his desk. "The Catholics are right when they forbid their priests to marry."

He placed the papers on the desk. "What brings that up?"

"The way we live," she answered. "You can't be a husband and a father as well as a minister. There just isn't enough time. You have to establish priorities. And by now I know what those priorities are."

"You know how much work I have to do," he said.

"I know," she said.

"It doesn't get easier," he said. "There's more and more work all the time."

"And less and less time for us," she said. "It used to be that at least once in a while we could share an evening together. But not anymore. In the last three or four months we've managed to have dinner together just once."

He was silent.

"And I can't remember when it was that we last made love," she said. "I'm not naive enough to believe that the fires that burned so brightly when we were first together would continue forever but it doesn't seem unreasonable to me to expect a spark now and then. I can't help thinking that maybe you're bored with me, maybe I don't excite you anymore, or even that you have others you find more exciting."

"It's nothing like that," he said seriously. "I'm forty-one years old now and I just don't have the drives or energies I used to."

"It's not your age," she said. "It's your work. That's where you burn yourself out."

"Maybe," he said.

"I don't like what's happening to me," she said, tears suddenly in her eyes. "Do you have any idea of what it takes for me to fall asleep every night? Some nights I take pills. Then other nights I light a joint, and when I get stoned enough I fantasize and masturbate myself into a state of exhaustion."

"I'm sorry," he said. "I didn't realize—"

She rose angrily to her feet. "Of course you didn't realize. How could you when you think of nothing else but your work? Next to that, nothing is important to you!"

She tore the robe from her shoulders and flung it violently across the desk at him, her naked body gleaming in the reflected light of the desk lamp. "Look at me!" she cried. "Nothing has changed. Everything's still the same. I haven't suddenly grown old and ugly overnight."

"No," he said, staring at her. "You're beautiful."

"No, you're beautiful," she repeated sarcastically, her chest heaving angrily. "Tell me, Mr. Preacher, if it were another woman standing here naked before you, would you still be sitting there behind your desk and politely saying 'you're beautiful'?"

Silently, he rose and started around the desk toward her, the robe in his hands. He began to place it around her shoulders.

She turned and the robe fell to the floor. "Keep away from me!" she snapped. "The last thing I want from you is a consolation fuck!"

She went to the door and opened it. "You were right," she said in a cold voice, looking back at him. "I was a fool. I should have had that abortion when you wanted it!"

He stared at the closed door for a moment, then picked up the robe and went back to his desk. The robe still held the faint scent of her perfume. He dropped it into an empty chair, then sat down behind his desk and stared at the robe for a long time. Finally he clasped his hands on the desk before him and bowed his head. "I don't understand it, Lord," he whispered with closed eyes. "Tell me. What is happening to me?"

For a change Jake Randle let someone else carry the ball. This time it was Dick Craig who did the talking. But as Preacher looked down at the neatly typed plan contained in the blue leather-bound folder that had been distributed to the board at the beginning of the meeting, he knew this was not something dreamed up overnight. More than a few months had gone into it.

Craig had been more than respectful in his presentation. "It is most important that all of us understand that this plan is not a reflection on the work of any of the board members and does not represent any dissatisfaction on our part with the tremendous leadership given the ministry by Dr. Talbot, which has brought us to the success we now enjoy."

Preacher deliberately kept his face expressionless. There was no way he would let them see that he knew this was a declaration of war. Let them think they had succeeded in their own version of Pearl Harbor. He continued to listen as Craig droned on.

"Instead, this is a realization that the problems and work of continuing our ministry have become more than any one man can bear and it is unfair on our part to allow Dr. Talbot, no matter how willing he is, to bear that burden on his shoulders alone. It is solely for that reason that we propose to add four members to our board, each of whom will take up an active working position in the ministry under the guidance and leadership of Dr. Talbot.

"Each of these men has been investigated thoroughly and has come to us with more than adequate credentials and experience in other ministries to do the job he has been selected for. Two of the gentlemen will have the position of associate pastor. They are Dr. Thomas Sorensen, former associate pastor of the Liberty Baptist Church in Lynchburg, and Dr. Mark L. Ryker, former associate dean of religious studies at Oral Roberts University. The third gentleman we recommend is Mr. Sanford Carrol, formerly of the Christian Broadcasting Network, to assume the position of program and marketing director. Last, but not least, we recommend Mr. Sutter Duncan, former partner of the accounting firm Price, Waterhouse and Company, to assume the position of secretary and treasurer made vacant by the resignation of Mrs. Beverly Washington last month.

"Complete resumés of these gentlemen are also included in the folder before you. I personally can assure you that Mr. Randle, Mrs. Lacey and I have personally spoken to them and have found them completely in accord with our aims and interests, and feel they will be completely compatible with our organization. Each of them has indicated his willingness to accept a one-year employment contract with us at a compensation of forty thousand dollars a year plus living allowances and ordinary business expenses. We will also have options to renew their employment agreements annually for the next six years at a nominal increase of ten percent per annum.

"I now throw the proposal open for discussion."

Craig sat down and no one spoke, all eyes on Preacher.

Silently Preacher riffled through the pages of the report. Deliberately he refrained from speaking until they began to stir restlessly in their seats. Then he looked up. "I like it," he said.

He could almost see the expression of surprise on their faces. He smiled to himself. If they thought he was going to fight them when there was no way for him to outvote them, they were crazy. "But there is one important factor that I think has been overlooked. The franchise operation. With a potential income of three million dollars for this year I feel that we should acknowledge Mr. Washington's value to this ministry by electing him also an associate pastor and member of the board. If the board could see its way clear to join me in that, I would have no hesitation in making it a unanimous vote for the entire proposal."

There was silence for a moment, then Randle's voice boomed across the table. "I see no objection to Dr. Talbot's proposal. Shall we put it to a vote?"

The motion was carried unanimously.

Craig rose to his feet again. "I move that we adjourn this meeting and call a special meeting of the board two days from now at which the new members can join us."

The motion was seconded and carried.

Marcus followed Preacher to his office. He waited until the door was closed behind him before he spoke. "Did you know anything about that?"

"No," Preacher said, walking behind his desk. "Did you?"

Marcus shook his head. "It came out of the blue as far as I was concerned. They played that one pretty close to their vests."

"I guess so," Preacher said, sitting down.

"Are you upset over it?"

"No," Preacher answered. "Should I be?"

"It could be interpreted that they're going to try to push you out," Marcus said.

Preacher smiled. "They can try. But it won't work. The Community of God Church Christian America Triumphant is incorporated in Los Altos, California, and all the stock is in my name."

"You mean—?"

Preacher nodded. "We're nothing but tenants here in Churchland. If push comes to shove I can call a stockholders' meeting and throw out the whole board."

"I wonder if the old man knows that," Marcus said.

"He would if he ever stopped to think about it. But he's too busy with his own plans for us to ever take the time."

"You must have had some sharp legal advice."

"Not really," Preacher said. "But I remember once when Beverly was talking to a lawyer friend of hers from New York, Paul Gitlin his name was, and what he told her I never forgot."

"What was that?"

"Never give them anything they don't ask for," Preacher smiled. "And Randle never asked me. If he had, I probably would have given it to him."

"That was a break," Marcus said. "I have an idea about that program we were talking about. Care to hear about it?"

"Of course."

"You've heard of Jimmy and Kim Hickox?"

"Who hasn't?" Preacher asked. Twenty years earlier they'd been a leading pop singing duo on records and television. Then their popularity waned unexpectedly and for years not much was heard about them. About seven years before, they began to appear again, born-again Christians, and now they were the most sought-after stars of the Christian television circuit. Still young-looking, clean-cut-Americans, they came on with a warm homespun style that people seemed to enjoy.

"I've had some talks with them. They're interested in doing a show of their own. Sing and talk, five days a week. And they both respect you very much."

"What would they cost us?"

"They would take five thousand a week on a year's contract. They get ten thousand dollars a show ordinarily. Figure it would cost us another ten thousand a week to tape their show and twenty thousand a week for air time. We could put them on the air for less than two million a year."

Preacher looked up at him across the desk. "Do you think you can bring in a signed contract with them in time for the next board meeting two days from now?"

"I think so," Marcus said. "But I'd have to go up to L.A. to see them. That's where they live."

"Then what are you waiting for?" Preacher smiled. "I'll call the field and have our jet standing by for you. You come back with that contract. We'll give them a little surprise of our own. At least they won't have the complaint that we're not trying to increase our audience then."

He looked down at the blue folder he had brought from the meeting when the door closed behind Marcus. Idly he opened it and leafed through the pages. Maybe it wasn't that bad an idea after all. These were all good men and highly qualified. If they could take over the bulk of the detail work from him, he would have more time for himself. Maybe then he could patch things up with Jane so she wouldn't feel so left out.

He called his apartment. A maid answered. "Is Mrs. Talbot around?" he asked.

"No, sir," the girl answered. "She done picked up the children and went out."

"Did she say where she was going?" he asked.

"No, sir."

He put down the phone. There would be time enough to tell her later. He pressed the call button. His secretary's voice came through the speakerphone. "Call Mr. Washington for me in Los Altos."

A moment later he had Joe on the telephone. "Congratulations, Reverend Washington, you're now a member of the board and an associate pastor of the church."

"How about that?" Joe laughed. "Does that mean I get more money?"

"Probably," Preacher laughed. "The really big thing is that you're the first black pastor of a white ministry."

"Yeah," Joe said. "And I got some news for you."

"What's that?"

"You remember the pastor of the Little River Church, the first one we went to see?"

"I sure do," Preacher said. "Pastor Willard."

"That's him," Joe said. "Remember how he cried and felt bad because he couldn't get it up for his young wife?"

"I remember."

"Well, he said a miracle happened that very first night he joined up with us. The crowd in his church gave him such a big high, he went right back after the service and gave it to his wife."

"That's wonderful." Preacher smiled. "How did you hear about it?"

"He just called me." Joe laughed. "His wife just had an eight-pound baby boy. He's even goin' to name it after me."

"Why you?" Preacher asked.

Joe laughed again. "He said what I did that night gave him back his strength."

CHAPTER
NINE

Preacher finished reading the message on the typewritten sheet before him and looked up as he laid the paper on his desk. He watched while the sound engineer ran the tape back, then locked it into playback as the director listened on the headset.

A moment later the director held up his hand in an okay sign. He took off the headset. "I think this last one does it, Dr. Talbot. If you'll pick up your telephone, we'll feed it directly into your line so that you'll hear exactly how it will come over the wire."

Preacher nodded and picked up his telephone. It took but a moment for the engineer to rewind the tape and begin the playback once again. His own voice came into his ear.

"Thank you for calling the Community of God Church. This is the recorded voice of Dr. C. Andrew Talbot speaking. We are sorry but all of our lines are occupied at the moment. Your call will be transferred to the first counselor available. Meanwhile, if you will be kind enough to take advantage of your toll-free call to listen to Sister Aretha Franklin's famous rendition of 'Amazing Grace' while waiting, we will be most grateful. But first, when you hear the beep, you will have thirty seconds to give us your complete name and address, so that we may be able to direct your call to a counselor familiar with your area in order to be of greater assistance to you."

The sound of a beep came through the telephone followed by a moment's pause, then his voice came back on. "Thank you. God Bless you. And, remember, Jesus loves you." A moment later the first bars of the song came to his ears and he put down the telephone.

"Is that okay with you, Dr. Talbot?" the director asked.

Preacher nodded. "Fine."

"Good," the director smiled. He turned to the engineer. "Wrap it up." He came to the desk and picked up the microphone. "You're getting better all the time, Dr. Talbot," he said politely. "We took care of the next three months in only eleven takes. That's four takes better than we ever did before."

Preacher smiled at him. "Thanks to you. You have a way of making it come very naturally."

"Thank you, sir," the director said, coiling the wire and walking back to the engineer. The engineer pulled the lead plug from the recorder and got to his feet. They walked to the door. The director looked back from the doorway. "Goodbye, sir. Have a nice evening."

"You too," Preacher said. "Thank you."

He watched the doors close behind them. Each month a new recording would go on the toll-free counseling line. The message would be changed slightly from the previous month, and the holding song would be replaced with another. Whether or not there was a free line available, the message was important. It was the one sure way they could obtain the caller's name and address so that it could be fed into the computer for future use.

The message center was located in Fort Worth in its own building. Churchland wasn't large enough to carry the personnel necessary to operate it. There were over one hundred paid employees and between eight and nine hundred volunteers, the largest number at any one time being the shift that worked as the hours from midnight to five A.M. rolled across the country. Those were the lonely hours, the hours when most television stations went off the air and people were left alone in their rooms with only their own doubts and fears to keep them company.

When the counselor picked up the telephone, the caller's voice was the first one heard. The counselors didn't press the button on their telephones to connect them with the caller until after they had typed his name into the keyboard of the computer and it was on the screen in front of them. Seventy percent of the counselors were women but, men or women, all were screened for warm, friendly and sympathetic voices. They would address the caller by his or her first name and identify themselves as Brother or Sister with their own given names, thank them again for calling and ask how they could be of help. They seemed to have all the time in the world but their principal function was to obtain all the information possible about the caller and his problems, which was immediately typed into the computer. They would offer common-sense advice, generally including quotations from the Bible that were pertinent to the caller, the quotations fed to them by the computer screen as the computer sorted and selected the problems into the general classifications programmed into it. If necessary, the counselor would even join the caller in a short prayer. The conversation would be ended when the counselor would inform the caller of the location of the affiliated church nearest him and tell him that he would soon receive a letter from the pastor of that church, inviting him to come in and have a person-to-person talk with no obligation either to join the church or to make a financial contribution to it. (The letter would actually be sent from the message center on the stationery of the local church over a facsimile signature of the pastor of that church, and the church itself would receive a copy of that letter for reference.) Of course, if the caller cared to, he could make a contribution directly to the Community of God Church in Churchland to help defray the costs of maintaining this worthwhile service of helping people like himself with their problems but it was not obligatory to do so. But contribution or no, the most important thing the caller should remember is: No matter how terrible things might seem at the moment, tomorrow will be better because Jesus loves you.

During the past several years there had been an average of one thousand calls a day but lately, since the recession and growing unemployment, the number of calls had increased by two to three hundred a day and was still increasing. And more than ninety percent of the callers made contributions of about five or ten dollars each. How much more they contributed by follow-up mailings or through the local churches was difficult to estimate but one study had shown that the total average contributions from each caller amounted to thirty dollars, which came to about eighteen million dollars a year based on six hundred thousand callers.

It was nine o'clock when he stepped from the private elevator that went directly from his office to the main floor. The uniformed guard in the corridor touched his cap respectfully. "Evenin', Dr. Talbot."

"Good evening, Jeff," Preacher answered. "How's the arthritis tonight?"

"Much better, Dr. Talbot," the guard said. "I been sayin' those prayers you gave me every night and, you know somethin', they been really workin'. Thank you, Dr. Talbot. I don't even have to take no aspirin no more to go to sleep. Thank you."

"Don't thank me, Jeff," Preacher said. "Thank Jesus for His mercy. It was He who answered your prayers. Not me."

"Thank you, Jesus," the guard said fervently.

"That's better," Preacher smiled. "God be with you. Good night."

"Good night, Dr. Talbot."

Preacher hesitated a moment, then walked down the corridor to the main entrance. He needed some fresh air before crossing to the parsonage and there was none in the tunnel walkway between it and the main building. The sounds of a chorale came to his ears as he entered the lobby. He crossed to one of the auditorium entrances and looked inside.

The guard at the door turned and saw him. He touched his cap. "Evening, Dr. Talbot," he whispered.

"Good evening, Morris," he whispered, his eyes surveying the auditorium. It was almost full. "Quite a crowd."

"Always is when we do *The Resurrection*," the guard whispered. "We got more'n thirty buses outside."

"Of course," Preacher nodded. "I forgot it was Tuesday."

Every Tuesday night the Churchland Amateur Theatre presented its weekly play. There were ten plays, each about a portion of Jesus' life, adapted freely from the Bible and the television series they distributed to the affiliated churches. At the moment it was intermission, and while the choir sang the wicker collection baskets were moving up and across the aisles.

"I'm always glad to be workin' nights when this play is on," the guard whispered. "It's a miracle how they can make those miracles happen on the stage right in front of your eyes. Even if you know all the equipment and technical things they got to do it with."

Preacher smiled. "Don't forget that Jesus made all those miracles happen Himself. And He didn't need any equipment and technical machinery to help Him."

"That's right," the guard nodded in agreement. "It really was a miracle."

"Good night, Morris," Preacher said. "God be with you."

He went out into the cool evening and breathed deeply of the crisp night air. It filled his lungs and he felt his strength and energy returning. He took the long way back to the parsonage, walking past the rows of buses to the back path, then down the slight hill to the parsonage.

He went inside and directly up the staircase to his study. He put his attaché case on the desk and then went into the bedroom. It was empty. He went from the bedroom directly to the dining room. She had probably started dinner without him. But that room too was empty, the table not even set. He picked up the telephone on the sideboard and pressed the button for the maid. "Where's Mrs. Talbot?" he asked as soon as she came on the wire.

"I don't know, sir," she answered. "They haven't come back yet. It's past the children's bedtime too. I been worryin'."

"Didn't she tell you where she was going?"

"I wasn't on when she left," she answered. "This was my morning off."

"She probably went to visit her father," he said. "And you know him. He doesn't like to let them go and probably made them stay for supper. But don't worry about it, I'll give him a call."

"Yes, sir," she said. "Shall I fix you some supper?"

"Please," he said. "I'll take it in my study."

He went back to his study and called the ranch. The butler answered. "Mr. Randle available?" Preacher asked.

"No, Dr. Talbot," the butler replied. "He's already gone to bed."

"What time did Mrs. Talbot leave?" he asked.

"Mrs. Talbot?" There was a note of surprise in the man's voice. "Mrs. Talbot hasn't been here at all today."

Preacher put down the phone and stared at it. None of it made sense. Where could she have gone? He called the garage where the cars were kept. "Is Mrs. Talbot's Mercedes there?" he asked.

"No, sir," the man answered.

"Anyone there who saw her leave?"

"No, sir. I'm the night man. I don't come on until eight. The day men are all gone."

Slowly he returned the receiver to the telephone. He rose from behind the desk and went to the bedroom. There wasn't even a note in the room. He crossed the hall to the children's room. It, too, was deserted.

He was in the hallway on his way back to the study when

he heard the telephone begin to ring. He ran into the room and picked it up. "Jane?"

"Yes," she answered.

"Where are you?" he asked. "I was beginning to worry. Your car isn't in the garage and I was beginning to imagine all kinds of accidents."

"No, we're fine," she said.

"Where are you?" he asked.

"In Dallas," she said. "At Aunt Jenny's."

He lost his temper. "What the hell are you doing in Dallas?"

"I needed some breathing space," she said. "I felt I was going crazy in Churchland."

"Breathing space?" he shouted. "If that's what you wanted, why did you drag the kids with you?"

She was silent for a moment. "Because we're not coming back."

"Wait a minute," he said, not believing his ears. "You can't do that."

"I've done it," she said.

"You can't do it," he said. "Not without talking it over."

"I knew better than that. I've had enough of your spellbinding. I've seen it work on too many people. I never would have left."

"Did you ever stop to think that you wouldn't have left because you knew it was wrong?"

"I won't listen to you," she said. "I've made up my mind. I'll call the maid in the morning and arrange to have her bring the clothes up here."

"You'll do no such thing," he said. "I'm coming up there and I'll bring you back myself."

"I don't believe you," she said in a tired voice. "Tomorrow morning there'll be something more important for you to do. You'll never come up here."

"I'll be there," he said, but he was already talking into a dead line. She had hung up.

The maid came into the study, carrying a tray, while he

was still staring at the telephone in his hand. "Was that Mrs. Talbot you were talking to?" she asked, placing the tray on the desk.

"Yes," he answered shortly.

"Is everything all right?" she asked.

"Everything's fine," he said, looking up at her. "She decided to visit her Aunt Jenny in Dallas at the last minute."

The maid looked at him for a moment, then nodded. "I'm glad they're all right," she said and left the room.

He stared at the tray for a long time and finally pushed it away. He wasn't hungry. He could fly up there early in the morning and have them all home before noon.

His mind made up, he opened his attaché case and took out the folder marked "Urgent." Quickly he skimmed through it. There was at least two hours' work he would have to leave on his secretary's desk in the morning. He switched on the desk lamp and began to read the first report.

CHAPTER
TEN

He was still at his desk almost two hours later when Marcus called. "They'll do it!" Marcus was excited. "I just got back to the hotel. We have the lawyers working on a memo agreement that will be ready tomorrow."

"Congratulations," Preacher said. "Their program will be a major asset to the church. They have a following that crosses all denominational lines. Methodists, Baptists, Presbyterians, even the Episcopalians like them."

"There's one hitch though," Marcus said. "They won't sign until you see them personally and reassure them that all the promises I made are true."

"I'll be glad to see them," Preacher said. "Bring them down on the plane with you tomorrow."

"They can't make it," Marcus said. "They're committed to Bob Shuller for a special program at the Crystal Cathedral tomorrow night. You'll have to come up to L.A. if you want that agreement for the board meeting."

"Can't do it," Preacher said. "I have to be in Dallas tomorrow morning."

"Put it off," Marcus said. "It can't be as important as this."

Preacher was silent. In a way, Marcus was right. And so was Jane. The church took precedence over his private life. But that was a fact of life that every minister's wife had to face. In another way, maybe it was just as well that he didn't go charging up to Dallas after her. Right now she was still angry. A few days to think it over and she might cool off. Maybe life in Churchland wouldn't seem so bad to her after all. "Okay," he said, taking a deep breath. "How long is the flight?"

"About three hours."

He calculated the time. Los Angeles was two hours back. He could still get a few things done in the morning and take off by ten A.M. "I'll be up on *Churchland 2*," he said. "Look for us at the airport around eleven in the morning."

"I'll be there," Marcus said.

Preacher put down the telephone, found a cigarette, and lit it. He blew the smoke out slowly. He didn't like himself right now. He didn't like having to admit that she was right in saying there would be something else for him to do that would keep him from coming to Dallas. But then, she had no reason to turn it into a battle between the church and herself. He didn't love her any the less because of his love for Jesus.

A sudden thought crossed his mind and he ground the cigarette angrily into the ashtray. Maybe what she felt was more true than even she realized. They hadn't married because he was passionately in love with her. In his own way he loved her, but no more than many other girls. Maybe the simple truth was that he was just not capable of the kind of love she demanded.

The white stretchout limousine with blackout windows pulled alongside the plane as *Churchland 2* rolled to a stop. The steward opened the door and pressed a button that automatically set down the steps.

Marcus was waiting as Preacher came down the steps. "Good flight?"

"Perfect." Preacher smiled and looked down at the limousine. "Flash?"

"It's called the rock star special." Marcus smiled. "Thought you deserved nothing but the best. It has everything; bar, television, two phones, even a pull-down writing desk if you want to make notes."

"Of course," Preacher said as the chauffeur opened the door. He got into the car and Marcus followed him.

"I have a draft of the preliminary memo with me. We can go over it on the way to the hotel and discuss any changes we want to make with their lawyers before we meet with them," Marcus said.

Preacher looked at him. "Why the hotel?"

"I thought you might want to shower and change first. I've taken a bungalow at the Beverly Hills Hotel for you. That way you can go right in from the street without going into the lobby. We're not meeting until after lunch, two-thirty at their house."

Preacher looked out the window. They were already on the freeway north. There was no chance that he could make it back to Dallas before nightfall now. "I thought all we had to do was sign the agreement."

"That's all we have to do," Marcus said. "But that's not the way it's done in show business. It's two hours of bullshit for every two minutes' work."

"Okay," Preacher said. "Let's see the memo."

Marcus pulled down the desk tray in front of them and opened his attaché case. He placed a set of papers in front of Preacher and one in front of himself. "Everything is pretty much what you and I talked about," he said. "But there are a few things they want."

"Like what?"

"They want to work only thirty-nine weeks a year and the right to select the guest hosts for the remaining thirteen weeks, subject to our approval, of course. I saw no problem in that since we had approval, so I okayed it."

Preacher nodded. "Next?"

266

"They want the program called 'The Jimmy and Kim Hickox Show'."

"Okay."

"They want executive producer credit for themselves."

"They got it."

"They want the show to be a joint venture between their company and us. The credit would read, 'A Hickox–Churchland Production,' and they wanted us to split the copyright. I said no to that one."

"Why?" Preacher asked.

"Because if we ever wanted to do anything with the show afterwards, we would have to get their approval. I said they could have the production credit but not the copyright."

"Did they agree to it?"

"Not yet," Marcus said. "They're going to try it on you. If you stand fast I think they'll cave in."

"I'm with you," Preacher said.

"Good," Marcus said. "There's just one more point open. And this one might be the deal breaker. They want to tape the show here. They say they wouldn't be able to get the guests they want if they taped in Churchland. If we have to rent space up here, it could double the production costs on the show. We couldn't afford it."

"How do we solve that one?" Preacher asked.

"I don't know," Marcus answered. "I tried everything I could but got nowhere. That one's up to you."

Preacher thought for a moment. "Have we anything to offer them in place of it?"

Marcus shook his head. "Not really."

Preacher looked at him. "What are they like?"

"He seems to be a nice-enough guy. You know, easy, relaxed, just like he is on the tube, but she's something else. A very tough lady. She's the wheeler-dealer in the family. Apparently she had to be because she took over when he blew his money and his career some years ago being Mr. Nice Guy." Marcus took a deep breath. "I can't be sure but I have the feeling that she moved him onto the gospel circuit because she saw the money in it and knew he didn't stand a chance on commercial television."

Preacher probed further. "Are you telling me that she's not for real? That God is more business than conviction for her?"

Marcus shrugged. "It's possible. But I can't say for sure."

Preacher nodded. He was silent for a moment, then he smiled. "We'll soon find out."

"How?" Marcus asked.

"Maybe I'll take her into another room and pray with her a little," Preacher said. He saw the expression on Marcus' face and laughed. "Don't be upset. It's just one of my private jokes. I know that this is not the time for prayer. If she's the kind of lady you think she is, let's see how tough she really is. Call her attorney and tell him that in no manner will I agree to have the show produced anywhere but in Churchland. If they won't agree to that, the deal is off. You can also tell him that I will be at the hotel until two o'clock and if I don't hear that they will agree to do the show from Churchland by then, there will be no point in my meeting with them and I will leave for the airport."

Marcus stared at him. "That's strong. You don't leave me any room for negotiation."

"There isn't any," Preacher said flatly. "One of the most important reasons for broadcasting from Churchland is that we can attract more people to come there. If we can't have that, fifty percent of their validity will be lost."

"We have nowhere to go if they turn us down," Marcus said.

"They can't be the only fish in the sea," Preacher said. He thought for a moment. "What about Pat Boone? He's very good and a bigger attraction than Jimmy Hickox ever was."

"The reason I didn't approach him first is that I heard he's committed a year in advance."

Preacher looked at him. "You're putting the cart before the horse. They haven't turned us down yet. Make the call first."

. . .

They were at the hotel at eleven-thirty. Marcus led him to the bungalow. It was just off the street on Crescent Drive. "Are you hungry?" he asked. "Shall I order lunch?"

Preacher shook his head. "No, thanks. But I am tired. I didn't sleep very well last night. Do you think I have time for a nap?"

"Of course," Marcus said. "I have a few errands to run. Why don't you lie down and I'll come back at one-fifteen to wake you?"

"That would be fine."

Marcus left and Preacher went into the bedroom, drew the drapes until the room was dark, then took off his clothes and stretched out on the bed in only his shorts. A moment later, he sat up and picked up the telephone.

The operator came on the line immediately. "Yes, Dr. Talbot?"

He placed a call to Jane in Dallas. The telephone rang twice and was answered, "Dawson residence."

"This is Dr. Talbot," he said. "Is Mrs. Talbot there?"

"No, Dr. Talbot," the maid's voice answered. "She took the children out shopping. May I take a message?"

"Please," Preacher said. "Would you be kind enough to tell Mrs. Talbot that I had to go to Los Angeles unexpectedly and that I will call later to explain."

"I'll do that," the maid answered.

"Thank you," Preacher said, putting down the telephone and lying back on the pillows. He stared up into the dark. Nothing seemed to be going exactly right. First, the board of directors, then Jane, and now the Hickoxes. It was strange. Ever since he had turned forty he'd had the feeling that time was running away from him and he could never catch up to it. He was tired. Very tired. He closed his eyes and fell off to sleep.

The faintly sweet odor of grass filtered into his sleep. At first he rejected it. It wasn't true. He was dreaming. But the odor persisted, growing stronger. Finally, he opened his eyes. In the dark all he could see was the outline of two girls seated at the foot of the bed and their cigarettes glowing.

He sat up, reaching for the lamp next to the bed. One of the girls reached over and stopped his hand. "Go back to sleep, Preacher. We didn't mean to disturb you."

He plucked the joint from her fingers and dragged on it. "You weren't disturbing me, Charlie," he said. "If I'm going to get stoned, I'd rather be awake to enjoy it."

"We love you, Preacher," the other girl said.

"And I love you, Melanie," he said. He gave the joint back to Charlie. "Now, can I turn on the light?"

"I'll do it," she said. The lamp clicked on.

He blinked his eyes and stared at them. They were smiling. "How did you know I was here?"

"Joe found out from Marcus and told us. We've been driving since dawn. We wanted to see you," Melanie said.

"After all, it's been almost a year," Charlie said.

He was silent for a moment. "Put out the joints," he said. "I've got an important meeting coming up and I can't afford to be tripping."

"Aren't you glad to see us, Preacher?" Charlie sounded hurt.

"You know I'm always glad to see you," he answered. He got out of bed. "I'd better take a cold shower and get my head straight."

"How about a warm fuck first?" Melanie asked. "At least, that'll relax you and take away all the tensions that are screwing up your head."

He looked at them, smiling. "You're both beautiful. You never change. But I haven't got the time."

"Then make the time, Preacher," Charlie said, beginning to step out of her clothes. "Your vibes tell us you need us."

"Tell her to stop," he said, turning to Melanie. But Melanie was already naked and crawling across the bed toward him. He began to turn back toward Charlie. She too was naked. "Hey—!"

Laughing, they pulled him down on the bed, and holding him down, they pressed themselves against him, their faces over his. He lay very still, his eyes going from one to the other. He took a deep breath. "It won't work, children."

"Nothing works if you won't let it, Preacher," Charlie said, her eyes beginning to moisten.

He turned his face to Melanie. There were tears in her eyes also. "Please, Preacher," she whispered. "Don't grow old on us."

He stared without speaking.

She brushed her nose with the back of her hand. "Because if you grow old, then we grow old too."

He felt his own eyes fill with tears and he pulled their faces down to his shoulders and they lay quietly, their tears mingling, for a long time. Finally, he dropped his hands to his sides and the girls rose from the bed. He lay there silently, watching them dress.

Charlie turned toward him. "I'm sorry," she said. "We shouldn't have come."

"We thought it would be like old times," Melanie said. "But we were wrong. Everything's changed. Even you. We know that now."

"We're not going back to the Community," Charlie said. "That's not the same either."

"Where will you go then?" Preacher asked, sitting up.

Melanie shrugged. "We were thinking of going back to Churchland with you if you would have us. But we know better now."

"We'll find a place," Charlie said. "If you should speak to Joe tell him we'll let him know where to send our things as soon as we settle down."

Preacher looked at them, then smiled slowly. "You can call him right now and tell him."

"What do you mean?" Melanie asked.

"Both of you are going back to Churchland on the plane with me tonight," he said. He saw the look of surprise on their faces and smiled again. "Now is it all right with you ladies if I take a cold shower?"

"How long is the flight?" Charlie asked.

"Three hours," he answered.

They both came toward him and kissed his cheeks. "Then don't make the shower too cold," Charlie said.

CHAPTER
ELEVEN

Jimmy Hickox opened the door for them. His youthful appearance belied his age. He looked no more than a man in his middle thirties though Preacher knew he was in his early fifties. "Dr. Talbot," he said, holding out his hand. "It's a great pleasure to meet you, sir."

Jimmy's handshake was firm and enthusiastic. Preacher smiled. "It's my pleasure, Mr. Hickox. I've been a fan for a long time."

"That makes me feel good," Jimmy said. "I'm an admirer of yours also. I'm very impressed with the manner in which you carry on the work of the Lord. This country needs more men like yourself who devote their lives to fighting the sins that threaten to corrupt the very structure of the American family and destroy our way of life."

Preacher shot a quick glance at Marcus. There was a hidden amusement in his eyes. It was obvious that Jimmy had never seen a program of his or he would know that wasn't the kind of thing that he did. "Thank you," he said. "All of us do the best we can, Mr. Hickox."

"Call me Jimmy," Jimmy said. "Kim and the others are waiting for us in the living room."

There were three other men with her, their agent, their business manager, and their attorney. Jimmy introduced them first. Preacher shook their hands and turned to Kim Hickox. He took her hand before Jimmy had a chance to introduce them, and she had to get out of her chair. He held her hand a moment longer than was necessary and looked into her eyes. "I thought he'd never get around to you," he said. "But now I understand, Mrs. Hickox. He was saving the best for last. It's a real pleasure."

She was blushing beneath her makeup as he let go of her hand. "It's a pleasure for me too, Dr. Talbot. I can't tell you how honored we feel that you called us to help you in your work for the Lord."

"I, too, am pleased that all the problems have been worked out. I'm sure that it's the Lord's will that we join together in working for Him," he said. He saw the slight flush rise into her cheeks again and knew that she had picked up the double entendre.

She tore her eyes away from him. "Would anyone care for a cold drink? Some coffee or tea?"

"Not for me, Mrs. Hickox," he said quickly. "I'm afraid I haven't the time. I have to be in Dallas tonight."

"I'm sorry, Dr. Talbot," she said. "I thought we might have time to chat a little about the program."

"We will, Mrs. Hickox," he said. "Perhaps you could find some time and spend a few days with me in Churchland. That way you'll be able to see for yourself how complete our facilities are and we can get down to some really constructive work."

She nodded. "I agree, Dr. Talbot. That's very important. I'd like it to be as soon as possible. Maybe next week?"

"That's fine with me, Mrs. Hickox," he answered.

"Just a minute, Kim," Jimmy said. "Have you forgotten I promised to join the Billy Graham crusade in Canada next week?"

She smiled but her voice had a quiet authority. "That's all right, dear. I'm sure it will be better for all of us if I spend my time working on the program rather than be sitting around the house doing nothing next week."

"That's true," Jimmy said, nodding. "I hadn't thought of that."

"Might I suggest that we go over the papers now?" Marcus said. "The sooner we get them signed, the quicker Dr. Talbot can go to the airport. He really has to be in Dallas tonight."

The attorney distributed the papers. Preacher handed his copy back to him. "I never read contracts. I leave that to Mr. Lincoln and just sign where he tells me."

He turned to Kim, who was holding her copy. "I'm sure that you do the same thing, Mrs. Hickox. Leave things like that in the capable hands of your husband and advisors."

"Of course, Dr. Talbot," she said. She placed the papers on the coffee table and stood there hesitantly.

"You have a lovely home, Mrs. Hickox." He smiled. "Is it true, as I've heard, that you have one wall in the house covered with all of your husband's gold records?"

"It's true," she said. "In the library. Would you like to see it?"

"I really would, Mrs. Hickox," he said. "Would you believe I've never seen a gold record?"

"Please call me Kim," she said. She turned to her attorney. "Call us as soon as you're ready."

Preacher followed her out of the room to the staircase in the foyer. She started up the steps, then turned and looked down at him. "The library is on the second floor," she said.

He looked up at her. "I read that in the same article I learned about the gold records."

She flushed again, then silently turned and led him to the library. She opened the door and entered the room, standing next to the open doorway. "The records are on the far wall behind the desk."

He went past her into the room, then around behind the

desk. He gave the records a perfunctory glance, then turned to look at her. "Close the door," he said.

She hesitated a moment, then shut the door and stood next to it.

He walked around the desk and stood in front of it. "You're too far away," he said.

Slowly, almost zombie-like, her eyes fixed on him, she crossed the room. She stopped in front of him. Her voice was almost frightened. "Why are you hitting on me?"

He put his hands on her shoulders and felt her trembling. "Before I answer that, I think you have something to tell me."

Her eyes fell. "I've never told anyone."

"Tell me," he said.

"I wasn't always like this. I used to laugh and have fun. Like everyone else. Then one day I woke up and found that I was married to a weak empty shell, an alcoholic who'd managed to lose everything we'd worked for, security and career. I had to take over. I tried everything and nothing helped cure him until he was born again in Christ. At the same time I saw the way to restore his career, a way to make use of the name he still had. For Christ." She looked up at him. "Is that what you wanted to hear?"

"Praise the Lord," he said in a mocking voice. "That story should go over big with Robertson or Bakker on their shows."

"You don't believe me?" she asked.

"I believe you," he said. "But you told me only what you thought I wanted to hear. Not what I wanted to know."

"I don't understand you," she said.

He looked at her. "Did you know he was gay when you were married?"

She shook her head. "No," she answered in a low voice.

"Is that why you want to do the show in Los Angeles?" he asked. "Because you were afraid he couldn't get lost in a small place like Churchland the way he does here?"

Her eyes fell again. "Yes."

He raised her chin with his hand so that she was forced to

look at him. "Maybe it's too big a risk for all of us to take," he said thoughtfully. "If it should get out, I have enough enemies to make mincemeat out of him in order to get at me."

"It won't get out," she said fiercely. "I can control him. How do you think we got this far? There's never been a word about him anywhere."

"You're a very tough lady," he said.

"I had to be but there were times I haven't been," she said. "I'm still a woman with a woman's desires. I haven't always been what I should be."

"I'm sure the Lord understands and forgives. His mercy is not for sinners alone."

"But I am a sinner," she said.

"We are all sinners," he said quietly. "That's why I hit on you."

She stepped away from him. "But not for the reason I thought?"

He didn't answer.

"You're a strange man, Dr. Talbot. Not like any minister I've ever met." She took a deep breath. "I should have known the moment we met not to play games with you." She started for the door, then turned back. "I'm going to my room. Do you mind telling them that we agreed to disagree? I'm not up to facing any of them right now."

"Without knowing the truth about either of you, Kim, I could not sign the agreement. But now I can. I know you won't let me down."

Her astonishment showed. "You mean—?"

"Yes," he smiled, walking toward her. "Let's go downstairs and take care of business."

By the time he thought of calling Jane, he was already on the plane returning to Churchland and it was too late.

The seat-belt sign went out as the plane reached cruising altitude. Preacher unbuckled and looked across the table at Marcus, sitting opposite him. "Thanks for thinking of sending the other plane for Joe. I had completely forgotten about it and if it weren't for you, he might never have made the meeting."

"You have enough on your mind," Marcus said.

"Any refreshment?" the steward asked.

Marcus looked up at him. "If this were a commercial flight I would have a double Scotch but since it isn't, I'll take a black coffee."

Preacher smiled. He looked up at the steward. "I'll have mine on the rocks." He turned to Marcus. "Of course it's off the record, but I keep a private locker on each of the planes for myself."

Marcus returned his smile. "For medicinal purposes."

Preacher nodded. "Absolutely, it's the only way to fly."

They laughed. Marcus glanced over his shoulder at the two girls seated forward. "The old man isn't going to like you bringing them back."

Preacher nodded. "Probably not."

"Do you have any idea where they will work?"

Preacher waited until the steward had put the drinks on the table in front of them and walked away. He picked up his glass and studied the pale golden color of the liquor. "Probably in V.I.P. reception. They're expert in making people feel important."

"I thought that department was turned over to public relations and done away with."

"Then we'll open it up again. We can afford it."

Marcus sipped at his drink. "I was surprised how quickly he agreed with your suggestion to add Joe to the board, weren't you?"

Preacher shook his head. "Not at all. Jake's a shrewd trader. He gave up one to get four. That's not bad."

"How do you think he'll take to the Hickox show?"

"I don't know that it matters," Preacher said. "The contract's already signed. He has no choice but to accept it."

"Doesn't the board have to approve the contracts though?"

"Ordinarily, yes. But as pastor and chairman of the board, any contract I sign is valid and binding on the church."

Marcus took another sip of his drink. "Even if he does like the idea of the show, he won't like the idea that I worked with you on it without telling him. After all, technically, I'm still president of Randle Communications."

"How much time did you buy on the Randle stations for the show?"

"A lot," Marcus answered.

"Then he won't object," Preacher said. "You can always tell him that I pushed the show on you and that you protected him by buying all that time. Just show how much money we all can make with it. That's the bottom line for him. He won't fight that."

"But we both know if we do the show as we plan, without any direct solicitations in it, we're not going to make any money."

"I'm not going to tell him," Preacher said. "Let him discover that for himself when he watches the show. If he ever does."

Marcus laughed suddenly. "Sanford Carrol's going to shit. He's been trying to get them for C.B.N. for a year now but they wouldn't come up with enough money for the Hickoxes."

"What kind of a man is he?" Preacher asked. "Is he good?"

"Very good," Marcus said. "Extremely capable and professional. He was with N.B.C. for ten years before moving to C.B.N."

"Then I suggest you have a little talk with him before the meeting. There's no reason why we couldn't share some of the credit for the idea with him. If it's a show he really wanted, he won't object to that."

Marcus stared at him. "Are you sure you're not a businessman disguised as a minister?"

"I'm sure," Preacher smiled. "I'm a preacher trying to play the game of being a businessman."

Melanie got out of her seat and walked back to them. She

held a lighted joint in her hand. "Do you mind if we smoke?"

Preacher looked up at her with a faint smile. "Why bother to ask? You already are."

"I was just being polite," Melanie said, holding out the joint to him. "Care for a toke?"

"That's the right question to ask," Preacher said, taking the joint from her. "Of course." He sucked the smoke deep into his lungs and let it out idly. He nodded in approval. "Yes."

She waited until he took another toke, then took it back and offered it to Marcus. "Marcus?" she asked.

He stared at the joint for a moment, then took it from her. "Why not? We're doing everything else on this plane."

She watched him take two expert hits, then took the joint back from him. "Hey," she said in admiration. "All these years I thought you were a snob and you turn out to be a real head."

He laughed. "What's in that joint? Two hits and I'm stoned." He fished in his vest pocket and came out with something concealed in the palm of his hand. "I can't be selfish. Preacher came up with the Scotch, you girls with the grass. I have a contribution to make." He opened his hand, showing the small brown vial. "Anybody care for a toot?" He smiled.

Melanie stared for a moment, then turned and called up the aisle. "Hey, Charlie! Come on back here. It's party time!"

None of them were feeling any pain by the time the plane touched down in Churchland.

CHAPTER
TWELVE

The alarm woke him at seven in the morning. With a groan, he sat up in bed. His eyes hurt and his head throbbed with the granddaddy of all hangovers. His mouth felt rug-lined.

He staggered out of bed and went into the bathroom, searching through the medicine cabinet for an Alka Seltzer. Finding it, he threw four of the tablets into a glass of water. The fizzing noise of the effervescence sounded like the roaring of a lion in his ears. Quickly he drank it and, resting his arms on the sink to support himself, stared into the mirror. His bloodshot eyes stared back at him. Sadly he shook his head. This wasn't exactly the sort of condition for him to be in when he opened the board meeting.

He went back into the bedroom and called downstairs for a large pot of black coffee. He sat on the edge of the bed and waited for the throbbing in his temples to cease. Idly he wondered how he got home. The last thing he remembered was leaving the plane.

There was a knock at the door and the maid came in with

the morning tray of orange juice and coffee. She placed it on the bedside table and turned to him with the glass of juice in her hand. "Feeling better this morning, Dr. Talbot?"

He looked at her as he took the juice from her hand, trying to gauge the sound of her voice. He couldn't tell whether she was just being polite, cool or disapproving. "I don't know yet," he said as she turned to pour the coffee into his big breakfast mug.

She took the glass from his hand and replaced it with the coffee. "I put the two ladies in the guest room," she said in an expressionless voice. She saw the blank look on his face. "You know, those two ladies who used to work here in reception," she added quickly. "They said you were feeling a bit under the weather."

He sipped silently at the hot black coffee. They weren't wrong about that even though it was a polite way of putting it.

"Between us we managed to get you upstairs and into bed," she said.

"Thanks," he said. The hot coffee was helping. "Are the ladies awake yet?"

She shook her head. "I haven't heard a word from them."

He nodded. "Were there any messages for me?"

"Mr. Randle called several times yesterday but didn't ask for you to call him back," she said. "And, oh yes, Mrs. Talbot called."

"What did she say?"

"I don't know, I didn't talk with her," she answered. "It was while we were trying to get you into bed. One of the girls answered the phone. When she told Mrs. Talbot who she was, Mrs. Talbot hung up."

He groaned inwardly as he drained his cup and held it out to be refilled. He sipped it again.

"Would you care for some hot breakfast, Dr. Talbot?" the maid asked. "Some food in your stomach will make you feel better."

He shook his head. There was no way he could face it. "No,

thank you. This will be fine." He rose from the bed. "Maybe when I come downstairs. A shave and a shower should wake me up."

He waited until she had left the room before he put down the coffee, holding it carefully with both hands. He didn't want her to see them shaking. He went back into the bathroom and turned on the shower. Very cold. Then holding his breath, he stepped quickly under it.

The cold water hit him like a needle spray of icicles. He let the water flood over him a long time until the cold went through him, clearing his head, then gradually he turned the water to warm while he lathered his body. He let the soap run off him with hot water, then turned it back to ice cold before he stepped from the shower.

He rubbed himself vigorously with the large turkish bath towel and, feeling more human once again, picked up the telephone near the john. He called the kitchen. Suddenly he was starving. "I'll have a stack of wheats, two fried eggs with bacon and sausages and lots of coffee," he told the cook. "I'll be down in ten minutes."

It wasn't until he had finished breakfast and was sitting with his coffee and a cigarette that he reached for the telephone that was always placed on the dining room table next to him and called Jane.

Her aunt's maid answered the telephone. "Mrs. Talbot is still asleep."

"Then wake her up," he said sharply.

"Yes, sir," the maid said quickly.

Almost as quickly as the maid had put down the phone, Jane picked it up. From the sound of her voice, he knew that the maid had been lying. Jane didn't sound the least sleepy. "I thought you said you would be up here yesterday."

"Did you get the message I left?"

"I got it." Her voice was as cold as his shower had been. "What was so important about going to Los Angeles? Or are those whores so important to you that you had to go and bring them back yourself?"

"It was business," he said. "We signed Jimmy and Kim Hickox to do a daily show from Churchland."

"You don't expect me to believe that," she said sarcastically. "Melanie answered the phone in our bedroom at one o'clock this morning. You didn't even give the bed a chance to cool after I was gone."

He felt himself growing angry but he controlled his temper and spoke slowly and deliberately. "Jane, I'm going to say this once, then never again. So listen carefully whether you believe it or not.

"Nothing happened between me and the girls last night. They were helping Susie get me to bed. I was bombed out of my skull. Right now, they're asleep in the guest room and were never in our bed.

"The reason I went to L.A. was exactly what I told you. They would not sign a contract unless I was there personally and I wanted that agreement for the board meeting today. I did not arrange, nor did I expect to see the girls there. They had come to ask me if they could return to Churchland. That's the whole of the story, nothing more, nothing less."

"Why did they want to come back?" she asked snidely. "Did they suddenly discover that they couldn't live without you?"

"I told you I wouldn't have anything more to say on that subject," he said quietly. "I have a heavy day coming up, so I can't come up there myself but I can send a plane for you."

"Don't bother, I'm not coming back," she said. "I'm not one of those whores. I can live without you."

"I'm sorry," he said. "Truly sorry." But he heard the click of the phone as he was speaking. The telephone went dead in his hands and he never knew whether she had heard him or not.

The old man was already waiting in his office when Preacher arrived at eight o'clock. He was sitting in a chair, his chin resting on his hands as they clasped the heavy gold-topped walking cane, staring dourly at Preacher while he walked around his desk and sat down.

"Good morning, Jake," Preacher said. "Would you like a cup of coffee?"

Randle didn't answer him.

Preacher pressed the intercom on his desk. "Might I have some coffee, please?" A moment later, the coffee was on his desk and his secretary had gone. He took a sip of his coffee and looked across the desk. "What's on your mind?" he asked.

"You know damn well what's on my mind," the old man rasped.

"It could be any one of a number of things but since I'm not a mind reader," Preacher said, "supposing you tell me."

"What the hell is Jane doing with the children in Dallas?" Randle asked.

"You didn't talk to her?" Preacher was curious.

"I spoke to her," the old man said heavily.

"Then you already know," Preacher said. He took another sip of coffee. "She's left me."

"Goddammit!" the old man exploded. "How could you let such a thing happen? Why didn't you stop her?"

"I was as surprised as you were," Preacher said. "She never told me what she was going to do."

"You've got to bring her back," Randle said.

Preacher looked at him. "Why?"

"Why?" the old man echoed. "I'll tell you why. Because you're the pastor of this ministry, that's why! And you can't have any talk about you without losing your credibility both for the ministry and yourself. How do you expect people to look to you for guidance when you can't even manage your own affairs? And if she decides to file for divorce, then we've really had it. Remember the problems Oral Roberts had when his son was divorced? It caused an upheaval in his ministry that we can in no way afford because we're nowhere near as established as he is."

Preacher stared at him. "Is your concern for the ministry or for your daughter?"

Randle got to his feet. "Both. I've worked too hard to make this ministry viable. And I don't like to see her acting as stupidly as her mother."

"She hasn't said anything about a divorce," Preacher said.

"Not yet. This is only the beginning. That's the next step. Take it from me, I've been through it," Randle said. He paused heavily. "Now, are you going up there to get her or do I have to have her brought back here?"

Preacher looked up at him. "Exactly how do you propose to do that?"

Jake glared at him. "There are ways. She took the children with her. She won't stay away if the children are brought back here."

"No," Preacher said coldly. He rose to his feet and leaned on the desk so that his face was on the same level as the old man's. "This is one time you're going to stay out of it, Jake. You've been pushing people around for so long you've forgotten they have a right to live their own lives as they please. She may be your daughter but she's my wife and they're my children and whatever happens is my concern, not yours. And if you make one move to interfere with our personal lives, I'll show you how fast I can take this ministry apart."

The old man looked at him, breathing heavily. "You're a fool!"

"Maybe." Preacher sank back into his chair and smiled at him. "Why don't you relax, Jake, and have a little more faith? The Lord will see to it that justice is done. Meanwhile, you and I have a great deal of work to do, so why don't we get on with it and not get into arguments that will only keep us from accomplishing what the good Lord intends for us?"

"You can't allow her to file for a divorce," the old man said.

"I'll try," Preacher said. "I don't want a divorce any more than you do, but she has something to say about it too."

"You can go up there and knock her up again," the old man said. "That would stop her."

Preacher laughed and walked around his desk to the old

man. "If that's such a good idea, how come you didn't do it when Jane's mother sued you for divorce?"

The old man's eyes crinkled as he looked up at Preacher. "I tried," he said heavily.

"And what happened?"

"She wouldn't uncross her legs."

Preacher laughed again. "Then what makes you think I'll have any better luck than you?"

CHAPTER
THIRTEEN

Preacher rapped the table with the small wooden gavel. "The special meeting of the board of directors of the Community of God Church of Christian America Triumphant is hereby called to order. The chair will entertain a motion to dispense with the reading of the minutes of the preceding meeting so that we may get on with the business before us."

The motion was made, seconded and unanimously approved in less than a minute. Preacher tapped the table again. "The motion is carried," he said. He rose to his feet and paused for a moment, his gaze covering the board as they sat looking toward him.

"The chair would like to express officially as well as personally its welcome to the new members of this board of directors. I know that all of you bring to this ministry the experience, the zeal, and the faith in our Lord Jesus Christ that will enable us to reach and bring more souls to His love. And I, for one, believe that you have come not a moment too soon.

"For the burden has become too heavy for one man to carry alone. In the six years since this ministry was founded, I have done my best to cope with its many problems but now I must admit that it has become more difficult and more complex than even I had thought. And like Jesus, who sought disciples to spread His Gospel, so I turn to you. Not as disciples but as fellow laborers in the vineyards of the Lord. Together we will forge a mighty power in His name.

"Gentlemen, let us pray."

He bowed his head and clasped his hands above the table before him. There was a faint rustle around the table as they followed his example. His voice rose clear and strong over them.

"O Lord, look down upon this gathering of men who are less than the least of all the saints and grant to us, like the Apostle Paul, the grace given to preach the unsearchable riches of Christ. And to make all men see that which from the beginning of the world hath been hid in God, who created all things by Jesus Christ. And to know the love of Christ, which passeth all knowledge, that we may be filled with the fullness of God. And grant to us the glory in the church by Christ Jesus, throughout all ages, world without end. Amen."

The chorus of Amens went around the table as he raised his head. They returned his gaze with serious expressions. After a moment, he smiled. "I only hope that Paul will forgive the liberties I took with his Epistle to the Ephesians."

The ice was broken and they all smiled and sat back more comfortably in their chairs. "And now for the first order of business," he said. "As you know, we have for a long time been desirous of increasing our presence on television in the form of a daily program such as other ministries have been doing. But until now, we had neither the necessary manpower nor the talent capable of maintaining a program of that sort. I am pleased to report to the board that yesterday we entered into an agreement which makes this step possible. Now, let me turn the floor over to Brother Marcus Lincoln, who far better than I will be able to tell you all about it. Brother Marcus."

Marcus rose to his feet. "Thank you, Dr. Talbot." He glanced around the table. "Before I begin let me inform you that our newly elected board member Brother Sanford Carrol was consulted throughout the progress of this project and has given us his enthusiastic support and the benefit of his expertise."

Marcus paused for a moment to let the information sink in. Preacher noted that Carrol was nodding his head in approval. He smiled to himself. Marcus had covered all his bets. With less than fifteen minutes of discussion the agreement with Hickoxes was unanimously approved.

Randle held up his hand for attention. "Mr. Chairman."

Preacher nodded. "The chair recognizes Brother Randle."

The old man didn't rise from his seat. "I have listened carefully to the opening statements made by Dr. Talbot and I must say that no one agrees with him more than I. It is true that this ministry has grown and become in many ways too great a burden for one man to oversee. I would like to recommend that this board appoint an executive committee which will undertake an independent survey of all the activities of this ministry—pastoral, administrative and financial—with a view to improving the quality of our services to the community at large. This committee will report directly to Dr. Talbot and to this board all results and recommendations that may result from their study."

"I think Brother Randle's recommendation is well taken," Preacher said. "I have only one suggestion to add. That the committee so appointed shall consist of the five new members of this board, because they will bring to their work a fresh and objective point of view, unencumbered by the habits and methods of the past. If Brother Randle agrees that this suggestion will serve the best interests of the church, the chair would be pleased if he would present this to the board in the manner of a motion for consideration."

The old man made the motion incorporating Preacher's suggestion. It was quickly seconded by Mr. Craig and Mrs. Lacey, then passed unanimously by the board with only the five members concerned abstaining.

Preacher rose to his feet. "I think this pretty well completes any official business before the board at this meeting, but before we adjourn I would like to inform the board that I plan to introduce in the course of my programs during the next few weeks each of my three associate pastors so that our vast television audience becomes aware of them and gets to know them. It is my personal conviction that it will demonstrate to all our strength and our depth of pastoral talent and convince everyone that this is a real church that will continue in its good work no matter what may happen to any one of us, that no one is indispensable to the Community of God Church except God Himself and His only begotten Son, our Savior Jesus Christ."

A chorus of Amens went around the table. Preacher rapped the gavel again. "The chair will entertain a motion to adjourn."

Joe paced angrily back and forth in front of Preacher's desk while Beverly sat quietly on the couch near the office windows. Finally, Joe stopped his pacing and stared down at Preacher. "Have you gone out of your cotton-pickin' mind, Preacher?" He didn't wait for an answer. "You know what you done? You just delivered yourself into the hands of the Philistines. You know the old man's just been waitin' to cut you down to size, so what do you do? You give him all the weapons he needs to do the job."

Preacher looked at him silently.

"If what you really want is out, Preacher, why didn't you just step aside and turn it all over to them? 'Cause that's what's goin' to happen anyway. They're goin' to get rid of you and take over."

Preacher looked at Beverly across the room. "Is that what you think?"

She hesitated a moment, then nodded. "It's a strong possibility," she said thoughtfully.

Preacher turned back to Joe. "What would you have done?"

"I would have told them all to go fuck 'emselves. I would

have told them this is *my* church and I built it an' I'm goin' to keep it."

Preacher's voice was soft. "It's not my church, it's not any man's church. It's God's church."

"God didn't have this church until you built it for Him," Joe said.

"God had this church long before any of us were born and He will have it long after all of us are gone," Preacher said. "Whatever I did was only carrying out His will."

"You can't tell me that now God is willin' for you to turn over His church to those money-grubbin', power-crazy Philistines," Joe said vehemently.

"I'm not telling you anything of the sort," Preacher said easily. "But before you pass judgment on them, think whether we haven't been guilty of the same things you accuse them of planning to do." He took a deep breath. "It seems to me that we have spent more time devising ways and means to gather a harvest of worldly goods rather than a harvest of souls."

"You can't do nothin' in this world without money," Joe said. "And you, better than anyone, know how expensive it is to do God's work." He glanced over his shoulder at Beverly, then back at Preacher. "Maybe you forgot how it was when we had no money but we haven't. Remember how we got chased out of the Community? Remember how we couldn't pay our bills with the gospel tent and how many times we went hungry so that we could give some money to the people who worked for us? Remember half the time we would have really been on our ass if Beverly hadn't dug into her sock to keep us goin'."

Preacher nodded. "I remember," he said quietly. "And I will always be in your debt. It's something I could never forget. But then was then and now is now. I also remember that it was Jake Randle who put up the money to make all this possible. And whatever his motives were for doing it, it was God who brought him to us."

"We always knew his motives," Joe said. "He never once took his eye off the ball. He wanted a certain kind of power and now he's plannin' to take it. That's why those new guys are here. He's got them jumpin' through his hoop like trained animals."

"I'm not ready to pass judgment on anyone," Preacher said. "I accept that God works in His mysterious ways. Perhaps it will be that they are better equipped than I to carry on His work. If that is so, I shall be happy to give it to them."

"And what if it turns out that they are doing Caesar's work, not God's?" Joe asked.

"We'll have to deal with that when we see it," Preacher said.

"It may be too late then," Joe said sourly.

"You're on the committee," Preacher said. "You'll know what they're doing."

Joe shook his head. "They'll let me know only what they want me to. I'm jes a nigger Daniel in a den of white lions."

"You won't be after you're on national television," Preacher said. "I've heard you preach. They haven't. You'll put them all away. One program and they'll be pussycats lying at your feet."

"Don't kid yourself," Joe said sourly. "I know how the old man feels about niggers. The only reason he puts up with me is because I'm money in the bank. But he ain't goin' to let me on the air and get any more important."

Preacher smiled. "You're wrong. There's nothing he can do to stop you."

Joe squinted at him. "Tell me."

"You heard what I told them at the meeting," Preacher said quietly, "that I would introduce you all on the air over the next few weeks? What I didn't tell them was that you're going on the air this Sunday. I've told no one up to now except you and I don't intend to tell anyone else. Not even the program director. That means they won't know until we're actually on the air. And then there will be nothing they can do about it."

Joe broke into a broad grin. He slapped at his knee and laughed. "I should have know better than not to trust you."

"You would do better to place your trust in God," Preacher said, "than in weak and foolish men." He rose from his chair behind the desk, walked to the window and stood there looking out. After a moment he turned and came back to them. "Besides, I've had it with the old man's secret war. He might as well learn right now that I intend to run this ministry as I believe God intends it to be run. And if he doesn't like it he's going to have to come out in the open and say so."

"He's tough. He's going to fight you," Joe said. "You might lose."

Preacher looked down at him. "I might," he nodded slowly. "But God never will."

CHAPTER
FOURTEEN

"It's over," Jane said, a tone of finality in her voice. "I've thought about it and thought about it but there's no use. It won't work. I know that now."

Preacher sat on the couch opposite her. "You know what's happening. We'll have more time. I'll only be doing one program a month now."

She looked at him steadily, then raised the glass of white wine to her lips. "You don't understand, Preacher," she said. "It's not that at all. Maybe I wasn't cut out to be a minister's wife. I guess I never really understood the commitment it takes, the restrictions we live under. I just never really felt free living in Churchland. It was like living in a fishbowl with absolutely nothing to do, just swimming aimlessly back and forth."

"It's not as bad as that," Preacher said.

"Maybe not for you," she said. "You are preoccupied with your work. You never stop. You travel, you move around. People pay attention to you, to what you do. I have nothing to do there. Just stay in the house and wait for you to come home and go to sleep."

Preacher was silent.

"I'm planning to buy a house here," she said. "Once we're settled in and the children are in their new schools, I'm going back to work. I have to feel useful. I don't like the idea of my brain turning into jelly."

"Are you going back to work for your father?" he asked.

"No," she answered. "I'm tired of his trying to run my life too. I won't have too much trouble finding the right job. I'm good at my work."

"I know that," he said.

She took another sip of her wine. "I told him that and he didn't argue with me. He only asked one thing."

"What?"

"Not to file for a divorce at this time. He said the church is going through a difficult period and that a divorce could do it a lot of harm." She paused for a moment, looking at him. "Do you feel that way too?"

"Not for the same reason," he said. "The church should be strong enough to withstand the problems of any of its members be they ministerial or lay people. I guess I don't want a divorce because I don't like to admit failure."

"But we have failed," Jane said without rancor. "We've never really built a marriage, we've never really had a marriage. We've had children together, we've lived in the same house together. But the only time we were on the same wavelength was when we got stoned and fucked. Outside of that we lived in different worlds. Your world was somewhere else, a world I could never share, a world in which I really never existed."

He was silent for a moment, then took a cigarette from the package on the coffee table between them. He lit it and let the smoke drift out slowly. "I'm sorry," he said.

"You shouldn't be," she said. "You didn't lie to me. You told me up front to get rid of the child. I was the one who insisted we get married. You never even once told me that you

296

loved me, not in the same way as people who are really in love."

He drew on his cigarette without answering.

"I was foolish, I guess," she continued. "Maybe even naive. I thought because I was pregnant it was a sign that we were in love—otherwise it couldn't have happened. I know better now."

"How are the children?" he asked.

"Fine," she said. "They like it here. There are more things for them to do, more places for them to go."

"Do they ask about me?"

"Not really," she answered. "Sometimes when they see you on TV they point and say That's Daddy, but that's about all. They do ask about Grandpa, though. After all, he spent more time with them than you ever did."

Again he was silent.

"Children are like animals. Instinctively they know their places in relationships. They respond to affection when affection is shown, to attention when it is given."

He ground out his cigarette. "You've made your case. I guess you've about said it all."

"Have I?" she asked. "I wonder. I've listened to your sermons often enough. I've heard you quoting from the Scriptures that the God you worship is a demanding God, a consuming God, that nothing in this world must be allowed to come between you. Did you ever wonder that Jesus died without even once declaring His love for a woman?"

"Jesus declared His love for all the world and all the people in it," Preacher said. "He died so that we might live."

"I don't argue that," she said. "But is it possible that Jesus gave so much love to all that he had none of His own left to give to any one woman?"

"If you're saying that I am like Jesus," Preacher said, "you're not making any sense at all."

"That's not what I'm saying," she said quickly. "What I am saying is that you give all the love you have in you to everyone in the name of Christ and that you have none left of your own to give to anyone. Not to yourself and not for yourself."

"I can't make you understand," Preacher said. "There is so much work to do and so little time in which to do it."

"You're wrong, Preacher," she said. "I do understand. Only too well. That's why I feel the way I do. I've finally come to realize that the only way in which you can do your work is to be free. Any personal life you might have would only be another millstone around your neck."

His voice was low. "That makes me seem pretty awful. And selfish."

"You're nothing of the sort, Preacher," she said. "You're just trying so hard to be all things to all men because you believe that's the way the Lord wants you to be. Maybe that's true. But I can't believe that Jesus Christ in His mercy asks anything more of you than to first be yourself."

He rose to his feet and looked down at her. He took a deep breath and spoke in a voice tinged with sadness. "I shall pray, Jane, that it is not the devil speaking through your lips, trying to turn me from God's work."

She returned his gaze evenly. "And I too shall pray, Preacher. That Jesus Christ, in His mercy, gives you the vision to see yourself as you truly are. A human being. Like all of us. Not a man trying to assume God's role on this earth."

Preacher stood on the pulpit platform elevator below the auditorium stage and listened to the choir as they sang above him. He watched as the small television monitor in front of him flickered and sprang into life with the helicopter view of Churchland, then panned to the crowds thronging their way into the theater and then, following the people down the aisles, gradually panned up to the stage and the huge golden cross hanging on the backdrop.

The choir faded as the professional voice of the announcer came through the speaker and the main titles began to appear on the screen. "Ladies and gentlemen, from Churchland, Texas, the Community of God Church of Christian America

Triumphant and its four thousand nine hundred and seventy-one affiliated churches throughout the United States are proud to welcome you to our weekly program, 'Sunday Morning at Churchland.' "

The announcer paused for a moment to allow the applause to swell and then, as it faded down, spoke again. "Ladies and gentlemen, your pastor, Dr. C. Andrew Talbot!"

The applause began to rise again and the director's voice in Preacher's earphone crackled. "You're on your way, Dr. Talbot." Unconsciously Preacher nodded as the elevator rose. The applause was still ringing in his ears as the platform came to position on the stage.

Preacher waited a moment, then held up both arms for silence. Gradually the applause died down. "Brothers and Sisters," he said, his voice echoing through the speakers, "in the name of our Savior Jesus Christ, I welcome you." The applause began again but he quickly held it down by continuing to speak. "Today is a very special day for me and, I hope, a very special day for all of us in the Community of God. For this is the first day in which I am no longer alone in this ministry. I have found three brothers, three good men, three wise men, three men whose faith in our Lord Jesus Christ will extend my strength and the church's strength to expand our work for the Lord."

The director's panic-stricken voice crackled in Preacher's earphone. "That's not the script for today, Dr. Talbot! We've just blown all the cues. Shall I put the script on your monitor?"

Preacher pressed the red button on the pulpit which connected him to the control booth high in the back of the auditorium. "No," he whispered. "Just take your cues from me as best you can."

He released the button and looked out at the congregation. "Today I take pleasure in bringing to you the first of these wise men who will share my ministry. This is a man I have known many years, a man who has steadfastly been at my side throughout the long years of struggle to establish this church.

A man who traveled the country with me, preaching the Gospel first from a van, later in a tent, in the rain and snow of winter and in the heat and drought of summer. A man whose faith and love in Jesus came not from words alone, but from struggle and doing battle with the forces of evil and the courage to confront Satan to his own face. A man who, more than any other, has helped build the affiliated churches of the Community of God into a viable and great force for the gathering of hundreds and thousands of souls for our Lord and Savior Jesus Christ. A man under whose leadership our newspaper, *The Major Minority,* has brought to the attention of everyone the real needs of the members of our congregation so that they may survive and be able to clothe and feed their families, do battle with all the injustices that man does to man under the influence of Satan, and deal with the realities of life in Jesus Christ and not in the vain promises and theories of pie in the sky offered by the ungodly.

"Brothers and Sisters, it gives me great pleasure to introduce and bring to you my beloved brother in Christ to preach the sermon for today, the Reverend Josephus Washington." Preacher stepped back from the pulpit, he extended one hand palm out toward the stage wings, the other hand he held out to the congregation, palm up to signal their applause.

Obediently the congregation followed his lead, the applause beginning to swell through the auditorium. The applause faltered for a moment as Joe stepped from the wings but Preacher would have none of it. With a commanding gesture he bade them to continue and they did as Joe walked across the giant stage, his flowing dark blue robe with white trimming falling below his ministerial collar, the special lighting makeup blended for his dark skin giving him the ideal image of a man of God.

They shook hands, embraced, and then Preacher escorted him to the pulpit and retired to a chair, seating himself behind the pulpit and slightly to the right so that he would always be in camera range in order to indicate his approval and acceptance.

A stillness fell across the congregation as Joe looked out at them. He stood straight and tall, his serious face high above the pulpit, making it seem almost too small for him. Still not speaking, he took a small wireless pin microphone and fastened it to his robe, then stepped around and in front of the pulpit. Again, he stood silently for a moment, looking at them before he spoke. When he did, his voice was rich and filled with all the musical beauty of the great ministers of the past.

"Brothers and Sisters, my sermon today will come from the First Psalm. Let me repeat those holy words to you before I begin.

> *Blessed is the man that walketh not in the counsel of the ungodly, nor standeth in the way of sinners, nor sitteth in the seat of the scornful.*
>
> *But his delight is in the law of the Lord, and in his law doth he meditate day and night.*
>
> *And he shall be like a tree planted by the rivers of water, that bringeth forth his fruit in his season; his leaf also shall not wither; and whatsoever he doeth shall prosper.*
>
> *The ungodly are not so: but are like the chaff which the wind driveth away.*
>
> *Therefore the ungodly shall not stand in the judgment, nor sinners in the congregation of the righteous.*
>
> *For the Lord knoweth the way of the righteous: but the way of the ungodly shall perish.*"

He let his voice fade away and walked back to the pulpit. He placed his large hands on the edges of the lectern and looked out at the congregation. Once more his strong, rich voice echoed in the auditorium.

"We live today in a world filled with the ungodly—those men who threaten the fabric of our lives and seek to take from us our rights, our liberties and our very freedom. The ungodly ones who seek to turn brother against brother, neighbor against neighbor, race against race, creed against creed. The ungodly who threaten to take from us the very food from the mouths of our children, the meager comforts of our aged. The ungodly who seek nothing more than to steal the whole world for the devil from the merciful grace of our beloved Christ Jesus!"

Slowly a ripple of applause began to grow until it swelled into a roar of approval. Behind him, seated in his chair, Preacher allowed himself a faint smile. Joe had them.

CHAPTER
FIFTEEN

Joe came to the end of his sermon to the roaring applause of the congregation and Preacher rose from his chair and walked toward the pulpit as Joe left it. They clasped hands warmly and Joe took his seat as Preacher stood behind the pulpit. Preacher held up his hand for silence. The congregation settled back.

Preacher smiled and nodded his head. "On behalf of the Community of God as well as myself, I want to extend my thanks and deep gratitude to Reverend Washington for his stirring and uplifting sermon to us today. I know that all of us will be inspired by his words to a greater effort to consecrate ourselves to our Lord Jesus Christ and I am sure that his example and his devotion to the Gospel will continue to inspire us in the future."

He paused for a moment, then continued. "As you know, at the beginning of these services I mentioned three wise men who have come to aid us in our work for the Lord. This week I introduced to you the Reverend Josephus Washington, the first of those good men. In weeks to come I will bring you the second, Dr. Thomas Sorensen, formerly associate pastor of the Liberty Baptist Church, and the third, Dr. Mark L. Ryker, formerly associate dean of religious studies at Oral Roberts University. Each of these men will bring to us the richness of their faith in the Lord, and together we shall forge the greatest army for Christ the world has ever known."

The director's voice crackled in his earphone. "Three minutes, Dr. Talbot."

Preacher held up his hand to hold back the applause that was beginning to swell through the auditorium. He began to speak almost before the sound died away.

"Now, for the first time since this ministry was started and because of the addition of these great men to share my burdens, it will be possible for the Community of God Church of Christian America Triumphant to make plans and engage in an even greater effort to bring Jesus Christ to the hearts and souls of all men than it ever has before.

"The first of these plans is to organize and achieve the first nationwide Crusade for Christ ever held in the United States on one day. Three months from now on Labor Day, the first Monday in September, at the same moment in time all over the United States, in churches, auditoriums, and stadiums, all linked together by the God-given miracle of satellite, hundreds of thousands, perhaps even millions, of people will gather together in Christian brotherhood and raise their voices to the heavens in prayer and homage to our Lord and Savior Jesus Christ and rededicate themselves and their lives once more to Him who died on the cross for all the sins of mankind."

The director's voice crackled again in his ear. "Thirty seconds."

Preacher held both arms in the air. "The time has come again to bring to a close our program, 'Sunday Morning at Churchland,' and until next Sunday at the same time and on the same stations, I pray that you will live in the Spirit of Christ Jesus. So, goodbye for now and may God be with you."

He remained in the pulpit, smiling and still holding his arms in the air as the choir broke into song behind them. A quick glance at the monitor screen revealed the camera zooming in close on his face as the credit lines raced across the screen.

The director's voice crackled in his earphone. "Your secretary called, Dr. Talbot, and asked that you come to your office as soon as the program is over."

He nodded, still smiling. It was not entirely unexpected. By now, all hell had to be breaking loose in the ranks of the ungodly. He waited until the screen had gone to black and the congregation began filing out before he left the stage.

The telephone messages were on his desk. He picked them up. Jake Randle. Marcus Lincoln. John Connors, the supervisor at the Fort Worth 800-line message center. Helen Lacey. Richard Craig. His mother. Jake Randle twice again. He returned his mother's call first.

"I thought what you did on the program today, Constantine, was wonderful," his mother said.

"Thank you, Mother," he said. "But I have the feeling that not many around here will agree with you."

She laughed on the telephone. "Did whatever others thought ever mean anything to you?" she asked. "Haven't you always listened to your own God?"

"Not my own God, Mother," he said. "Everyone's God."

"That's true, Constantine," she said, "but somehow you seem to hear Him say things that other people do not."

"Maybe they listen only to what they want to hear."

"I don't know," she said. "I just wanted you to know that I am very proud of you and I'm sure that Jane is too."

He was silent for a moment. "I wouldn't know how she feels, Mother. Jane's left me."

305

"I'm sorry, Constantine." His mother's voice was shocked. "When did it happen?"

"About a week ago. She took the children and went up to Dallas. She plans to buy a house there and go back to work."

"Did you talk to her?"

"Yes."

"Perhaps she'll come back when she's had a chance to think it over," his mother said.

"I think not, Mother. Her mind seems made up. She told me that she wasn't cut out to be a minister's wife, that she doesn't like living in Churchland because she feels like a prisoner in a fishbowl."

"It has to be more than that," his mother said shrewdly.

"She said that I use all the love in me to give everyone in the name of Christ and that I have none of my own to give to any one person, including myself."

His mother was silent for a moment. "She's not altogether wrong, son."

Preacher's voice was weary. "I didn't say she was, Mother."

"You can change, Constantine. Other ministers make time for their personal lives."

"I wish I could, Mother." He felt his voice near the breaking point. "I've lived all my life with one dream. To make God real. To show the world that God lives. I don't know any other way. And if I take anything away from that dream to make room for my own selfish needs then my life will be nothing and I might as well have never lived. If I do not belong to God and give all my love to Him, then who do I belong to?"

"You also belong to those who love you, Constantine," she said softly.

"I know, Mother," he said. "But God's love is greater than any in this world have to give."

A hint of sadness came into her voice. "Many times, Constantine, I have wondered whether you were really my son."

"I have always been your son, Mother," he said softly. "Just as I have always been God's child. As we all are."

She hesitated a moment. "Would you mind if I spoke with Jane?"

"Not at all, Mother," he said. "As a matter of fact I think she would appreciate it. She too needs friends to love her."

He put down the telephone after giving his mother Jane's number in Dallas and stared silently at the instrument for a long while. Then he reached for it again and asked his secretary to get Connors at the Fort Worth telephone center for him.

"I'm sorry to disturb you, Dr. Talbot," Connors said. "But I thought it important to let you know what's happening here."

"I'm glad you called, John," Preacher said. "Please go ahead."

"As you know, sir, we always have extra personnel on the phones when the program is on the air but this time it was impossible to keep up with the calls. Shortly after Reverend Washington began to speak the phones started coming off the wall. At one point near the end of the program we had almost a thousand calls stacked up. We're still five hundred calls behind."

"How do you rate the calls, John, favorable or unfavorable?"

"We're programming the computer for that right now, sir," Connors answered. "Unfortunately, due to the pileup there were many calls we couldn't pick up in time and lost completely. And, for the first time in our experience, there were many anonymous calls that we picked up where the caller never gave a name." He paused for a moment, then came back on the line. "The breakdown is coming up now, sir. You can pick up the information on your desk computer screen. The access code we assigned to the breakdown is FW-800-316-248."

Preacher pressed the computer switch on and tapped out the access code. The figures rolled onto the screen in front of him at the same time that Connors began to read them aloud.

Total calls registered at air time plus thirty minutes	6,142
Total calls lost	2,961
Total calls answered	3,181=100%
Anonymous calls answered	1,060–33% U
Normal calls answered	2,121–67%
Normal calls breakdown	320–10% U
Normal calls breakdown	1,801–57% F

Coding: U–Unfavorable F–Favorable End Breakdown Report.

Preacher turned off the computer and the screen went blank. "How long would it take to get a geographical point of origin for the calls, John?" he asked.

"We can have the normal calls for you in a few minutes, sir," Connors replied. "But we have to get the anonymous call register from the telephone company, sir, and I doubt whether we could have that much before the day after tomorrow. They would have to pull a special-billing run for us."

"Do it," Preacher said. "I want to know where in the country the anonymous calls came from."

"I do too, sir," John said. "Our people are still in a state of shock. You just cannot believe the language many of those callers used. The most foul and abusive language any of us have ever heard."

"You track that information, John," Preacher said. "People who use language like that are sick. And it is just as well for us to know the location of our enemies."

"I'll get right on it, Dr. Talbot."

"Thank you, John," Preacher said. "You've done an excellent job and I want you to know I personally appreciate it."

"Thank you, Dr. Talbot." John seemed pleased. "Goodbye."

"Goodbye, John." Preacher put down the telephone. He jotted some figures on his pad and stared at them thoughtfully. He wondered how many of the anonymous callers were members of the church and if it would ever be possible to find out. But the figures themselves were scary. An unfavorable re-action of 43 percent of the total calls logged could in no way be interpreted as good for the church.

Marcus Lincoln was his next call. "You came out of left field with that one, Preacher," he said. "Ten minutes after you were on the air, the old man was on the wire screaming for me to pull you off the air."

"That sounds like par for the course," Preacher said.

"That was only the beginning," Marcus said. "You should have heard him when I told him there was no way we could do it. That there were at least a hundred stations around the country that would sue our balls off for leaving them with dead air and they would probably win. In addition to that they would jump at the chance to cancel our time contract, which has another three years to run at '79 rates and which they could turn right around and sell at today's rates, which are almost three times as much."

Preacher laughed. "That had to send him up the wall."

"It did," Marcus said. "Then he took off on me and wanted to know why in hell I wasn't riding herd on you and how come I didn't know you were going to do a program like that and if I did, why wasn't he informed.

"I explained to him that the script we had seen wasn't any-thing like that which went on the air, and that I had checked with the director in the control booth, who had told me that you pulled the switch on him the moment you went on the air."

"That was true," Preacher said. "I'm sorry I had to put you on the spot like that, but if I had talked about it in advance I might never had been able to do it. It would have been meet-inged to death." He paused for a moment. "Anyway, it's done now and that's the end of it."

"Not according to him. He's going to get that nigger's ass are his exact words, then he's going after you. Another quote from him. You're getting too big for your britches, you're for-getting that he put you up there and that he can take you down just as fast. He's not going to stand by and let the

Christian principles that he believes in be torn down by pot-smoking adulterers who desert their wives and children."

"Is that all he said?" Preacher asked quietly.

"No," Marcus answered. "He said if I let one more incident like that get by me, I could consider myself fired. I told him if he really felt like that he could have my resignation right now, but he backed away from that one."

"Thank you, Marcus," Preacher said genuinely. "That took real guts."

"Not really," Marcus replied. "I've about reached the point where I've taken as much of his bullshit as I could. This isn't the only job in the world."

"It still took courage," Preacher said.

"I don't know," Marcus answered. "I'm not completely stupid. I can read the writing on the wall. He's going to get me sooner or later. For what other reason would he bring in Sanford Carrol? You don't need two men to do the same job and I think he's already convinced himself that I'm in your corner."

"You may not know it, Marcus," Preacher said, "but you're not in my corner; we're both in God's."

"I'll accept that," Marcus said.

"Good," Preacher answered. "Now, I want you to get some information for me in a hurry. I need the overnight Nielsens from the major markets in a hurry. First half-hour of the program against the second. I have to know whether we lost any audience after Joe went on the air."

"Expect any trouble?" Marcus asked.

"I'm afraid so," Preacher replied seriously. "But I hope I'm wrong."

"I'll try to have them for you by noon tomorrow."

"Good. I'll talk to you then," Preacher said.

"One more thing," Marcus said. "Don't forget that Kim Hickox is coming in on *Churchland 1* tomorrow afternoon at three o'clock and you promised to meet her."

"I'll be there," Preacher said. "Thanks again, Marcus."

The intercom buzzed as soon as he put down the telephone. "Mrs. Talbot is on line two, Dr. Talbot."

"Tell her that I'll call her back immediately on my private line," Preacher said. He waited a moment to give her time to hang up, then dialed her number.

She answered immediately. "Preacher?"

"Yes," he said.

"I've just finished speaking with my father," she said. "He was ranting and raving so much that I could hardly make out what he was saying. He's changed his mind completely. Now he wants me to start divorce proceedings right away and he'll furnish me with all the evidence I need to prove you guilty of adultery in any court in the land before you turn the church completely over to the blacks."

"Blacks?" Preacher asked. "Was that the word your father used?"

"No. You know the word he uses but because he uses it doesn't mean that I have to," she said. "What did you do that got him so crazy?"

"Did you see the program this morning?"

"No," she answered.

"I put Joe on the air to give the sermon," he said.

"I don't see anything wrong in that."

"Neither do I," he said. "But apparently your father doesn't see things the way we do."

She was silent for a moment before she spoke. "Well, the reason I called was that I wanted you to know that I have no intention of filing for divorce at this time. No matter what else you may hear from anyone. Including my father."

"Thank you, Jane," he said humbly.

"You don't have to thank me," she said. "Whether you and I can live together is one thing. I still have to do what I believe is right. And, after all, you still are the father of my children and there is no way I'm going to allow any mud to be smeared over them."

She put down the telephone before he had a chance to say

any more. Slowly he turned to the window and looked out as he put his receiver down. Suddenly, he was very tired. He stared out the window for a long moment, then got to his feet.

He left his office and stopped at his secretary's desk on the way out. "I'm going to the parsonage to take a nap," he said. "Hold all the calls for me. I'll be back in a few hours."

"But, Dr. Talbot," she cried, "you haven't returned Mr. Randle's calls yet and now there are a half a dozen more. And what if Mr. Randle calls again?"

"You just tell the truth," he said. "Tell them that I'm tired and I've gone to take a nap and that I'll call them back when I return."

CHAPTER
SIXTEEN

He felt a weariness heavy within him. He turned restlessly on the bed, unable to find the elusive rest he sought. For a moment he seemed to doze, then a pinpoint of light seemed to penetrate the darkness of the room. The light seemed to be growing stronger and he opened his eyes, searching for its source. But it was nowhere to be found; the blackout drapes covering the windows were completely drawn. Still the room seemed to be growing lighter, bathed in a strange golden glow that appeared to be in the air of the room itself. A peculiar surge of power seemed to flow through him, carrying away the heavy weariness.

He sat up in the bed, his eyes suddenly wide, trying to see into the golden light around his bed. He felt himself trembling. "Father?" he asked.

The voice he heard was not a physical sound but words that seemed to form themselves in his brain. "My son."

"I am lost, Father," he said. "I have sinned and I do not know which way to turn."

"I know, my son. The path you have chosen is long and

lonely." The golden light seemed to swirl closer around him. "But the way to truth has always been strewn with thorns and rocks."

"I have tried, Father. But nothing seems to be the way I wanted it to be. I know I have committed many wrongs, Father. But I can't seem to discover what they are."

"Have you looked within yourself, my son?"

"Yes, Father. And many times have I prayed for Your guidance and searched for my answer in Your words. Still when I thought I had found what I sought, it was never all I had prayed it would be." He felt himself still trembling. "Is it possible, Father, that the sins I feared have taken possession of me? That the millions I hid from the church were hidden not to preserve the church but my own power? That my children were conceived by my lust, not my love, and my marriage by my greed?"

The golden light seemed to swirl and ebb and flow with the words forming in his brain. "The answers you seek are not always to be found in my words alone. Sometimes they can be found almost anywhere. Even in the words of your enemies. Though they may give voice to the words of Satan, they may reveal to you the very fears of Satan himself."

"I am too unworthy and too ignorant, Father. I hear in their words only the evil and the sin with which he seeks to entrap the world. I still don't understand."

"Listen again, carefully, to the words of your enemies, my son. And the innermost fears of Satan will reveal themselves to you. And when understanding finally comes to you, let your actions be according to the light you have within you and the love we bear for one another."

The golden glow of light began to soften and fade into the dark of the room. A sudden panic rose in Preacher. "Father! Father! Do not leave me!"

The words in his brain seemed to come from a distance. "I shall never leave you, my son. We shall be together once again."

Then the golden light was gone and Preacher sank back to

his pillow, a strange and beautiful peace and strength inside him. He closed his eyes and slept.

His secretary looked up as he entered the outer office. "Mr. Randle and Dr. Sorensen and Dr. Ryker are waiting in your office."

He paused for a moment, frowning. "Mrs. Hill, I would be very pleased in the future if you would be kind enough to remember that my office is private and that no one, absolutely no one, is to be admitted unless I have given my prior permission. We have a waiting room for just that purpose."

She was flustered. "But, Dr. Talbot, Mr. Randle always—"

He cut her short. "I meant exactly what I said, Mrs. Hill. And that includes Mr. Randle."

The two ministers jumped to their feet as he entered the office but Jake Randle remained seated. Silently Preacher walked behind his desk and sat down. The two ministers remained standing, awkwardly. He gestured to them to take their seats, and didn't speak until they were seated again. He glanced at them. "Gentlemen," he said in a cool voice.

"You didn't return my calls," the old man rasped.

He looked at Randle directly. "I had other things to do."

"Like taking a nap?" Randle asked sarcastically.

"I always attend to matters in the order of their importance," he replied quietly.

Randle flushed. "Why did you choose not to inform the board of your intention to introduce that nigger on the program this morning?"

Preacher met his eyes. "I presume you're referring to Reverend Washington?"

"You know goddamn well who I'm talking about," Randle said angrily. "That nigger is no more a minister than I am."

"Mr. Randle," Preacher said coldly, "Reverend Washington has been officially ordained by this church. That makes him a minister as far as anyone is concerned."

"By whose standards does he qualify to be a minister?"

"By God's standards, Mr. Randle. Our Lord Jesus Christ asked nothing of his disciples except that they have faith in Him and go forth to preach His Gospel. Reverend Washington's faith in our Lord and his ability to preach the Gospel is second to no man's. All of that plus the fact that he, personally, is responsible for bringing many souls to Christ as well as more than six million dollars in contributions to the church in the past two years."

"That still does not explain why you chose not to inform the board of your intention," Randle snapped.

"Mr. Randle," Preacher said, his voice suddenly hard and cold, "I did inform you, but as pastor of this church I am under no obligation to inform the board about anything I may or may not do. Neither do I have the obligation to be bound by any action or recommendation made by the board on behalf of this church. If you will take the trouble to read the articles of incorporation and the by-laws of this church, you will realize that I, alone, have the sole authority to act on behalf of the church and that every appointee to that board as well as the board itself functions at my personal discretion."

The old man's face grew flushed and angry. "You seem to conveniently forget, Dr. Talbot, that it was I who made it possible for you to establish this ministry."

"I haven't forgotten, Mr. Randle, and I shall always be the first to acknowledge the great debt this church has to you. I have said so publicly many times."

"And that the lease under which this ministry occupies these premises known as Churchland has a clause within it that allows for its termination without reason at any time at *my* sole discretion." The old man drew a triumphant breath and glanced at the two ministers, whose silence throughout the meeting had been so absolute that they might as well have not been there.

Preacher came right to the point. "Mr. Randle, if you are suggesting that you would like the Community of God Church of Christian America Triumphant to vacate the premises all you have to do is to send us a letter to that effect and we will do so immediately."

Randle was silent for a moment, staring at Preacher. He knew immediately that his bluff had been called. There was not another ministry with the financial resources available to take over Churchland and the property itself would soon become as worthless as the land on which it had been built. "I didn't suggest that, Dr. Talbot. I proffered that information merely as part of the discussion of our mutual rights. I have no intention of terminating the lease."

"I am pleased to hear that, Mr. Randle," Preacher said quietly.

"I still don't intend to stand quietly by, Dr. Talbot," the old man said harshly, "and permit you to turn this ministry over to the niggers."

"Mr. Randle, I think it about time that you joined the present century," Preacher said in an annoyed voice. "I find your use of that word extremely objectionable, as do many of our ministry and viewers as well, and I am sure, as do my colleagues here in this meeting. I would prefer very much if in the future you will refer to the black people of our ministry in more respectful and acceptable terms."

Randle glanced at the two pastors. They still remained silent. He turned back to Preacher. "I am sure, however, that they agree with me that it was not fair to them to bring the nig—I mean, the black man—on before them. You've placed them both in a very embarrassing position."

Preacher turned to the ministers. "Do you agree with Mr. Randle, gentlemen?"

Dr. Sorensen glanced at Ryker, then spoke. His voice was smooth and conciliatory. "I do feel, Dr. Talbot, that if we all had had an opportunity to go over this matter a much more balanced presentation might have been made."

"What do you mean by 'balanced,' Dr. Sorensen?"

"One that might have mitigated the shock a white audience might feel at seeing and hearing a black minister on a program as important as this one."

Preacher nodded. "I see." He turned to the other minister. "And you, Dr. Ryker, I would like your opinion."

Dr. Ryker's voice was professorial in texture. He sounded like a man who had spent years in a classroom. "One of the important parts of our work in Christian schools and colleges has been the study of what we loosely designate as cultural shock. This is a classic case of the wrong man in the wrong place at the wrong time. Asking a basically white congregation to listen to a black man preach to them about God, who created man in His own image, is essentially a very difficult thing for them to accept because it is a psychological affront to the man he sees in the mirror every morning."

Preacher was casual. "But the reverse does not create a problem?"

"Not at all, Dr. Talbot," Ryker said. "It is a role that has been made acceptable by years of tradition."

"Does that make it right, Dr. Ryker?" Preacher asked. "After all, in the Scriptures it does say that God created man in His own image. But nowhere in the Scriptures have I ever read that the man He created was white, black, yellow, red or green."

"We're trying to be practical, Dr. Talbot," Sorensen said smoothly, "not theological." He took a deep breath. "The fact remains that if we alienate a large portion of our white audience we may also suffer a sizable loss of income."

Preacher looked at him. "Dr. Sorensen," he said dryly, "this is a ministry, not the Harvard School of Business. Our principal concern is saving souls for Christ, not the accumulation of large bank balances."

"Without those balances, Dr. Talbot," Randle said, "you know from your own experience how much more difficult it is to reach those souls who are in most need of saving."

Preacher looked at each of them in turn and then spoke slowly. "Gentlemen, more than seventy percent of the churches affiliated with the Community of God Church are black ministries. I cannot believe that the soul of any man is different from the soul of any other man because of the color of his skin. And as long as these people are part of the Community of God, I feel they are entitled to representation in our ministry."

"You let them in now," Randle said angrily, "and the next thing you know they'll take over the whole church. You know how they are. Sell them one house on a street and in a few months the whole neighborhood is swarming with them. Dick Craig and Helen Lacey are already threatening to pull the support of their organizations away from us. That's more than two million white people who will turn their backs on this ministry. These people are the backbone of the conservative Christian majority and in no way are they going to allow themselves to be seated in a pew next to a nig—a black person."

"Then we are wasting time squabbling among ourselves, gentlemen," Preacher said. "We really have our work cut out for us. In that nationwide Crusade for Christ that I plan for next Labor Day one of our most important objectives will be to make every Christian see that the God he loves is the same God who loves all men."

"You don't expect me to go along with that?" Randle snapped.

"Think about it carefully, Mr. Randle," Preacher said. "In just one day we have the opportunity to gather a million souls for Christ. And, in that same day, the opportunity to raise perhaps as much as fifty million dollars to enable us to continue our labors for Christ."

Randle stared at him for a moment, then settled back in his chair. "You never explained that."

"It's simple enough," Preacher smiled. "If one championship prizefight can get twenty-five million dollars, try to imagine how many millions of dollars more one championship fight between our Lord and Satan will draw?"

Randle didn't answer but Preacher could almost see the computer in his head clicking away behind the old man's veiled eyes. "With the proper organization and planning we should be able to command a television audience of fifty million people via satellite relay as well as fill every major sports arena in the country."

"It's an extremely ambitious plan, Dr. Talbot," Sorensen said, "and one I am highly in favor of. But I wonder, isn't it perhaps too large a project for any single ministry to undertake? I feel our chances of success would be even greater if several of the other large television ministries could be persuaded to join us."

"A point very well taken, Dr. Sorensen," Preacher said. "I would appreciate it if you could form an ad hoc committee to approach other ministries about joining the Crusade. I think a fair share of the total proceeds could be arrived at for their participation."

"If that approach is taken, I feel we have to offer the pastors of those ministries an important position on the program," Ryker said.

"An excellent suggestion, Dr. Ryker. I would be honored to have many of those ministers whose work and devotion to Christ I have for so long admired join with me in this great Crusade."

Ryker glanced at Sorensen. "I am sure that Dr. Sorensen will agree with me when I say that such great ministers as Jerry Falwell, Oral Roberts, Rex Humbard, Bob Shuller and perhaps even Dr. Billy Graham would give this project their most attentive personal consideration."

"And I wouldn't forget Paul Crouch and Fred Price out in California either," Preacher said. "They pack a heavy clout out there." He waited for their reactions. The Reverend Price was the black minister in Los Angeles who was already on thirty-five stations and whose church in Crenshaw wasn't large enough to contain all the well-to-do middle-class blacks of his congregation who began lining up in the street long before the church opened its doors every Sunday morning.

"Of course," Sorensen said quickly. "It's a most exciting project and the more stars we can get, the better."

Preacher smiled. There was no mention of the fact that the Reverend Fred Price was black at all. Apparently money had the power to cut across all color lines. Something clicked in his head. Exactly what was it that the voice in his strange dream had told him? "Listen again, carefully, to the words of your enemies, my son."

The smile left his lips. "I am listening, Father," he whispered almost to himself. "I only pray that I'll know the right use to make of them."

"Were you speaking, Dr. Talbot?" Ryker asked.

Preacher shook his head. "Not really. I was just thinking aloud."

Randle got to his feet. He was not about to be left out of this discussion. "I'm sure that my television station group can also persuade many television and motion picture stars to appear on the show. I can almost see it before my eyes right now. The greatest preachers in the world, all together, on one big show. It will make religious television history." He paused suddenly as if struck by an idea. "We'll have to go two hours," he said. "There's no way a show like that can be done in one hour. Maybe we'll even have to go longer."

"That's entirely possible," Preacher agreed. "But we'll have to find the time."

"That's only money," Randle said disdainfully. "What's a million or two more when you're shooting for the moon?"

Preacher looked at them and smiled. "Isn't it better, gentlemen, to work together in peace and creative harmony than to meet with each other with bitter recriminations and destructive anger?"

CHAPTER
SEVENTEEN

"Just because you made him stop callin' us niggers ain't goin' to stop that man," Joe said. "He's a born hater, that one. He ain't goin' to let go until he got me swingin' from a tree with a rope around my neck and you cookin' over a fire nailed to a burnin' cross."

Preacher watched him take a massive bite from the rare half-pound cheeseburger that left less than half the giant sandwich in his hand. It seemed as if he almost didn't chew it at all before it went down. Preacher glanced at Beverly, picking daintily at her salad, then back at Joe. "I'm glad all that talk of gore hasn't affected your appetite," he said, smiling.

Joe washed his throat with half a bottle of beer before he spoke. "You know what I say is true, Preacher. That man is bad. The only reason he ain't dumpin' down on us right now is because he smells money."

"I'm not disagreeing with you, Joe," Preacher said. "But if I spend my time worrying about all the haters in this world, I'll never have time to get my work done."

"Mark my words," Joe said darkly. "Just as soon as that Crusade is over, he's goin' to make his move."

"You're wrong." Preacher shook his head. "He's going to move before that."

Joe stared at him. "You know somethin' I don't?"

"No," Preacher answered. "But it's logical. He's only going to wait until he's sure that nothing can stop the Crusade from going forward. Then he's got to get rid of us. Because he knows that if we get the credit for pulling this off, there's nothing he can ever do to touch us."

"Shit!" Joe said in disgust. "And here I been thinkin' I got three months at least in which to play it safe."

Preacher smiled. "There's nothing that says that we can't prepare ourselves for him, though."

"How can you prepare yourself when you don't know what he's goin' to do?" Joe asked. "That man's a snake. You don't know from which direction he's goin' to come at you."

"True enough," Preacher said. "All we can do is shore up our defenses so that we're ready no matter how he attacks."

"Like in 'Nam," Joe said. "String wire all around the perimeter, front and back. He's got to trip over at least one of them."

"Hopefully," Preacher said.

"I got a better idea and it's simpler," Joe said. "Let me plant a plastic cookie under the back seat of that big stretch-out of his. Then the next time he gets in the car and puts his ass down on that seat, boom! It'll be the biggest bowel movement that son of a bitch ever had."

Preacher laughed, shaking his head. "You never change, Joe. Can't you just once remember that you're a man of God now? And that isn't what men of God do."

"Okay," Joe said. "Give me a better idea."

"Let's try to take care of ourselves," Preacher said, "and leave him to heaven."

"Amen," Joe said. "Now tell me what we're going to do."

"First, lock the door," Preacher said. "I don't want anyone walking in on us."

They had been having lunch in the library at the parsonage. Preacher waited until Joe had locked the door and come back to the table. Then he rose from his own chair and pushed aside a panel on the bookshelf wall, revealing a safe. Quickly he spun the dial, opened the door, took out some papers, then returned everything to its normal position and came back to the table. He handed the papers across the table to Beverly, who looked at them. "Recognize them?" he asked.

She raised her head and nodded silently.

"A long time ago we decided to prepare ourselves in case something like this was ever going to happen," he said. "Well, it's happening right now."

She nodded again.

"I don't know what the hell you two are talkin' about," Joe said.

Preacher looked at him. "I want to give the Community of God Church to the affiliates."

Joe stared at him. "Now I know you're nuts, man. You're givin' away fifty million dollars. Maybe more."

"I don't need the money," Preacher said. "And I want it set up so that each church that acquires a share sets it up in a trust for the poor of its community."

"Then what do you get out of it?" Joe asked.

"If everything goes the way I planned it," Preacher said, "I'll have exactly what I started out with. Nothing."

Joe shook his head sadly. "Preacher, Preacher, you don't change neither. You got about as much sense now as when I met you in 'Nam. None at all."

Preacher looked at Beverly. "It will be a lot of work. First, you'll have to arrange to get the money to the affiliated churches. Then a trust has to be set up which will acquire the shares in the Community. I think you know how to do that."

"Yes," Beverly answered. "We make an anonymous donation to the churches from this account. At the same time the church trust turns this money back to us for your shares in the Community."

"That's right," Preacher said.

"Then what do you want done with that money?" she asked. "It's made a round trip right back to you."

"Put it in a bank account in trust for my children with their mother as trustee," he said. "I also want you and Joe to have a share." He turned to Joe. "You'll have to work out the agreements with the affiliates," he said. "But I don't think you'll have any problem with that."

"What problem?" Joe laughed shortly. "Shit, man. By the time I finish givin' them all that money, they goin' to think I'm Santa Claus."

"There is just one thing though," Preacher said. "I want it all signed, sealed and delivered before the Crusade."

"That doesn't give us much time," Beverly said. "It means that for the next three months Joe and I will have time for nothing else."

"That's right," Preacher nodded. He looked at them. "Can you do it?"

Beverly and Joe looked at each other for a moment. Then Joe nodded and she turned back to Preacher. "We'll do it."

He smiled. "Good."

Suddenly her eyes misted over and she ran into his arms. She kissed his cheek and he felt the wetness of her tears. "You know we love you, Preacher."

Joe came and put his giant arms around both of them. His voice was husky. "That's right, you crazy man. We sure do love you. But tell me why, man. Why you givin' everything away? Nobody'll appreciate it and in the end you'll get nothing but shit for it."

Preacher felt the warmth of their love. His eyes misted over. He wanted them to understand.

"Remember when we had the gospel tent and we used to fight about giving money to the local churches?" he asked. He didn't wait for them to answer. "Don't you see? This is the same thing. We're only returning the money to the churches and the congregations it rightfully belongs to."

Marcus was in the waiting room when he got back to his office after lunch. "I have those figures for you," he said.

"Come inside," Preacher said, leading the way into his office. He closed the door behind him and walked around his desk. He looked into Marcus' face for a moment. "Okay, how bad was it?"

"We got hurt," Marcus said. "Nationally we normally lose ten percent of our audience the second half-hour as against the first, this time twenty-three percent. Do you want the breakdown by market?"

Preacher nodded.

Marcus read from the typewritten sheet in his hand. "I'll begin with the worst and work my way up," he said. "The South, normal loss 5 percent, this time 46 percent; the Southwest, normal loss 15 percent, this time 37 percent; the Midwest, normal loss 2 percent, this time 31 percent; the Coast, normal loss 2 percent, this time 20 percent; the Mid-Atlantic, normal loss 7 percent, this time 19 percent; the Northeast, normal loss 15 percent, this time 17 percent. The only bright spots were the urban centers. Philadelphia, New York, Boston, Detroit, Chicago and L.A., mostly all were normal, with Detroit and Chicago even up a little."

Preacher nodded. The figures checked out with all the other reports, the telephone message center, and the overnight letters and collections. Based on the first day's collection report, the computer extrapolated a drop this week of at least forty percent. He looked at Marcus and smiled wryly. "Maybe I was in too much of a hurry," he said. "Perhaps I should have taken the time to build the audience up to it. Doing the right thing doesn't always work out that way."

"I think the results would have been the same whenever you did it," Marcus said. "The crackpots and lunatics are always out there waiting to tear you up. Anyway, you did it and it's behind you now. Let's wait and see what happens next week. Who are you putting on?"

"Sorensen," Preacher said.

"A perfect choice," Marcus said. "He's a special favorite of the far right, the dyed-in-the-wool conservatives and the Moral Majority. I suggest that we hit heavy with advertising and on-the-air radio promos all this week and he'll get you numbers."

Preacher nodded. "You take care of it."

"I've already put it in the works," Marcus said.

"Good," Preacher said. "How long do you think it will be before these numbers get around?"

"If I know Carrol," Marcus said, "he's on his way out to the Randle Ranch right now."

Preacher shook his head. "That's not going to help our case much."

"We've got a saying in the television business that we took from the newspaper business," Marcus said. "The hell with it. It's yesterday's news. We've got another show to get on."

"Can't argue with that," Preacher said. The telephone on his desk rang. He picked it up, listened for a moment, then handed it to Marcus. "It's for you."

"Yes," Marcus said into the phone. He listened for a moment, then put it down and looked at Preacher. "The tower just called to let us know that our lady's six minutes away from touchdown, so I guess we might as well get on out there."

"Might as well," Preacher said despondently.

"Don't be so down," Marcus said, trying to change his mood. They stepped into the private elevator. "You might have some fun. I have a feeling the lady's hot to trot. Living with a fag can't be all that easy."

Preacher shot him a glance. Apparently it wasn't as much of a secret as she thought, or maybe she'd meant it was a secret only as far as the public was concerned. "If she is," he said, "then you're going to have to put her through her paces."

"But she's not interested in me," Marcus laughed. "She's got big eyes for you."

They came out of the elevator and went out the side entrance, where the chauffeur was waiting with the limousine. "It's not going to do her much good then," Preacher said as they got into the car. "I've got about all the trouble I can handle."

But he was wrong. He didn't know how she did it but Kim managed to have him ask her to dinner at the parsonage that night. They had coffee in the library and she came up with a couple of super sinsemillas. They were in bed together before midnight.

CHAPTER
EIGHTEEN

The two men were leaving his office the next morning as he came in. He paused at his secretary's desk. "Who are they?" he asked.

"Telephone men, Dr. Talbot," she answered in an excited voice. "We're the first office to get the new phones. They're on their way to the parsonage now to make the installation there."

"I was perfectly happy with the old phones," he said.

"You'll love these, Dr. Talbot," she said. "They're completely automatic and so easy to operate. And best of all, they're voice-activated. You don't have to pick up the receiver to answer it, just the sound of your voice alone will do it and if you want to speak privately when there's someone in the office, all you do is pick up the receiver. Then there's a printout screen that shows the number you just dialed and if you get a busy, it will redial the same number automatically for you every fifteen seconds until it's answered. It has everything, including an answering device that will take messages when you're away from your desk. All the secretaries are as excited about it as I am. It will make our work so much easier for us."

"That's good," he said. "By the way, Mrs. Hill, who ordered this equipment?"

"The new treasurer, Mr. Duncan," she answered. "There was a team of efficiency experts in here the week before last and Friday we received a memo that a new phone system was going to be installed starting today and that the installation throughout all the offices should be completed in less than two weeks."

"That's wonderful," he said unenthusiastically. "Would you get Mr. Duncan on the phone for me? Or do I just have to snap my fingers at it?"

"No, Dr. Talbot," she giggled. "There are some things we secretaries still have to do."

He went into his office and sat behind the desk. The new instrument looked like a miniaturized version of a call director. While he was staring at it, it began to ring. He didn't touch the phone, as she had directed him. "Yes?"

"I have Mr. Duncan for you on line one."

"Good," he said. "Put him on." He paused for a moment. "Sutter?"

The indicator light for line one stopped flashing and turned into a steady glow. "Dr. Talbot, how do you like the new equipment?"

"It's something else," Preacher said. "It had to cost a lot of money."

"Close to a million dollars," Duncan replied. "But the resulting efficiencies will recover the cost for us in less than eighteen months and the savings after that could run between three hundred fifty and five hundred thousand a year. The telephone company equipment rental charges amounted to a quarter million a year alone—against a service and maintenance contract for the new system of a hundred thousand."

"That sounds good," Preacher said. "But what guarantees do we have that the company will still be in business when we need them?"

Duncan laughed. "I can't imagine Mr. Randle would enter

into a fly-by-night proposition. He has the sole sales and distribution rights to this line for the entire state of Texas and is
negotiating with the manufacturers in Japan for the rights to
all of the Southwest."

"That's good enough for me, Sutter," Preacher said.
"Thanks for putting me first on your list."

"Wouldn't have it any other way, Dr. Talbot. As a matter
of fact, Mr. Randle insisted on it."

"Thanks anyway, Sutter. Goodbye."

"Goodbye, Dr. Talbot." The indicator light went out.

Preacher leaned back in his chair. The old man was no fool.
If he was going to lift a million-dollar contract, he was going
to make sure that Preacher could not object to it. Once the
equipment was installed in his office, there was no way he
could have it removed. Still, a contract of that size should
have been brought before the board for approval, but the old
man had been shrewd enough to calculate that if Preacher
objected to the expenditure he could always backtrack and
agree to let them have the new equipment for the same
amount they were paying the telephone company.

The telephone rang again. "Mrs. Hickox, Mr. Lincoln and
Mr. Carrol are here for their appointment."

"Show them in," he replied, rising.

The door opened and Kim came in first, the others following. He came around his desk and kissed her cheek, then led
them to a conversational grouping at the far side of the office.
He waved them to the couch and seated himself in a chair
opposite them. "Well." He smiled. "How did it go?"

"Unbelievably well, Dr. Talbot," she said. "Marcus and
Sanford couldn't have been nicer and the technical staff they
have assembled are second to none I have ever seen, even in
Hollywood. I'm so excited that I'm ready to begin even sooner
than we agreed if you want."

"That is good news," he said. He turned to Marcus. "How
do you feel about it?"

"Both Sanford and I agree that it might not be a bad idea,"
Marcus replied. "We've had a fantastic week. We've already

worked out the show format and the set is under construction right now. We also have Kim's two writers collaborating with three of our own on storyboards and scripts. And Kim came up with a genius of an idea that will take the show right through the roof. I think you ought to hear it from her."

Preacher turned back to her. "It must be something very special to turn him on like that."

She played it modestly. "It's really not that much. The idea itself was so simple and so obvious one of us would have picked it up in a matter of time."

"Maybe," Sanford said. "But still you saw it first."

Preacher smiled. "Now tell me."

"As you know we plan to shoot the five shows in two days. Two the first day and three the next," she said. "There are many reasons, including costs, which make that a very practical way to operate. Also we have more time to plan the following week's programs. That was how I got the idea. Since it involved only two days' work, why shouldn't we have an important star as guest of the week? First, it will be easier to get someone of the caliber we seek for two days than for the whole week simply because we don't demand that much of their time and second, we can make it attractive to them because we pay them way over scale for the two days—which massages their ego—while we might not be able to afford them if we kept them for a full week."

"That is a fantastic idea," he said. "What kind of stars are you talking about?"

"Not the stars you usually see on the usual TV gospel circuit. I've already called my agents in Hollywood as well as a number of personal friends, and it's just possible we can get people like Charlton Heston, whose most famous role was that of Moses in *The Ten Commandments,* to do selected readings from the script of that film, Carol Burnett to talk about her fight against drug abuse in children and the personal struggle to free her own daughter from the problem, Danny Thomas about his work for St. Jude's Children's Hospital, singers like

Aretha Franklin, Johnny Cash, Tammy Wynette, recreating the inspirational songs of their old gospel days."

"You got me." Preacher smiled. "When do we start?"

"With luck and God's help," she said, "I could be ready to shoot a pilot the week after next. The big problem as I see it is, if we do decide to start earlier, can we get air time?"

"That's not my department," Preacher said. "Gentlemen, what do you think?"

Marcus passed on that question. "I think Sanford is much closer to the market situation than I am."

Sanford cleared his throat. "We might have a better chance than we think. After all, we are going into the summer months and the recession has hurt the sale of television time as much as it has everything else. If you'll give me a few days to investigate the situation thoroughly, I'll be able to get you a better fix on it. But I have to approach it cautiously. I wouldn't want any of the stations to think that we have to have the time or they'll push their rates through the roof."

"You take all the time you need," Preacher said. "Meanwhile let's all of us keep on working as if we're going to make it on the air this summer."

The telephone rang. "Dr. Talbot," his secretary's voice said, "your next appointment is here."

"Show them to the waiting room," he said. "I'll be just a few minutes more." He turned back to them. "I can't tell you how pleased and excited I am about the tremendous enthusiasm and progress you have shown on this project. I just know we're going to have a very big hit on our hands."

He got to his feet and they rose with him. "Now, remember to keep me posted. I want to be right with you all the way."

He walked with them to the door and opened it. "We'll talk some more soon," he said.

Marcus and Sanford were already outside the office when Kim turned back to him. "I'm flying back to L.A. tomorrow morning," she said in a low voice. "Do you think we can manage dinner tonight?"

"I don't see why not." He smiled. "Eight o'clock at the parsonage?"

"I'll be there," she whispered. "I can almost taste your cock right now."

She was gone before he had a chance to reply. The door to the waiting room opened and Melanie and Charlie came out just as Kim left the secretary's office. He waited at the open door for them to come into his office. He closed the door and kissed both girls on the cheek.

He led them to the conversational grouping and took his place again on the chair facing the couch. "Have they been keeping you busy, children?"

"Not as much as we'd like," Charlie said. "I don't know whether it's because someone's put the word out on us or there's just not much to do."

He didn't answer.

"Been seein' much of that lady, Preacher?" Melanie asked.

"A little," he answered. "On and off."

"Better watch out for her," Melanie said. "She's real bad news."

"That's right," Charlie added. "She's a bona fide minister groupie. They say she's balled the ministers of every show she's ever been on and it's cost some of them a lot of bread to get rid of her."

He was silent for a moment, looking at them, then rose to his feet. "How would you girls like to take a little walk outside with me? I feel like a little fresh air."

Mrs. Hill's voice came from the telephone. "Dr. Sorensen's on the line. He would like to talk to you."

"I'll get back to him in about fifteen minutes," he said. He looked at the girls. "Just for once I would like to be able to talk without being bugged by the telephone."

The girls nodded their understanding. "We'd love a little fresh air ourselves, Preacher."

They came out of his private entrance and walked down the path on the rolling lawn to the fountain. "Pretty, isn't it?" he asked, watching the sunlight dancing in its spray.

"Beautiful," Melanie said.

"It's nicer from that hill over there," he said.

Silently, they followed him about five hundred yards up the hill. He turned and looked down at the fountain, then up at the building. Nothing could be seen behind its black windows. "There's a bench just behind that cluster of trees," he said.

The bench could not be seen from the building. He sat down and they sat next to him. He turned toward them, his face serious. "I've got a very important job for you to do for me."

They nodded attentively, without speaking.

"I'll have to be brief," he said, "because I've got appointments stacked up like crazy, so listen carefully. I want you to leave here, each of you separately, one of you tomorrow, the other a few days later. Say nothing to anyone, just pack your things and go. Arrange to meet in San Antonio and, wherever you stay, register under false names. When you are together, call Beverly at home in Los Altos. She will wire you fifty thousand dollars under whatever name you use. Use that money to buy the most completely equipped Winnebago you can find, one big enough for the three of us to live in. Register it under a false name and move into a trailer park. Then call Beverly again and let her know where you are and wait there for me."

"What's it all about, Preacher?" Charlie asked in a concerned voice.

"I haven't got the time to go into it, but don't worry. We're not in any danger." He looked at them. "Do you understand what I want you to do?"

"We've got it, Preacher," Melanie said. "Do you want me to run it back for you?"

"Please."

Quickly, she repeated his instructions without missing a point. "Okay?" she asked when she had finished.

"Perfect," he said, taking an envelope out of his pocket. "There's a thousand dollars in cash in there to cover your expenses. Just one more thing. Go there by a roundabout way and don't forget to tell each other what names each of you is going to use."

They laughed together. "We won't forget, Preacher," Charlie said.

He got to his feet and looked down at them. "Thanks," he said. "If you don't mind, I'll leave you here, children. I've got to get back to the office."

"Preacher," Melanie called as he started away, "is your office bugged?"

He stopped to look back at her. "I think so. They just installed new phones today. And I didn't order them."

She was silent for a moment. "When can we expect you?"

He shook his head. "I don't know, but I have the feeling it won't be long."

They watched him turn down the path and didn't begin to rise from the bench until he had disappeared behind the cluster of trees.

CHAPTER
NINETEEN

"The board meeting will begin in ten minutes, Dr. Talbot."
Mrs. Hill's voice came from the phone.

"I'm just checking some papers, Mrs. Hill. I'll be ready to leave in just a few minutes."

"Don't forget they're planning to run the pilot of the Hickox show before the official business."

"I haven't forgotten, Mrs. Hill," he answered. "Thank you." He finished putting the last of the papers in his folder when the phone rang again. "Yes, Mrs. Hill?"

"Mrs. Washington is on the line from Los Altos," his secretary said. "She says that it's extremely important that she speak with you before the meeting."

"I'll take it, Mrs. Hill." He pressed the button. This time he picked up the telephone. "Yes, Beverly?"

She sounded frightened and out of breath. "Some men were just here and took Joe away."

"What are you talking about? What men?" he asked.

"I don't know," she half sobbed. "They said they were police when we opened the door. There were three of them. One of them took a piece of paper out of his pocket and said it was a warrant for his arrest on the charge of acts of terrorism he committed years ago and a charge of bigamy by his ex-wife in South Carolina. He told them they were full of shit, he had never been legally married, and besides there was no way those two charges could be on a single warrant because they came under the jurisdiction of different courts. The man who told him about the warrant took a pair of handcuffs from his pocket and told him not to give him any nigger crap and hold out his hands. 'You ain't no cops, you sons of bitches, you never even read me my rights,' Joe yelled, and he swung at the man with the handcuffs and knocked him down. One of the other men hit Joe over the head with the butt of his gun, knocking him unconscious. Then the first man got to his feet and put the handcuffs on Joe and they began to drag him to the door. I began to scream and one of the men came back and slapped me on the face. 'You better shut your mouth, you chink bitch,' he said. 'And get on the phone to your friend, Dr. Talbot. He's the only man who can get your husband back to you alive.' Then they dragged Joe out the door and dumped him into the back seat of a car and drove off with him."

"Did you see the make of the car or the license plate?"

"It was a black car," she said. "I couldn't tell what kind. And the license plate was all smeared over with mud." She began to cry into the receiver. "What's happening, Preacher?"

"I don't know," he said. "But you stay there and calm down. And don't worry. I'll find out and get him back to you."

"But he was bleeding. The blood was running all down his face from a cut on his head."

"He'll be all right," Preacher said soothingly. "I know him. He's got a skull made of cast iron. Now you wait there until I call you back."

He put the receiver down slowly and picked up the folder. This was only the first gun fired. He wondered what would be next. And, oddly enough, he didn't think he would have to wait very long to find out.

He looked down the long director's table at Randle as the picture faded from the giant projection screen and the lights came up. The old man's eyes were closed. From the glimpses Preacher managed to catch of him during the program, he seemed to have slept through most of it.

"I think it's a very good show, gentlemen. The Hickoxes came across as sincerely warm and likable people. And best of all, it was really entertaining. It has a little of everything that makes successful television. A little game show, some very good songs by Jimmy, a great deal of heart from that lady whose strength was sustained by Jesus while her little boy was dying of cancer, and a fine touch of comedy in the skit where the Hickoxes deal with the plumber fixing their dishwasher. The show should get good ratings." Preacher glanced around the table. "I would like to go with the show for the summer."

"I, for one, am a little disappointed, Dr. Talbot," Sorensen said. "Personally I would prefer a greater emphasis on religion and less on fun and games. After all, this is a church-sponsored program."

"That's exactly the point we're trying to make, Dr. Sorensen," Preacher said. "There are enough personality programs on the air right now with a heavy religious slant. I think people are fed up with them and turn them off. People want to be entertained today; they have too many problems of their own to be lectured to constantly. Don't forget we'll have four full commercial minutes on every show. That will get our message across."

"I'm not that sure," Sorensen said.

"Why don't we try it this way for a few shows? If it doesn't work, we can change it quickly enough."

"Is there some way we could incorporate a number of references about the Crusade into it?" Sorensen asked. "If we could do that, I would be inclined to go along with you."

"That's up to our experts," Preacher said. "Mr. Lincoln, Mr. Carrol, what are your thoughts?"

"I think Dr. Sorensen's idea can be accommodated without interfering with the flow of the program," Carrol said.

"I agree," Marcus said. "It would take a little work but it can be done."

"Good," Preacher said. "Then if Dr. Sorensen agrees, the chair will entertain a motion to put the show on the air as soon as possible."

Dr. Sorensen made the motion, it was seconded by Dr. Ryker and Mrs. Lacey and carried by a unanimous vote with only Lincoln and Carrol abstaining for propriety's sake, since it was their work. As usual, the chair had no vote unless it was needed to break a tie.

Preacher looked down at his notes. "Dr. Ryker has agreed that Dr. Sorensen will give us the progress report on the Crusade."

Dr. Sorensen rose. "It gives me great pleasure to report to this board that of the fifteen major television ministries on the air, eleven have given their consent to join us. Five of the pastors of those ministries have agreed to join us here on the dais in Churchland, the others will contribute short videotape clips to be incorporated into the program because of their commitments on the same day to their own ministries. Contracts have been submitted to more than thirty-one major arenas and theaters throughout the land to carry the Crusade, giving us a potential live audience of more than two million people. An average admission of five dollars will be charged, of which we will receive forty percent, a potential receipt from this source alone of four million dollars. No admission will be charged, of course, in our affiliated churches. However, in addition to our regularly programmed stations, various cable systems and normal television stations have expressed interest in also broadcasting our Crusade and various financial arrangements are in the process of negotiation. But I can safely say that we can conservatively estimate receipts of ten million dollars from these sources. We are also entertaining offers for syndication from various religious broadcasting companies both here and abroad and there is a possible additional million dollars in income from this source. Of course, none of the foregoing includes any income we might receive from the normal broadcasting of this Crusade whose present audience potential could be as much as forty million people. I don't have to tell you that an average contribution of one dollar per person is not too much to expect. The guest committee has received over six hundred acceptances from important officials of national, state and local governments and other important public personalities to attend the Crusade here in Churchland. The program committee has now begun its work and we expect to have the final breakdown on the time allotted to each facet of the Crusade, speakers, music and entertainment." He sat down to a ripple of applause from around the table.

Preacher rose to his feet. "The chair expresses its personal appreciation to Dr. Sorensen for his fine report and to him, Dr. Ryker and their various committees and assistants our gratitude for their magnificent and unselfish efforts on behalf of this ministry." He paused for a moment. "If there is no further business to come before this board, the chair will entertain a motion to adjourn."

The meeting over, members of the board began to file from the room as Preacher put his papers back into the folder. He picked it up and was about to rise from his chair when Randle spoke to him.

"Do you have a moment for us?"

Preacher looked down the table at the old man. Dick Craig and Mrs. Lacey were seated on either side of him. Drs. Sorensen and Ryker had remained in their regular seats. "Of course," he answered, sinking back into his own chair.

Randle gestured at the door and Ryker, who was nearest, jumped up and closed it. He returned to his seat. For a long while Randle looked across the table at Preacher. When he finally began to speak, his voice held a curious mixture of power and triumph. "Certain information has come to our attention, Dr. Talbot, that makes us question the future value of yourself and your associate, Reverend Washington, to this ministry. As a matter of fact, this is an understatement. The information of which I speak convinces us that you and your associate are unfit to be associated with this ministry and that if this information should become public knowledge it would lead to the destruction of this church and put an end forever to all its potential to continue its work to bring the Gospel of our Lord Jesus Christ to the people of America."

Preacher's voice was calm. "I presume you have that information of which you speak available."

"Of course," Randle said. He opened his folder and pushed a bound report to Ryker, who in turn handed it to Preacher.

Preacher opened the report and looked down at it. It was a report by a well-known private detective firm. The subject of the report was Reverend Josephus Washington aka Ali Elijah. The brief summary of the report contained in a paragraph stated that Joe had committed acts of violence while a member of the Black Muslims and had been on the wanted list of the FBI, and that during that time he had been living with a woman, Leah Turner, who bore him two children. Recently he was married to a Beverly Lee.

He closed the report, having read enough. He gestured to the report. "Are these the same people who kidnapped Reverend Washington from his home this morning and are holding him illegally against his will?"

"Not kidnapped, Dr. Talbot," Randle said. "Detaining him so that he can be turned over to the authorities."

"In that case, why haven't they done so?"

"Because I made them aware of the harm that could do to this ministry," Randle replied. "They are decent Christian men and see no reason to bring harm to many for the crimes of one man, even one as despicable as he."

"They are good men," Preacher said sarcastically. "Of course, you had nothing to do with this affair?"

Randle stared at him without answering, his mouth tight and grim. He seemed to be scarcely breathing.

"Do I assume your silence means that you did?"

"You can assume whatever you please," Randle said heavily. He took a folded package of papers from in front of him. Ryker picked it up and gave it to Preacher.

Preacher looked down at it. The green heavy legal binding over the folded papers was an unfiled petition for divorce in the matter of *Talbot* v. *Talbot*. He opened the papers. The grounds were repeated and various counts of adultery and cruel and inhuman treatment. He put them down. "My wife told me that under no circumstances would she file for divorce at the present time, no matter what I might hear from anyone, even you."

"She hasn't—yet," the old man said. "But I think she will change her mind when she sees this." He took a videotape cartridge and gave it to Ryker, who placed it in the videotape player. Randle turned to Mrs. Lacey. "You might want to leave the room, Mrs. Lacey. You do not have to subject yourself to perversions of this sort."

"No," Mrs. Lacey said firmly. "As one of the founding board members of this ministry I feel it is my duty to know all the facts no matter how much I may feel repulsed by them."

Preacher was impassive. Suddenly he knew what was coming. Randle had not only bugged his telephones, he'd had a videotape camera placed in his bedroom.

Randle nodded. Ryker started the tape, at the same time turning off the lights in the room. He went back to his chair and sat down.

The screen spit black-and-white flashes, then suddenly rapid spots of color. A moment later the picture came on. But there was very little to be seen, just faint outlines of bodies moving almost indistinguishably in the dark; then a woman's voice was heard. "Your cock feels so big in my mouth I have to see it."

Suddenly light flooded the screen. Now the figures could be plainly seen. He was naked on his knees in the bed, his back to the camera, hiding Kim, her head on the pillow before him, her hands hidden by his pelvis. She moved suddenly, turning him, so that now he was facing into the camera while she held his erect phallus in her hands, then she rolled over on her back and, raising her legs high, guided him into her. She closed her eyes as he began to thrust.

"You can stop now," Randle said. "I think we've seen enough."

Preacher was silent. Kim had set him up. He could see by the way she'd positioned him so that he faced directly into the camera that she had known exactly where it was.

Randle looked at him. "Do you still think she will not file for divorce after seeing that?"

"I can't answer for Jane," Preacher said. "What I would like to know is what you promised Kim Hickox for doing that?"

Again Randle didn't answer.

"Or could it be that she is merely a good Christian woman sacrificing herself for the benefit of the ministry?" He laughed shortly. "I had been warned about that lady. Apparently this was not the first time she sought God in a minister's bed."

Randle broke his silence. "We do not want to be too harsh on you. And we are interested in protecting the ministry. So we will not ask you and your friend to resign at this particular time. We will settle for your resignation to take effect the day after the Crusade. Of course, we expect to have the letter of resignation in our hands immediately."

"And if I don't?"

"Your wife will get the tape," Randle said. "And the nigger will be turned over to the police."

Preacher was silent for a moment. "What if I tell you that I don't give a damn? Go ahead."

Randle stared at him. "You'll destroy the church."

"No," Preacher said. "I won't. You will. From the very beginning I should have known that it was not God's word you cared about. Only the money and the power His word could give you."

"One of those men with your friend lost two members of his family in a bomb blast set by the Black Muslims," Randle said, ignoring Preacher's words. "Your friend's wife will be lucky if all they do is turn him over to the police. She may never see him alive again."

Preacher looked into his eyes. "You're a strange man, Jake. Murder one. Murder two. That means nothing to you, does it?"

"My only concern is this church," Randle said.

"And your daughter?"

"She chose to marry you. I didn't," Randle answered. "She'll have to pay for her own sins."

"And whose sins will you pay for, Jake?" Preacher asked. "You don't intend to pay for your own."

Randle didn't answer.

"First, there's one thing I want from you, Jake," Preacher said. "I want to announce on the air next Sunday that I'm going into a retreat for rest and meditation until the day of the Crusade."

"I won't object to that," Randle said.

"Thanks," Preacher said sarcastically.

"Now, do we get the letter of resignation?"

"Yes," Preacher said. He got to his feet. He walked to the door and opened it, looking back at them. "Quite a telephone company you have, Jake. What other goodies do you have installed around here that even your friends don't know about?"

Randle shrugged off the remark. "When can we expect the letter?"

"Just as soon as I hear from Beverly that Joe is home, safe and sound," Preacher said, walking out and closing the door behind him.

CHAPTER
TWENTY

The green Buick sedan turned into the RV park on the Pacific Coast Highway just north of San Diego and drove down the narrow paved road to where the silver-and-black Winnebago was parked at the edge of a bluff overlooking the beach and the ocean. The car stopped and Joe, who had been driving, was the first to get out. A moment later Beverly and Tarz stood beside him.

Joe squinted at the Winnebago. "That must be it. The only silver-and-black one I see."

"Why don't we just knock on the door and find out?" Beverly suggested.

They walked up to the Winnebago and Joe knocked gently on the door. There was no answer. He knocked again. A little more loudly this time.

A moment later a woman's muffled voice came through the closed door. "Who is it?"

Joe recognized it. "It's Joe, Charlie. Open up."

The door was flung open and Charlie came down the steps

and threw herself into Joe's arms. "You're here!" she laughed. "You're really here! I can't believe it!"

"Didn't Preacher tell you we were coming?"

"Yes, yes," she said. "But we've been waiting here more than a week. I was beginning to think you would never show up."

"It took time to get everything he wanted together," Joe said. He glanced up as Melanie appeared in the doorway. "Hey, baby," he said. "You're lookin' good."

She came down into his arms as Charlie turned to Beverly, hugging and kissing her, then finally to Tarz. For a moment they were all talking at once, then Joe looked around. "Where's Preacher?"

"He's down on the beach," Melanie said. "He goes down there every morning for meditation."

"Is he all right?" Beverly asked.

"Beautiful," Charlie said. "Come over here. You can see for yourself."

They followed her to the edge of the bluff and looked down to where she pointed. Preacher was seated on a rock, his back to them, staring out at the ocean, absolutely motionless.

"He's let his hair grow long again," Beverly said.

"Yes," Charlie answered. "And his beard is back. He's grown younger. Just like the Preacher we used to know."

"Was he upset about the divorce last month?" Beverly asked.

"No," Melanie answered. "I guess he expected it, so he wasn't surprised when he telephoned Jane and she told him. He told us that he thought it was all for the best."

"What surprised me was that there was nothing in the papers about it," Charlie said.

"That's her old man," Joe said. "He kept everything quiet." He turned to look down at Preacher again. "How long will he be?"

"Maybe another half-hour," Charlie said. "If you want, I'll go down and get him."

"No," Joe said. "We waited two months to see him; we can wait a half-hour more."

"Then come on back to the Winnie. We've got some cold beer in the refrigerator," Charlie said.

It was cool inside the motor home; the air conditioner's silent hum was soft and soothing in its own way. Joe sipped at his beer. "So what have you guys been doin' with yourselves every day? I know I kept getting your calls from all over the place. Like each week you'd be in another state."

Melanie sipped at her iced tea. "Going to church mostly. Every day a different church. Then Preacher would stand around and talk to people. He never said very much. Just listened. Then the next day the same thing in another town, another church."

"He didn't do any preaching?" Tarz asked.

"None at all. He said that this time, for once, he was doing what his mother had told him to do many times. Just talk and listen to people."

Beverly nodded. She looked at Joe. "He should be coming back real soon now. Maybe we ought to get those papers he wants from the trunk of the car?"

Joe nodded and got to his feet. "Come on, Tarz," he said. "No reason to leave all the heavy work to the black man."

Tarz laughed and followed him outside.

Beverly turned to the girls. "Is Preacher really all right?"

Melanie nodded. "Yes. Only thing is that he's more quiet than he used to be. It almost seems like he's talking to someone inside himself most of the time."

"It's weird," Charlie said. "You can be telling him something but half the time you aren't sure that he even heard you. But then he'll answer and you know that he did."

"And the rest of the time," Melanie added, "he'll be reading the Bible. By now I figure he's gone through it so many times he's worn the print off the pages."

Beverly was silent for a moment. Her voice was soft. "The Buddhist priests tell us that each word has a thousand meanings but only one of them is the right one for you. Maybe what Preacher is searching for is the meaning that is right for him."

The file folders and the papers were spread neatly on the table before him. Preacher sat quietly between Beverly and Joe while Tarz and the girls sat across from them.

Beverly opened the first folder. "This is the computer print-out from Churchland until the fifteenth of June. After that we couldn't get any more information."

"Why?" Preacher asked.

"They changed the access code," she answered. "I think they became suspicious that someone had tapped into their lines."

"Is there any way they could trace it to you?" Preacher asked.

She shook her head. "Impossible. We changed our base each time we went in on their line. And the computer doesn't store records of who asked for the information."

Preacher nodded. "Without my reading the whole thing, can you tell me the highlights?"

"I think so," Beverly said. "The first thing Randle did was take care of himself. He sold Churchland and all the buildings on it to the Community for twenty-five million dollars in cash. Title and money were both due to be transferred on June thirtieth."

"That's not so bad for about six million dollars' worth of buildings and a thousand acres of worthless prairie land," Preacher said.

"Five hundred acres," Beverly corrected him. "He kept the airport and the land beyond it for himself. Churchland's leasing that for two hundred thousand a year."

Preacher was silent.

"Approximately eight million dollars was donated to the Jake Randle Foundation for distribution to various other ministries and social and political action groups. One million dollars each was given to Mr. Craig's Americans for a Better Way and Mrs. Lacey's Christian Women's Council. Also, new contracts were drawn for Drs. Sorensen and Ryker, increasing their salaries and expense accounts to one hundred and fifty thousand a year each, and a bonus of two hundred and fifty thousand dollars was paid to Mrs. Kim Hickox for her special assistance in securing additional talent for the Crusade for Christ." Beverly paused for a moment to sip at her glass of iced tea, then continued. "As of our cutoff date, which was June fifteenth, approximately seven million dollars was paid out as advances on air time and advertising for the Crusade."

Preacher looked at her. "What was the balance in the surplus account?"

"Between six and seven million dollars," she answered. "Based on current collections and expenditures that should dwindle by at least half by the day of the Crusade, but if the computer predictions are correct they will pick up twenty-five million dollars or more from it."

Preacher picked up the printout folder and flipped through it. "Everybody got their pound of flesh," he said.

"Not yet they haven't," Joe said.

"What do you mean?" Preacher asked.

"You know too much," Joe said. "Don't you think for a minute the old man doesn't know it. He can't take no chances and let you blow the whistle on him." He turned to Tarz. "Tell him what you found out."

"One night last week I went to a movie in Los Altos. I was thirsty when I came out, so I went into a bar for a drink. The bar was crowded, so I sat down at a table and ordered a beer. Before I could even get it, two men came and sat down next to me. One look and I knew they were flatfeet. They didn't say anything until the waitress brought my beer and left. I didn't say anything either.

"Finally one of them spoke. 'You're an assistant pastor over at the Community?' 'That's right,' I said. 'You're an old friend of the Preacher, aren't you?' 'One of the oldest,' I said. 'Heard from him lately?' he asked. 'Nope,' I said, 'not since he went for his retreat.'

" 'You don't believe that bullshit, do you?' he asked. 'I believe what they tell me,' I said. 'Well, believe me, it's bullshit,' he said. 'He took off with half the church's money.' 'No,' I said, hoping I sounded shocked enough. 'Who would ever think a man like him would do a thing like that?'

"He eyeballed me. 'You wouldn't happen to know where he is, would you?' 'No,' I said. 'I don't even know where he's makin' his retreat.' He looked at the other guy and the other guy nodded. He turned back to me. 'Mr. Randle would like to talk to him and settle this whole business quietly. He don't want no scandal for the church.' 'Neither do I,' I said. 'Mr. Randle will pay ten thousand dollars to anyone who can tell us where to pick him up.'

"I take a deep breath and a sip of my beer. 'That's a lot of money.' 'Mr. Randle's real concerned,' he said, 'real concerned.' 'Have you checked out his mother?' I asked, knowing you weren't there. 'We got her place under twenty-four-hour surveillance and her phone bugged besides. Nuthin,' he answered. 'We even got his ex-wife's place covered but she hasn't heard from him in a month, not since she told him about the divorce.' 'I can't think of anywhere else then,' I said.

" 'What about that nigger preacher who keeps movin' around to all those little churches?' he asked. 'I don't hear from him either,' I said. 'I have nothing to do with that end of it.' He was silent for a moment. 'How do you like ten grand?' 'Real good,' I said. 'Who don't?'

"He took a card from his pocket and pushed it toward me. I looked at it. 'If you hear anything call that number. If we get him, it's worth ten grand to you.' 'Ten grand for sure?' I asked. 'Ten grand,' he said, getting up. 'Real money. Don't lose the card.'

" 'I won't,' I said, sticking it in my pocket. And I didn't." He took the card from his wallet and gave it to Preacher.

Preacher looked down at it. Special Security Services, Inc., Houston, Texas. The telephone number was a toll-free 800 line.

"That's the same bunch that picked me up," Joe said.

Preacher nodded silently and put the card in his shirt pocket. He looked at Tarz. "Thanks."

Tarz smiled. "For what? I didn't do anything."

"For loving. And caring," Preacher said. He turned back to Joe and Beverly. "How about our plan for the affiliates?"

Joe smiled. "We got over ninety percent of them signed, sealed, and delivered. The rest should come through in a few weeks. That pile of ten file folders over there has a copy of every agreement."

"Good," Preacher smiled. He looked at Beverly. "And the trust for the children?"

"That's done too," she said. She moved a heavy brown legal envelope toward him. "It's all in there. Notarized and approved by the bank. All that has to be done now is to send your ex-wife a copy."

He pushed the envelope back to her. "You send it to her by registered mail the day before the Crusade."

"Okay," she said.

"What about the ministers' petition to the court?" he asked.

"That's ready too," Joe said. "They all signed the same time we gave them the shares. But our lawyers advise us to file it in a federal court in California. One, because we are incorporated here in California and, two, if we file in Texas, Randle's got so much clout he'll have it buried. Right now they're checking out the federal judges here in San Diego to pick one they feel will be the most favorable toward us."

Preacher nodded.

"They also advise us to file the Friday before the Crusade so that the court order will be effective on the day after because Labor Day is a legal holiday. That way we freeze everything, including the collections from the Crusade."

Preacher took a deep breath. "Then you'll have to go into court for me. I won't be here."

Joe stared at him. "Where the hell will you be?"

"In Churchland, where I'm supposed to be," Preacher said.

"After all, they're still carrying me in all their advertising. I'm supposed to deliver the closing sermon."

"Are you crazy?" Joe's voice was shocked. "After what you heard from Tarz do you think they'll let you get anywhere near the place?"

"They can't keep me out," Preacher said calmly.

"Then I'll go too, and I better get a few of the brothers to come with us," Joe said. "I can have them start makin' up a few goodies right away."

"No one is going in with me," Preacher said calmly. "I won't have anyone hurt on my account. Either those for me or those against me. I don't believe in killing."

"Do you think they feel the same way?" Joe asked angrily.

"Then I pity them."

"That does you no good if you're dead."

Preacher nodded. There was a finality to his words they had never heard before. One that brooked no argument. "Jesus knew that when he went to face the Romans, yet he was not afraid. And it still took Pontius Pilate to order his death." He looked around the table at each of them. "Do not fear for me, my children. I will survive even as our Lord survived."

CHAPTER
TWENTY-ONE

The ringing telephone blasted into his sleep. He rolled over in his bed, fighting its insistent call to consciousness. Finally he opened his eyes. The digital clock at his bedside read 5:55. He groaned and looked toward the window. The gray light of dawn didn't even cast a shadow. He groaned again. Less than three hours' sleep and they were on his back again. He could hardly move. It took all his strength just to pick up the telephone. His voice rasped into the instrument. "Lincoln."

The whispering voice was faintly familiar in his ear. "Abraham?"

He was sick of the joke. It had plagued him since childhood. "No, Goddammit! Marcus!"

"What's the trouble, Marcus? Did I wake you up?" The voice laughed.

Suddenly he was wide awake. He knew the laugh. "Are you—?"

The voice cut him off. "No names, please. Go out to the public telephone booth at the corner and I'll call you in three minutes."

"All right," Marcus said.

Three minutes later Lincoln was standing in the narrow telephone booth when the phone rang. "Is that you?" he said breathlessly as he picked up the receiver. "How are you?"

"Never better."

"Where the hell have you been?" he asked. "I tried to find you everywhere."

"Around. Learning. Thinking. Praying."

"You should have called me," Marcus said. "I am your friend."

"I know. But I couldn't. I was busy getting all the shit out of my head. I need some information. And a favor."

"Go."

"Are the wireless mikes still on the same frequency as before?"

"Yes. We've never changed it."

"Would a superpowered pin mike running off twenty-four volts drown out all the others?"

"Easily. They're only one point five volts. It will easily put away all the hand-held wireless mikes. They're only three volts. Twenty-four volts will take out everything within a thousand yards."

"Still use only one panel for the wired mikes?"

"Check."

"And a separate rebroadcast unit for the wireless?"

"Check."

"How many video cameras are you using?"

"Twenty. Our monitor board can't carry more than eight. We'll have to keep pulling in and out according to the cue sheet."

"Can you lock your best Zoomar onto the cross and fix it so that it can't be pulled out?"

"Yes. Care to give me a focus?"

"Do you have a good man for it?"

"I'll stay on it myself."

"Dead center of the cross where the panel slides into the arms so that the battery of night floods can roll out on their platform."

"Got it."

"Can you kill every monitor except that one when the panel begins to open?"

"Easy."

"And the wire mike panel?"

"Zap."

"Okay. Then you got it."

"Wait a minute. When does all this action start?"

"When you see me."

"You'll never get in here."

"Why not? They still have me listed on the program, haven't they?"

"Of course they have. But you know better than that. They never intended to let you get on the air. They've already got Sorensen down on the cue sheet to take your place."

"He's going to be awfully disappointed, then."

"The old man's got three hundred special police crawling all over the place and each of them has a picture of you. The minute you show your face, even anywhere near the gate, they grab you."

"They're never going to see me."

"They sure as hell will. The only way you'll ever make it is if you take invisible pills. Please, do me a favor and don't try to get inside. Those guys are rough. And they have orders to really hurt you."

"Too bad. That means I can't even try to get out."

"What the hell are you talking about?"

"I've already been inside for the last three days." The warm familiar laugh chuckled in his ear. "May God be with you, Marcus."

The phone went dead in his hand. Slowly he came out of the booth. The sun was already coming up. It was going to be a beautiful day for a Crusade.

By noon, four hours before the Crusade was to begin, the ten-thousand-seat amphitheater built in the parking lot in front of the main building was already jammed. Every parking lot was filled with cars and every green patch of lawn was swarming with people. There was a gay festive air over it all. The popcorn, hot dog and cold drink vendors were already doing a land-office business. Even the people in the lines in front of the hundred Johnny on the Spots were in a good humor as they waited their turns to enter the sanctum of relief.

From the control booth, specially erected, high behind the amphitheater, Marcus looked out. Below him there was nothing but a landscape of moving and flowing colored bodies. On the roof of the black-windowed building he saw the guards with their binoculars swinging from the straps around their necks and their rifles with the telescopic sights in their arms. Reflected in the mirror-like glass of the building, he could see the guards pacing on the roof of the control booth over his head.

Forward in front of the building was the newly built stage, large enough to accommodate the more than six hundred specially invited guests under its brand-new red-white-and-blue-striped canvas sun shelter. He looked up at the giant golden cross that reached into the sky, suspended between the two towers of the building. His eyes squinted to make out the lines of the sliding panels. For a long moment he stared at them, then he turned and went back into the control booth.

Quietly he turned on remote camera one, suspended outside, just under the overhang of the control booth. Watching the monitor, he focused it on the sliding panels, then zoomed in tight until it filled the monitor screen. He locked it into position, watched it for a moment more on the monitor, then turned off the switch and the monitor screen went to black. Suddenly soul-weary, he went into the tiny bathroom. He closed and locked the door behind him. He turned and looked into the mirror. He never knew that his eyes could hold so much pain. After a moment, he took a small vial of cocaine from his pocket and took two giant snorts in each nostril. Then he closed the vial, clasped his hands, bowed his head and closed his eyes and prayed.

"Please, dear God. Don't let him do it."

Marcus looked at the program clock on the panel. There were six minutes left of the two-hour program, one minute left to final cue time. There was no doubt about it. This had truly been the greatest revival meeting of all time. Reports coming in on the clattering telex indicated that everywhere in the country the results had been the same. It seemed as if the love of God had reached out and touched all of America. Preacher's great dream had become reality.

He moved in closer to the panel. "I'll take over," he said to the engineer. "You must be beat."

The engineer nodded. "Yeah. And I gotta take a piss or I'll bust."

Marcus put the head mike on over his ears. He spoke into the mouthpiece. "Camera seven, in tight on Randle. He's the man in the white suit with dark glasses, just behind the pulpit left." He watched Randle appear on the monitor, the old man's bodyguard towering behind him. Randle seemed to be dourly staring into the ground, no expression visible at all behind the glasses. He didn't even seem to care what was happening in the pulpit before him as the announcer moved into place.

Marcus stole a glance at the panel clock. Thirty seconds. The announcer began on cue as the giant smiling face of California's most famous minister, beamed in directly from his own pulpit on the Coast, faded from the moving-picture-sized screen behind him.

He switched on remote camera one and watched the sliding panels in the center of the cross while listening to the announcer. The announcer's face and voice were going out on the relay. Marcus dropped both hands to the switches, the announcer's professional voice booming in his ear.

"—the man whose love of Jesus Christ led to this first great nationwide Crusade for Christ, the great pastor of the Community of God Church of Christian America Triumphant, Dr. C. Andrew Talbot, unfortu—"

Marcus hit all the switches, cutting the announcer off the air as the panel doors slid away and the floodlight platform rolled out from inside the cross. The floodlights were partly hidden by an almost seven-foot-tall dark wooden cross. A man dressed in a loose white wool robe, belted with white rope and falling almost to his bare feet, moved slowly to the center of the platform, his hands holding lightly to the guard railing around it.

Marcus stared with unbelieving eyes at the monitor. The man's hair was long, falling below his shoulders; his beard almost reached his breast. He stood there silently for a moment, looking down at the crowd. It wasn't until Marcus heard his voice that he really believed it was Preacher. Marcus hit the switch that threw the picture onto the giant movie screen down on the stage so that Preacher could be seen there as well as all over the country.

Preacher's voice boomed through all the loudspeakers in the amphitheater. "Brothers and Sisters in Christ—" Then the roaring and screaming love rising from the crowd reached up, drowning out his voice.

The panic-stricken voice of the stage director came through the earphone. "What the hell is going on up there? You've blown your cue. Get back to Dr. Sorensen on the pulpit!"

Marcus stole a glance at the stage monitor. Randle was on his feet, screaming at the bodyguard behind him, while staring up at the screen. Then he pushed his way angrily to the pulpit, shouting at Sorensen, who was standing there apparently in a dazed shock at what was happening. "Fuck you, Jake," Marcus whispered to himself and turned his eyes back to Preacher.

Preacher held up his hands for silence. Quickly the crowd began to quiet down, many falling to their knees in prayer, some fainting with their love for Christ. His voice boomed once again through the many loudspeakers.

"I have not come here today to preach to you to love God. Because this you already do. I have not come here today to tell you that He loves you. Because this you already know. I have come here today instead to tell you about Judas. Not the miserable Judas who betrayed our Lord and Savior Jesus Christ. But the hundreds of Judases who selfishly use your love of Christ Jesus to betray both you and Him.

"Look with your hearts into the faces of the men you trust, those men who promise to lead you to His heaven for the pittance you send them and then use that money to enrich themselves and to gain the power they seek. I know these men well, for once I was one of them.

"For the past months I have been wandering among you, listening to your pains, your sorrows, your struggles and your dreams. And in so doing, I learned that I have sinned. Not only against Him whom I love but also against you who are my brethren. And because of that I have doubly sinned. And I pray to the Savior Christ Jesus, who died on the cross for my sins and yours, that hearing my confession, He gives me of His mercy.

"This ministry, as well as many others, was built on the tiny bricks of dollars that you, in your desire to show your love of God, have given to us. And what did we do with that money to show our love of God? We bought limousines to ride in, airplanes to fly in, rich homes to live in, fine clothes to wear and fine food to eat. This we had. You did not. Even though it was your money that made it possible. Then, not content enough with that, we began to build monuments to our names; we called them schools and hospitals, churches and cathedrals. And when these things drained our resources we turned again to you and sold you pieces of land which you did not own except symbolically. We pled for you to match gifts of large sums of money we knew we would never get; we asked you to become faith partners with us, to send tithes, love gifts, and to support our radio and television programs, which were basically designed—like all radio and television—to sell a product. Only this time we were our own product—wrapped in the latest package design of our Lord. We spent half the money you gave us to persuade you to give us more money.

"Then there are the other uses we make of your money. We buy power. We make gifts to those politicians who make it possible for us to gain power over your minds, your thoughts, your lives. In just the last few years we have brought to power men who have taken from you the food you eat, the jobs at which you work, the education you sorely need, the medical care you deserve, the security of your old age that you have worked all your life to gain. We have given money to men who wish to deny you your God-given rights to equality because of your race, your creed, your color or your sex. We have given money to these men who, while spending untold billions of dollars on weapons of destruction, tell us that we must tighten our belts and suffer the pangs of hunger so that the budget may be balanced while they meet the threat of Communism.

"And by so doing, by supporting and condoning all these things with the money we take from you in the name of the Lord and thereby assuring ourselves of our power in the structure of our society, are we also not unlike the Communists we cry out against in the name of God? If we must find a name for ourselves should not that name be 'religious Communists'? Should not our creed be called 'religious Communism'? Because do we not do the very same things we charge the others are doing in the name of atheistic Communism?

"I have in my hand a piece of paper taken from the computer of this church. In the past few months we have used God's money, your money, to buy this land on which we presently stand for twenty-five million dollars. The very same land and the buildings on it that cost no more than six million dollars six years ago. Another ten million dollars of God's money, your money, went to political causes not in your interest and to propaganda or so-called educational programs designed to assure certain people that their stature in society will not be threatened by non-Christians—whose prayers we are told God does not hear—by human beings of other colors who threaten our purity, by men and women whose sexuality does not happen to agree with ours. If what this church has done is not religious Communism, I do not know the meaning of the word.

"But perhaps the greatest of all the sins we have committed is the one we commit most often. Every day many churches like ours keep you from your local house of prayer and give you instead a graven image to worship. The image on your own television screen. Think. The Lord has commanded us not to make graven images of anything on this earth to worship. And is that which we see on the screen not also an image?

"Because of all these things I have done and all these sins I have committed, three days ago I petitioned a federal court on behalf of you and the affiliated churches who are the rightful owners of the Community of God Church to ask the court to appoint a receiver for the assets of this church and determine whether or not there has been an improper or illegal use of these moneys you gave us to enrich certain of us or to gain illegal powers for ourselves. I have learned that this court has appointed a receiver and, I, too, will face the proper authorities for any crimes that I may have committed."

He paused for a moment. Not a sound came from the crowd of people. He clasped his hand on the railing. "Brothers and Sisters in Christ, please join with me in a prayer for His mercy—"

Marcus pushed the switch to pick up the prayer of the audience. A rasping voice came roaring through the loudspeakers. Startled, Marcus turned to the stage monitor. Randle was screaming, "I don't give a damn what you think! Kill the son of a bitch!"

The sound of the three rifle shots seemed to come almost together. With horror-stricken eyes, Marcus stared at the screen. The first bullet had torn through Preacher's robe, ripping a wide hole in his side; as his body spun from the impact, the second tore through both his hands, still clasped in prayer. He grabbed at the wooden cross behind him for support. The third bullet blew him off his feet and he fell backward over the railing, still clinging to the cross. His body tumbled over and over in the air, hitting the canvas sun roof with a sound like a roar of thunder, the cross beneath him. The left arm of the cross tore partly through the canvas and Preacher rolled lifelessly onto his back, arms outstretched on the cross.

Automatically, Marcus zoomed in on Preacher. At the same moment the rays of the sun crested between the towers, bathing his body in glowing gold. A strangely painful moan seemed to rise from the bowels of the people who could see him on the giant screen. Many of them fell to their knees, tears mingling with their prayers.

Marcus stared in an almost hypnotic state. There was a hole in the open palm of each outstretched hand, a gaping torn-open space in Preacher's side, through which the last few drops of his blood flowed, and a hole in his crossed ankles where the bullet inside still held them pinned together. Marcus zoomed the camera in on Preacher's face, then felt himself choke as his eyes filled with tears.

There was a look of loving peace on Preacher's face that he had never had in life.

10 For the love of money is the root of all evil: which while some coveted after, they have erred from the faith, and pierced themselves through with many sorrows.

11 But thou, O man of God, flee these things; and follow after righteousness, godliness, faith, love, patience, meekness.

12 Fight the good fight of faith, lay hold on eternal life, whereunto thou art also called, and hast professed a good profession before many witnesses.

13 I give thee charge in the sight of God, who quickeneth all things, and before Christ Jesus, who before Pontius Pilate witnessed a good confession;

14 That thou keep this commandment without spot, unrebukeable, until the appearing of our Lord Jesus Christ:

15 Which in his times he shall shew, who is the blessed and only Potentate, the King of kings, and Lord of lords;

16 Who only hath immortality, dwelling in the light which no man can approach unto; whom no man hath seen, nor can see: to whom be honor and power everlasting. Amen.

I TIMOTHY VI